P9-APT-363

THE ULTIMATE Zombie

Other Ultimate Monster Books from Dell

THE ULTIMATE DRACULA

THE ULTIMATE FRANKENSTEIN

THE ULTIMATE WEREWOLF

THE ULTIMATE WITCH

THE ULTIMATE
Zombie

BYRON PREISS
& JOHN BETANCOURT
EDITORS

ILLUSTRATED BY
MICHAEL DAVID BIEGEL

BOOK DESIGN
BY FEARN CUTLER

A BYRON PREISS BOOK
A DELL TRADE PAPERBACK

A Dell Trade Paperback

Published by Dell Publishing, a division of Bantam Doubleday Dell Publishing Group, Inc., 1540 Broadway, New York, NY 10036

Special thanks to Leigh Grossman, Jeanne Cavelos, and Leslie Schnur

Design: Fearn Cutler

ISBN: 0-440-50534-8

Printed in the United States of America

Published simultaneously in Canada

October 1993

10 9 8 7 6 5 4 3 2 1

CONTENTS

INTRODUCTION: LIVING WITH DEATH

▼▼▼

Dennis Etchison

HORROR writers spend a lot of time thinking about fear—what it is, where it comes from, what it means. In other people such a preoccupation might indicate an unhealthy, morbid personality, or a level of anxiety that cries out for professional help. But if you make your living writing horror stories, this kind of thinking is a normal part of your daily life, and represents nothing more than job-related research.

I write horror stories. That means I worry about shadows in doorways, the rustling on the roof, voices in the walls and the darkness under the bed. I am compelled to do this out of professional necessity rather than any perverse interest. It is my job to worry, and to wonder why, and to try to understand the mechanism behind the feeling so that I may use it to trigger a similar sense of unease in my readers, whose reactions are crucial to my success or failure.

It is not enough to say, *This frightens me.* That does not necessarily mean it will frighten you, as well. It would be arrogant to assume that my experiences and responses are universal. The emotions, yes; we do have a common ancestry and a nervous system that reflects our shared evolution. But the associations, the specifics, are never quite the same. If we were all identically conditioned, we could be relied upon to buy the same product, vote for the same candidate, embrace war or peace or jump off cliffs like lemmings at a given signal. Were it so simple—if so absolute a link between stimulus and response could be isolated—then there would be no further need for competition in the marketplace, or for democracy.

And yet there are archetypes. Certain primal images survive, at least in our time and culture. If it were not so, my job would be hopeless. It is my task to find those archetypes and utilize them to create suspense, terror and catharsis.

So I think about fear, its nature and origins.

And when I do, I think about my childhood.

It was not a particularly fearful time, as far as I can remember. The summers were long, the playing went on for hours, and there were always hot meals and the kind faces of my parents and grandmothers and aunts and uncles waiting for me inside the house. It all tends to blur together in a seamless memory of warmth and reassurance that exists outside of time in a place I call the Bradbury Dimension.

But Bradbury also wrote a great many horror stories about that place, at least in the early years of his career, when the memories were fresh and not yet tinged with a golden glow, like a vision of paradise slipping away with the setting sun.

And sometimes, in those moments late at night when I am about to slip away into a dream of my own, it comes back to me:

The way it really was.

Those times may not have been filled with dread, but there was an undercurrent of anxiety as real as a heartbeat that never stopped, not even in sleep. It was born of childhood uncertainties about the meaning of things that grown-ups already understood but would not tell, and what was expected of me, what I was supposed to do until I had the knowledge I needed to act on my own, without being told. There were lessons I ought to be learning on the way, but the explanations I received were tantalizingly incomplete, an instruction manual given out one chapter at a time with no answer page at the back of the book. So the anxiety took shape as dreams, nightmares of pursuit by monsters, one of which I still find it hard to talk about without a shudder and the sound of my own blood pulsing in my ears.

It had many faces.

One was *Frankenstein*.

The next was *Dracula*. . . .

When my father took me to a double bill of movies featuring both characters, they appeared more real than any others I had seen on the screen, and strangely, hauntingly familiar, like the figures one is most afraid to meet in dreams.

Since then they have become even more familiar, icons of popular culture. I have seen them portrayed in many other films—too many—and I must admit that, for me, the years have somewhat dimmed their mythic power.

I have made it my business to understand such myths. I know now that *Frankenstein* was Mary Shelley's cautionary talk about human pride, written at a time when scientific reductionism and the industrial revolution were about to reshape Western civilization, and based on the fable of Prometheus, who stole fire from the gods. The Monster's vengeance is the retribution that will come if we dare to see ourselves as gods and assume dominion over life and death.

And *Dracula*? The vampire has its origins in Jewish tradition as well as the Biblical account of Genesis, and draws from Goethe, Coleridge, Le Fanu and the Romanian stories of *nosferatu* and the historical Vlad the Impaler. Bram Stoker's version was about repressed sexuality in Victorian England, and a metaphor for the fear of disease caused by seduction and the unleashing of the libido.

So I no longer dream of Frankenstein's Monster and Dracula, despite the occasional *frisson* when a modern writer or filmmaker manages to inject new blood into a revisionist retelling of the stories. And though these symbols have lost their edge for me, the originals do retain some of their cultural potency; otherwise they would not continue to be re-examined. I sense an ongoing process at work every time I see the rubber-fanged Count Chocula and the cute, cuddly Frankenberry on the breakfast cereal shelf or Saturday morning cartoon shows. In their pure form, these characters still have a vestige of their old power to disturb and frighten. Were it not so, they would have been forgotten long ago, their demystification complete.

There is, however, another face of the monster that I cannot so easily dismiss.

Can you guess its name?

Zombies are a relatively new addition to the pantheon of horror archetypes. Unlike vampires and the Frankenstein Monster, their story does not derive from a classic novel. Though legends about the living dead have long been a part of folklore the world over, and may have a factual basis in Haitian voodoo, almost all of what we know about them comes from movies. The fad started in 1932 with the film *White Zombie*, followed by a great many fast-and-cheap successors, one of which was a masterpiece of style and atmosphere: *I Walked with a Zombie* (1943).

I was too young to have seen these in theaters, but when they began to show up on television in the early fifties, they left their mark. The ones I remember most vividly starred Bela Lugosi (the Count himself), and Mantan Moreland usually seemed to be somewhere close by, his eyes bugging out and his chauffeur's cap pushed back nervously to reveal a brow beaded with cold sweat. The central image was invariably the army of the undead—plantation workers, laborers, nameless minions of the night—shambling ever forward in an unstoppable wave, oblivious to any opposition and without concern for their own lives, which were already forfeited. Nothing could deter them, their gray, unseeing eyes staring blindly ahead, mindless legions in the service of another master. . . .

Later they might appear as servants of an alien race (*Invaders from Mars, Enemy from Space*) or sinister copies of the people next door (*Invasion of the Body Snatchers*), but they were always easy to spot by their vacant, unfocused eyes, their imperviousness to pain, in fact their total lack of feeling. They were Bad News. You couldn't outwit them because they had no strategy other than relentless brute strength and the force of numbers; neither could you hope to reason with them or plead for mercy because they had no capacity for emotion. They were beyond caring, beyond humanity, beyond the last borderline that separates life from death.

And that was what was most frightening. Frankenstein's Monster was ultimately a pathetic creature, a product of man's hubris and more to be pitied than feared; Dracula was a deformed, almost tragic soul doomed to wander the Earth in search of nourishment to sustain the curse of immortality. But zombies lacked any trace of elegance or dignity. They were caricatures of human beings, moving with no purpose of their own and toward no reward save oblivion. Like the seven-foot police officers in George Lucas's *THX 1138*, who were incapable of being swayed from their course by reasons or even bribery because they were not men but robots, zombies resembled automatons more than flesh and blood. They were Philip K. Dick's *simulacra*, which were in turn a science-fiction metaphor for those brain-dead entities we encounter from time to time who are really only pretending to be our friends or lovers.

It does not much comfort me to know that psychologists now term such individuals *schizoid* because they lack normal "affect" and do not respond in appropriately human fashion, or that *The Serpent and the Rainbow* has offered a quasi-medical explanation of zombieism. Their numbers only seem to be increasing, encouraged by the need to feed our war machine, just as they fed the factory production line, where men and women and children were treated as interchangeable parts to meet the needs of industry.

This monster still walks in my dreams and in my stories (cf. "The Late Shift" and "The Blood Kiss," to name two), just as it continues to proliferate on movie screens, with no end in sight. If George Romero's *Night of the Living Dead* (adding a new twist, borrowed from Richard Matheson's vampire novel *I am Legend*, to make them flesh-eaters bent on spreading their infection) was a bitter comment on Vietnam and the futility of human intelligence in the face of an insatiable war, his sequels were even darker. *Dawn of the Dead* presented a blackly comic picture of America as a nation of classically-conditioned sleepwalkers who will go on shopping and consuming long after those habits have lost any meaning; and *Day of the Dead* imagined what might happen when the zombies finally take over, with the few remaining humans left to fend for themselves against the hordes while attempting to co-exist between the military-industrial complex and pure science. And whether the humans' apparent escape at the end was only one more manifestation of a desperate dream or the beginnings of a new Garden of Eden, I am not at all sure. Vlad was a real tyrant who skewered his enemies on poles; he died centuries ago; and Frankenstein was only a morality play. But my latest dreams, I am afraid, may be the waking nightmares of a generation pressed inexorably toward absorption by the masses of the walking dead in a society of debased pluralism. It may be no mere coincidence that I worry as I do, and cannot get this newest monster out of my mind. For the handwriting is on the wall. The zombie has not gone away, and will not. He is *us*.

THOUGH I WALK THROUGH THE VALLEY

▼▼▼

S.P. SOMTOW

UNCLE Will never meant no harm. Dude, he was *down.* Last Christmas he gave me a Super Nintendo and a dirt bike. Once a month or so we'd like get drunk and stoned and shit. When my brother was gunned down in a drive-by, he took me down to Hollywood after the funeral and bought me a big old chocolate sundae, and he told me I could come and live with him if I wanted to. And I'm all, "Thanks, but like I don't want to hurt Mom's feelings even if she don't got no feelings since she became a junkie."

He's all, "I hear you, but don't be such a stranger anymore. I only live two floors down. I like you, Oz. You really have your head screwed on straight for a kid who's had so much shit happen to him in his life. So maybe you can do me a favor, talk some sense into Little Ferdie; he's so fucking stubborn."

That's how I come to see a lot more of my cousin Ferdie, and how I found out that Uncle Will was a child abuser.

Cousin Ferdie was twelve like me but he was totally skinny with big bulging eyes like a hunger poster. When I started hanging out at Uncle Will's apartment after school, or when I would ditch, I didn't see much of him. His door'd be closed and there wasn't no reason for me to go in and see him and maybe he wasn't even home, maybe he was like out cruising with his own friends somewheres. I didn't like Ferdie. He was so quiet he made you nervous, and when he would say something it would be like sudden, out of nowhere, something that had nothing to do with anything . . . like when my grandmother would do her speaking-in-tongues thing in church.

I didn't go to Uncle Will's to see Ferdie anyways. I was there to see Will. He was always there because he'd been laid off for three months. His girlfriend, a directory assistance lady, was paying all the bills, except his liquor bill which he would get the money for by standing at the entrance to the Sacramento Freeway with a big old sign that said he was homeless. By lunchtime he would always have enough for a couple of forty-ouncers.

He often had his homies over. There was Bill and Ted, forty-year-old surfers, from the apartment next door, and Armando, who was dying of AIDS, and Lupe the hooker, and Jungle George the loan shark, but most of all there was Mr. Death, an old black dude with long white hair. His real name was Daniel Moreau. Mr. Death was his professional name. He was a *houngan*—a voodoo witch doctor. Retired that is. Used to hang out with Baby Doc in Haiti. Told wild stories: political prisoners getting burning tires hung around their necks, magic potions, and zombies, naturally, except, the way he told it, there wasn't nothing supernatural about them. He was my favorite of Uncle Will's friends, but his stories about Haiti made the East Valley sound like buttfuck Egypt, I mean *nothing* happens here except like, drive-bys and drug busts and shit.

My cousin Ferdie was usually nowhere to be found. That was fine with me. Then, one too-hot day in April, I totally saved his life.

It was kind of an accident. I was at the 7-Eleven trying to buy a pack of cigarettes. Usually the dude just sells them to me but this time I think it was a different person even though it's like hard to tell them apart. He stood there, six feet six in his turban, and he's all, "You cannot be purchasing cigarettes here, young man."

I'm all, "Why not?" and he's all, "Because you are being too young," so I'm all, "You motherfucking camel jockey," and slamming the hardpack on the counter and jamming out of the store. But because I'm in such a hurry, everything I've jacked starts tumbling out of my pocket: two Twix bars, a packet of condoms, a bag of peanuts, and a Bic lighter.

"Shoplifter!" he screamed, and started loping out from behind the counter.

But I'm all, "So what are you gonna do about it, fag?" because I knew I could outrun anybody, and I started running, but he pushed some kind of alarm button and I didn't make it out of the parking lot before a cop car pulled in and two big dudes jumped out with big old PR-24s. They started chasing me but they didn't know the alleys like I did. I lost them but then I heard the sirens and I knew they were going to try and head me off somewheres. I hopped a chain-link fence and dove through a hole in a churchyard shrubbery and I came out behind our apartment building. I was in an alley that was too narrow for the squad car to squeeze through but I seen it through the gap and the lights flashing and I knew that they'd be running after me again and I didn't feel like getting beat up. Them plastic ties they put around your wrists can really cut you.

I shimmied up the wall where an orange tree grew, swung over the branch, and found myself on the balcony outside my cousin's room. I could tell they hadn't seen me because I heard them running all the way past the complex shouting, "Stop, you little cholo shit, stop or I'll shoot your fucking face off," and I knew I'd gotten clean away. They'd never even gotten a good look at me since they thought I was a cholo; I may dress like one but I don't look like one.

So I slide open the door into Ferdie's room and there he is, standing on a chair with a belt around his neck, tightening the buckle and getting ready to kick. His eyes were all empty and he had wet his boxers.

I didn't waste no time, I just grabbed a hold of him and yanked the belt out of the buckle. There was like a red bruise all around his neck where the leather had cut it. I lifted him up real easy (he was a head shorter than me) and carried him to the lower bunk and I'm all, "What do you think you're doing, dude?" and pulling off his boxers and drying him off with a Ren and Stimpy towel.

"Jesus, Ferdie," I said, "you could at least have pissed in the bathroom."

"Not allowed in the bathroom."

"What do you mean?"

"Not allowed to leave my room for two weeks on account of I'm stubborn."

"Not even to go to the bathroom?"

"Sometimes there ain't no one out there to let me out in time."

I tried Ferdie's door. It was locked from the outside. Then I heard my Uncle Will's voice: "Don't you try the door, it's no use; I'll double your time if I even hear you breathe."

I held my breath. This was another Uncle Will than the down dude I could get stoned with. I'd never heard Uncle Will scream like that before. Never even heard him raise his voice.

Ferdie was all shivering even though it was probably 106 outside and the swamp cooler wasn't working too well because of the humidity. I looked around the room for some clean underwear, but when I found it he wouldn't let me take away his towel. I had to trick him and whisk it away and that's when I saw all the bruises because he stepped out from the shadow of the bunk, into the harsh light. There were some thin red stripes, like maybe an electric cord, and some wide purple ones with punctures, like the buckle end of a belt, and a couple of cigarette burns. I was too shocked to say anything at first, and then all I could say was "Why?" because something this bad had to have a reason, it couldn't just happen.

And he's all, "I dunno." And he shrugged. "I guess it's because I'm stubborn, that's all, stubborn."

"How stubborn?"

"I forget. I think I wouldn't eat my cereal." He gave a sharp giggle, like a girl. "I don't like Captain Crunch."

There had to be more to it than that. I figured maybe he wasn't thinking straight seeing how he'd just been this close to history. Uncle Will wasn't like one of them dudes on *Geraldo*, you know, one show they had with like kids who had been locked up in cages, used in satanic sacrifices, shit like that. Was he? I've known Uncle Will since the fourth grade, when we moved down to the Valley from the trailer park in Lancaster. Maybe Uncle Will had gotten weird from being laid off so long.

"You still shouldn't of tried to kill yourself," I said. "It's a sin."

"I know, Oz," Ferdie said, "but hell can't be no worse than this."

Then he looks at me with big sad sunken eyes and picks at a scab on the back of his hand. The way he looks at me is all, *I'm in hell now, Oz, and you gotta help me, cuz I'm sinking fast*. But I still couldn't believe that Uncle Will would have done that to him. I didn't like Ferdie, you understand, on account of he could stare anyone down and he made you nervous just being around him. And he read books, too, and he could toss of a string of facts that would make you feel totally stupid and want to punch his head in. But he was my cousin and, you know, family is all you have, and less and less of it because they keep getting gunned down in your backyard.

"You don't got to help me any," Ferdie said, "next week they're gonna put me on Ritalin and maybe I won't be so stubborn no more."

I'm all, "Shit, Ferdie, of course I'll help you." I gave him a piece of bubble gum that I'd jacked along with the other stuff, that hadn't fallen out of my pocket. He swallowed the whole thing. "Me and Uncle Will are homies. Maybe I can find out what's making him act this way." Because I still thought that it was just some kind of temporary craziness and I could get Will to come to his senses, and I knew we couldn't turn him in, because that would tear the family apart forever.

▼▼▼

So I waited for a couple of hours and I snuck back over the balcony and around to the front of the apartment building. Mr. Death and Uncle Will were sitting in the living room chugging their forty-ouncers. They were talking in whispers and they didn't see me come in. So I sat down on the bean bag behind Will's armchair and pretended like I wasn't there.

Uncle Will's all, "I don't know what to do, I try so hard, he's so stubborn."

"I would say you was probably stubborn too," Mr. Death said. "Stubborn runs in families." His voice was deep and it rolled like a tubular wave. The way he talked wasn't like the black people in my school exactly. I mean it had like a foreign lilt to it, French or something.

"Yeah," Uncle Will said, "I reckon I was. Stubborn I mean. My Dad used to whip the shit out of me. But Ferdinand's a different kind of stubborn. He's stubborn like a block of granite that you want to carve into a statue and it won't give. Drugs don't help him; whipping don't make it any better."

It's weird. *Stubborn* ain't a word you hear people use much about kids, well, just old people, and they're more'n likely talking about a mule or a dog when they say it. When I heard Uncle Will talking this way it was, you know, like when I heard his voice booming through Ferdie's locked door—it didn't sound like the Will I knew, my bud. Suddenly I realized that it sounded like Grandpa.

And like I'm all cold suddenly, cold and clammy, even though the air from the electric fan is as burning hot as the smoggy air outside. Because I seen my grandfather dead, at the wake. They made me kiss the corpse on the cheek. The makeup rubbed off on my lips and I sucked in a cold and bitter-tasting wind. Even though that had been a totally hot day too, a heat wave, and me six years old and standing on a crate and sweating like a motherfucker.

Uncle Will said, "I wish there was another way." And popped the cap off the second forty-ouncer. "Jesus I try so hard but him and me, it's like I'm butting my head against the biggest-ass wall in the world."

And Mr. Death said, "Well, Will, there *be* other ways. There is things in the world you can only see if you choose to open your eyes. There is doors you can unlock but only if you know they there."

I could tell that like, Mr. Death was about to totally launch into one of them stories of his. Maybe if Uncle Will got all involved in the story I could slip out from behind the armchair and act like I just arrived. But Will cut him off and he just said, "Daniel, I got no patience for your bullshit today. I'm scared, man, scared for me and my son. What if I accidentally kill him one of these days? I ain't a bad man, I ain't a murderer, but the kid just plain makes me go berserk."

"Well, back at home there is a little trick I do," Mr. Death said. "And after I do this little trick, my patients they all calm, they do what they told, they never ever complain no more."

"What is it, some kind of voodoo therapy?"

"Maybe you call it that."

"Is it expensive?"

"Not for you. You can't afford not to have it done. You drinking yourself into the grave because how much it trouble you. You want to feel that love God say you got to feel for the child of your own loins."

"I'd give anything."

"And you will. Not just anything. Everything."

"But what will you give Ferdie in return?"

"I will give him a new life," Mr. Death said. "A kind of being born again, starting with a clean slate."

That's when I really got scared, because before you can kind of be born again, you have to kind of die. And I knew Mr. Death was talking about turning Ferdie into a zombie.

▼▼▼

I didn't come out from behind that armchair until long after Daniel Moreau had gone home and Uncle Will dozed off after his second forty-ouncer. I crept up the stairs to my mom's apartment. She was lying on the living room floor, past noticing anything.

I dreamed about my brother. I never saw him dead because they couldn't fix his face and so they had a closed coffin funeral. Then I dreamed Ferdie was dangling from the end of a noose, swinging like a busted naked light bulb. Then I dreamed about Grandpa. Bending down to kiss the body. His eyes popping open. Staring straight at me. Fixed. Like the lens of a camcorder. Staring. Videotaping me, my lips still freeze-dried from brushing his cheek, too scared to scream.

Then I dreamed it was me in that coffin, and I'm all rigid but not from death, only from terror because the three of them are standing around me and all of them are dead and all of them with their fixed-focus eyes. . . .

I woke up and I thought: Uncle Will didn't come to the funeral. I didn't meet him for another three years. I wondered why he didn't come. I'm all, I think I'll ask him tomorrow. I looked over at the VCR and the timer said 3:30 in the morning. I tried to go back to sleep.

But like, every time I closed my eyes, I would see all three of them again. *Night of the Living Dead*-style, with their arms hanging limp and shambling around my grave. And their heads swiveling like the security cameras at the K-Mart. And that's how it goes on, all night long, so I can't get to sleep, so when I finally do it's almost dawn and I know I'm going to have to sleep through first period or totally ditch.

▼▼▼

I got up around twelve. I couldn't leave the house because there's always a cop prowling around somewheres and they can't wait to truss your wrists with them plastic ties and haul you off to school. So I decided to go down to Uncle Will's apartment.

Actually I went down the fire escape first, slipped Ferdie a couple of cookies and a wine cooler—he just sat staring into a broken television set—then worked my way back around to the front, let myself in.

Uncle Will gave me a big old hug and I told him I had nightmares all night long and he's all, "It's okay, son, I'm here for you. Calm down now."

And I'm all, "Dude, I dreamed everyone was dead."

"You've had it rough, kid." He steered me toward the sofa and gave me a couple of Valium. "You want to hang out here for a while? Your mom don't give a shit."

I sat on the sofa juggling the Valium from hand to hand. "Uncle Will? Why didn't you go to Grandpa's funeral? Like, he was your dad, wasn't he?"

"Don't got no father," said Uncle Will.

"Well but . . . Uncle Will? Why do you beat up on Ferdie so much?"

"Because he's a stubborn little motherfucker."

"Yeah, but . . . over not eating his cereal? I mean like, cigarette burns and shit?"

"How d'you find out?"

"I saw him yesterday."

"Saw him? I told him to stay in his room!"

"I know, I went in through the balcony."

"I told him not to—" I could see that Uncle Will was getting real pissed. Frothing at the mouth almost. He strode down the corridor to Ferdie's room and started trying to kick it in.

I'm all, "Don't you have a key?" and he like calms down, but only a little bit, and fumbles in his jeans and pulls them out and unlocks the door. There's Ferdie, sitting on the bunk in just a pair of *Terminator 2* boxer shorts and crisscrossed with cuts, and I see what Uncle Will means when he says *stubborn* because there ain't one shred of fear or self-pity in Ferdie's eyes; he just glares at Will and there's more anger coiled up in them eyes than you can imagine. Will just throws himself on Ferdie and he's all punching him and Ferdie just sits there, taking it, but no matter how hard he's hit he never gives up one little bit of that fury that's in his eyes. After a while I couldn't stand it no more and I'm all trying to pull Will off of him and I'm all, "You're crazy, dude, you're not yourself, you're fucking possessed or something."

And then it all suddenly snaps to. Ferdie, rigid, Uncle Will stepping back, looking away from those blazing eyes. "It's them eyes," he said, "it's all because of them eyes. Devil eyes. They just keep daring me and daring me. They taunt me and they haunt me."

He grabbed my shoulders and pushed me out of Ferdie's room and then he slammed the door shut behind us and locked it again. "I got to do something," he said. "Or else I'm going to murder him, I really am."

Once Ferdie was out of sight, he started changing back into the Will I knew. "Let's go cruising," he said. "I can't stay cooped up here. I'll keep thinking about *him*."

So we took off down the San Fernando Road toward Sun Valley, past Foothill Division, with speed metal all blaring on the stereo. I had to shout and he did too. And he's got his arm around me the whole time, and he's all, "Ozzie, I wish you were my kid. We have such good times together."

"Don't you love Ferdinand, Uncle Will?"

"I love him with all my heart." But there's no tenderness in his voice when he says it, only fear. "I don't know why I want to kill him so bad. He's got some devil in him."

"Maybe it's in *you*, Uncle Will. You know"—we turned a sharp corner, bounced across the railroad tracks somewhere around Tuxford, nothing but big old gray warehouses covered with taggers' writings, and the smog totally hiding the San Gabriel Mountains from sight—"when you were all screaming and shit, you sounded like another person. You sounded almost like Grandpa."

"Your grandfather was a good man. He never laid a hand on me. Do you hear that? Don't you ever forget that."

The tape was getting chewed up, so I had to stop the stereo and pull out the cassette and wind the little ribbon back with the end of a Pilot marker. So we caught the end of some news thing and it was the cops were all found not guilty up there in Simi Valley, and then Uncle Will switched the radio off. "Motherfuckers," he said softly.

"Uncle Will, where are we?"

We were threading down a narrow winding road, half paved, half dirt, and weeds waist-high on either side of us, and like, it was suddenly getting dark. Then, poking out of them weeds, there's a big old sign that reads *Daniel Moreau, Doctor of Divinity*. I get that chilly feeling inside me again because of what I heard them talking about last night, which I've been trying to forget all day.

"I'll be damned," Uncle Will said. "It's Mr. Death's place."

After we parked we had to walk through a path winding through trees and weeds and here and there little piles of rocks, pyramids kind of, decorated with bunches of wildflowers. Like the place was a kind of homemade graveyard. The house wasn't much more than a shack, and it was set way in back of the lot. It looked abandoned, but when we got closer we could see the TV flickering behind closed blinds, and Uncle Will knocked on the door. There wasn't no answer, but we went in anyways.

Mr. Death was in a Lazyboy rocking back and forth and looking at the television. "Gone be riots," he said softly. "I just know it."

Uncle Will's all, "Gosh, Daniel, I don't know what happened. We were just cruising is all, and the road twisted and turned and we somehow ended up here."

"I been expecting you." Mr. Death's voice was all booming and hollow. On TV, the sun was setting and the streets were totally filling with angry black dudes and they were shouting and breaking store windows and beating up Koreans and shit. "You come for that service we done talked about."

"No, Mr. Death," Uncle Will said, "I swear, we were just passing by."

"You at your wits' end, Will. And Mr. Death he at the end of every road."

Now I was getting totally scared because the way Mr. Death was talking, it was like this house, this whole encounter, was supernatural somehow. And I was staring at TV, it was Fox 11, and I could see fire running down the streets of South Central, and once in a while they cut to the videotape of the Rodney King thing; I remembered us driving past Foothill Division, I thought of my dream and my grandfather's shambling toward me with camcorder eyes.

"Don't be ashamed you come to me," said Daniel Moreau. "You done tried everything you can. You a good man, Will, but you have one streak of darkness in you, and maybe this gone lighten your darkness, maybe not."

"I just . . . want to be able to love my son . . . you know. The way I love Ozzie, my nephew."

And the way he said it, it made me feel like me and Ferdie were more alike than I'd of ever thought; like Ferdie was my own self's shadow, locked up in a dark room, sucking the hatred out of Uncle Will so that all that was left for me was his love. We were different like night and day, but the sickness in Uncle Will's mind had made us Siamese twins, joined at the heart.

"Give me a few minutes," said Mr. Death, "and I'll get all my tools."

"How much is this going to cost me?"

"It against the law for me to charge for this kind of thing. But you make a voluntary donation, that's fine."

"How much?" said Uncle Will, who always counted every dime, even when he was panhandling for change next to the freeway.

"You will know what the price will be," Mr. Death says, "and it will be the right price."

We followed him into the kitchen, which was totally filthy. On the counter there was a bell jar with a big old frog inside, and hanging from the ceiling where a light bulb should be there was a bunch of dried puffer fishes. At first I thought the frog was dead but he was only sleeping, and Mr. Death lifted the jar and made me hold him in both my hands, and then he jabbed it in the head with a needle, so it was dead and undead at the same time, and then he cut down one of the puffer fishes and got a whole mess of other shit off the shelves and then he throws everything, including the dead twitching frog, into like this big old blender, and he like turns it on.

While it's whirring all I can think of are frog-in-a-blender jokes.

Okay so then he pours this gooey mass out of the blender and then he does something with it in the microwave and finally he's all pounding it in a mortar and he's all mumbling in some kind of foreign language. After a while the chemicals and the dead animals were reduced to about a handful of dark powder and Mr. Death used a flour scoop to fill a Ziploc bag with it. A black-and-white TV on top of the microwave was on the whole time and the riots were getting uglier every minute, but so far they hadn't mentioned San Fernando; it was all like mostly downtown.

"You know," Mr. Death said, "if we cruise up to Mulholland Drive, we'd see, the whole city she a sea of fire."

He closed his eyes like he was remembering that sea of fire. But I knew that Mr. Death had been here the whole time. Maybe he had an inner eye for seeing things like that. Or he could send his spirit out hovering over the city. Maybe that was how we been led to his house . . . shit all I know is he scared me, and I couldn't take my eyes off the things he was doing, and maybe it was the words he mumbled and maybe it was the two Valium, but my mind was all fuzzed up and I couldn't see straight.

Mr. Death put the powder in a black tote bag and took a human skull out of the refrigerator and he stuck that in the bag too. Then we drove back to the apartment and what was weird was it only took a minute or two to get back and I never seen the road we took before. In front of the complex there wasn't nobody cruising, only a patrol car with its lights flashing at the corner of Aztec and Hubbard. We went indoors and the TV was on and it showed a helicopter view of the city and, like Mr. Death said, it was a ocean of flames and the people were streaming down the streets like termites.

We went to Ferdie's room and we found him exactly where he'd been sitting before, on the bunk bed facing the television.

Mr. Death is all, "We must introduce the *coup poudre* through a cut in the skin; it has to get into the bloodstream before it start to work."

"Come here, Ferdinand," said Uncle Will.

Ferdie comes toward us. He's thin as a shadow and there's his eyes, clear blue and deep sunken and full of rage, and some of his welts are bleeding a little bit where he's been picking scabs.

"And now," says Mr. Death, "please remember, my homies, there is no magic, no superstition. This an ancient and venerable science that come all the way from BaKongo times. The *coup poudre* gone send the boy into the sleep of no dreaming, and then, when he come back, he don't be stubborn no more."

I'm all, "You're gonna kill him, dude!"

Mr. Death said, "Death is transformation."

Ferdie comes up to Uncle Will. He only comes up to his chest. His sandy hair is all matted. I'm all, "What the fuck do you think you're doing, Uncle Will?" but he pushes me away real rough like. I never seen him be this rough to me before; he sends me reeling across the carpet and I hit my head against the bunk post. I'm all, "Why are you hurting me, Uncle Will," but then I look across the room and I see a strange thing in the cold light of the street lamp through the orange tree that leans against the balcony: I see Uncle

Will take Ferdie into his arms with all the tenderness that he shows me, sometimes, when I knows I'm going through a lot of pain, and he hugs him, and he's all, "Ferdie, I'm only doing this because I want us to be a real family, I'm doing this for you as much as for me," and while he's hugging him his fingernail is searching out a long thick scab that goes diagonally all the way across Ferdie's back like a burned-on shoulder strap, and he's all digging his fingernail into it, flicking off the dry blood and exposing the quick, slick flesh. And the weird thing is there is a kind of love between them, or anyways a kind of dependency, because they are like each other's liquid sky, they are each other's addiction. Uncle Will still has Ferdie in his arms and he turns his back to me so I can see right into Ferdie's eyes and them eyes are all shiny, like the contact lenses a monster wears in a cheesy horror movie. But Ferdie's smiling too, like he's telling me, *This is what I've been waiting for. Yeah, maybe you like saved my life yesterday, but you couldn't snatch me away from Mr. Death forever.* And I'm all like standing with pain pounding in my skull from hitting the post and breaking out in a cold sweat because now Mr. Death has crept up behind Ferdie, with his cupped hands full of the powder, and even bending down he's a head taller than them, and standing against the balcony door he's all black and shadowy and big and terrifying, and then I guess when there's enough raw flesh showing he like blows the powder all over Ferdie's back and he begins to chant and the powder goes everywhere; it wraps itself around the three of them like a cloud for a moment and then it all gets totally swallowed up in the dust and darkness of the room.

That's when Ferdie starts to scream.

Uncle Will's all, "God damn it, bitch, stop whining or I'll whip your motherfucking ass to kingdom come," but Mr. Death puts his hand on Will's shoulder and says, "It too late, my friend, you already have."

▼▼▼

We left him screaming and went into the living room, and Uncle Will broke out a brand-new bottle of Jack Daniel's. We drank the whole thing in less than fifteen minutes. Then we got totally fucked up on weed and downers. We had to. Because that screaming went on and on and it made me feel cold all the way into my guts. I don't know how long it went on but when I finally woke up it was because Uncle Will was prodding me with an empty bottle, and he's all, "Help me load him into the car, dude."

"Where's Mr. Death?"

"Gone already. But he's left us a note."

The note read:

Bring him to my house
Bury him in my yard
Wait

And that's what we did. We found an open wooden box lying out under the trees, all ready to receive the body, and we dug a hole and buried Ferdie, and we set up a pile of stones like we seen other places in Mr. Death's yard. We hung around all day. It got to late afternoon and Uncle Will kept going up to the house and knocking, but the whole place was locked up. When the sun got near to setting Will was all pacing up and down and he's all, "We can't stay after sunset; there's a fucking curfew on and we'll have to spend the fucking night if we don't leave now."

"But we can't just leave Ferdie behind."

Just when Will was about ready to explode, this beat-up old Packard comes screaming into the driveway and there's Mr. Death. He's all dressed in black. He has a bottle of pills in his hand and he throws it to me and the bottle says on it, *Datura*. "Sorry I'm so late," he said, "I had to see my pharmaceutical contacts. It difficult to trace anybody down with all them riots going on."

"What's that stuff for?" said Uncle Will.

"Insurance," said Mr. Death. "Now let's dig up your new son."

Digging him up took a lot longer than burying him because every now and then Mr. Death stopped to chant. Then, when the moon came out, he went into like a trance and his eyes totally rolled up into their sockets and he danced around us, hollering and shrieking.

But we finally pulled the coffin back out of the ground and opened the lid, and there was Ferdie, his eyes wide open, trying to breathe, and his knuckles and knees were all bloody from clawing and kicking at the coffin lid. Mr. Death forced a pill down his throat and he calmed down, and Mr. Death's all, "Ferdinand, you a zombie now. You one of the living dead. You understand what that mean?"

Ferdie nods, slowly, and yeah, I can tell that he's changed. It ain't that he looks much different. There ain't no smell of dead things on him, just the usual toilet smell because he didn't have nowhere he could go in that box we buried him in. His eyes have that look though. The look I remember from my grandpa. The camcorder look. The eyes suck in, but they give nothing out.

"Now," Mr. Death says, "embrace your father, and don't you be stubborn again, cuz next time you dead for good."

"I won't be stubborn," Ferdie says, and he sounds more like a toddler than a twelve-year-old. "I love my father."

We went back to the house and camped out on the living room floor because of the curfew. Ferdie lay on the floor and slept with his eyes open and didn't move a muscle. Maybe Mr. Death was right when he said this was all science, not magic, and maybe it was true that Ferdie wasn't really dead but had only been called back from a coma caused by the nerve poison in the puffer fish, but I knew that Ferdie didn't think so. Ferdie had watched zombie movies before. He knew that he didn't have his soul no more. He knew he was just an animated corpse.

▼▼▼

I didn't ditch too much that week because of the riots and there was so much to talk about with my homies. A lot of them had taken the bus down to South Central and did their own looting and they were all telling me about their new watches, Sega Genesises, boomboxes, shoes they jacked. I couldn't tell them I had spent the last two days raising the dead so I pretended I didn't care. In fact, whenever they tell me about all the shit they stoled, I'm all, "Who cares? It ain't no challenge looting a big old Circuit City with five hundred other people and the cops too scared to come in. Me, I can jack a CD player right from under the security guard's eyes. I'm down and you ain't."

So anyways I didn't see too much of Uncle Will that week. But whenever I would go there, the apartment was totally different. It was all clean and vacuumed and all the forty-ouncer bottles were all neatly lined up against the wall ready to be recycled. The blinds were all up and the living room was flooded in sunlight. At first I thought Uncle Will must have a new girlfriend but actually she had dumped him and it was just him and Ferdie living there now. And it was Ferdie cleaning the house. One time I caught him at it. He was all dusting the blinds and he was dressed different, too, in freshly laundered Bugle Boys and a white T-shirt.

"Yo, Ferdie," I said.

And he's all, "Hello, Ozzie, can I get you something to drink?" like he's a fucking waitress at Denny's or something. I was amazed and I just let him fetch me a wine cooler from the refrigerator. Then he went back into the kitchen and I followed him. He didn't walk like a zombie. He wasn't all shambling. He held his shoulders back and stood straight and didn't slouch around like a wuss. And he was all smiling. I mean, all the time. Only his eyes didn't smile. His eyes took everything in, gave out nothing.

I'm all, "What the fuck's happened to you?"

"I think I'm enjoying being dead."

"Ferdie, you ain't dead. Mr. Death explained the whole process to us. The datura makes your mind all fuzzy, but you ain't *dead.*"

He's all, "Of course I am. It's what I been praying for all my life. I'm happy now and so is my dad. You should try it, Oz. I look at you and I see, you're so unhappy."

"I seen dead people before," I said. I thought of Grandpa. I thought of my brother, which I never saw dead but they all told me about his brains being splattered on the pavement and his eyeball impaled by the hood ornament of a parked Impala. "You ain't one of them." But his eyes, his eyes . . . "And I don't want to be one neither."

"Suit yourself," he said, and scrubbed the counter with a sponge, scrubbed it to death even though it was already shiny except the spots where his scrubbing had wore off the laminate.

Uncle Will came home.

Ferdie's all "Daddy!" and he runs over to embrace him. Uncle Will kisses him on the cheek. He takes a pill out of his pocket and feeds it to Ferdie. They hug each other again. It's kind of sickening actually, like *The Waltons*.

"Shit," he says, "last one. I'll have to ask Mr. Death for more." Then he sees me and he's all, "Oh, it's you."

I'm all, "I stopped by to see what's up."

Uncle Will looks me over and then he's all, "Look at you, Ozzie, jeeze you're a disgrace. Look at them jeans. What are you doing wearing them jeans, they look like they're about ten sizes too big."

"It's the style, Uncle Will."

"Fucking cholo style. You want people to think we're nothing but white trash?"

I backed away in a real hurry. I looked at Ferdie but he didn't seem to think anything was wrong; he was hanging on every word Uncle Will spoke, like a ten-year-old girl at a NKOTB concert.

"And what are you doing drinking that wine cooler anyways?"

"You always let me drink wine coolers, Uncle Will."

He knocked the bottle out of my hand and Ferdie dove after it, caught it one handed, got on his hands and knees to sponge the mess off of the carpet. While I was all standing there stunned, Uncle Will slaps me hard right across the mouth a couple of times. I can't believe this is happening to me even when I start to taste blood.

And Ferdie's all smiling.

"Uncle Will," I said softly, "you never done this to me before."

"I'm seeing you with new eyes, you good-for-nothing juvenile delinquent scumbag."

"Come on, Uncle Will, you said yourself every kid has to steal a few cars and jack a few stereos once in a while, and get drunk. You said it was just a phase, that I'd get over it, that it was like harmless."

"Don't sass me."

But it's hard to get out of the habit of answering back because it's always been this close between me and Uncle Will and I can't understand why he's turned against me until I realize that it's the Siamese twin thing, that Will can't love his zombie son without hating me. So I'm all backing out of there real fast because I think any minute now he's going to starting laying into me with his belt or his fists or a cigarette. I get out of there as fast as I can and I go sprinting up the stairs three steps at a time to my mom's apartment, the place where I most hate to be.

▼▼▼

Mom was sitting at the counter and what was weird was she was actually making dinner when I arrived. The whole living room smelled of enchiladas. She was all dressed up, too. I realized she had been out looking for a job, and she didn't look wasted. She was all shredding lettuce and watching television, which was showing the riots, naturally.

"How's the job market, Mom?"

She's all, "I actually *got* a job today, Oz, they're going to train me to be a checkout lady at Alpha Beta."

"Coolness."

"I get a discount on food, too. We're not gonna be hungry no more."

"We wouldn't be hungry, Mom, if you would have spent them disability checks on food instead of—"

"I know, I know. Let's not argue about it no more. I want to start again. I done a lot of things I regretted in my life. And Jesus, I don't know how to tell you this, but . . . there was this lady from the rehab program, she got my name off some mailing list, she was over here to talk about shared needles and . . . Jesus, Oz, do you think I have it?"

"Don't say that, Mom."

"I'm scared to take the test, son. I'm scared to stick another needle in me and I'm scared not to because if I didn't then I know I'm going to be scared by everything around me, the whole world."

She's all crying and the oven timer goes *dingdingding*, so I took the enchiladas out. Then I put my arm around Mom's waist and let her cry for the longest time, and dinner was totally cold when we finally got around to it; but it's the thought that counts and it was like the first dinner she'd made in six months.

After we ate I asked her what Grandpa was like. "Was he ever mean to you?" I said. "Did he like hit you and stuff?"

"No. I got everything I ever asked for. It was Will he hated. He always said Will was stubborn. He'd lock him up in the toolshed for days at a time. Me, though, he loved me. He loved me to death. His love was a scary thing. It engulfed me. It ate me up. I guess that's why I became a junkie."

And then I understood everything. Uncle Will's sickness didn't just come from nowhere. It had been handed down through the generations and maybe, one day, it would even come down to me. Grown-ups are always all, what a big deal it is to grow up, to become mature, to set aside childish things as my grandma says, quoting the Bible . . . I ain't grown up yet but I already know that growing up is a big old joke . . . you don't grow up. You just live through your childhood again and again and again until the day you die. Your childhood is who you are.

"I'm going back down to Uncle Will's place," I said. "There's something I just got to tell him."

"All right," she said. "But don't go outside. The curfew hasn't been lifted yet and you don't know what the cops will do, they're in such a state over these damn riots."

Yeah. We could hear sirens in the distance. Mom switched channels and an anchorman was talking about the fires again . . . behind him, the city was burning . . . in a little window on the screen, they were replaying the video of the Rodney King beating for the millionth time. They had preempted the fucking *Simpsons*. They showed a clip of Pat Buchanan visiting South Central. He might just as well have been an alien from *Close Encounters*.

I went down to Uncle Will's to tell him my big new insight. I figure if he would have known that he was just slow-motion-replaying a scene from his childhood over and over, he could maybe step back from it, get it in perspective, and then maybe we could pull Ferdie back from his so-called death and Will out of his madness. But when

I got to Will's I could tell that things had gone wrong, more wrong than they ever were before.

Will and Ferdie were standing on opposite sides of the living room. Between them, on the big TV, was the bird's-eye view of the ocean of fire. Will was shouting into his portable phone. "God damn it," he was saying, "I need the fucking pills *now*. He's getting stubborn again, and I'm gonna fucking lose control!"

He had run out of datura. But what difference did it make? Ferdie was standing there and he was all submissive, all smiling, didn't seem like he was doing nothing wrong.

I heard Mr. Death's voice, "You know I can't come out there now. The curfew. And my supplier he way out in South Pas."

And Uncle Will's all, "Fuck, fuck, fuck, I'm fucking desperate!"

He slammed the portable phone against the wall. Then he turned and saw me. "Kid's being stubborn again," he shouted. "He won't mind, he just stands there, won't do what he's told." Then he turned to Ferdie and screamed, "I want you to whine, you hear! I want you to wipe that grin off your face! I'm sick of watching that smile day in day out!"

Ferdie tried to frown but the smile was soldered on his face. He said, "But I can't be unhappy, Dad. I have the kindest father in the world. I have a great life."

"You don't even *have* a life, you're just an animated corpse, and I want you to obey me!"

Ferdie's all, "Okay, Dad. I'm as sad as you want me to be." And he goes on smiling. And Uncle Will's going berserk. I mean like, more berserk than he's ever been before, he's like frothing at the mouth and shit. And Ferdie just goes on smiling. And Will's all, "I'm gonna hurt you, Ferdie," but Ferdie's all, "I don't hurt anymore, Dad. There ain't no hurting where I am, the dead country." And he goes on smiling.

Uncle Will picks up the first thing he sees, which is one of the empty bottles lined up against the wall. He strides over to Ferdie and he starts swinging it and it cracks against the wall and he cuts Ferdie's face a couple of times, and Ferdie goes on smiling. Will socks him in the jaw and a bloody tooth flies on to the carpet, and

Ferdie smiles a gap-toothed smile, wider than ever. Will's weeping with rage and he just goes on punching and punching and for a long while I'm all standing there and staring because I can't believe it's happening, it's worse than I've ever seen before. I forget all about the big old revelation I was going to make. I think maybe even though it's true, that we're all together in this generational cycle of violence, that just saying it isn't going to make it stop because we're stuck in it, we're part of it; we're the spokes of the wheel and when the wheel turns we can't just turn the other way. I'm so full of despair I want to go hang myself like Ferdie was trying to. I want to be dead.

While I'm all standing there with these terrible emotions raging through me, Uncle Will's never stopped trying to whip that smile off Ferdie's face. And now he's all, "You ain't dead, you ain't dead, it's just your stubbornness speaking, and I'm going to *shock* you back to the way you are. You can't escape from me by playing possum cuz I know you're inside there and you're laughing at me, laughing at me . . ." and he sounds just like Grandpa used to sound sometimes. I stand there and watch while he ties Ferdie to a chair with an extension cord and now he's all getting more cords out of a drawer and I realize that when Uncle Will says *shock* that's exactly what he means; he's going to fry Ferdie's brains and this time he'll *really* be dead. And finally this shocks *me* out of my despair and I do what I should have done the first day I saw my cousin cut and bruised and caged . . . I crawl over to where the phone's lying on the carpet and I pull up the antenna and I dial 911.

It takes forever to get through because of the riots I guess. And the whole time Uncle Will's all storming through the house and throwing things around, and there's blood all over Ferdie's white shirt but Ferdie's all smiling, smiling, smiling, and even I can feel a piece of Uncle Will's madness in me, the smile that goes on and on and driving you all crazy and shit. Then there's a lull in the shouting. Uncle Will's out of breath or something maybe, and that's when I get through to the police and I give them our address and tell them there's a child beating going on right now and please come, please Jesus come fast or I think my cousin's going to get fucking killed.

I put down the phone and I see the two of them, face-to-face, frozen in a moment of concentrated rage. Uncle Will turns to me and says, real soft like, "Traitor."

I'm all, "I'm sorry, Uncle Will." And I'm thinking of the times Uncle Will's been good to me, put his arm around me, wiped my tears with his sleeve, and all the time there's been a mirror image of this love between us, locked up like a dirty secret. And I'm all crying. We can hear sirens in the distance. They're already coming.

"I've gotta get out of here," says Will. "Can't let them catch me. There's a warrant on me, parking tickets and shit, car registration, I don't know."

"You got nowheres to go, Uncle Will. There's a curfew."

Someone is knocking on the door.

Uncle Will bolts past both of us toward Ferdie's room. I let the officer in and she takes one look at Ferdie, tied to the chair and covered in blood, and she's all pulling out her gun and running toward the back of the house.

I untie Ferdie and then me and him follow. We hear the rustle of the orange tree and we know he's going down into the alley. The sirens are wailing from every side now. The police officer's all, "Stay right here, kids. I'm going down to radio for help."

So there's me and there's Ferdie standing on the balcony looking down through the branches of the orange tree into the alley below. And there's Uncle Will. Staggering. Confused. Two police officers come in from Aztec and two from Astoria, and they have their PR24's out. They don't read him no rights, they don't call out to him to surrender. They just surround him and start beating the shit out of him with their power strokes. The whistling of the nightsticks and the crunching of bones blend in with the other sounds of the night, the swaying of the orange branches, the rattling of garbage cans, the thrum of helicopters, the wail of sirens and stray cats. The night air totally smells of citrus and smog and garbage and gunsmoke. Though this is all happening for real and not on television, there's something about it that's less real than television: it's because we're standing in the warm wind of night and seeing the San Gabriel Mountains through the veil of smog and we feel small and we feel powerless, not like TV where you're bigger than the people on the screen and you can turn them on and off with a flick of a remote. I look down and I don't see a man I used to love, I only see flesh and bone and blood, and I try to feel but I don't feel nothing, *nothing*.

And like, now I understand why Ferdie prefers being dead.

The beating goes on and on, and afterwards Uncle Will isn't moving no more and I'm sure that he's not gonna see the morning.

And I'm all, "Ferdie, come back from the dead now. You don't have to be dead no more. We've killed him."

But Ferdie doesn't come back from the dead. I look into his eyes and they have the lifeless look of a camcorder lens. There won't be no videotape of Uncle Will to play on national television. No, there'll just be the videotape that's burned into me and Ferdie, with the erase tab popped forever.

Ferdie smiles. And smiles.

And smiles.

▼▼▼

Me and my mom and Ferdie are in family counseling now. We were on a waiting list for a foster home for a while, but nobody wanted us. Mr. Death has disappeared, and we've never been able to find his house again.

Our counselor says it's true what Mr. Death said: that there's no magic to what happened, that Ferdie never was dead or came back from the dead. He says that Uncle Will wove a tapestry of illusion around us, that we were trapped inside his warped reality. He says that coming to terms with this will help us to change, to heal.

Well like, *I've* changed. I hardly drink no more and I never shoplift. I try to read books sometimes, like Ferdie used to. Ferdie don't read books. I don't think he's even growing any. He's all frozen in time.

But Ferdie hasn't stopped smiling. He smiles through everything:

happy times, sad times. A defense mechanism, the counselor calls it. My mom says, "Give him time and one day he'll feel again."

Sometimes I ask him if he's ever going to come back. And always he's all, "Nu-*uh*."

"Why not, Ferdie?" I'll ask him. Because like, there's no reason for him to play dead no more. Mom's in rehab and we're getting taken care of, and he don't have to feel pain all the time like he used to.

But he'll just look at me with them dead eyes, and he'll say, "I like it better here."

THE DOCTOR

ANNE RICE

THE doctor had never been inside an antebellum mansion until that spring in New Orleans. And the old house really did have white fluted columns on the front, though the paint was peeling away. Greek Revival style they called it—a long violet-gray town house on a dark shady corner in the Garden District, its front gate guarded it seemed by two enormous oaks. The iron lace railings were made in a rose pattern and much festooned with vines—purple wisteria, the yellow Virginia creeper, and bougainvillea of a dark, incandescent pink.

He liked to pause on the marble steps and look up at the Doric capitals, wreathed as they were by those drowsy fragrant blossoms. The sun came in thin dusty shafts through the twisting branches. Bees sang in the tangle of brilliant green leaves beneath the peeling cornices. Never mind that it was so somber here, so damp.

Even the approach through the deserted streets seduced him. He walked slowly over cracked and uneven sidewalks of herringbone brick or gray flagstone, under an unbroken archway of oak branches, the light eternally dappled, the sky perpetually veiled in green. Always he paused at the largest tree that had lifted the iron fence with its bulbous roots. He could not have gotten his arms around the trunk of it. It reached all the way from the pavement to the house itself, twisted limbs clawing at the shuttered windows beyond the banisters, leaves enmeshed with the flowering vines.

But the decay here troubled him nevertheless. Spiders wove their tiny intricate webs over the iron lace roses. In places the iron had so rusted that it fell away to powder at the touch. And here and there near the railings, the wood of the porches was rotted right through.

Then there was the old swimming pool far beyond the garden—a great long octagon bounded by the flagstones, which had become a swamp unto itself with its black water and wild irises. The smell alone was frightful. Frogs lived there, frogs you could hear at dusk, singing their grinding, ugly song. Sad to see the little fountain jets up one side and down the other still sending their little arching streams into the muck. He longed to drain it, clean it, scrub the sides with his own hands if he had to. Longed to patch the broken balustrade, and rip the weeds from the overgrown urns.

Even the elderly aunts of his patient—Miss Carl, Miss Millie, and Miss Nancy—had an air of staleness and decay. It wasn't a matter of gray hair or wire-rimmed glasses. It was their manner, and the fragrance of camphor that clung to their clothes.

Once he had wandered into the library and taken a book down from the shelf. Tiny black beetles scurried out of the crevice. Alarmed, he had put the book back.

If there had been air-conditioning in the place it might have been different. But the old house was too big for that—or so they had said back then. The ceilings soared fourteen feet overhead. And the sluggish breeze carried with it the scent of mold.

His patient was well cared for, however. That he had to admit. A sweet old black nurse named Viola brought his patient out on the screened porch in the morning and took her in at evening.

"She's no trouble at all, Doctor. Now, you come on, Miss Deirdre, walk for the doctor." Viola would lift her out of the chair and push her patiently step by step.

"I've been with her seven years now, Doctor, she's my sweet girl."

Seven years like that. No wonder the woman's feet had started to turn in at the ankles, and her arms to draw close to her chest if the nurse didn't force them down into her lap again.

Viola would walk her round and round the long double parlor, past the harp and the Bösendorfer grand layered with dust. Into the long broad dining room with its faded murals of moss-hung oaks and tilled fields.

Slippered feet shuffling on the worn Aubusson carpet. The woman was forty-one years old, yet she looked both ancient and young—a stooped and pale child, untouched by adult worry or passion. *Deirdre, did you ever have a lover? Did you ever dance in that parlor?*

On the library bookshelves were leather-bound ledgers with old dates marked on the spines in faded purple ink: 1756, 1757, 1758 . . . Each bore the family name of Mayfair in gold lettering.

Ah, these old southern families, how he envied them their heritage. It did not have to lead to this decay. And to think, he did not know the full names of his own great-grandparents or where they had been born.

Mayfair—a vintage colonial clan. There were old paintings on the walls of men and women in eighteenth-century dress, as well as daguerreotypes and tintypes and faded photographs. A yellowed map of Saint-Domingue—did they call it that still?—in a dirty frame in the hallway. And a darkening painting of a great plantation house.

And look at the jewels his patient wore. Heirlooms surely, with those antique settings. What did it mean that they put that kind of jewelry on a woman who hadn't spoken a word or moved of her own volition in over seven years?

The nurse said she never took off the chain with the emerald pendant, not even when she bathed Miss Deirdre.

"Let me tell you a little secret, Doctor, don't you ever touch that!"

"And why not " he wanted to ask. But he had said nothing. He watched uneasily as the nurse put on the patient's ruby earrings, her diamond ring.

Like dressing a corpse, he thought. And out there the dark oaks wind their limbs toward the dusty window screens. And the garden shimmers in the dull heat.

"And look at her hair," said the nurse lovingly. "Have you ever seen such beautiful hair?"

It was black all right, and thick and curly and long. The nurse loved to brush it, watching the curls roll up as the brush released them. And the patient's eyes, for all their listless stare, were a clear blue. Yet now and then a thin silver line of saliva fell down from the side of her mouth, making a dark circle on the bosom of her white nightgown.

"It's a wonder somebody hasn't tried to steal those things," he said half to himself. "She's so helpless."

The nurse had given him a superior, knowing smile.

"No one who's ever worked in this house would try that."

"But she sits all alone on that side porch by the hour. You can see her from the street."

Laughter.

"Don't worry about that, doctor. No one around here is fool enough to come in that gate. Old Ronnie mows the lawn, but that's because he always did, done it for thirty years now, but then old Ronnie isn't exactly right in the head."

"Nevertheless . . ." But he had stopped himself. What was he doing, talking like this right in front of the silent woman, whose eyes only now and then moved just a little, whose hands lay just where the nurse had placed them, whose feet rested limply on the bare floor. How easy it was to forget oneself, forget to respect this tragic creature. Nobody knew what the woman understood.

"Might get her out in the sun sometime," the doctor said. "Her skin is so white."

But he knew the garden was impossible, even far away from the reek of the pool. The thorny bougainvillea burst in clumps from beneath the wild cherry laurel. Fat little cherubs, streaked with slime, peered out of overgrown lantana like ghosts.

Yet once children had played here.

Some boy or girl had carved the word *Lasher* into the thick trunk of the giant crepe myrtle that grew against the far fence. The deep gashes had weathered so that they gleamed white against the waxy bark. Strange word that. And a wooden swing was still hanging from the branch of the distant oak.

He'd walked back to that lonely tree, and sat down on the swing for a moment, felt the rusted chains creak, then move as he pushed his foot into the crushed grass.

The southern flank of the house looked mammoth and overwhelmingly beautiful to him from this perspective, the flowering vines climbing together all the way up past the green shuttered windows to the twin chimneys above the third floor. The dark bamboo rattled in the breeze against the plastered masonry. The glossy banana trees grew so high and dense they made a jungle clear back to the brick wall.

It was like his patient, this old place—beautiful yet forgotten by time, by urgency.

Her face might be pretty still if it were not so utterly lifeless. Did she see the delicate purple clusters of wisteria, shivering against the screens, the writhing tangle of other blooms? Could she see all the way through the trees to the white columned house across the street?

Once he had ridden upstairs with her and her nurse in the quaint yet powerful little elevator with its brass gate and worn carpet. No change in Deirdre's expression as the little car began to rise. It made him anxious to hear the churning machinery. He could not imagine the motor except as something blackened and sticky and ancient, coated with dust.

Of course he had questioned the old doctor at the sanitarium.

"I remember when I was your age," said the old doctor. "I was going to cure all of them. I was going to reason with the paranoiacs, and bring the schizophrenics back to reality, and make the catatonics wake up. You give her that shot every day, son. There's nothing there anymore. We just do our best to keep her from getting worked up now and then, you know, the agitation."

Agitation? That was the reason for these powerful drugs? Even if the shots were stopped tomorrow it would be a month before the effects had fully worn off. And the levels used were so high they might have killed another patient. You had to build up to a dosage like that.

How could anyone know the true state of the woman when the medication had gone on for so long? If only he could run an electroencephalogram. . . .

He'd been on the case about a month when he sent for the records. It was a routine request. No one noticed. He sat at his desk at the sanitarium all afternoon struggling with the scrawl of dozens of other physicians, the vague and contradictory diagnoses—mania, paranoia, complete exhaustion, delusions, psychotic break, depression, attempted suicide. It went all the way back to the girl's teens apparently. No, even before. Someone had seen her for "dementia" when she was ten years old.

What were the specifics behind these abstractions? Somewhere in the mountain of scribble he found that she had borne a girl child at eighteen, given it up, suffered "severe paranoia."

Is that why they had given her shock treatments in one place and insulin shock in another? What had she done to the nurses who over and over again quit on account of "physical attacks"?

She had "run away" at one point, been "forcibly committed" again. Then pages were missing, whole years uncharted. "Irreversible brain damage" was noted in 1976. "Patient sent home, Thorazine prescribed to prevent palsy, mania."

It was an ugly document, telling no story, revealing no truth. And it discouraged him, finally. Had a legion of other doctors talked to her the way he did now when he sat beside her on the side porch?

"It's a beautiful day, isn't it, Deirdre?" Ah, the breeze here, so fragrant. The scent of the gardenias was suddenly overpowering, yet he loved it. Just for a moment, he closed his eyes.

Did she loathe him, laugh at him, even know he was there? There were a few streaks of gray in her hair, he saw that now. Her hand was cold, unpleasant to touch.

The nurse came out with a blue envelope in her hand, a snapshot.

"It's from your daughter, Deirdre. See? She's twenty-four years old now, Deirdre." She held the snapshot out for the doctor to see too. A blond girl on the deck of a big white yacht, hair blowing in the wind. Pretty, very pretty. "On San Francisco Bay, 1983."

Nothing changed in the woman's face. The nurse brushed the black hair back from her forehead. She thrust the picture at the doctor. "See that girl? That girl's a doctor, too!" She gave him a great superior nod. "She's an intern, going to be a medical doctor just like you someday, that's the truth."

Was it possible? Had the young woman never come home to see to her own mother? He disliked her suddenly. Going to be a medical doctor, indeed.

How long had it been since his patient had worn a dress or a real pair of shoes? He longed to play a radio for her. Maybe she would like music. The nurse had her television soap operas on all afternoon in the back kitchen.

He came to distrust the nurses as he distrusted the aunts.

The tall one who wrote the checks for him—"Miss Carl"—was a lawyer still though she must have been in her seventies. She came and went from her offices on Carondelet Street in a taxicab because she could no longer climb up on the high wooden step of the St. Charles car. For fifty years, she had told him once when he had met her at the gate, she had ridden the St. Charles car.

"Oh, yes," the nurse said one afternoon as she was brushing Deirdre's hair very slowly, very gently. "Miss Carl's the smart one. Works for Judge Fleming. One of the first women ever to graduate from the Loyola School of Law. She was seventeen years old when she went to Loyola. Her father was old Judge McIntyre, and she was ever so proud of him."

Miss Carl never spoke to the patient, not that the doctor had ever seen. It was the portly one, "Miss Nancy," who was mean to her, or so the doctor thought.

"They say Miss Nancy never had much chance for an education," the nurse gossiped. "Always home taking care of the others. There used to be old Miss Belle here too."

There was something sullen and almost common about "Miss Nancy." Dumpy, neglected, always wearing her apron yet speaking to the nurse in that patronizing artificial voice. Miss Nancy had a faint sneer on her lips when she looked at Deirdre.

And then there was Miss Millie, the eldest of them all, who was actually some sort of cousin—a classic in old lady black silk and string shoes. She came and went, never without her worn gloves and her small black straw hat with its veil. She had a cheery smile for the doctor, and a kiss for Deirdre. "That's my poor dear sweetheart," she would say in a tremulous voice.

One afternoon, he had come upon Miss Millie standing on the broken flags by the pool.

"Nowhere to begin anymore, Doctor," she had said sadly.

It was not his place to challenge her, yet something quickened in him to hear this tragedy acknowledged.

"And how Stella loved to swim here," the old woman said. "It was Stella who built it, Stella who had so many plans and dreams. Stella put in the elevator, you know. That's just the sort of thing that Stella would do. Stella gave such parties. Why, I remember hundreds in the house, tables over the whole lawn, and the bands that would play. You're too young, Doctor, to remember that lively music. Stella had those draperies made in the double parlor, and now they're too old to be cleaned anymore. That's what they said. They'd fall apart if we tried to clean them now. And it was Stella who had paths of flagstones laid here, all along the pool. You see, like the old flags in the front and along the side . . ." She broke off, pointing down the long side of the house at the distant patio so crowded by weeds. It was as if she couldn't speak anymore. Slowly she looked up at the high attic window.

He had wanted to ask, But who is Stella?

"Poor darling Stella."

He had envisioned paper lanterns strung through the trees.

Maybe they were simply too old, these women. And that young one, the intern or whatever she was, two thousand miles away. . . .

Miss Nancy bullied the silent Deirdre. She'd watch the nurse walking the patient, then shout in the patient's ear.

"Pick up your feet. You know damn good and well you could walk on your own if you wanted to."

"There's nothing wrong with Miss Deirdre's hearing," the nurse would interrupt her. "Doctor says she can hear and see just fine."

Once he tried to question Miss Nancy as she swept the upstairs hallway, thinking, well, maybe out of anger she'll shed a little light.

"Is there ever the slightest change in her? Does she ever speak . . . even a single word?"

The woman squinted at him for a long moment, the sweat gleaming on her round face, her nose painfully red at the bridge from the weight of her glasses.

"I'll tell you what I want to know!" she said. "Who's going to take care of her when we're no longer here! You think that spoilt daughter out in California is going to take care of her? That girl doesn't even know her mother's name. It's Ellie Mayfair who sends those pictures." She snorted. "Ellie Mayfair hasn't set foot in this house since the day that baby was born and she came to take that baby out of here. All she wanted was that baby because she couldn't have a baby of her own, and she was scared to death her husband would leave her. He's some big lawyer out there. You know what Carl paid Ellie to take that baby? To see to it that girl never came home? Oh, just get her out of here, that was the idea. Made Ellie sign a paper." She gave a bitter smile, wiping her hands on her apron. "Send her to California with Ellie and Graham to live in a fancy house on San Francisco Bay with a big boat and all, that's what happened to Deirdre's daughter."

Ah, so the young woman did not know, he thought, but he said nothing.

"Let Carl and Nancy stay here and take care of things!" The woman went on. "That's the song in this family. Let Carl write the checks and let Nancy cook and scrub. And what the hell has Millie ever done? Millie just goes to church, and prays for us all. Isn't that grand? Aunt Millie's more useless than Aunt Belle ever was. I'll tell you what Aunt Millie can do best. Cut flowers. Aunt Millie cuts those roses now and then, those roses growing wild out there."

She gave a deep ugly laugh, and went past him into the patient's bedroom, gripping the broom by its greasy handle.

"You know you can't ask a nurse to sweep a floor! Oh, no, they wouldn't stoop to that, now, would they? Would you care to tell me why a nurse cannot sweep a floor?"

The bedroom was clean all right, the master bedroom of the house it appeared to be, a large airy northern room. Ashes in the marble fireplace. And what a bed his patient slept in, one of those massive things made at the end of the last century, with the towering half tester of walnut and tufted silk.

He was glad of the smell of floor wax and fresh linen. But the room was full of dreadful religious artifacts. On the marble dresser stood a statue of the Virgin with the naked red heart on her breast, lurid, and disgusting to look at. A crucifix lay beside it, with a twisting, writhing body of Christ in natural colors even to the dark blood flowing from the nails in his hands. Candles burned in red glasses, beside a bit of withered palm.

"Does she notice these religious things?" the doctor asked.

"Hell, no," Miss Nancy said. Whiffs of camphor rose from the dresser drawers as she straightened their contents. "Lot of good they do under this roof!"

There were rosaries hung about the carved brass lamps, even through their faded satin shades. And it seemed nothing had been changed here for decades. The yellow lace curtains were stiff and rotted in places. Catching the sun they seemed to hold it, casting their own burnt and somber light.

There was the jewel box on the marble-top bedside table. Open. As if the contents weren't priceless, which of course they were. Even the doctor, with his scant knowledge of such things, knew those jewels were real.

Beside the jewel box stood the snapshot of the pretty blond-haired daughter. And beneath it a much older and faded picture of the same girl, small but even then quite pretty. Scribble at the bottom. He could only make out: "Pacific Heights School, 1966."

When he touched the velvet cover of the jewel box, Miss Nancy had turned and all but screamed at him.

"Don't you touch that, Doctor!"

"Good Lord, woman, you don't think I'm a thief."

"There's a lot you don't know about this house and this patient.

Why do you think the shutters are all broken, Doctor? Almost fallen off their hinges? Why do you think the plaster's peeling off the brick?" She shook her head, the soft flesh of her cheeks wobbling, her colorless mouth set. "Just let somebody try to fix those shutters. Just let someone climb a ladder and try to paint this house."

"I don't understand you," said the doctor.

"Don't ever touch her jewels, Doctor, that's what I'm saying. Don't touch a thing around here you don't have to. That swimming pool out there, for instance. All choked with leaves and filth like it is, but those old fountains run into it still, you ever think about that? Just try to turn off those faucets, Doctor!"

"But who—?"

"Leave her jewels alone, Doctor. That's my advice to you."

"Would changing things make her speak?" he asked boldly, impatient with all this, and not afraid of this aunt the way he was of Miss Carl.

The woman laughed. "No, it wouldn't make *her* do anything," Nancy answered with a sneer. She slammed the drawer into the bureau. Glass rosary beads tinkled against a small statue of Jesus. "Now, if you'll excuse me, I have to clean out the bathroom, too."

He looked at the bearded Jesus, the finger pointing to the crown of thorns around his heart.

Maybe they were all crazy. Maybe he would go crazy himself if he didn't get out of this house.

▼▼▼

Once, when he was alone in the dining room, he'd seen that word again—Lasher—written in the thick dust on the table. It was done as if by fingertip. Great fancy capital L. Now, what could it possibly mean? It was dusted away when he came the following afternoon, the only time in fact that he had ever seen the dust disturbed there, where the silver tea service on the sideboard was tarnished black. Faded the murals on these walls, yet he could see a plantation scene if he studied them, yes, that same house that was in the painting in the hall. Only after he had studied the chandelier for a long time did he realize it had never been wired for electricity. There was wax still on the candle holders. Ah, such a sadness, the whole place.

At night at home in his modern apartment overlooking the lake, he couldn't stop brooding on his patient. He wondered if her eyes were open as she lay in bed.

"Maybe I have an obligation—" But then what obligation? Her doctor was a reputable psychiatrist. Wouldn't do to question his judgment. Wouldn't do to try anything foolish—like taking her out for a ride in the country, or bringing a radio to the porch. Or *stopping the sedatives to see what would happen?*

Or picking up a phone and contacting that daughter, the intern. *Made Ellie sign a paper.* Twenty-four years old was plenty old enough to be told a few things about one's own mother.

And surely common sense dictated a break in Deirdre's medication once in a while. And what about a complete reevaluation? He had to at least suggest it.

"You just give her the shots," said the old doctor. "Visit with her an hour a day. That's what you're asked to do." Slight coldness this time around. Old fool!

No wonder he was so glad the afternoon he had first seen the man visiting her.

It was early September, and still warm. And as he turned in the gate, he saw the man on the screen porch beside her, obviously talking to her, his arm resting on the back of her chair.

A tall, brown-haired man, rather slender.

The doctor felt a curious possessive feeling. A man he didn't know with his patient. But he was eager to meet him actually. Maybe the man would explain things that the women would not. And surely he was a good friend. There was something intimate in the way he stood so close, the way he inclined toward the silent Deirdre.

But when the doctor came out on the porch there was no visitor. And he could find no one in the front rooms.

"You know, I saw a man here a while ago," he said to the nurse when she came in. "He was talking to Miss Deirdre."

"I didn't see him," the nurse had said offhandedly.

Miss Nancy, shelling peas in the kitchen when he found her,

stared at him for a long moment, then shook her head, her chin jutting. "I didn't hear anybody come in."

Well, isn't that the damnedest thing! But he had to confess, it had only been for an instant—a glimpse through screens. No, but he *saw* the man there.

"If only you could speak to me," he said to Deirdre when they were alone. He was preparing the injection. "If only you could tell me if you want to have visitors, if it matters . . ." Her arm was so thin. When he glanced at her, the needle ready, she was staring at him!

"Deirdre?"

His heart pounded.

The eyes rolled to the left, and she stared forward, mute and listless as before. And the heat, which the doctor had come to like, seemed suddenly oppressive. The doctor felt light-headed in fact, as though he was about to faint. Beyond the blackened, dusty screen, the lawn seemed to move.

Now, he'd never fainted in his life, and as he thought that over, as he tried to think it over, he realized he'd been talking with the man, yes, the man was here, no, not here now, but just had been. They had been in the middle of a conversation, and now he'd lost the thread, or no, that wasn't it, it was that he suddenly couldn't remember how long they'd been talking, and it was so strange to have been talking all this time together, and not recall how it started!

He was suddenly trying to clear his head, and have a better look at the guy, but what had the man just said? It was all very confusing because there was no one there to talk to, no one but her, but yes, he'd just said to the brown-haired man, "Of course, stop the injections . . ." and the absolute rectitude of his position was beyond doubt, the old doctor—"A fool, yes!" said the brown-haired man—would just have to listen!

This was monstrous all this, and the daughter in California . . .

He shook himself. He stood up on the porch. What had happened? He had fallen asleep in the wicker chair. He had been dreaming. The murmur of the bees grew disconcertingly loud in is ears and the fragrance of the gardenias seemed to drug him suddenly.

He looked down over the railing at the patio to his left. Had something moved there?

Only the limbs of the trees beyond as the breeze traveled through them. He'd seen it a thousand times in New Orleans, that graceful dance, as if one tree releases the breeze to another. Such lovely embracing heat. *Stop the injections! She will wake.*

Slowly, awkwardly, a monarch butterfly climbed the screen in front of him. Gorgeous wings. But gradually he focused upon the body of the thing, small and glossy and black. It ceased to be a butterfly and became an insect—loathsome!

"I have to go home," he said aloud to no one. "I don't feel right exactly, I think I should lie down."

The man's name. What was it? He'd known it just a moment ago, such a remarkable name—ah, so that's what the word means, you are—actually, quite beautiful—but wait. It was happening again. He would not let it!

"Miss Nancy!" He stood up out of the chair.

His patient stared forward, unchanged, the heavy emerald pendant gleaming against her gown. All the world was filled with green light, with shivering leaves, the faint blur of the bougainvillea.

"Yes, the heat," he whispered. "Have I given her the shot?" Good Lord. He had actually dropped the syringe, and it had broken.

"You called for me, Doctor?" said Miss Nancy. There she stood in the parlor door, staring at him, wiping her hands on her apron. The colored woman was there too, and the nurse behind her.

"Nothing, just the heat," he murmured. "I dropped it, the needle. but I have another, of course."

How they looked at him, studied him. *You think I'm going crazy, too?*

It was on the following Friday afternoon that he saw the man again.

The doctor was late, he'd had an emergency at the sanitarium. He was sprinting up First Street in the early fall dusk. He didn't want to disturb the family dinner. He was running by the time he reached the gate.

The man was standing in the shadows of the open front porch.

He watched the doctor, his arms folded, his shoulder against the porch column, his eyes dark and rather wide, as though he were lost in contemplation. Tall, slender, clothes beautifully fitted.

"Ah, so there you are," the doctor murmured aloud. Flush of relief. He had his hand out as he came up the steps. "Dr. Petrie is my name, how do you do?"

And—how to describe it? There was simply no man there.

"Now, I know this happened!" he said to Miss Carl in the kitchen. "I saw him on that porch and he vanished into thin air."

"Well, what business is it of ours what you saw, Doctor?" said the woman. Strange choice of words. And she was so hard, this lady. Nothing feeble about her in her old age. She stood very straight in her dark blue gabardine suit, glaring at him through her wire-rimmed glasses, her mouth withered to a thin line.

"Miss Carl, I've seen this man with my patient. Now the patient, as we all know, is a helpless woman. If an unidentified person is coming and going on these premises—"

But the words were unimportant. Either the woman didn't believe him or the woman didn't care. And Miss Nancy, at the kitchen table, never even looked up from her plate as she scraped up the food noisily onto her fork. But the look on Miss Millie's face, ah, now that was something—old Miss Millie so clearly disturbed, her eyes darting from him to Carl and back again.

What a household.

He was irritated as he stepped into the dusty little elevator and pressed the black button in the brass plate.

The velvet drapes were closed and the bedroom was almost dark, the little candles sputtering in their red glasses. The shadow of the Virgin leaped on the wall. He couldn't find the light switch immediately. And when he did, only a single tiny bulb went on in the lamp beside the bed. The open jewel box was right next to it. What a spectacular thing.

When he saw the woman lying there with her eyes open, he felt a catch in his throat. Her black hair was brushed out over the stained pillowcase. There was a flush of unfamiliar color in her cheeks.

Did her lips move?

"Lasher . . ."

A whisper. What had she said? Why, she'd said Lasher, hadn't she? The name he'd seen on the tree trunk and in the dust of the dining table. And he had heard that name spoken somewhere else . . . That's why he knew it was a name. It sent the chills up his back and neck, this catatonic patient actually speaking. But no, he must have been imagining it. It was just the thing he wanted so to happen—the miracle change in her. She lay as ever in her trance. Enough Thorazine to kill somebody else . . .

He set down the bag on the side of the bed. He filled the syringe carefully, thinking as he had several times before, what if you just didn't, just cut it down to half, or a fourth, or none and sat by her and watched and what if— He saw himself suddenly picking her up and taking her out of the house. He saw himself driving her out into the country. They walked hand in hand on a path through the grass until they'd come to the levee above the river. And there she smiled, her hair blowing in the wind—

What nonsense. Here it was six-thirty, and the shot was long overdue. And the syringe was ready.

Suddenly something pushed him. He was sure of it, though where he had been pushed he couldn't say. He went down, his legs buckling, and the syringe went flying.

When he caught himself he was on his knees in the semidark, staring at motes of dust gathered on the bare floor beneath the bed.

"What the hell—" he'd said aloud before he could catch himself. He couldn't find the hypodermic needle. Then he saw it, yards away, beyond the armoire. It was broken, smashed, as if someone had stepped on it. All the Thorazine had oozed out of the crushed plastic vial onto the bare boards.

"Now, wait a minute!" he whispered. He picked it up and stood holding the ruined thing in his hands. Of course he had other syringes, but this was the second time this sort of thing. . . . And he found himself at the bedside again, staring down at the motionless patient, thinking, now how exactly did this—I mean, what in God's name is going on?

He felt a sudden intense heat. Something moved in the room,

rattling faintly. Only the rosary beads wound about the brass lamp. He went to wipe his brow. Then he realized, very slowly, even as he stared at Deirdre, that there was a figure standing on the other side of the bed. He saw the dark clothes, a waistcoat, a coat with dark buttons. and then he looked up and saw it was the man.

In a split second his disbelief changed to terror. There was no disorientation now, no dreamlike unreality. The man was there, staring at him. Soft brown eyes staring at him. Then the man was simply gone. The room was cold. A breeze lifted the draperies. The doctor caught himself in the act of shouting. No, screaming, to be perfectly frank.

▼▼▼

At ten o'clock that night, he was off the case. The old psychiatrist came all the way out to the lakefront apartment house to tell him in person. They had gone down to the lake together and strolled along the concrete shore.

Even as the men nearby went on with their conversation, the doctor felt the keening terror he had known in Deirdre Mayfair's darkened room.

The man sat perfectly still gazing at him. Not twenty feet separated him from the doctor. And the white daylight from the front windows of the bar fell quite distinctly over the man's shoulder, illuminating the side of his face.

Really there. The doctor's mouth was filling with water. He was going to be sick. Going to pass out. They'd think he was drunk in this place. God only knew what would happen— He struggled to steady his hand on the glass. He struggled not to panic completely as he had done in Deirdre's room.

Then, without warning, the man appeared to flicker as if he were a projected image, then vanish before the doctor's eyes. A cold breeze swept through the bar.

The bartender turned to keep a soiled napkin from blowing away. A door slammed somewhere. And it seemed the conversation grew louder. The doctor felt a low throbbing in his head.

". . . Going mad!" he whispered.

No power on earth could have persuaded him to pass Deirdre Mayfair's house again.

But the following night, as he was driving home to the lakefront, he saw the man again, standing under a street lamp by the cemeteries on Canal Boulevard, the yellow light shining full upon him against the chalk white graveyard wall.

Just a glimpse but he knew he wasn't mistaken. He began to tremble violently. It seemed for a moment he could not remember how to work the controls of his car, and then he drove it recklessly, stupidly, as if the man were pursuing him. He did not feel safe until he had shut his apartment door.

The following Friday, he saw the man in broad daylight, standing motionless on the grass in Jackson Square. A woman passing turned to glance at the brown-haired figure. Yes, there, as he had been before! The doctor ran through the French Quarter streets. Finding a cab at a hotel door, he ordered the driver to get him out of there, just to take him anywhere, he did not care.

As the days passed, the doctor had ceased to be frightened so much as horrified. He couldn't eat or sleep. He could concentrate on nothing. He moved perpetually in utter gloom. He stared in silent rage at the old psychiatrist whenever their paths crossed.

How in God's name could he communicate to this monstrous thing that he would not come near the miserable woman in the porch rocker? No more needles, no more drugs from him! *I am no longer the enemy, don't you see!*

To ask the help or understanding of anyone he knew was to risk his reputation, even his entire future. A psychiatrist going mad, like his patients. He was desperate. He had to escape this thing. Who knew when it might next appear to him? What if it could come into these very rooms!

Finally on Monday morning, his nerves frayed, his hands shaking, he found himself in the old psychiatrist's office. He had not made up his mind what he would say, only that he could stand the strain no longer. And he soon found himself rattling on about the tropical heat, headaches and sleepless nights, the need for quick acceptance of his resignation.

He drove out of New Orleans that very afternoon.

Only when he was safe in his father's office in Portland, Maine, did he at last reveal the whole story.

"There was never anything menacing in the face," he explained. "On the contrary. It was strangely unlined. It was as bland as the face of Christ in the portrait on the wall of her room. Just staring at me. But it didn't want me to give her the injection! It was trying to scare me."

His father was a patient man. He did not answer at once. Then slowly he began to talk of the strange things he'd witnessed over the years in psychiatric hospitals—doctors seemingly infected with the neuroses and psychoses of their patients. He'd seen a doctor go catatonic one day in the midst of his catatonic patients.

"The important thing, Larry, is that you rest," his father said. "That you let the effects of this whole thing wear off. *And that you don't tell anyone else about it.*"

▼▼▼

Years had passed. The doctor's work in Maine had gone well. And gradually he had built a solid private practice independent of his father.

As for the specter, he had left it behind him in New Orleans, along with the memory of Deirdre Mayfair, sitting eternally in that chair.

Yet there remained in him a lingering fear that if such a thing had happened once, it might happen another time for entirely different reasons. The doctor had tasted real horror in those damp, dark New Orleans days, and his view of the world had never been the same.

DEAD RIGHT

GEOFFREY A. LANDIS

ALI danced left, right, but I had his number, I had the unbeatable combination; I hit him where he dodged and dodged him where he hit. Not even the Champ at his prime could stand against me. He danced back—as expected—and I started into the knockout sequence, counting under my breath (Left! Left! Duck!) to keep the timing (Cross! Half pace back!) and *there*!

Muhammad Ali froze in mid-punch and the lights came on. I took off the glasses and looked at the tally screen: *Ali by knockout*. "What?"

Jim Mallok was standing in the door. "You were a quarter-second late on the A3 sequence, and a half second on the C3. A fighter like Ali, you have to be right in the groove; the bandwidth is too tight for anything else." He flipped a switch, and the video image of Muhammad Ali vanished into the sweat-filled air. A punching bag stood forlorn where he had been. "What the hell you doing fighting Ali, Dave? You got real work to do."

"Yeah, I know. Just sharpening up my moves."

"Can't you sharpen 'em up on your own time? This is business, not a video arcade. We got work to do."

I shrugged. "Can't train against this Sobo guy until you get some videos of him fighting."

"You can still practice your basics. Forget the fancy stuff; you're not going up against Ali. Practice knocking down some real human beings like you might see in the ring."

"Yow-SUH, Mr. Boss-Man suh! Ah's working, Ah's working jes as hard as I can."

Jim smiled.

▼▼▼

I used to fight golden-gloves when I was in high school. I was pretty good, but—let's face it—golden-gloves Minneapolis isn't quite the same league as golden-gloves New York or Chicago. The kids who hung out at the gym were dead-enders from the projects, kids whose only ways to leave the inner city were with their fists or on a slab. I liked it anyway; the jive talking and no-nonsense attitudes were a welcome change from the suburban intellectuals of high school. And besides, there is a pure visceral satisfaction in going into the gym and beating the hell out of a speed bag, walloping the thing until you fall into the flow, a rhythm that goes on effortlessly, until suddenly you wake up covered with sweat and tired right down to your kneecaps.

I boxed at the Naval Academy, too, at least until they told me I was too tall to go into flight training and I opted out to finish my degree at Cleveland State. State didn't have boxing, so while I still kept in shape working out at the Y, I stopped fighting. I didn't think I missed it. Boxing is a young man's sport anyway.

I figured that was the end of my fighting career. Just goes to show how wrong you can be.

I met Mallok during my first, and last, year in grad school, the year I spent slowly discovering that I didn't have any desire to spend the rest of my life as an electrical engineer. I used to go over to the west side to the bouts down on Worthing Street every Saturday afternoon. Alone, of course: the girl I was dating considered any hint of macho something unutterably gauche and the fights absolutely barbaric. One of those Saturdays—a welterweight match—I ran into Mallok. I'd seen him around the fights, but never really noticed what he'd been doing. He was sitting right up by the ring, flicking his attention from the fight to his laptop computer and back, tapping frenetically at the keyboard. I came over to watch, and soon we got to talking fights. By the end of the evening Kid Rutano had downed Corregio with an overhand right, and Mallok had invited me back into his place, a gym and computer lab in one, to look over his fight analysis software.

Until he'd failed to get tenure and dropped out of academia, Jim Mallok had had all the Air Force contracts he could handle. He'd been big in computer conflict modeling, based on a network theory of games. Network theory says that every sufficiently complicated system must have poles and zeros. Put simply, this means that every strategy has a weakness, every opponent has a blind spot. If he knew the physiology and the tactics of a boxer, Mallok said, he could find a strategy that would put him down as easily as tapping him on the shoulder.

I tried a couple of rounds with the video-boxing simulator he'd hacked together, and tried some of the combinations he showed me. It wasn't as realistic as the one he trained me on later, but it was still surprisingly effective. The computer pulled images from a CD ROM library, and twin video projectors put a separate image onto each eyepiece of a set of special glasses. Anybody looking at me would see me circling around a video projector, but to me it looked like the video image had puffed up and started throwing punches.

We made a peculiar pair, Mallock and I; him short and dapper and full of enthusiasm, dark hair slicked back; me the ex-jock in faded sweatshirts, stocky and slow speaking, but always moving. We complemented one another perfectly.

▼▼▼

We were at the ring, and Mallok still hadn't gotten any videos of this Sobo. I was ready for him, though, limbered up and ready with a hatful of winning combinations.

I was dressing down when Sal walked back to the car to get his kit and Jim had gone to talk business with some backers. An old black man in a beat-up felt hat sidled up to me, grabbed my biceps, and looked me earnestly in the eye. "This Sobo, he bad *baka*," he said, with an odd lilting accent that it took me a few seconds to understand. "You understand? He not person. No heart. You fight him, he going kill you. Better you drop out, you sick."

I yanked away, disgusted. "Thanks, guy. I'll do okay." A lot of weird stuff goes on in the fight game. Drugs, legal and illegal, and bribes of all kinds, of course, but not just that. Anything for an edge. Had Sobo's trainer put this guy up to this, or did he have money on the fight? Either way, I wasn't going to buy into it.

"I serious." His look was intense, almost fearful. Maybe he owed money to the mob, needed to win a bet. "Sobo, he different. You not know his type in America. He once dead man, no can die."

Jim had promised that we would be different, we wouldn't play those games, and I wasn't going to be played with, either. "Go away, old man, or I call security. You shouldn't be here."

"I just ignorant man, sir," he said. "But, please, you think it, okay? You be smart."

Sal pushed through the door and stopped. He took one look at me, then threw the tape down on the floor in disgust, and grabbed the man with one hand on his collar and the other on the seat of his pants. "You. Out." He shuffled the man toward the door and gave him a boost outward, then turned to me. "You shouldn't let guys like that talk trash to you, kid. What did he want, ask you to throw the fight?"

I held out my hands to be taped up, and shook my head slightly. "Just trying to scare me, I think," I said. "Didn't work. We don't play those games."

▼▼▼

The damn ring was too hot, and I was sweating before I'd even stood up. Sobo looked tough. He was a tall, stringy guy, skin black as graveyard dirt, thin as a cadaver, but with plenty of reach. He sat there unmoving as his trainer fussed over him, staring straight forward as if he'd forgotten how to use his eyelids. I've seen 'em like that before, brain damaged from too many punches, but still, something about the complete emptiness in his eyes unnerved me. What the old black man had said still ran through my head. "You heard anything about this guy Sobo?" I whispered to Sal.

He didn't look up. "Not much." He continued to rub oil into my back, loosening me up for the bout. "Hasn't been in the country long. Fought twice, won 'em both by wearing the other guy down."

"Umm." I probably knew more than he did; I'd read the dossier. But Sal had street smarts, and we didn't have a good lock on this guy. I'd been hoping for something better.

Sal slapped me on the back. "You can take him, kid. Show him how a red-blooded American fights."

The trainer was muttering to him. From across the ring I could barely hear it, unusual, urgent cadences in a whispered, distorted Creole. At the same time he was wiping Sobo down. I squinted. What was that fluid he was wiping him with? It glistened with an evil shine on Sobo's preternaturally black skin.

The ref made the announcement and I stood up. We looked at each other for a moment, and then the bell rang. Sal punched me softly. "Kill 'im, kid."

Sobo moved out slowly, with a trace of hesitation between movements giving him a jerky look. I memorized that. If he moved with the same rhythm in the ring, I'd have to compensate, or I'd be punching in places where he wasn't.

He had a slow guard, and barely even tried to duck punches. I did the basic sequence: one, two, pause, three, four, down! I stepped back to let the ref in as he fell.

Sobo was still on his feet.

Whap, whap, whap; I licked out a few fast lefts to the face. He raised his guard. Whap, whap; I hit him a couple of times in the stomach. He lowered his guard. He didn't seem to notice, just kept plugging away with his right, pumping like a slow piston. Mostly I blocked 'em, but he put in a couple every now and then.

In the clinches his skin felt cool and squishy. I was breathing hard now, and sweating like a horse. Sobo didn't seem to be sweating at all. Nor breathing, either, as far as I could tell. And he had that same dead, impassive expression on his face. His eyes were funny—flat, almost dusty. No matter where I dodged, he stared straight ahead. I was wearing myself out hitting him, and he didn't even seem to notice it.

This was no projection. This was the real thing, and I didn't like it.

I hate these sleazy, second-rate arenas. The lights hang down low, the air is stagnant and full of smoke; you get hot and soaked in sweat in no time. I was beginning to tire, but Sobo hadn't slowed down a whit. He didn't seem to notice any of my blows, though I was landing three for every one he hit me with. My hands were beginning to hurt. I was sweating rivers, but he hadn't started to sweat at all. The bell rang, at last. I gave him one final lick where the ref couldn't see, then headed back to my corner.

"I gotta talk to Mallok, Sal." When Jim came over, I said, "got anything new?"

Jim shook his head.

"I got a bad feeling about this one, Jim. He's not responding right."

"Keep on it, Dave. We'll get a make on him yet. We got the technology, dig it? Hang in there."

"I got a bad feeling, Jim." Then the bell rang, and I was back in the ring.

Second round was worse. I was killing him on points, but he was wearing me down. The combinations I used had been optimized and fine-tuned and should have been able to knock over a horse, but he kept on moving. I'd gotten in one good one to the face and cut him bad over one eye, but instead of blood, the open edges of the wound oozed a sickly pale yellow fluid, and he took no notice. My throat was raw from panting; bile like stale piss burned in the back of my mouth. I couldn't stand up any longer, and then the bell came.

Third round was worse yet. Sal was yelling advice—"hands high! Head down!"—but I was too tired to keep up. My hands were too heavy, sliding down of their own will. My nostrils were clogged with the tang of sweat and linament, but under those familiar smells was another, a rank odor of decay, like a whiff of rotten meat. I was beginning to feel an awful certainty about the word the old man had been too frightened to say. The bell rang, and I called for Jim.

"He's a zombie, Jim! I mean, a real, live zombie! I mean, a dead one! From Haiti. He's not alive!"

In the opposite corner Sobo stared unmoving, unblinking, the voodoo man chanting over him and rubbing his skin with fresh blood.

Jim didn't even blink. "Isn't that some sort of blowfish poison they use? Should slow him down—what's the problem?"

"No, Jim. I don't mean some poor drugged-out crazy. I mean, he's a zombie. Dead, and I mean D-E-A-D, dead."

"Zombie, like the walking dead? I don't think I believe in zombies, kid."

"You've been updating the program, right? What have you come up with?"

He shook his head. "According to my model, he should be dead twice over by now. Just keep hitting him in the same places, and sooner or later—"

"Negative, Jim. It's voodoo. He *is* dead. Feed it into the computer. Tell me—how can you knock out a fighter who's *already dead*?"

The bell rang. He blinked, and nodded. "I'll try."

▼▼▼

The job market for people to play around with computers, the only profession I was decently prepared for, had quietly gone soft while I was wasting time flunking out of grad school. My girlfriend had drifted off with a vague "we'll stay friends, okay?"; my secondhand Plymouth vanished when the bank noticed I hadn't made any payments for six months. I didn't have any idea of what to do next. I certainly hadn't planned to go back into the fight scene, never even considered going pro. But that summer there was nothing, not even any openings flipping burgers, and I was getting desperate. I'd been hitting the bags at the Y when Jim caught up with me and made his offer. Jim believed that fighting was a thinking man's sport, and he wanted a partner who could think as well as fight.

I could barely believe him. Unless you're up there with Ali, prizefighting is a lousy way to make a living. On the bottom of the card it's hard work and constant training for a shot at a hundred, maybe two hundred, dollars. He wasn't even a trainer, not a real trainer, he was an ex-professor with a theory.

His theory was simple. He claimed that network theory guaranteed that for any system, there was an input that it couldn't respond to. For every fighter there exists some combination of moves that he can't respond to, that leaves him waltzing right into the knockout blow. He could input videotapes of a fighter's past fights into the computer, and have it model the fighter and tell us the moves.

With a piece of software that could train any boxer to beat anybody, he could just name his price, right?

Wrong. An out-of-work college professor? Just who was he trying to scam, anyway? Before he could win fights, he had to win some fights. He needed a demo model.

Me.

I was in no condition for extended bouts, but that made little difference to his strategy.

The computer was programmed with all the great fighters of the past . . . and videos of all the fighters I was going to meet. I was programmed, too: programmed with the moves to beat them.

It was crazy to accept it, but what else did I have? I told him I'd think it over. The next day he'd hired Sal, an old guy who'd been working the corner since the forties, until he got squeezed out by the mob. Sal came in for nothing but a cut of the prize and Mallok's promise that we were going to play straight. When I came by that afternoon to tell him I was in, he was already setting up for the first bout.

The first few fights were upsets—surprise victory by knockout in the first round. It had been so easy it surprised even me; I knew what they were going to do before they did, and they walked into my knockout punch like they were following a script. Suddenly we were getting the attention Mallok needed. With one more win to show that the first two were more than a fluke, I'd be able to get out of the ring and the money would start rolling in. But we were stymied with Sobo. No videos. Most boxers were glad to supplement their income with the little bit of money they'd get from selling videos, but there was a wall of secrecy about the new Haitian fighter. We were going in blind.

No big deal, since we still had the physiology, the nerve connections and blood flow. If you hit him right, not even necessarily very hard, just *right*, any fighter would have to go down. Any fighter alive.

We had never counted on meeting a fighter who wasn't.

His smell was making me retch; something in my hindbrain said that it was wrong, evil, unclean. I was in shape for a sprint, and the match had turned into a marathon. I'd barely stayed upright last round, much less done any damage, and he'd been impassive, steady as a stiffened corpse. As I collapsed onto the stool, I could hear the voodoo man start to mutter his chant in the opposite corner. Jim's voice seemed to come from far away. "I've got it set. Get him off balance to the left, and then knock him over with an A3-A3-B13 combination."

I blinked. A3-A3 was a classic feint combination, footwork opposite to left jab, which would certainly get him off balance—this guy Sobo was no Fred Astaire when it came to dancing—but a B13 wouldn't do anything. Knock him over? Possible, even likely, but tripping him wouldn't hurt him any. What was the point, when he would just get back up again punching? I started to say something when the bell rang.

"Go!" Sal lifted me up off the bench and pushed me toward the ring. Somewhere I found enough energy to stagger forward.

Sobo stepped forward, pistoning away tirelessly. I stepped left, he stepped left, I crossed and jabbed, and then whacked him. It was a soft blow, I was too tired; I had no power left to put behind it. He tripped over his misplaced feet, and his own momentum carried him down. He started to get up—

"Stop the fight!"

The ring medic jumped the rope and ran to Sobo. Sobo was already stumbling to his feet, his right still pumping away, even though I wasn't anywhere in range. "Stop the fight!" The ref looked confused, and then the medic pulled out a hypodermic.

Sobo's trainer shrieked.

The ring medic had to hold Sobo down to examine him. He didn't have a pulse, and his flesh was cold as a shock victim, but he was still trying to get up when the medic jabbed him full of adrenaline to restart his heart.

▼▼▼

Sobo may or may not have been clinically dead when he entered the ambulance. For certain, though, after the paramedics tried adrenaline injections, CPR, electroshock, and all the rest in a frantic effort to restart his heart, he was good and dead by the time he got to the hospital.

There was a big commotion for a while—that's how I picked up the nickname "Killer"—but the coroner's statement said Sobo had been in such bad shape that he never should have been in the ring in the first place. "I don't understand why he was even walking, much less fighting," the doctor said, and nobody ever quite figured out how he'd ever won his first two fights. His trainer was deported back to Haiti as an undesirable alien.

I was feeling nothing: no triumph, no pity, no pain. Just weary. Jim came in as Sal was cutting the tape off my hands. I looked up slowly. "So?"

"So he was already dead. It wasn't exactly illegal, kid. We heard what you said. We figured, if he was a zombie, he couldn't stand up to even a cursory med exam. Sal had to bribe the ring medic to get him to jump in in the middle of the fight, but once he got close to Sobo, the show was over. We didn't intend to kill the guy, but, hell, he was already dead. Should of figured it. Stands to reason, if he was dead to start with, starting his heart wouldn't do him any good."

"What do you mean, not exactly legal?"

"So, new philosophy: if you can't win by the rules," he shrugged, "bribe an official."

I winced as Sal touched up a ripening bruise. "I thought we didn't play that way."

"Hell, kid, you think they were playing by the rules? They must of paid to get somebody to look the other way."

"Then the program's wrong." I just looked at him.

There's a lot of weird stuff that goes down. Fighting a dead man was a new one, but it wouldn't be the weirdest thing to happen in the ring, or outside of it.

"Well, of course. I mean it's not exactly *wrong*, it's just . . . it's that it couldn't . . . it . . ." He paused. "Yeah. Wrong. Dead wrong."

I nodded. "So you know."

We looked at each other, but I was tired, too dead tired to think now, too tired to make fine moral distinctions. In the morning I'd see it clearly.

"I think," Jim said, slowly, "we have some work to do." And, after a long while, he began to laugh.

PASSENGERS

ROBERT SILVERBERG

THERE are only fragments of me left now. Chunks of memory have broken free and drifted away like calved glaciers. It is always like that when a Passenger leaves us. We can never be sure of all the things our borrowed bodies did. We have only the lingering traces, the imprints.

Like sand clinging to an ocean-tossed bottle. Like the throbbings of amputated legs.

I rise. I collect myself. My hair is rumpled; I comb it. My face is creased from too little sleep. There is sourness in my mouth. Has my Passenger been eating dung with my mouth? They do that. They do anything.

It is morning.

A gray, uncertain morning. I stare at it awhile, and then, shuddering, I opaque the window and confront instead the gray, uncertain surface of the inner panel. My room looks untidy. Did I have a woman here? There are ashes in the trays. Searching for butts, I find several with lipstick stains. Yes, a woman was here.

I touch the bedsheets. Still warm with shared warmth. Both pillows tousled. There are other indications of the night's pleasures. A woman, yes.

I have no recollection of any of it, of course. I never do. Helen of Troy could have spent the night with me, or Marilyn Monroe's ghost, or Aphrodite herself, and the next morning I would know nothing of what had taken place. All I know is that a woman was here, and that we made love. And now she is gone, and the Passenger has gone also, and I am alone.

How long did it last, this time?

I pick up the phone and ring Central. "What is the date?"

The computer's bland feminine voice replies, "Friday December fourth, two thousand seven."

"The time?"

"Nine fifty-one, Eastern Standard Time."

"The weather forecast?"

"Predicted temperature range for today, thirty to thirty-eight. Current temperature, thirty-one. Wind from the north, sixteen miles an hour. Chances of precipitation slight."

"What do you recommend for a hangover?"

"Food or medication?"

"Anything you like," I say.

The computer mulls that one over for a while. Then it decides on both, and activates my kitchen. The spigot yields cold tomato juice. Eggs begin to fry. From the medicine slot comes a purplish liquid. The Central Computer is always so thoughtful. Do the Passengers ever ride it, I wonder? What thrills could that hold for them? Surely it must be more exciting to borrow the million minds of Central than to live awhile in the faulty, short-circuited soul of a corroding human being!

December fourth, Central said. Friday. So the Passenger had me for three nights.

I drink the purplish stuff and probe my memories in a gingerly way, as one might probe a festering sore.

I remember Tuesday morning. A bad time at work. None of the charts will come out right. The section manager irritable; he has been taken by Passengers three times in five weeks, and his section is in disarray as a result, and his Christmas bonus is jeopardized. Even though it is customary not to penalize a person for lapses due to Passengers, according to the system, the section manager seems to feel he will be treated unfairly. We have a hard time. Revise the charts, fiddle with the program, check the fundamentals ten times over. Out they come: the detailed forecasts for price variations of public utility securities, February–April 2008. That afternoon we are to meet and discuss the charts and what they tell us.

I do not remember Tuesday afternoon.

That must have been when the Passenger took me. Perhaps at work; perhaps in the mahogany-paneled boardroom itself, during the conference. Pink concerned faces all about me; I cough, I lurch, I stumble from my seat. They shake their heads sadly. No one reaches for me. No one stops me. It is too dangerous to interfere with one who has a Passenger. The chances are great that a second Passenger lurks nearby in the discorporate state, looking for a mount. So I am avoided. I leave the building.

After that, what?

Sitting in my room on this bleak Friday morning, I eat my scrambled eggs and try to reconstruct the three lost nights.

Of course it is impossible. The conscious mind functions during the period of captivity, but upon withdrawal of the Passenger nearly every recollection goes too. There is only a slight residue, a gritty film of faint and ghostly memories. The mount is never precisely the same person afterward; though he cannot recall the details of his experience, he is subtly changed by it.

I try to recall.

A girl? Yes: lipstick on the butts. Sex, then, here in my room. Young? Old? Blonde? Dark? Everything is hazy. How did my borrowed body behave? Was I a good lover? I try to be, when I am myself. I keep in shape. At thirty-eight, I can handle three sets of tennis on a summer afternoon without collapsing. I can make a woman glow as a woman is meant to glow. Not boasting; just categorizing. We have our skills. These are mine.

But Passengers, I am told, take wry amusement in controverting our skills. So would it have given my rider a kind of delight to find me a woman and force me to fail repeatedly with her?

I dislike that thought.

The fog is going from my mind now. The medicine prescribed

by Central works rapidly. I eat, I shave, I stand under the vibrator until my skin is clean. I do my exercises. Did the Passenger exercise my body Wednesday and Thursday mornings? Probably not. I must make up for that. I am close to middle age, now; tonus lost is not easily regained.

I touch my toes twenty times, knees stiff.

I kick my legs in the air.

I lie flat and lift myself on pumping elbows.

The body responds, maltreated though it has been. It is the first bright moment of my awakening: to feel the inner tingling, to know that I still have vigor.

Fresh air is what I want next. Quickly I slip into my clothes and leave. There is no need for me to report to work today. They are aware that since Tuesday afternoon I have had a Passenger; they need not be aware that before dawn on Friday the Passenger departed. I will have a free day. I will walk the city's streets, stretching my limbs, repaying my body for the abuse it has suffered.

I enter the elevator. I drop fifty stories to the ground. I step out into the December dreariness.

The towers of New York rise about me.

In the street the cars stream forward. Drivers sit edgily at their wheels. One never knows when the driver of a nearby car will be borrowed, and there is always a moment of lapsed coordination as the Passenger takes over. Many lives are lost that way on our streets and highways; but never the life of a Passenger.

I began to walk without purpose. I cross Fourteenth Street, heading north, listening to the soft violent purr of the electric engines. I see a boy jigging in the street and know he is being ridden. At Fifth and Twenty-second a prosperous-looking paunchy man approaches, his necktie askew, this morning's *Wall Street Journal* jutting from an overcoat pocket. He giggles. He thrusts out his tongue. Ridden. Ridden. I avoid him. Moving briskly, I come to the underpass that carries traffic below Thirty-fourth Street toward Queens, and pause for a moment to watch two adolescent girls quarreling at the rim of the pedestrian walk. One is black. Her eyes are rolling in terror. The other pushes her closer to the railing. Ridden. But the Passenger does not have murder on its mind, merely pleasure. The black girl is released and falls in a huddled heap, trembling. Then she rises and runs. The other girl draws a long strand of gleaming hair into her mouth, chews on it, seems to awaken. She looks dazed.

I avert my eyes. One does not watch while a fellow sufferer is awakening. There is a morality of the ridden; we have so many new tribal mores in these dark days.

I hurry on.

Where am I going so hurriedly? Already I have walked more than a mile. I seem to be moving toward some goal, as though my Passenger still hunches in my skull, urging me about. But I know that is not so. For the moment, at least, I am free.

Can I be sure of that?

Cogito ergo sum no longer applies. We go on thinking even while we are ridden, and we live in quiet desperation, unable to halt our courses no matter how ghastly, no matter how self-destructive. I am certain that I can distinguish between the condition of bearing a Passenger and the condition of being free. But perhaps not. Perhaps I bear a particularly devilish Passenger which has not quitted me at all, but which merely has receded to the cerebellum, leaving me the illusion of freedom while all the time surreptitiously driving me onward to some purpose of its own.

Did we ever have more than that: the illusion of freedom?

But this is disturbing, the thought that I may be ridden without realizing it. I burst out in heavy perspiration, not merely from the exertion of walking. Stop. Stop here. Why must you walk? You are at Forty-second Street. There is the library. Nothing forces you onward. Stop a while, I tell myself. Rest on the library steps.

I sit on the cold stone and tell myself that I have made this decision for myself.

Have I? It is the old problem, free will versus determinism, translated into the foulest of forms. Determinism is no longer a philosopher's abstraction; it is cold alien tendrils sliding between the cranial sutures. The Passengers arrived three years ago. I have been ridden five times since then. Our world is quite different now. But we have adjusted even to this. We have adjusted. We have our mores. Life goes on. Our governments rule, our legislatures meet, our stock exchanges transact business as usual, and we have methods for compensating for the random havoc. It is the only way. What else can we do? Shrivel in defeat? We have an enemy we cannot fight; at best we can resist through endurance. So we endure.

The stone steps are cold against my body. In December few people sit here.

I tell myself that I made this long walk of my own free will, that I halted of my own free will, that no Passenger rides my brain now. Perhaps. Perhaps. I cannot let myself believe that I am not free.

Can it be, I wonder, that the Passenger left some lingering command in me? Walk to this place, halt at this place? That is possible too.

I look about me at the others on the library steps.

An old man, eyes vacant, sitting on newspaper. A boy of thirteen or so with flaring nostrils. A plump woman. Are all of them ridden? Passengers seem to cluster about me today. The more I study the ridden ones, the more convinced I become that I am, for the moment, free. The last time, I had three months of freedom between rides. Some people, they say, are scarcely ever free. Their bodies are in great demand, and they know only scattered bursts of freedom, a day here, a week there, an hour. We have never been able to determine how many Passengers infest our world. Millions, maybe. Or maybe five. Who can tell?

A wisp of snow curls down out of the gray sky. Central had said the chance of precipitation was slight. Are they riding Central this morning too?

I see the girl.

She sits diagonally across from me, five steps up and a hundred feet away, her black skirt pulled up on her knees to reveal handsome legs. She is young. Her hair is deep, rich auburn. Her eyes are pale; at this distance, I cannot make out the precise color. She is dressed simply. She is younger than thirty. She wears a dark green coat and her lipstick has a purplish tinge. Her lips are full, her nose slender, high-bridged, her eyebrows carefully plucked.

I know her.

I have spent the past three nights with her in my room. She is the one. Ridden, she came to me, and ridden, I slept with her. I am certain of this. The veil of memory opens; I see her slim body naked on my bed.

How can it be that I remember this?

It is too strong to be an illusion. Clearly this is something that I have been *permitted* to remember for reasons I cannot comprehend. And I remember more. I remember her soft gasping sounds of pleasure. I know that my own body did not betray me those three nights, nor did I fail her need.

And there is more. A memory of sinuous music; a scent of youth in her hair; the rustle of winter trees. Somehow she brings back to me a time of innocence, a time when I am young and girls are mysterious, a time of parties and dances and warmth and secrets.

I am drawn to her now.

There is an etiquette about such things, too. It is in poor taste to approach someone you have met while being ridden. Such an encounter gives you no privilege; a stranger remains a stranger, no matter what you and she may have done and said during your involuntary time together.

Yet I am drawn to her.

Why this violation of taboo? Why this raw breach of etiquette? I have never done this before. I have been scrupulous.

But I get to my feet and walk along the step on which I have been sitting until I am below her, and I look up, and automatically she folds her ankles together and angles her knees as if in awareness that her position is not a modest one. I know from that gesture that she is not ridden now. My eyes meet hers. Her eyes are hazy green. She is beautiful, and I rack my memory for more details of our passion.

I climb step by step until I stand before her.

"Hello," I say.

She gives me a neutral look. She does not seem to recognize me. Her eyes are veiled, as one's eyes often are, just after the Passenger has gone. She purses her lips and appraises me in a distant way.

"Hello," she replies coolly. "I don't think I know you."

"No. You don't. But I have the feeling you don't want to be alone just now. And I know I don't." I try to persuade her with my eyes that my motives are decent. "There's snow in the air," I say. "We can find a warmer place. I'd like to talk to you."

"About what?"

"Let's go elsewhere, and I'll tell you. I'm Charles Roth."

"Helen Martin."

She gets to her feet. She still has not cast aside her cool neutrality; she is suspicious, ill at ease. But at least she is willing to go with me. A good sign.

"Is it too early in the day for a drink?" I ask.

"I'm not sure. I hardly know what time it is."

"Before noon."

"Let's have a drink anyway," she says, and we both smile.

We go to a cocktail lounge across the street. Sitting face-to-face in the darkness, we sip drinks, daiquiri for her, Bloody Mary for me. She relaxes a little. I ask myself what it is I want from her. The pleasure of her company, yes. Her company in bed? But I have already had that pleasure, three nights of it, though she does not know that. I want something more. Something more. What?

Her eyes are bloodshot. She has had little sleep these past three nights.

I say, "Was it very unpleasant for you?"

"What?"

"The Passenger."

A whiplash of reaction crosses her face. "How did you know I've had a Passenger?"

"I know."

"We aren't supposed to talk about it."

"I'm broadminded," I tell her. "My Passenger left me sometime during the night. I was ridden since Tuesday afternoon."

"Mine left me about two hours ago, I think." Her cheeks color. She is doing something daring, talking like this. "I was ridden since Monday night. This was my fifth time."

"Mine also."

We toy with our drinks. Rapport is growing, almost without the need of words. Our recent experiences with Passengers give us something in common, although Helen does not realize how intimately we shared those experiences.

We talk. She is a designer of display windows. She has a small apartment several blocks from here. She lives alone. She asks me what I do. "Securities analyst," I tell her. She smiles. Her teeth are flawless. We have a second round of drinks. I am positive, now, that this is the girl who was in my room while I was ridden.

A seed of hope grows in me. It was a happy chance that brought us together again, so soon after we parted as dreamers. A happy chance, too, that some vestige of the dream lingered in my mind.

We have shared something, who knows what, and it must have been good to leave such a vivid imprint on me, and now I want to come to her conscious, aware, my own master, and renew that relationship, making it a real one this time. It is not proper, for I am trespassing on a privilege that is not mine except by virtue of our Passengers' brief presence in us. Yet I need her. I want her.

She seems to need me, too, without realizing who I am. But fear holds her back.

I am frightened of frightening her, and I do not try to press my advantage too quickly. Perhaps she would take me to her apartment with her now, perhaps not, but I do not ask. We finish our drinks. We arrange to meet by the library steps again tomorrow. My hand momentarily brushes hers. Then she is gone.

I fill three ashtrays that night. Over and over I debate the wisdom of what I am doing. But why not leave her alone? I have no right to follow her. In the place our world has become, we are wisest to remain apart.

And yet—there is that stab of half-memory when I think of her. The blurred lights of lost chances behind the stairs, of girlish laughter in second-floor corridors, of stolen kisses, of tea and cake. I remember the girl with the orchid in her hair, and the one in the spangled dress, and the one with the child's face and the woman's eyes, all so long ago, all lost, all gone, and I tell myself that this one I will not lose, I will not permit her to be taken from me.

Morning comes, a quiet Saturday. I return to the library, hardly expecting to find her there, but she is there, on the steps, and the sight of her is like a reprieve. She looks wary, troubled; obviously she has done much thinking, little sleeping. Together we walk along Fifth Avenue. She is quite close to me, but she does not take my arm. Her steps are brisk, short, nervous.

I want to suggest that we go to her apartment instead of to the cocktail lounge. In these days we must move swiftly while we are free. But I know it would be a mistake to think of this as a matter of tactics. Coarse haste would be fatal, bringing me perhaps an ordinary victory, a numbing defeat within it. In any event her mood hardly seems promising. I look at her, thinking of string music and new snowfalls, and she looks toward the gray sky.

She says, "I can feel them watching me all the time. Like vultures swooping overhead, waiting, waiting. Ready to pounce."

"But there's a way of beating them. We can grab little scraps of life when they're not looking."

"They're *always* looking."

"No," I tell her. "There can't be enough of them for that. Sometimes they're looking the other way. And while they are, two people can come together and try to share warmth."

"But what's the use?"

"You're too pessimistic, Helen. They ignore us for months at a time. We have a chance. We have a chance."

But I cannot break through her shell of fear. She is paralyzed by the nearness of the Passengers, unwilling to begin anything for fear it will be snatched away by our tormentors. We reach the building where she lives, and I hope she will relent and invite me in. For an instant she wavers, but only for an instant: she takes my hand in both of hers, and smiles, and the smile fades, and she is gone, leaving me only with the words, "Let's meet at the library again tomorrow. Noon."

I make the long chilling walk home alone.

Some of her pessimism seeps into me that night. I seems futile for us to try to salvage anything. More than that: wicked for me to seek her out, shameful to offer a hesitant love when I am not free. In this world, I tell myself, we should keep well clear of others, so that we do not harm anyone when we are seized and ridden.

I do not go to meet her in the morning.

It is best this way, I insist. I have no business trifling with her. I imagine her at the library, wondering why I am late, growing tense, impatient, then annoyed. She will be angry with me for breaking our date, but her anger will ebb, and she will forget me quickly enough.

Monday comes. I return to work.

Naturally, no one discusses my absence. It is as though I have never been away. The market is strong that morning. The work is challenging; it is mid-morning before I think of Helen at all. But once I think of her, I can think of nothing else. My cowardice in standing her up. The childishness of Saturday night's dark thoughts. Why accept fate so passively? Why give in? I want to fight, now, to carve out a pocket of security despite the odds. I feel a deep conviction that it can be done. The Passengers may never bother the two of us again, after all. And that flickering smile of hers outside her building Saturday, that momentary glow—it should have told me that behind her wall of fear she felt the same hopes. She was waiting for me to lead the way. And I stayed home instead.

At lunchtime I go to the library, convinced it is futile.

But she is there. She paces along the steps; the wind slices at her slender figure. I go to her.

She is silent a moment. "Hello," she says finally.

"I'm sorry about yesterday."

"I waited a long time for you."

I shrug. "I made up my mind that it was no use to come. But then I changed my mind again."

She tries to look angry. But I know she is pleased to see me again—else why did she come here today? She cannot hide her inner pleasure. Nor can I. I point across the street to the cocktail lounge.

"A daiquiri?" I say. "As a peace offering?"

"All right."

Today the lounge is crowded, but we find a booth somehow.

There is a brightness in her eyes that I have not seen before. I sense that a barrier is crumbling within her.

"You're less afraid of me, Helen," I say.

"I've never been afraid of you. I'm afraid of what could happen if we take the risks."

"Don't be. Don't be."

"I'm trying not to be afraid. But sometimes it seems so hopeless. Since *they* came here—"

"We can still try to live our own lives."

"Maybe."

"We have to. Let's make a pact, Helen. No more gloom. No more worrying about the terrible things that might just happen. All right?"

A pause. Then a cool hand against mine.

"All right."

We finish our drinks, and I present my Credit Central to pay for them, and we go outside. I want her to tell me to forget about this afternoon's work and come home with her. It is inevitable, now, that she will ask me, and better sooner than later.

We walk a block. She does not offer the invitation. I sense the struggle inside her, and I wait, letting that struggle reach its own resolution without interference from me. We walk a second block. Her arm is through mine, but she talks only of her work, of the weather, and it is a remote, arm's-length conversation. At the next corner she swings around, away from her apartment, back toward the cocktail lounge. I try to be patient with her.

I have no need to rush things now, I tell myself. Her body is not a secret to me. We have begun our relationship topsy-turvy, with the physical part first; now it will take time to work backward to the more difficult part that some people call love.

But of course she is not aware that we have known each other that way. The wind blows swirling snowflakes in our faces, and somehow the cold sting awakens honesty in me. I know what I must say. I must relinquish my unfair advantage.

I tell her, "While I was ridden last week, Helen, I had a girl in my room."

"Why talk of such things now?"

"I have to, Helen. You were the girl."

She halts. She turns to me. People hurry past us in the street. Her face is very pale, with dark red spots growing in her cheeks.

"That's not funny, Charles."

"It wasn't meant to be. You were with me from Tuesday night to early Friday morning."

"How can you possibly know that?"

"I do. I do. The memory is clear. Somehow it remains, Helen. I see your whole body."

"Stop it, Charles."

"We were very good together," I say. "We must have pleased our Passengers because we were so good. To see you again—it was like waking from a dream, and finding that the dream was real, the girl right there—"

"No!"

"Let's go to your apartment and begin again."

She says, "You're being deliberately filthy, and I don't know why, but there wasn't any reason for you to spoil things. Maybe I was with you and maybe I wasn't, but you wouldn't know it, and if you did know it you should keep your mouth shut about it, and—"

"You have a birthmark the size of a dime," I say, "about three inches below your left breast."

She sobs and hurls herself at me, there in the street. Her long silvery nails rake my cheeks. She pummels me. I seize her. Her knees assail me. No one pays attention; those who pass by assume we are ridden, and turn their heads. She is all fury, but I have my arms around hers like metal bands, so that she can only stamp and snort, and her body is close against mine. She is rigid, anguished.

In a low, urgent voice, I say, "We'll defeat them, Helen. We'll finish what they started. Don't fight me. There's no reason to fight me. I know, it's a fluke that I remember you, but let me go with you and I'll prove that we belong together."

"Let—go—"

"Please. Please. Why should we be enemies? I don't mean you any harm. I love you, Helen. Do you remember, when we were kids, we could play at being in love? I did; you must have done it too. Sixteen, seventeen years old. The whispers, the conspiracies—all a big game, and we knew it. But the game's over. We can't afford to tease and run. We have so little time, when we're free—we have to trust, to open ourselves—"

"It's wrong."

"No. Just because it's the stupid custom for two people brought together by Passengers to avoid one another, that doesn't mean we have to follow it. Helen—Helen—"

Something in my tone registers with her. She ceases to struggle. Her rigid body softens. She looks up at me, her tear-streaked face thawing, her eyes blurred.

"Trust me," I say. "Trust me, Helen!"

She hesitates. Then she smiles.

▼▼▼

In that moment I feel the chill at the back of my skull, the sensation as of a steel needle driven deep through bone. I stiffen. My arms drop away form her. For an instant I lose touch, and when the mists clear all is different.

"Charles?" she says. "*Charles?*"

Her knuckles are against her teeth. I turn, ignoring her, and go back into the cocktail lounge. A young man sits in one of the front booths. His dark hair gleams with pomade; his cheeks are smooth. His eyes meet mine.

I sit down. He orders drinks. We do not talk.

My hand falls on his wrist, and remains there. The bartender, serving the drinks, scowls but says nothing. We sip our cocktails and put the drained glasses down.

"Let's go," the young man says.

I follow him out.

BRINGING THE FAMILY

KEVIN J. ANDERSON

BOTH coffins shifted as the wagon wheels hit a rut in the dirt road. Mr. Deakin, sitting beside his silent passenger, Clancy Tucker, clucked to the horses and steered them to the left.

The rhythmic creak of the wagon and the buzz of flies around the coffins were the only sounds in the muggy air. Over the past three days Mr. Deakin and Clancy had already said everything relative strangers could say to each other.

Clancy rocked back and forth to counteract the motion of the wagon. A sprawling expanse or prairie surrounded them, mile after mile of green grassland broken only by the ribbonlike track heading north. Clancy looked up at the early afternoon sun. "Time to stop."

Mr. Deakin groaned. "We got hours of daylight left."

Clancy made his lips thin and white. "We gotta be sure we get those graves dug by dark."

"Do you realize how stupid this is, Clancy? Night after night—"

"A promise is a promise." Clancy pointed to a patch of thin grass next to a few drying puddles from the last thunderstorm. "Looks like a good place over there."

With only a grunt for an answer, Mr. Deakin pulled the horses to the side and brought them to a stop. The rotten smell settled around them. Clancy Tucker had insisted on making this journey in the heat and humidity of summer; in winter and spring, he said, the ground was frozen too hard to keep reburying his Ma and Dad along the way.

Clancy grabbed a pickax from the wagon bed and sauntered over to the flat spot. By now they had this ritual down to a science. Mr. Deakin said nothing as he unhitched the horses, hobbled them, and began to rub them down. These horses were the only asset he had left, and he insisted on tending them before helping Clancy on his fool's errand.

Clancy swung the pickax, chopping the woven grassroots. His bright bulging eyes looked as if someone with big hands had squeezed him too tightly at the middle. He slipped one suspender off his shoulder, and a dark, damp shadow of perspiration seeped from his underarms.

As he worked, Clancy hummed an endless hymn that Mr. Deakin recognized as "Bringing in the Sheaves." The chorus went around and around without ever finding its way to the last verse. Over the hours, between the humming and the stench from the unearthed coffins, Mr. Deakin wanted to shove Clancy's head under one of the wheels.

When he finished with the horses, he pulled a shovel from between the two coffins and went over to help Clancy. To make the daily task more difficult, Clancy insisted on digging two separate graves, one for his Ma and one for his Dad, rather than a single large pit for both coffins.

They worked for more than an hour in the suffocating heat of afternoon, surrounded by flies and the sweat on their own bodies. Mr. Deakin had run out of snuff on the first day, and his little pocket jar held only a smear or two of the camphor ointment he kept for sore muscles, which he also used to burn the putrid smell from his nostrils.

Mr. Deakin's body ached, his hands felt flayed with blisters, and he did his best to shut off all thought. He would work like one of those escaped slaves from down south, forced to labor all day long in the cotton fields. Clancy Tucker's family had kept a freed slave to tend their home, and she had spooked Clancy badly, filling his head with strange ideas. Or maybe Clancy just had strange ideas all by himself.

A month before, Mr. Deakin would never have imagined himself stooping to such crazy tasks as digging up coffins and burying them night after night on a slow journey to Wisconsin. But an Illinois tornado had flattened his house, knocked down the barn, and left him with nothing.

Standing in the aftermath of that storm, under a sky that had cleared to a mocking blue, Mr. Deakin had wanted to shake his fist at the clouds and shout, but he only hung his head in silent despair. He had worked his whole life to compile meager possessions on a homestead and some rented cropland. It would be months before his harvest came in, and he had no way to pay the rent in the meantime; the tornado had crushed his harvesting equipment, smashed his barn. After the storm, only two horses had stood surrounded by the wreckage of their small corral, bewildered and as shocked by the disaster as Mr. Deakin.

His life ruined, Mr. Deakin had had no choice but to say yes when Clancy Tucker had made his proposition. . . .

"Make it six feet deep now!" Clancy said, throwing wet earth over his shoulder into a mound beside the grave. Fat earthworms wriggled in the clods, trying to grope their way back to darkness. Mr. Deakin felt his muscles aching as he stomped on the shovel with his boot and hefted up another load of dirt. "What difference does it make if they're six feet under or five and a half?" he muttered.

Beside him, standing waist-deep in the companion grave, Clancy looked at him strangely, as if the answer were obvious. The floppy brim of his hat cast a shadow across his face. "Why, because anything less than six feet, and *they could dig their way back up by morning!*"

Mr. Deakin felt his skin crawl and turned back to his work. Clancy Tucker either had a sick sense of humor, or just a sick mind. . . .

Only a day after the tornado had struck, when things seemed bleakest, Mr. Deakin stood alone in the ruins of his homestead. He watched Clancy Tucker walk toward him across the puddle-dotted field. "Good morning, Mr. Deakin," he had said.

"Morning," Mr. Deakin said, leaving the "good" off.

"You know my brother Jerome recently founded a town up in Wisconsin—Tucker's Grove. Can I hire you to help me bring the family up there? You look like you could use a lucky break right about now."

"How much is it worth?" Mr. Deakin asked.

Clancy folded his hands together. "I can offer you this. If you'd give us a ride on your wagon up to Wisconsin, my brother will give you your very own farm, a homestead as big as this one. And it'll be yours, not rented. Lots of land to be had up there. In the meantime, we can loan you enough hard currency to take care of your business here." Clancy held out a handful of silver coins. "We know you need the help."

Mr. Deakin could hardly believe what he heard. The Tuckers had no surviving family—Clancy and his broad-chested brother Jerome were the only sons. Who else would they be taking along?

Clancy nodded again. "It would be the Christian thing to do, Mr. Deakin. Neighbor helping neighbor."

So he had agreed to the deal. Not until they were ready to set out did he learn that Clancy wanted to haul the exhumed coffins of his recently deceased mother and father. By the time Mr. Deakin found out, Clancy had already paid some of Mr. Deakin's most important debts, binding him to his word. . . .

It was deep twilight by the time they had two graves dug and both coffins lowered into the ground with thick hemp ropes. They finished packing down the mounds of earth, leaving the rope ends aboveground for easy lifting the next morning. Mr. Deakin built a small fire to make coffee and warm their supper.

He felt stiff and sore as he bedded down for the night, taking a blanket from the wagon bed. Now that the cool night air smelled clean around him, with no corpse odor hanging about, he wished he had saved some of that camphor for his aching muscles.

Clancy Tucker lay across the fresh earth of the two graves. Mr. Deakin grabbed another blanket and tossed it toward him, but the other man did not look up. Clancy placed his ear against the ground, as if listening for sounds of something stirring below.

▼▼▼

One of the townspeople had used a heated iron spike to burn letters on a plank. *WELCOME TO COMPROMISE, ILLINOIS*. The population tally had been scratched out and rewritten several times, but it looked as if folk no longer kept track. The townspeople watched them approach down the dirt path.

The flat blandness of unending grassland and the corduroy of cornfields swept out to where the land met the sky. On the horizon, gray clouds began building into thunderheads.

"Don't see no church here," Clancy said, "not one with a steeple anyway."

"Town's too small probably," Mr. Deakin answered.

Clancy set his mouth. "Tucker's Grove might be small, but the very first thing Jerome's building will be his church."

Mr. Deakin saw a building attached to the side of the general store and realized that this was probably a gathering place and a saloon. Some townspeople wandered out to watch their arrival, lounging against the boardwalk rails. A gaunt man with bushy eyebrows and thinning steel-gray hair stepped out from the general store like an official emissary.

But when the storekeeper saw the coffins in back of the wagon, he wrinkled his nose. The others covered their noses and moved upwind. Without a word of greeting, the storekeeper wiped his stained white apron and said, "Who's in the coffins?"

"My beloved parents," Clancy said.

"Sorry to hear that," the storekeeper said. "Not common to see someone hauling bodies cross country in the summer heat. I reckon the first thing you'll want is some salt to fill them boxes. It'll cut down the rot."

Mr. Deakin felt his mouth go dry. He didn't want to say that they had little to pay for such an extravagant quantity of salt. But Clancy interrupted.

"Actually," he looked at the other townspeople, "we'd prefer a place to bury these coffins for the night. If you have a graveyard, perhaps? I'm sure after our long journey—" he patted the dirt-stained tops of the coffins, "they would prefer a peaceful night's rest. The ground is hallowed, ain't it?"

The storekeeper scowled. "We got a graveyard over by the stand of trees there, but no church yet. A Presbyterian circuit rider comes along every week or so, not necessarily on Sundays. He's due back anytime now, if you'd like to wait and hold some kind of service."

Mr. Deakin didn't know what to say. The entire situation seemed unreal. He tried to cut off his companion's crazy talk, but Clancy Tucker wouldn't be interrupted.

"Presbyterian? I'm a good Methodist, and my parents were good Methodists. My brother Jerome is even a Methodist minister, self-ordained."

"Clancy—" Mr. Deakin began.

Clancy sighed. "Well, it's only for the night, after all." He looked at Mr. Deakin and lowered his voice. "Hallowed ground. They won't try to come back up, so we don't need to dig so deep."

The storekeeper put his hands behind his apron. "Digging up graves after you planted the coffins? If you want to bury them in our graveyard, that's your business. But we won't be wanting you to disturb what's been reverently put to rest."

Mr. Deakin refrained from pointing out that these particular coffins had been buried and dug up a number of times already.

"You wouldn't be wanting me to break a sacred oath either, would you?" Clancy turned his bulging eyes toward the man; he didn't blink for a long time. "I swore to my parents, on their deathbeds, that I would bring them with me when I moved to Wisconsin. And I'm not leaving them here after all this way."

Seemingly from out of nowhere, Clancy produced a coin and tossed it to the storekeeper, who refused to come closer to the wagons because of the stench. "Are you trying to buy my agreement?" the storekeeper asked.

"No. It's for the horses. We'll need some oats."

Though the graveyard of Compromise was small, many wooden crosses protruded like scarecrows. The townspeople did not offer to help Mr. Deakin and Clancy dig, but a few of them watched.

Mr. Deakin pulled the wagon to an empty spot, careful not to let the horses tread on the other graves. As the two of them fell to work with their shovels, Clancy kept looking at the other grave markers. He jutted his stubbled chin toward a row of crosses, marking the graves of an entire family that had died from diphtheria, according to the scrawled words.

"My parents died from scarlet fever," Clancy said. "Jerome caught it first, and he was so sick we thought he'd never get up again. He kept rolling around, sweating, raving. He wouldn't let our Negro Maggie go near him. When the fever broke, his eyes had a whole different sparkle to them, and he talked about how God had showed him a vision of our promised land. Jerome knew he was supposed to found a town in Wisconsin.

"He kept talking about it until we got fired up by his enthusiasm. He wanted to pack up everything we had and strike off, but then Ma and Dad caught the fever themselves, probably from tending Jerome so close."

Mr. Deakin pressed his lips together and kept digging in the soft earth. He didn't want to wallow in his own loss, and he didn't want to wallow in Clancy Tucker's either.

"When they were both sweating with fever, they claimed to share Jerome's vision. They were terrified that Jerome and I would leave them behind. So I promised we would bring them along, no matter what. Oh, they wanted to come so bad. Maggie heard them and she said she could help."

Clancy didn't even pause for breath as he continued. "I could see how bothered Jerome was, because he wanted to leave right away. Our parents were getting worse and worse. They certainly couldn't stand a wagon ride, and it didn't look like they had much time left.

"One day, after Jerome had been sitting with them for a long time, he came out of their room. His face was frightful with so much grief. He said that their souls had flown off to Heaven." Clancy's eyes glowed.

"He left the day afterward, going alone to scout things out, while I took care of details until I could follow, bringing the family. Jerome is waiting for us there now."

Clancy looked up. He had a smear of mud along one cheek. His eyes looked as if they wanted to spill over with tears, but they didn't dare. "So you see why it's so important to me. Ma and Dad have to be there with us. They have their part to play, even if it's just to be the first two in our graveyard."

Mr. Deakin said nothing; Clancy didn't seem to want him to.

▼▼▼

The sun began to rise in a pool of molten orange. Mr. Deakin dutifully went back to Clancy Tucker, who had slept up against a wagon wheel. Mr. Deakin's head throbbed, but he had not gotten himself so drunk in the saloon that he forgot his obligations, bizarre though they might be.

He and Clancy set to work on the dewy grass with their shovels, digging out the loosened earth they had piled into graves only the night before.

Mr. Deakin looked toward town, sensing rather than hearing the group of people moving toward them. Clancy didn't notice, but Mr. Deakin halted, propped the shovel into the dirt where it rested against the coffin lid. Clancy unearthed the top of the second coffin, and then stopped as the group approached. He went over to stand by the wagon.

The people carried sticks and farm implements, marching along with their faces screwed up and squinting as they stared into the rising sun. They swaggered as if they had just been talked into a fit of righteous anger.

At the front of the group strode a tall man dressed in a black frock coat and a stiff-brimmed black hat. Mr. Deakin realized that this must be the Presbyterian circuit rider, just in time to stir up trouble.

"We come to take action against two blasphemers!" the circuit rider said.

"Amen!" the people answered.

The preacher had a deep-throated voice, as if every word he uttered was too heavy with import to be spoken in a normal voice. He stepped close, and the sunlight shone full on his face. His weathered features were stretched over a frame of bone, as if he had seen too many cycles of abundance and famine.

The bushy-browed storekeeper stood beside him. "We ain't letting you dig up graves in our town."

"Grave robbers!" the circuit rider spat. "How dare you disturb those buried here? You'll roast in Hell."

"Amen!" the chorus said again.

Mr. Deakin made no move with his shovel, looking at the group and feeling cold. He had already lost everything he had, and he didn't care about Clancy Tucker's craziness—not enough to get lynched for it.

Clancy stood beside the wagon, holding Mr. Deakin's shotgun in his hands and pointing it toward the mob. "This here gun is loaded with bird-shot. It's bound to hit most everybody with flying lead pellets. Might even *kill* someone. Whoever wants to keep me from my own parents, just take a step forward. I've got my finger right on the trigger." He paused for just a moment. "Mr. Deakin, would you kindly finish the last bit of digging?"

Mr. Deakin took the shovel and went to work, moving slowly, and watched Clancy Tucker's bulging eyes. Sweat streamed down Clancy's forehead, and his hands shook as he pointed the shotgun.

"I'm done, Clancy," Mr. Deakin said, just loud enough for the other man to hear him.

Clancy tilted the shotgun up and discharged the first barrel with a sound like a cannon. Morning birds in the outlying fields burst into the air, squawking. Clancy lowered the gun toward the mob again. "Git!"

The circuit rider looked as if he wanted to bluster some more, but the townspeople of Compromise turned to run. Not wanting to be left behind, the circuit rider turned around, his black frock coat flapping. His hat flew off as he ran, drifted in the air, then fell to the muck.

▼▼▼

Clancy Tucker shivered on the seat of the wagon, pulling a blanket around himself. He had cradled the empty shotgun for a long time as Mr. Deakin led the wagon around the town of Compromise, bumping over rough fields.

"I would've shot him," Clancy said. His teeth chattered together. "I really meant it. I was going to kill them! 'Thou shalt not kill!' I've never had thoughts like that before!"

Mr. Deakin made Clancy take a nap for a few hours, but the other man seemed just as disturbed after he awoke. "How am I going to live with this? I meant to kill another man! I had the gun in my hand. If I had tilted the barrel down just a bit I could have popped that circuit rider's head like a muskmelon."

"It was only bird-shot, Clancy," Mr. Deakin said, but Clancy didn't hear.

As the horses followed the dirt path, Mr. Deakin reached behind to the bed of the wagon where they kept their supplies. He rummaged under the tarpaulin and pulled out a two-gallon jug of whiskey. "Here, drink some of this. It'll smooth out your nerves."

Clancy looked at him, wide-eyed, but Mr. Deakin kept his face free of any expression. "I traded my little silver mirror for it last night in the saloon. You could use some right now, Clancy. I've never seen anybody this bad."

Clancy pulled out the cork and took a deep whiff of the contents. Startled, stinging tears came to his eyes. "I won't, Mr. Deakin! It says right in Leviticus, 'Do not drink wine nor strong drink.' "

"Oh, don't go giving me that," Mr. Deakin said, pursing his lips. "Isn't there another verse that says to give wine to those with heavy hearts so they remember their misery no more?"

Clancy blinked, as if he had never considered the idea. "That's in Proverbs, I think."

"Well, you look like you could forget some of your misery."

Clancy took out a metal cup and, with tense movements as if

someone were about to catch him at what he was doing, he poured half a cupful of the brown liquid. He screwed up his face and looked down into the cup. Mr. Deakin watched him, knowing that Clancy's lips had probably never been sullied by so much as a curse word, not to mention whiskey.

As if realizing that he had reached his point of greatest courage, Clancy lifted the cup and gulped from it. His eyes seemed to pop even farther from his head, and he bit back a loud cough. Before he could recover his voice to gasp, Mr. Deakin, hiding a smile, spoke from the corner of his mouth. "My gosh, Clancy, just pretend you're drinking hot coffee! Sip it."

Looking alarmed but determined, Clancy brought the cup back to his lips, then squeezed his eyes shut and took a smaller sip. He didn't speak again, and Mr. Deakin ignored him. Morning shadows stretched out to the left as the wagon headed north toward Wisconsin.

Mr. Deakin made no comment when Clancy refilled the metal cup and settled back down to a regular routine of long, slow sips.

By noon the sky had begun to thicken up with thunderheads, and the air held the muggy, oppressive scent of a lumbering storm. The flies went away, but mosquitoes came out. The coffins in back of the wagon stank worse than ever.

Clancy hummed "Bringing in the Sheaves" over and over, growing louder with each verse. He turned to look at the coffins in the back of the wagon, and giggled. He spoke for the first time in hours. "Can you keep a secret, Mr. Deakin?"

Mr. Deakin wasn't sure he wanted to, and avoided answering.

"I don't think I know your Christian name, Mr. Deakin."

"How do you know I even have one?" he muttered. He had lived alone and made few friends in Illinois, working too hard to socialize much. The neighbors and townsfolk called him Mr. Deakin, and it had been a long time since he'd heard anyone refer to him as anything else. Clancy found that very funny.

"Yes, I can keep a secret," Mr. Deakin finally said.

"Promise?"

"Promise."

Clancy dropped his voice to a stage whisper. "Jerome lied!" He paused, as if this revelation were horrifying enough.

"And when did he do that?" Mr. Deakin asked, not really interested.

"When he came out of my parents' room and said that their souls had flown off to Heaven—that wasn't true at all. And he knew it! When he went into that room, after Ma and Dad were sick for so long, after he wanted to go found the new town so bad, Jerome smothered them both with their pillows!"

Mr. Deakin intentionally kept his gaze pointed straight ahead. "Clancy, you've had too much of that whiskey."

"He did Dad first, who still had some strength to struggle. But Ma didn't fight. She just laid back and closed her eyes. She knew we had promised to take them both to Tucker's Grove, and she knew we would keep our word. You always have to keep your word.

"But when Jerome said their souls had flown off to Heaven, well, that just wasn't true—because by smothering them with the pillow, he trapped their souls *inside*!"

Clancy opened his eyes. Mr. Deakin saw bloodshot lines around the irises. "What makes you say that, Clancy?" Mr. Deakin asked. He wasn't sure if he could believe any of this.

"Maggie said so." Clancy stared off into the gathering storm. "Right after they died, our Negro Maggie sacrificed one of our chickens, danced around mumbling spells. Jerome and I came back from the coffin makers and found her inside by the bodies. He tried to whack her on the head with a shovel, then he chased her out of our house and said he'd burn her as a witch if she ever came back."

"And so Jerome left while you packed everything up and made ready to move?" Mr. Deakin asked. He had no idea what to make of killing chickens and chanting spells.

"I'm the only one who didn't see the vision. But Ma and Dad wanted to come so bad. Maggie said she was just trying to help, and it worked. That's why we have to keep burying the coffins—so the bodies stay down!" Clancy glanced at Mr. Deakin, expectant, but then his own expression changed. With a comical look of astonishment at himself, he covered his mouth with one hand, still grimy from digging out the graves at dawn.

"I promised Jerome I wouldn't tell *anybody*. and now I broke my promise. Something bad's bound to happen for sure now!" He closed his eyes and began to groan in the back of his throat.

In exasperation, Mr. Deakin reached over and yanked on the floppy brim of Clancy's hat, pulling it over his face. "Clancy, you just take another nap. Get some rest." He lowered his voice and mumbled under his breath, "And give me some peace, too."

▼▼▼

Clancy slept most of the afternoon, lying in an awkward position against the backboard. Mr. Deakin urged the horses onward, racing the oncoming storm. He hadn't seen another town since Compromise, and the wild prairie sprawled as far as he could see, dotted with clumps of trees. The wagon track was only a faint impression, showing the way to go. A damp breeze licked across Mr. Deakin's face.

The first droplets of water sprinkled his cheeks, and Mr. Deakin pulled his own hat tight onto his head. As the storm picked up, the breeze and the raindrops made a rushing sound in the grasses.

Clancy grunted and woke up. He looked disoriented, saw the darkened sky, and sat up sharply. "What time is it? How long did I sleep?" He whirled to look at the coffins in the back. The patter of raindrops sounded like drumbeats against the wood.

Mr. Deakin knew what Clancy was going to say, but maintained a nonchalant expression. "Hard to tell what time it is with these clouds and the storm. Probably late afternoon . . ." He looked at Clancy. "Sunset maybe." A boom of thunder made a drawn-out, tearing sound across the sky.

"You've got to stop! We have to bury the—"

"Clancy, we'll never get them dug in time, and I'm not going to be shoveling a grave in the middle of a storm. Just cover them up with the tarp and they'll be all right."

Clancy turned to him with an expresssion filled with outrage and alarm. Before he could say anything, a *thump* came from the back of the wagon. Mr. Deakin looked around, wondering if he had rolled over a boulder on the path, but then the thump came again.

Out of the corner of his eye he saw one of the coffins move aside just a little.

"Oh no!" Clancy wailed. "I told you!"

An echoing thump came from the second coffin. Another burst of thunder rolled across the sky, and the horses picked up their pace, frightened by the wind and the storm.

Clancy leaned into the back of the wagon. He took a mallet from the pack of tools and, just as the first coffin bounced again, Clancy whacked the edge of the lid, striking the coffin nails to keep the top closed. The rusted and mud-specked nailheads gleamed bright with scraped metal.

Mr. Deakin had his mouth half-open, but he couldn't think of anything to say. He kept trying to convince himself that this was some kind of joke Clancy was playing, or perhaps even the townspeople of Compromise.

Just as he turned, the first coffin lid lurched, despite Clancy's hammering. The pine boards split, and the lid bent up just enough that a gnarled gray hand pushed its way out. Wet and rotting skin scraped off the edge of the wood as the claw-fingers scrabbled to find purchase and push the lid open farther. Tendons stuck out along yellowed bones. A burst of stench wafted out, and Mr. Deakin gagged but could not tear his eyes away.

The second coffin lid cracked open. He thought he saw a shadow moving inside it.

Clancy leaped into the back of the wagon and straddled one of the coffins. He banged again with the mallet, trying to keep the lid closed; but he hesitated, worried about injuring the hands and fingers groping through the cracks. "Help me, Mr. Deakin!"

A flash of lightning split across the darkness. Rain poured down, and the horses began to run. Mr. Deakin let the reins drop onto the seat and swung over the backboard into the wagon bed.

Clancy knelt beside his mother's coffin. "Please stay put! Just stay put! I'll get you there," he was saying, but his words were lost in the wind and the thunder and the rumble of wagon wheels.

One of the pine boards snapped on the father's coffin. An arm, clothed in the mildewed black of a Sunday suit, thrust out. The fingers had long, curved nails.

"Don't!" Clancy said.

Mr. Deakin was much bigger than Clancy. In the back of the wagon he planted his feet flat against the side of the first coffin. He pushed with his legs.

The single rotting arm flailed and tried to grab at his boot, but Mr. Deakin shoved. He closed his eyes and lay his head backward—and the coffin slid off the wagon bed, tottering for an instant. As the horses continued to gallop over the bumpy path, the coffin tilted over the edge onto the track.

"No!" Clancy screamed and grabbed at him, but Mr. Deakin slapped him away. He pushed the second coffin, a lighter one this time. The lid on this coffin began to give way as well. Thin fingers crept out.

Clancy yanked at Mr. Deakin's jacket, clawing at the throat and cutting off his air, but Mr. Deakin gave a last push to knock the second coffin over the edge.

"We've got to turn around!" Clancy cried.

The second coffin crashed to the ground, tilted over, and the wooden sides splintered. Just then a sheet of lightning illuminated the sky from horizon to horizon, like an enormous concussion of flash powder used by a daguerreotype photographer.

In that instant, Mr. Deakin saw the thin, twisted body rising from the shards of the broken coffin. Lumbering behind, already free of the first coffin, stood a taller corpse, shambling toward his wife. Then all fell black again as the lightning faded.

Mr. Deakin wanted to collapse and squeeze his eyes shut, but the horses continued to gallop wildly. He scrambled back to the seat and snatched up the reins.

"This weather is going to ruin them!" Clancy moaned. "You have to go back, Mr. Deakin!"

Mr. Deakin knew full well that he was abandoning a farm of his own in Tucker's Grove; but the consequences of breaking his agreement with Clancy seemed more sane to him than staying here any longer. He snapped the reins and shouted at the horses for greater speed.

Lightning sent him another picture of the two scarecrow corpses—but they had their backs to the wagon. Walking side by side, Clancy Tucker's dead parents struck off in the other direction. Back the way they had come.

With a sudden, resigned look on his face, Clancy Tucker swung both of his legs over the side of the wagon.

"Clancy, wait!" Mr. Deakin shouted. "They're going the other way! They don't want to come after all, can't you see?"

But Clancy's voice remained determined. "It doesn't matter. I've got to take them anyway." He ducked his head down and made ready to jump. "A promise is a promise," he said.

"Sometimes breaking a promise is better than keeping it," Mr. Deakin shouted.

But Clancy let go of the wagon, tucking and rolling onto the wet grass. He clambered to his feet and ran back toward where he had last seen his parents.

Mr. Deakin did not look back, but kept the horses running into the night.

As he listened to the majestic storm overhead, as he felt the wet, fresh air with each breath he took, Mr. Deakin realized that he still had more, much more, that he did not want to lose.

RESTORATION COMEDY

▼▼▼

CHELSEA QUINN YARBRO

THEY were nearing the end of the first act of *Tannhäuser*, the lush Venusberg music warring with the chorus of pilgrims: Melchior had never sung more passionately and Traubel was in superb voice. The two handsome singers showed to real advantage in their roles, and their highly controversial graphic lovemaking looked better and more erotic than the director had dared to hope it would. As the curtain fell and the thunderous applause erupted, the director turned to the tall, distinguished man beside him and said, "Okay, Leo; you were right. I admit it works."

The tall man smiled confidently. "Gene grafting does work. It works here as well as on the athletic fields. We're proving it every day."

"Yes. I saw Babe Ruth last week," the director said, lowering his eyes. "What does he think, being brought back this way?"

"So far as anyone can tell, he's very pleased to keep playing, and in a much better body than he had to work with originally. This time he's in great shape: the host is six-one and one-eighty-eight, with great running strength as well as real playing skills. And fewer bad habits, at least so far."

"I noticed how strong he is," said the director, moving back to permit the chorus members to file past him. He heard one of them mutter about ersatz singers and he pursed his lips with displeasure. "There are people who don't accept the gene grafts yet."

"They will, in time, when they see what we can do," said the tall man, Dr. Leo Holdstrom, who had received his Nobel Prize four weeks ago, as he looked out at the two handsome singers in front of the golden curtain, taking their bows to the enthusiastic audience reception.

"How much of a difference will that make, do you think?" The director nodded toward the singers as they came back from their curtain calls.

"The public is the mediator in our work, without doubt; it is public support that makes the program possible, and the public will determine how the gene grafts are used in society," said the tall man as if addressing a diplomatic reception. "It ought to help, having such reactions." He put his hands into his pockets, disrupting the flawless line of his dinner jacket. "Those singers of yours should prove the point we're trying to make: that we can take the best that were and make them better."

The director made a gesture of concession. "Well, these two are a hell of a lot prettier than the originals, and they know how to act. Cosmetically they read better in their roles than—"

The stage manager interrupted. "We need this space, gentlemen," she said.

The two moved aside at once. "As I was saying," the director went on, "they look better, but they get very tired. The talent makes demands."

"Is that a problem?" asked the tall man.

"It could be, in time," the director said. "If they don't have enough strength to do the work, it might make all this gene grafting questionable for some of the current singers—the living ones, not the restored ones. You know there is a long tradition in opera of hefty singers, and many of them have said that the weight was necessary to have the voice. But these restored singers are in much more appealing bodies, and they don't seem to hold up as well."

"Well, with gene grafting we can always duplicate the singers again when these are exhausted." He said it casually, as if he thought this was no more a problem than recycling glass. "Restoration is easily accomplished."

The director stared at his guest. "Leo, we're talking about great, legendary artists. I don't see how you can just turn them out like so much sausage."

"But why not? We lost two athletes to injuries this last year and already there are new hosts to take them over, so the playing contracts can be fulfilled. Red Grange has been restored in four hosts. So has Willy Jones, the rodeo champion and stunt trainer; his heirs are delighted." Leo Holdstrom gestured toward the last of the chorus members lingering backstage. "We don't bother with people like that; we only deal with the true greats, and we make sure that they continue their greatness, so that people who would not otherwise have the chance to see them will be able to know why they are great."

"But if the hosts are so . . . sacrificeable?" the director asked.

Leo shrugged, saying, "We have more volunteers for the host program than we know what to do with already, and it looks like we'll have many more over the next few years. I don't think we're going to have any trouble keeping up with the market, not for a while yet, until the market expands."

Lauritz Melchior, a tall, fair man with a shock of light brown hair and bright blue eyes, stopped beside the director and sighed. "The second act is going to need real strength to top what we've already done." He held out his hand to Helen Traubel. "You were great," he said warmly and suggestively. "Just great."

"I wasn't that great," she answered, moving his hand away from her. "You may get to paw me on stage, but you don't get to do it here." She was stunningly voluptuous, a blonde with green-tinted eyes and a full mouth. In her stage finery as Venus she had the appearance of a grand courtesan of two centuries ago. "You can do what you like on stage. Now keep your hands to yourself."

Melchior put a philosophical face on. "If that's what you want. You were getting into it for a while there; I could tell."

"It's what I want," said Traubel, ignoring the director and her creator, Leo Holdstrom. "I know your reputation, Lauritz. I'm not going to be one of the many, not to satisfy your ego or your libido."

"Can you imagine what opera would have been like back in the last two centuries with singers looking like these hosts instead of the way most of them looked? And acted?" Leo said as much to himself as to the director, as Helen Traubel swept past him. "It would have been bigger than rock ever was."

"There weren't too many gorgeous singers, it's true, not until later in the last century when film made everyone beauty-conscious, that is," the director said as he watched Melchior and Traubel disappear into their dressing rooms.

"Now we can give them great voices and great bodies at the same time. Talent alone isn't enough anymore, and gene grafting makes it possible to achieve the best of both worlds." Leo Holdstrom beamed.

"You don't have to sell me," said the director. "But I have to admit that there are times I wonder about the wisdom of it."

"What is there to wonder about?" asked Leo.

"The ethics of it, I suppose," said the director, as if he were not entirely comfortable with the notion. "And the legality. Do genes ever enter public domain?"

"But what's the matter with what we're doing?" asked Leo. "We have the permission of the heirs, and contracts with the hosts. The world is full of beautiful people who are willing to trade their looks for being the host to monumental talent." He strolled away from the space behind the stage manager's station, getting out of the path of the stagehands who were moving the Hall of Song into position in the process. "The biggest problem is working out the royalties with the estates of the subjects we want to use. If they don't mind, why should you?"

"I don't know; it bothers me a little, still." The director shook his head, then said rather sheepishly, "When you finally get Jussi Bjoerling, let me know. I want to use him with Mary Garden in *Manon Lescaut* and Nellie Melba in *Andrea Chenier*." There was an eager light in his eyes. "I know we could do great things with him."

"We have volunteer hosts for him already. But his heirs are very demanding. They want the money that the families of rock stars demand." He sighed. "The jazz people are getting just as bad. Tell me how I can justify giving them what I've given Louis Armstrong's heirs."

"Well, the careers should be about the same length," said the director. "I might be able to find a grant to help you out."

"For Jussi Bjoerling, or for the program?" asked Leo.

"For Jussi Bjoerling."

"All right." Leo thought a moment. "If we make all three of the best of the host volunteers, we might be able to justify the cost, amortizing it over the three," said Leo, taking up his position by the vast rear doors. "Milanov should be a great Elizabeth."

"Oh, she is," said the director, his tone growing warm. "You've done yourself proud on her. She sings like an angel and she's lovely to look at. The host has a fey quality that comes across well."

"The intention is to make the best combination possible." Leo Holdstrom smoothed the front of his shirt, fussing with the studs as he did. "Coming into the formal music world was the biggest risk we've taken so far. And so far it seems it's working."

"You mean that music is harder than sports?" exclaimed the director in mock horror.

"Certainly. There are so many factors to be considered." He puffed out his cheeks. "And we had to make sure that the hosts were very well prepared to receive the gene grafts. They needed the training and the mechanics of the job. We had half a dozen good violinists willing to host Menuhin when we brought him back. We had to audition them before we made our selections."

"And you auditioned the singers as well?" the director inquired.

"Certainly. We needed the right voice range and some experience in voice technique, and a knowledge of the literature. Just as we've matched up our athletes carefully, too." He chuckled. "What's the point of putting a world-class swimmer into a wrestler? Or a first-class linebacker into a tennis pro? Or a weight-lifter into a gymnast. Or for that matter, why put Chaliapin into a tenor host?"

"Point taken," said the director, who went on sheepishly, "Who do you think you might have coming up?"

"Well, we're getting Leonard Warren in a month or so; we have six good volunteers for him. And Marti Talvela in a year—Christoff and Pinza, too."

"Basses are doing well," the director said with a smile. "If you get me Bjoerling and Pinza, I could do one hell of a *Faust*. And if Tebaldi ever becomes available, let me know; she'd make it perfect."

"Of course. And in the meantime, I want you to tell me whatever you can about the way the singers are working out." He gave the director his vulpine smile. "I'm very proud of these restorations. We're trying now to make arrangements in advance, to have the genes available for transplant while the artists are still alive, so that when they retire they can be continued. So far, none of the artists have been willing to cooperate, though most are willing to make contracts for after their deaths. We've been able to set up very favorable terms with some formidable talent, arranging in advance the number of restorations possible, and the length of time we will be allowed to make the restorations. There are questions of rights. We settle all this up front. We even let them choose the sort of host they want to be restored with." He indicated the half-dozen chorus members on the far side of the rear door. "Don't you think any of them would give up everything to be the next Kiri Te Kanawa or Placido Domingo?"

One of the chorus members who had overheard this said, "No. I think what you're doing is obscene." He straightened up in his Gothic finery. "Bringing back the dead this way is an act of sacrilege." He glanced at the director. "Sorry, but that's how I feel about it."

Leo stared at him in disbelief. "But don't you want to sing with the greats?"

"Sure," said the chorus member with alacrity. "And I won't deny that it is a real thrill to sing with Melchior and Traubel. But the truth is that they aren't really Melchior and Traubel—they're just pretty boxes for the talent to be put in. And it's not the same as the real thing." He looked abashed. "You asked."

"I asked," Leo agreed. He moved aside and said nothing more to the chorus member.

After a moment the director followed Leo Holdstrom to the edge of the cyclorama on which would be projected the images of the Venusberg orgy while Tannhäuser and Elizabeth meet in the Hall of Song.

"They look better in the roles than the originals: more believable," said the director, attempting to compensate for what the chorus member had said. "It's always been the problem with opera—getting the images straight so that the audience can accept what they see. Two middle-aged, overweight people carrying on about grand passions looks a little absurd, you know."

Leo accepted this as his due. "That's part of our purpose, of course, to make them the best possible."

"And you've done a great job. Better than I expected you could." The director tugged Leo's sleeve and got him out of the way of part of the set as it was rolled into position.

"That's a compliment, coming from you," said Leo Holdstrom. "I know you have high standards to keep up."

"Certainly. In opera, you have to be very, very good just to be acceptable." He rubbed his hands together. "How long can you continue to restore the singers, do you know yet?"

"Not yet. The program's still new. With the athletes we're getting about ten years of solid work out of the restorations. And the prospects are good for extending that period." He grinned. "That's what made us think about going into the arts. We wanted to show that the principles work everywhere."

"What's next?" asked the director.

"You mean what area do we tackle now that we have the arts and athletics covered?" asked Leo with an I'm-so-glad-you-asked smile.

"You have other plans?" the director prompted.

"Certainly. We're looking at the possibilities of restoring some of the real greats of academia and politics. We'd like to start with Lincoln, but there are problems with that." He lowered his eyes. "You can't believe the hassles we've encountered in that area. There are people who want Kennedy before Lincoln, and some who think we should leave well enough alone."

"But you're going ahead," said the director with certainty. "I can see it in your eyes."

"Of course." Behind him the set was almost complete. The chorus was gathering at the rear entrance and the stage manager had given the call to Zinka Milanov and Lauritz Melchior in their dressing rooms to be prepared to get on stage.

"And when do you think you'll have the first restorations ready? Of the politicians and intellectuals?"

"In the next two years is our best guess. It's too bad that Dag Hammarskjold was killed the way he was. It would have been a coup to start the program off with him. As it is, we're trying to get some of the former Secretary-Generals to commit to restoration before they die, so we will have access to their knowledge and experience when we need them." He watched the stagehands check the set, then added, "We're going to have Toscanini available in a year. Are you interested?"

"Certainly, if I can stand his temperament," said the director. "I don't know that you can get the talent without the temperament."

"It doesn't seem to be possible, as we're finding out with Callas," said Leo, making a gesture of defeat. "The same thing is true of the athletes. The ones who were hard to deal with when they were alive in the original form are still hard to deal with in the restorations. You don't change the personality just because you house it in another person; the host becomes recessive to the talent grafted. It's part of the process, it turns out. Whatever they were when the talent was alive is what they are when they're restored."

"What about the host personality?" asked the director with a trace of alarm. "Isn't there some psychological risk?"

"Not that we've discovered yet. The host personality is still there, but it is subsumed by the genetic graft." He opened his hands to express his innocence.

"Sounds pretty depressing for the host," said the director, looking over his shoulder as the sound of chimes reminded them that the next act was about to start.

"The house is full tonight," Leo observed as they made their way backstage. "Everyone wants to hear Melchior and Traubel. And I understand that you're scheduled for three recital tours in the off-season." Leo beamed with pride.

"Caruso, of course, and Kirsten Flagstad after, and then Beniamino Gigli. A trio to dream over." He grinned. "You can be very proud of yourself for what you've done."

"Oh, I am," said Leo Holdstrom, as if the curtain-muted applause for the conductor was actually for him.

▼▼▼

"What do you mean, they won't sing?" Leo Holdstrom asked the woman on the other end of the line. "Is there something wrong with them? Have the hosts become ill? Is there some reason they're doing this, other than money?"

"I mean what I said," she answered. "The restorations are refusing to do tonight's performance of *I Lombardi*. They all claim they're too tired. They're demanding an adjustment in their schedules. They say that they are being exhausted by the talents they host and they want compensation."

"Compensation," Leo repeated, as if he had only a vague notion as to the meaning of the word. He added in a mutter, "It's about money. They've already made an agreement with this company. They're supposed to host the talent, not agent for it."

"They say that they aren't going to perform again until they have a contract giving them the right to decide when the talent can be exercised." The woman's voice was tight from being upset. "The musicians union is looking into a sympathy strike. We can't have this. It could ruin everything."

"They're as bad as the football pros," Leo complained, having spent the morning dealing with representatives of the restored athletes, not successfully. The notion of more of the same soured his outlook on the day.

"They're determined, I warn you. When you have half a dozen opera singers in agreement, you have a formidable force to contend with." She sounded annoyed now, and perplexed. "They're insisting on conditions I can't deal with."

"They'll listen to reason, if you remind them of their original contracts," said Leo in the same tone he had used with the football players, hoping it would work this time.

"I doubt it," she countered. "They want guarantees I can't make in regard to their schedules and performances."

"More than what you've told me?" Leo rubbed his forehead and wished his headache would vanish.

"More," said the woman. "My boss is going nuts. You have to do something."

"But what?" Leo asked. "We can take them to court, but there would be adverse publicity from a suit. Don't you think?"

"I don't know. You're the one who started this restoration business. You should know how to handle this situation." She paused. "If this is going to become a regular event, we'll have to go back to living singers. Restorations are wonderful, but they aren't worth this trouble. And we can't afford to pay them more than we are already."

This annoyed Leo greatly. "They're worth everything we have to do to keep them going," he said unsympathetically. "We've got something valuable here, and I don't intend to throw it away."

"That's because it's your baby," said the woman in disgust. "All your profits and fame come from the restorations. You'd be the last person to want to discontinue using them." She paused. "But something has to be done."

"What? They aren't slaves, are they?" asked Leo. "Restorations have certain rights we need to define, for their own sakes," said Leo, thinking as quickly as he could in order to diminish his responsibility in the matter. "With the kind of restorations we're doing now, it matters that we be prepared to negotiate with the restorations, so that the program can improve. Otherwise we might run into trouble. If we show that we're willing to make reasonable accommodations, we can avoid trouble in future. That's the way we'll get current talent to contract with us." He looked at the list of international high-power scientists he had been planning to approach to get them to make arrangements to restore them after they died. He had already decided to offer them a more comprehensive contract than what he had given the athletes and performers, including some say in what manner their restorations would be used.

"And you want me to tell the singers that?" she demanded.

"Certainly," he said, making up his mind quickly. "Tell them I want to meet with them, and their heirs, to work something out we can all live with." He smiled at his own ironic joke.

"All right, but they'll be suspicious," said the woman.

"That's fine with me, so long as they're willing to talk and bargain in good faith." He shrugged once, as if he thought he had made the best of a bad situation.

"I'll tell them what you've said," she promised, and lowered her voice. "I think you better be ready for a lot of resistance."

"I'll keep that in mind," said Leo, remembering that it was opera singers who he would have to deal with, not the more canny restorations his firm had undertaken in the last few months. He had something to be grateful for, he reminded himself. Opera singers were malleable compared to some of the restorations he had made recently.

Leo Holdstrom faced the wiry, energetic young man with the short red beard with dismay. "How do you mean, we can't restore anyone else?" he asked.

"You haven't the authority," said Clarence Darrow. "You are licensing the use of the dead without the consent of the dead themselves."

"I have the permission of the heirs," said Leo defensively.

"Not the same thing, since you are restoring the dead through gene grafting. Have you obtained their permission once they are restored? I don't think so. None of them said you had, and that was a serious oversight. You made no arrangements with the restorations, and you neglected to define the purpose of the restoration to the restored person. You didn't make any such arrangements with me, and that was a serious mistake."

"I can tell," said Leo angrily, then remembered who he was talking with and mastered his temper. "Keep in mind what this program accomplishes. We are enabling, through gene grafting, the continuation of some of the most illustrious careers of the last two centuries. Work that ended can be resumed and improved. There are dozens of programs underway now—in the sciences as well as athletics and art—that would have been impossible without the restorations."

"Wrong," said Darrow emphatically. "You are profiting from the talents of some of the most illustrious careers of the last two centuries. Your profits have been enormous, and you have gained tremendous prestige at the expense of those you have restored." He tapped his old-fashioned briefcase which contained the latest in notebook computers. "You have done this without having a specific grant from those restored. The heirs are profiting, not the restored talents and their hosts. I have been talking to a few of the restorations, in preparation to presenting their case, and many of them feel that you have done a great wrong."

"What do you mean, a great wrong?" Leo demanded. He had not wanted to let this offensive young man into his office and now he wished he could cause him to vanish.

"A double wrong, both to the restoration and to the host," Darrow insisted. "You have placed some of the hosts at risk because of the demands being made on the restorations they're hosting. There are psychological as well as physical traumas the hosts have experienced. That danger was not defined at the time the restoration was agreed to, and—"

"We weren't aware of any dangers, not that have been proven," said Leo defensively. "And the hosts are volunteers, remember. They want to host a talent. They aren't being coerced."

"Some of them aren't being treated very well, either. Stirling Moss has already crashed twice and he's been restored after each crash. That's a little hard on the hosts, wouldn't you say?" said Darrow. "Most of them are forced to maintain a schedule they are not able to handle, all because of your desire to make money from them."

"That's not true," Leo protested with heat. "All right. Yes, I make money from the restorations. I use the money to continue the project. We're providing a service to humanity with them. If you'll consider who we have restored, you'll know it's true; you're a case in point, Mr. Darrow."

"Do you think so?" Clarence Darrow countered. "It seems to me that you're indulging in sophistry, Dr. Holdstrom."

"What makes you say that?" asked Leo, hoping to get Darrow off his attack.

"You'll find out in court," said Darrow bluntly.

Leo glared at him. "I don't think that would be very wise," he warned. "Court is very expensive, and this company has the resources to fight you for years if we have to. I intend to protect this program any way I must, no matter what. And don't believe I won't do it if you make it necessary." This last was said softly, with menace.

But Darrow was unimpressed. "Oh, I believe you're prepared to act. I believe that you could make this costly," he said. "But the longer you force us to face you at the bar, the greater our awards will be in the end. You will be stuck with high settlements and massive court costs. It could ruin your company."

"Do you think so?" asked Leo in an attempt to sound unworried.

"I am certain of it. I have prepared a full brief including an analysis of your assets, so I have a good idea of how long you can hold out, and I know the patterns your investors have used in similar cases." He patted his briefcase. "The system you have going now for research makes my job easier than when I was first in practice. I am in a much better position to deal with this case than I would have been a hundred years ago. And luckily my host has enough court experience to know how to handle juries and voir dire. I think we can tie your company into knots, Dr. Holdstrom, and make it bleed."

For the first time Leo faltered. "You want the hosts given more say in what happens to them, and you want contracts with the restored talents? After restoration?"

"As a first few steps, yes. There are other issues requiring redress as well." The redheaded young man grinned with enthusiasm. "There are some technical questions that the courts will have to decide, in any case. Such as who owns the title to works completed by restorations? Is a restoration a collaboration, or do the heirs of the restored talent have primary rights to what their restored people have done, as a group of them have claimed."

Leo shook his head. "The judge ruled that the restorations were to be regarded as collaborations and all proceeds gained were to be divided equally."

"That may be changed on appeal. It will go to a higher court, and on up the line to Washington, and to The Hague, as well." He rocked back on his heels. "And if Europe and the U.S. disagree, it will take a long time to straighten it all out."

"And you think that would be a wise idea?" asked Leo, openly aghast.

"It is necessary. It should have been taken into account from the first. Your technique of gene grafting may be wonderful in its potential, but the reality has been a cock-up from the first." Darrow gave him a tight smile. "And since you aren't going to attend to this yourself, you're making the restorations force the issue."

"Because you've put ideas in their heads, and in the heads of their heirs," said Leo angrily.

"I have done nothing of the sort," said Darrow in an emotionless tone of voice. "I have been retained to represent certain parties who have been taken advantage of, and I will do that to the limits of my abilities, as any ethical attorney would." He lifted one eyebrow. "I don't want to ruin you, Dr. Holdstrom, but if you compel me to do it, I will."

"Why?" Leo demanded. "What is the point of all this?" He rose and began to pace. "What are you going to accomplish by ruining me? The process of gene grafting is licensed all over the world. You won't be able to stop it with a court battle, not now."

Darrow watched Leo pace. "I think that some of these issues should have been addressed from the first restoration. You went along thinking that it would make no difference to you, that you would be able to handle the whole restoration business by fiat. Well, Dr. Holdstrom, you're wrong. You aren't the great puppet-master you thought you were, and I'm going to prove it."

"I never thought I was a puppet-master," said Leo. "I thought I was doing a service for . . . everyone. From the first tennis star to the last mathematician we have restored, it has been with the intention of providing the world with the best it has to offer." It had also made him a fortune, but he made no mention of that.

"But without the permission of those you consider the best," Darrow reminded him. "That's the part that is the most troubling."

"You keep ignoring the fact that we have the permission of the heirs," said Leo, pausing in his restless striding. "How else are we to get it, but through the heirs? Until the subjects are restored there is no way whatsoever to consult them."

"That would be correct, as far as it goes," said Darrow. He folded his arms. "Luisa Tetrazini has been trying to get her host to gain weight, in order for her to sing comfortably. The host was chosen for cosmetic reasons as much as anything, and she resents what Tetrazini is trying to do. How do you plan to settle that?"

Leo nodded, doing his best to seem cooperative. "I can see your point in that case."

"There are dozens of others. Paavo Nurmi doesn't like the food his host eats and thinks that the routine for condition the runner keeps up is foolish." Darrow shrugged eloquently. "Even this host you've given me hates cigars."

"Is that an important issue?" asked Leo.

"Not for me, but there are other restorations who have bigger problems with the hosts than that. You have to establish some means of making reasonable concessions for the program or your supply of hosts is going to vanish, no matter what you think." Darrow picked up his briefcase once more. "Well, this should give you something to think about for the next few days. Talk to your lawyers, Dr. Holdstrom. And listen to them."

Leo wanted to protest this calm instruction, but could think of nothing to say. He watched Clarence Darrow leave his office, and stood for some little time once he was alone, trying to make up his mind which of his company attorneys should be spoken to first. At last he picked up the phone and called Sam Erwin.

"Sorry, Dr. Holdstrom," said the secretary. "He's in conference."

"Oh?" said Leo at his most depressing. "And why can't you interrupt him?"

"Because he said not to," the secretary responded.

Leo began to bluster. "And who is so important that his—"

"Justice William O. Douglas," the secretary said. "And Clarence Darrow."

▼▼▼

As he left the courtroom Leo Holdstrom felt faint. He had been listening to testimony from musicians for more than four days, hearing how the hosts were unprepared for the eccentricities and foibles of their talents; the week before the athletes had done the same thing, and Leo was getting heartily sick of it. He hoped that the jury felt the same way.

Wilson Trager, the formidable jurist, walked beside him, frowning deeply. "It will be worse when they have the scientists and statesmen on the stand," he warned. "Those people are able to make a better case. The public always assumes artists are a little crazy, and if they have problems, it doesn't seem as important as it does with intellectuals."

"You told me that yesterday," said Leo with ill grace.

"You had better keep it in mind," Trager stated. "When they put that young woman hosting Albert Einstein on the stand, there will be fireworks, I warn you." He thrust his free hand into his pocket. "It's unfortunate so much of the news media is covering this. And that they were able to use Harry Reasoner's restoration to anchor the coverage. If his wit weren't so mordant, our position would look better."

"Is there anything we can do about that?" asked Leo, remembering how he had chuckled at Reasoner's description of the body he currently inhabited, comparing it to the one he had had before, talking about getting used to having another four inches in height and seeing a black face when he looked in the mirror.

"Not if we want to underplay it, no," said Trager. "The trouble is, what Reasoner says makes sense, and most of the people watching this trial know it. They know how hard it can be to accustom oneself to driving a new car, and they appreciate that learning to use a new body would be much more difficult. To say nothing of the shock of coming back into this time, which is different than what they left behind."

"We have counselors for that. We offer therapy when it's needed," said Leo defensively. "There was no indication at first that there would be this kind of trouble for the hosts."

"Your program of gene grafting is nine years old. You've offered therapy for what? Five years? They're asking questions about what took you so long." Trager stared at the traffic. "The novelty is gone. It's no longer special to see a great athlete from the past performing in a new body. It's taken for granted that you can hear the greats of rock and roll, and jazz, and classical music. Now we're getting used to having the great minds of the past available to us, living with us through gene grafts. So people no longer regard the restorations as unusual, and they want a better life for them, since they seem to be here to stay. And you will have to guarantee that there will be no more simultaneous restorations. From the testimony we've heard, it sounds as if those are the most risky of the lot."

"But the heirs—" Leo began.

"Damn the heirs. They are a secondary problem right now."

"But don't they have a claim, as well? And don't they share some of the responsibility for authorizing the restorations in the first place?" Leo asked, gesturing toward a restaurant in the opposite corner. "I've got us reservations in there," he explained as he stepped off the curb.

Trager was right beside him. "It makes it harder to work out terms with the opposition, since they're all restorations themselves, and most of them have had a few unkind words to say about their heirs." He sidestepped one of the cars completing a turn. "We'd better be prepared with something to offer the restorations and hosts that will make it apparent that you do not intend to take too much advantage of them."

"But it's my process," Leo protested as they entered the restaurant.

"No question of that," said Trager. "But the fact is, that puts more of the trouble we're having now on your plate, as it were." He was silent as the waiter led them to their table, and then he spoke again. "You will have to do something, Leo, or you'll probably lose a lot of what you've gained for yourself. The restorations are right—you are profiting from their expertise. You wouldn't have restored them if they didn't have something of worth to license."

"All right," said Leo, who had resigned himself to just such a development some time before. "What do you suggest?"

Trager grinned as he made his suggestions; it was like watching a wolverine. "To begin with, I think it would be best to have a secondary level of contracts with the restorations, describing what they have been restored to do, and what they will need to negotiate in regard to their hosts. Second, I think it would be wise to offer some monetary incentive to the restorations to fulfill their work. It's possible that you could make a fund available to pay for any harm done the host by the actions of the restoration, something along those lines, anyway. We'll worry about what to do with the heirs later." He glanced up at the waiter and ordered an abalone sandwich and a bottle of mineral water.

Leo ordered a steak and a glass of wine, then said to Trager, "What if we do a restoration who will not do the work we want?"

"There has to be some arrangements for that, yes. Because you can't ungraft the genes, and no matter what the restoration does, it is in place in the host until the end, no matter how unwelcome. Just because it hasn't happened yet doesn't mean that it will not happen ever. And you want to be prepared. If you're not, who knows what could develop."

"I'll do what I can," said Leo.

"You'd better," said Trager with a serious nod of his head. "I think you'd be wise to have something to offer before the end of the week, or Darrow is going to take you apart."

"You can stop that," Leo reminded him.

"I don't know. Darrow is about the canniest courtroom fighter who was ever around. He had a way with him. He still does. He's making the restorations look like your personal bonded servants, and you an exploiter driven by greed, not the altruism you claim." He looked up as his lunch was set in front of him. "It would be a good idea to try to show you're not using the restorations to line your pockets."

"But the company—" Leo protested.

"You're the inventor of the process, and you will be held accountable for it; the heirs can be made to seem your victims," said Trager. "The stockholders are going to have to accept some adjustment in their earnings, or this process could end up outlawed." He saw the shock in Leo's eyes. "Yes. That is a possibility, and you had better face it. Your company could cease to exist entirely."

"But the process is known," said Leo. "I couldn't stop gene grafting now if I wanted to."

"As your attorney, I have to advise you that you had better find some way to make amends to the restorations and hosts, then, or you're apt to be tied up in civil suits for the next decade." He stared at the ceiling. "The heirs would sue you, too, if the judgment went against you for the restoration. The cost would be horrific."

Leo's lunch seemed nothing more than paper with indigestible lumps of glue in it. He ate with steady determination and a complete lack of savor. He said nothing more to Trager as he contemplated his predicament.

They were on their way back to the courthouse when the blue sedan went out of control, careened onto the sidewalk and struck down half a dozen pedestrians. Leo Holdstrom was dead on arrival at Sutton Memorial Hospital.

▼▼▼

The body was chunkier and shorter than the one he remembered, and more muscular. He stretched out his arm and stared at it, realizing from the color that he must be Asian. He tried to sit up, and heard someone nearby move toward him.

"He's waking up," said a voice Leo did not recognize.

"Great. I want him checked out by noon." This second voice was low and harsh, as if the speaker were under pressure.

"Okay," said the first voice. "He'll be ready to travel."

"The plane will be here this evening," said the second voice.

"We'll be paid as soon as we deliver this first Dr. Holdstrom to Santiago."

"Great," said the first, and chuckled. "It's pretty funny, isn't it? The great Leo Holdstrom, a restoration himself now, and on his way to Chile where restorations are still legal."

"Keep an eye on him. He might be listening. He's awake enough for that." The second voice was sharp with disapproval.

"I will," said the first.

Leo was thinking quickly, trying to sort out what had become of him. He tried to speak and was appalled at the sound he made. He tried to sit up, but could not make his body cooperate.

The first voice sounded in his ear as he was helped to sit. "Steady now, take it easy."

"I will," said Leo in a husky whisper.

"How are you feeling?" The first voice belonged to a middle-aged woman with heavy bags under her eyes and a faded smile.

"Rocky," said Leo, doing his best to speak normally.

"Don't try to force yourself," said the woman. "It takes time. You know more about that than I do."

"Sure," said Leo, better satisfied with how he sounded. Did all restorations feel as disoriented as he did? He wiggled his fingers and tried to move his legs.

"The gene grafts took very well on him," said the second voice. The speaker was a slight man in a lab coat with thinning, light-colored hair.

"Good," said the woman. "With these facilities, it isn't easy." She looked over at Leo. "You're in a warehouse, Dr. Holdstrom. We use it as our lab."

"Your lab? For gene grafting?" He stared up at the girders overhead and fought down a sudden flare of dread.

"You're going to Santiago in Chile tonight," said the man in the lab coat. "You and about ten other restorations. You'll be put to work there."

"In Chile?" Leo repeated, having trouble making sense out of what he heard.

"We have a contract to deliver you. And we will." There was hard determination in the man's voice now.

"But—" Leo began.

The man interrupted him. "And you know what I think?"

Leo shook his head, not daring to speculate now.

The man leaned over him with a brittle grin, laughing as Leo shrank from him. "I think it serves you right."

CORPORATE TAKEOVER

MATTHEW J. COSTELLO

WE commiserated over martinis occupying our usual window seats at Spat's Steak House, 5:15—the perfect time to study the secretaries scurrying in their sneakers for the subway.

Mark, sucking on an olive, clocked the ladies dashing underground and shook his head, distracted.

"It's no fuckin' good, Colin. Two into one won't go, and believe me—heads will roll, buddy."

Mark glanced around, his eyes shark-like, trolling the crowd at Spats. He spotted a trio of young women sitting at a table and then he nudged me with a chunky elbow—so suave and debonair. He grinned and put on his best Dan Ackroyd, Eastern Europe accent.

"Hey, Yortek . . . fox-es!"

Too much Nick at Nite for old Mark. Too little social life, too little of that magic stuff that could soothe a corporate financial officer at day's end.

Mark was perpetually on the make, always searching for Ms. Right—or at least someone, *anyone* who would settle down with him.

"I like the brunette," he said. "Nice tan."

His bar talk was out of date.

"Very cute," I said. I was also between relationships. At least, I assumed I was between relationships, the assumption being that there was, in fact, a new significant other waiting in the wings.

"So when are they sending you down there?" I said, trying to steer the conversation back to our earlier topic—namely, how the merger of Morra Communications with Island Pineapple & Sugar would affect our own particular stars. These were not good days to be out on our asses searching for jobs.

"Friday." Mark turned and looked at me. "Ever been to Purgatory?"

I saw a woman, not so young, look over at us. Must sound strange—Purgatory. Except there were a lot of oddball islands in the Caribbean. Hell was a great place, or so I've been told. Sunburned tourists, human lobsters, come back to Kennedy Airport with their straw hats and T-shirts declaring "I've been to Hell."

I hadn't heard much about Purgatory, though. The entire island, one hundred miles east of Aruba, belonged to Island Pineapple & Sugar, a successful packager and producer of tropical fruits and sugarcane. There were no resort facilities but, our office manager told us, there was a wonderful city with two luxurious hotels.

"Bring your swim fins," I said.

Mark downed his martini. "Right. I tell you, Col, some of us will be out on the street because of this. A stupid goddamn pineapple company. . . ."

He looked up for the bartender who hovered nearby.

Yes, I thought. Some of us may end up pounding the pavement, but not you, Markie. You're going down to Purgatory. You're all set.

Yes, I thought . . . Mark's in great shape. . . .

▼▼▼

His week-long visit stretched to two weeks and then three, until I thought that he'd never come back.

Good for you, old buddy, I thought. Enjoying the sun, the waves, the dark-haired women, and all those pineapples. Good for you. . . .

At the end of the third week, two executives from the island, tall, dark-skinned Purgatory natives, toured our office while we stood up in our white shirts, watching them slowly inspect our banks of computers, our cubicles. Their faces were solemn, impassive.

"Cheerful lot," I muttered to my secretary, a plump little meatball with three kids and a husband who drove a truck for the *Daily News*, New York's picture newspaper.

She shushed me. And I saw one of the Island P&S executives look up, hearing the whooshing noise she made. I felt his eyes, dark eyes set in pale pools, studying me, wondering—perhaps—is this someone who we can cut?

It was a merger. But we knew that Morra was the one strapped for cash and Island was *loaded*. Low overhead, high productivity in the pineapple and sugar cane business. Now they were joined to a struggling conglomerate that owned a magazine division, a string of TV and radio networks, a fast food chain (Pizza Pronto—"Your pizza in ten minutes or—boing!—it's free!"), and an assortment of quiet, slumbering industrial holdings that were, circa 1993, dying in the economic barrens of the Northeast.

The recession may have ended—but not here, sports fans.

The Island executives moved along. I took a breath, surprised at the sudden fear I felt. My secretary shook her head.

"You should be careful," she said.

"And you should control your—"

I looked down the hallway and I saw Mark. He was back—and the bastard hadn't even called me. He was shaking hands, saying hello to the other bean counters in our division. He was tanned, peeling, and flecks of his skin curled off him like parchment. He wore an oversized grin.

Mark was *back* . . . he must have flown in with the executives from Purgatory. I walked toward him and he looked up.

"Colin—" he came to me and gave me an exuberant bear hug. Mark was not reserved with his displays of affection. "Good to see you, buddy."

I nodded, feeling pale, wan next to his robust color. "Looks like you had some fun."

Mark pulled me tighter, conspiratorially drawing me close. "Fun isn't the word, buddy. Purgatory is a beautiful island. *Beautiful!* They got some sweet operation down there, runs like clockwork. Cheap happy labor, almost no overhead, and—"

Mark looked around and I smiled, seeing his beady shark eyes, a familiar sight at last. "And the women, Colin. The women are from heaven. Eyes to get lost in, skin like satin . . ." his voice lowered. "Tits to die for." He repeated the words. "To *die* for."

Good, I thought, Mark got laid. Good for him.

He pulled me away from the other cubicles, off to a corner.

"Like I said, sounds as if you had fun."

Mark held me at arm's length, the proud boy demanding that I see. *Look what I've done*. "No, Colin. You don't get it."

I waited, letting his shit-eating grin hang there, the human Cheshire cat.

"Don't get what?" I said. I still felt confused. I saw one of our new corporate partners glance over, seeing Mark literally frothing over—

"I'm married! I met someone, a dream—and we got married."

Oh, shit, I thought. That's great. Mark was providing an American green card to another pearl of the Caribbean. I was reluctant to yank him off his cloud.

"Hey, I know what you're thinking. It's too fast. But she worked in the hotel, she was the concierge. I took her out, drinks and stuff. I tell you, Myra's wonderful." His shark eyes returned. "To die for, buddy."

I nodded. Everyone else had returned to their work. The large room was filled with the chipmunk clattering of keyboards. I had a lot of work to do, dealing with taxes, getting forms filed in the wake of the merger.

I looked at Mark and wondered if this was the end of our post-game cocktail hour.

He looked up, thinking. "Tell you what. Why don't you come by tonight? Meet Myra. Yeah, come for dinner, drinks. What do you say?"

What could I say?

And, I had to admit, I was more than a little curious to see what Mark brought home from Purgatory.

"Sure." I smiled and then went back to my work.

▼▼▼

Mark's apartment was only four stops on the Seventh Avenue subway, and for the entire bumpy ride he extolled the virtues of Purgatory for me.

"You see, Col, they got a *great* system there. I guess, hell, it's like communism, or a dictatorship. But, shit, everyone has what they need, everyone's happy. The workers all live close to the factories and the plantations. You haven't seen a cleaner place, it's spotless." Mark nodded, "I tell you, we could use some of that efficiency here."

The subway screeched to a halt at the 14th Street station. I followed Mark out.

"Myra's whole family works for the company, her father, mother, brothers, sisters, uncles, aunts. Some in the plantation, others in the packing or business end. And—"

"But not Myra?"

"Eh?"

"Not Myra—she didn't work for Island?"

"Oh, sure. Not in the pineapple or sugar end. But the company owns the hotels, damn fine hotels, and she worked in the one I stayed at."

"And she just left her job?"

"Sure." Mark grinned, happy with his prowess at luring such a find to America. "Guess love will do that for you, Colin. You should try it."

I was about to remind him that I had, in fact, tried it—far too many times—when we arrived at his apartment. The elevator whisked us up to the third floor, to apartment 3-G, and a hallway filled with the dizzying smell of onions and spices.

Mark turned the key in the door. "And wait till you taste her cooking. . . ."

He threw open the door and the full aroma of dinner surrounded me, way too strong, and my appetite retreated. I felt the need to get to the window and gulp some good old New York air.

"Myra, sweetheart. We're here."

Mark had thoughtfully notified his wife that he was bringing someone home for dinner.

He called for her, and we waited. That should have been the first tip-off, the first peculiar thing.

"Get you a drink, Col? A beer, gin and tonic—"

I was looking toward Mark's small kitchen area, waiting for Myra to make her much heralded appearance.

"Maybe she's not—" I started to say, when she slipped out into the hall. The light was behind her so I didn't get to really see her. She was simply a silhouette . . . but a very nice one. She took a step closer, and some light from the living room caught her eyes. They were beautiful—sleepy, dark eyes that stared right through me. Myra wore a simple black shift, short and sleeveless, and sandals. Another step, and the light caught her sleek legs, the caramel texture of her skin, and—for sure—the wondrous swell of her breasts.

Mark was going to be a very happy man.

"Myra, babe. This is Colin, my good buddy."

She slowly extended her hand. She was close to me now and—though the smell of onions, and paprika, and things more exotic was still overpowering—I could smell Myra, some perfume on her, perhaps her shampoo. She was a mixture of Spanish and African and Anglo, and her beauty was stunning.

I had to wonder: what the hell is she doing with Mark?

And: why the hell is she moving so slowly, so deliberately?

I took her hand, her slim fingers. I squeezed gently, but even my gentle handshake seemed too strong. Her eyes were locked on mine. Her stare seemed full of promise, as if Mark wasn't there and I could just pull her close, press her close. . . .

I knew that it would be a wonderful experience.

I squeezed her hand. Her fingers felt cold as if she had been at the sink, running cold water on them. Her lips opened.

"I'm very glad to meet you."

And—at that moment—I was equally glad to meet her.

Mark didn't show up at work the day after our dinner. Can't say that I blamed him—must be hard to leave the little love nest with such a limpid beauty waiting there for you.

I thought about the dinner . . . Mark had rambled on about Purgatory, while I nodded and looked over at Myra, watching her slowly remove the plates from the table, leaning toward me, looking up. When her eyes locked on mine, it was electric. And though I was probably Mark's best friend, I could burn for what I wanted to do with his wife.

And she acted as if she *knew*, looking at me, her dark eyes on mine, hanging there until I felt all hot and sweaty. It was as if I was back to high school again.

When Mark came back to work, he looked a little green around the gills.

"What's wrong?" I said. "Too much honeymooning?" I imagined pear-shaped Mark rolling on top of Myra, an unlikely image to be sure.

He nodded, smiled wanly, his normal ebullience gone. "The food I think." Another smile. "Too strong, the spices. I—I don't feel so good."

Just then his intercom buzzed. They wanted him in the main office, three flights up.

Big stuff, I thought. Mark is rising up in the business. Maybe I should wangle an invite to Purgatory. . . .

In those first days, Mark didn't have time for our after-work cocktails. Okay, I thought. That's understandable. Sure, a new wife, coming home to that creamy skin and black pearl eyes. Myra continued to dance in my fantasies.

But I started to worry.

Mark didn't look so good. In fact, he looked worse every day. He quickly lost his color from his trip south. His skin still peeled and flaked, only now the new skin below was chalky white and mottled. His eyes had trouble making contact with mine. They seemed to float in his head, buoyant marbles inside a milky globe.

He looked sick. When I asked him about it, asked him if he had seen a doctor, he brushed the thought away.

"Just a little fever," he said. "Probably picked up something on the island."

I nodded. It wasn't my job to push. But I wondered what was happening to my friend. . . .

▼▼▼

Then he was gone. I came to work one day and his cubicle was empty. I asked his secretary and she told me that Mark had been sent back to Purgatory to look at some more things connected with the merger.

"Oh," I said, surprised that Mark hadn't told me. My concern over his health was replaced with concern that Mark was leaving me behind. When the shakeout came—and we all knew there would be a shakeout—he was definitely in. And me? Well, I was beginning to feel that I was *out*. . . .

I began to see new faces in the office, people obviously connected to Island. IP&S was bringing some of their people to New York. I kept waiting for my chance to go to Purgatory and still there was no word from Mark.

Until—one morning—there was a message from Myra. "Please call me," it said.

▼▼▼

I did. She asked me to come and see her. She said that she was worried about Mark. I was too, but that wasn't the reason I went to see her. No, I still harbored those fantasies. . . .

After work, I went to the apartment, feeling like a traitor. I knew what I hoped might happen, didn't I?

Myra opened the door. She wore a red sheathe dress; a sere purple scarf pulled back her long black hair. She invited me in. She offered me a drink, fixing a gin martini that was wondrously cold.

Myra told me that she hadn't heard from Mark in weeks. She told me she was worried that he had taken up with someone else.

"There are so many island girls," she said.

I nodded, thinking that Mark would have to be nuts to walk away from this one. I knew that I wouldn't. She looked at me again, and it was like getting a gift, having those eyes fall on me, devour me. She made me another drink and then sat down—even closer, I thought.

I'm a traitor, I told myself.

I didn't care.

I sipped my drink, and it felt hot in the apartment. I smelled her perfume, so spicy, exotic—not what the little legal secretaries in their Anne Klein suits dab between their ears.

Suddenly, Myra reached out and covered my hand with hers.

My mouth fell open, a stupid trapdoor. She whispered to me.

"I'm so lonely here." A pause, a breath. A tropical breeze. "I miss my island. This apartment, this city is so cold."

Her body touched mine. And I was not surprised that I was instantly aroused. I felt no embarrassment, though. Especially not when she leaned closer, put her lips against my ear, whispering . . .

"So lonely. . . ."

There wasn't a moment's hesitation on my part. I touched her face. My hands caressed her bare arms; then, like eager puppies, they were all over her.

▼▼▼

I spent that night in the apartment. And the next. I tried to stay away the third night—after all, what if Mark came back and found me there, his best friend, making love with his wife?

But even with that resolve, I ended up at her door. And on that night, as if aware that I was battling her siren call, she answered the door naked, with aromatic candlelight flickering behind her.

I was lost.

▼▼▼

I started to feel lost at the office, too. While Mark seemed ensconced in Purgatory, buried by legal paperwork, more Island people showed up at the office. A few of the other workers—men and women—went to the island and hadn't come back. Life was sweet in Purgatory. . . .

I also found I had less and less to do—so much of the day-to-day accounting had been moved out of my office. I didn't care . . . I was delirious in my burning lust for Myra. Nothing seemed to matter.

Then I had a brief moment of awareness.

One morning, my stomach felt horrible. It had been bothering me daily, and I attributed it to Myra's spicy island cuisine. But now it started to torture me. It was in knots, pulled tighter every hour.

My secretary looked at me as if wondering if she should call an EMS ambulance. I couldn't very well tell her that I was eating meals prepared by Mark's wife—

Among other things. . . .

I hobbled to the men's room and fell toward one of the glistening sinks, puking my guts out like I hadn't since college. Still, no light bulb went on. I hacked at the sink, spraying it with rainbow bits of meats, spices, and wild rice.

Someone came into the men's room and did a quick U-turn when they saw my colorful display.

And when it was finally over, I stood up, wiping at my greasy mouth. For all the wrenching horror, I felt a spot of relief.

Then I looked in the mirror. . . .

I looked like a guy who had just been tossing his cookies—and then some—at the speed of light. But there was something else. My skin looked pale and mottled. Was it the fluorescent lights? I looked up. Sure, that must be—

I looked back to the mirror. And I saw my eyes. They reminded me of something. I stood there, arms propped on the basin, thinking . . . until:

"Mark." I said the word.

Sure, that's how his eyes looked, when he got sick, before he left, before—

He disappeared. Admit it . . . he disappeared.

I recoiled from the mirror.

I wiped my mouth, feeling confused, the thing taking so long to come together for me. I cleaned the basin and then walked out of the men's room. I saw all the new faces, all the dark island people. A few looked at me as I came out.

You *know*, I thought. You know what's happening to me . . . what happened to Mark. I kept walking, right to the elevator, down to the street, out to the icy January air.

It was January, and I was in my shirt sleeves. But I didn't seem to feel it. In fact, I felt sweaty. People looked at me. There goes a crazy person, they must have thought.

I kept walking until I came to the stone lions standing guard outside the New York Public Library. I walked and a bug-eyed reference clerk with electric white hair made a rumpled face at me. Is it my appearance, I wondered, my smell . . . ?

"I'd like to find out . . ." I licked my lips. "About an island called . . ."

I looked around the cavernous library, lit by the glow of small lamps at the reading tables. The white-haired woman kept her lips locked tightly. If this was a bank, she would have already hit the alarm.

"Purgatory," I said. "I'd like to learn about Purgatory."

She nodded, glad to have reason to turn away from me, and she turned to her computer.

"There are some reference books . . ." She looked up. "But I can get you current information from *The New York Times*."

Current information. I smiled. That would be good.

An old man came close, a stack of books under his arm. I looked at him and he looked at me. Got a problem, buddy? Something wrong?

He kept on moving.

The woman handed me found microfilm boxes with dates on them, from 1967, 1977, 1978, and 1988.

I looked at the microfilm boxes. "The machines are back there," she said, pointing at a dark area off to the side. I nodded and walked away with my newspapers on microfilm.

▼▼▼

I read the first story, ignoring the ads for bell bottoms and *Barbarella*, before Jane Fonda went to Hanoi.

Purgatory had a revolution in 1967 and, after bloody battles in its two small cities, a military dictator, Simon Duvic, was installed.

I skipped to the next reel, the next stories in 1977. And Purgatory was again having problems, probably with the CIA's help, *New York Times* reporter Sidney Hersch speculated. Open gunfire between government troops and the people left their small island a tiny war zone.

Then—disaster. The dictator, Duvic, ordered total annihilation of the rebel population. But who were rebels and who were loyal? There was a photo of Duvic, then a shot of the island, dotted with fires, the cities smoking ruins.

In an act of suicidal genocide, Duvic had nearly wiped out everyone. Purgatory turned into hell.

I stopped for a moment. I heard whispered voices, the sound of the other people using the microfilm display machines. I thought of Myra. I could just walk away from here, simply leave, go back to her. She'd make me feel better, and—

I put on the last roll of microfilm. It took a while to find the story in *The New York Times Sunday Magazine*. "The Miracle of Purgatory" marveled at how the island recovered from all the violence of previous decades, how it evolved into a rich and successful island paradise. There were photos of the cities, the shiny new hotels, stories about the burgeoning tourist industry.

There was a photo of Duvic.

It's the same photo, I thought, from twenty years ago. They used the same photo. But no—

He was standing in front of one of the shiny new hotels.

I stared at the screen.

Everyone had been killed, massacred, gassed. Shit, the island had been blown into submission.

So where did everyone come from?

My stomach tightened again.

I got up, turned to the exit, leaving the microfilm in the machine. And I walked back to the Morra Building . . . because I didn't know what else to do.

▼▼▼

And they seemed to be waiting for me, those unfamiliar faces, now with same sloe eyes I had seen on Myra. They looked at me, and I thought I saw a few grin.

"Welcome back, Col," I heard a dull voice say.

I turned, and there was Mark. He looked so thin, he was almost unrecognizable, and there was no mistaking his unhealthy pallor. He moved toward me, slowly. Of course, he'd move slowly, I thought. He shook my hand and it was like grabbing a fish plucked from the coldest, deepest abyss in the Atlantic.

"Welcome," another voice said. Low, sensuous.

I turned and saw Myra. I shook my head, telling her no . . . I don't want anything to do with her, no more home-cooked meals that—

But there was no time to say *no.*

Mark touched my shoulder, his fish hand resting on my shoulder, dull, cold. . . . dead.

"Are you dead?'" I whispered to him, as if it was a secret. Did she kill you, poison you so you could be like them, an island of dead people—

The fish hand stayed there.

"The new boss wants to say hello," Mark said. His voice gurgled, as if speaking was difficult, a skill still being integrated into this new existence he had.

I heard steps.

There was a moan. No, not a moan, a mumbling chatter, and I realized it was a chant. The entire group was mumbling something to whoever was walking behind me.

Mark gave me a small push to turn around.

My mouth opened. The low chanting filled my ears like the buzz of mosquitoes.

I turned and saw Simon Duvic standing there.

Mark's hand pulled away. "Meet the new CEO, Col." The chanting swelled. My mouth was open. I had to say something, to break the spell. I didn't know that it was already too late—

"Are you ready?" Duvic said. I started to say something. Duvic grinned. "Are you ready to go to Purgatory?"

I looked around the office.

A business trip. A chance for a vertical promotion. To become part of the A-Team for the new combined Island-Morra holdings. . . .

I wanted to say *no*. That's what I tried to do . . . as if I could still make my own decisions. But when I made a sound, all I could hear—from my own lips—was the same mumbling chant, the gibberish now so soothing.

Maybe I'm dead already, I thought . . . or maybe that's still to come. And did it really matter?

I kept chanting . . . *Ade due, Zamballa. Ade. . . .*

Over and over.

After all—in this economy—how could I walk away from such a secure job?

EMMA'S DAUGHTER

ALAN RODGERS

EMMA went drinking the night after the cancer finally got done with her daughter Suzi. Suzi was eight, and she'd died long and hard and painful, and when she was finally gone what Emma needed more than anything else was to forget, at least for a night.

The bar Emma went to was a dirty place called the San Juan Tavern; she sometimes spent nights there with her friends. It was only four blocks from home—two blocks in another direction from the hospital where Suzi died. A lot of people who lived around where Emma did drank at the San Juan.

It made her feel dirty to be drinking the night after her daughter died. She thought a couple of times about stopping, paying up her bill, and going home and going to sleep like someone who had a little decency. Instead she lit cigarettes, smoked them hard until they almost burned her lips. She didn't usually smoke, but lately she felt like she needed it, and she'd been smoking a lot.

The cigarettes didn't help much, and neither did the wine. When she was halfway through her third tumbler of something that was cheap and chalky and red, Mama Estrella Perez sat down across from her and clomped her can of Budweiser onto the Formica tabletop. Emma expected the can to fall over and spill. It didn't, though—it just tottered back and forth a couple of times and then was still.

Mama Estrella ran the bodega downstairs from Emma's apartment. She was Emma's landlord, too—she owned the building. Her bodega wasn't like most of them; it was big and clean and well-lit, and there was a big botanica in the back, shelves and shelves of Santeria things, love potions and strange waters and things she couldn't figure out because she couldn't read Spanish very well. Emma always thought it was cute, but then she found out that Santeria was Cuban voodoo, and she didn't like it so much.

"Your daughter died today," Mama Estrella said. "Why're you out drinking? Why aren't you home, mourning?" Her tone made Emma feel as cheap and dirty as a streetwalker.

Emma shrugged. She knocked back the rest of her glass of wine and refilled it from the bottle the bartender had left for her.

Mama Estrella shook her head and finished off her beer; someone brought her another can before she even asked. She stared at Emma. Emma kept her seat, held her ground. But after a few minutes the taste of the wine began to sour in her throat, and she wanted to cry. She knew the feeling wasn't Mama Estrella's doing, even if Mama was some sort of a voodoo woman. It was nothing but Emma's own guilt, coming to get her.

"Mama, my baby *died* today. She died a little bit at a time for six months, with a tumor that finally got to be the size of a grapefruit growing in her belly, almost looking like a child that was going to kill her before it got born." She caught her breath. "I want to drink enough that I don't see her dying like that, at least not tonight."

Mama Estrella was a lot less belligerent-looking after that. Ten minutes later she took a long drink from her beer and said, "You okay, Emma." Emma poured herself some more wine, and someone brought Mama Estrella a pitcher of beer, and they sat drinking together, not talking, for a couple of hours.

About 1 A.M. Mama Estrella got a light in her eye, and for just an instant, just long enough to take a breath and let it out, Emma got a bad feeling. But she'd drunk too much by that point to feel bad about anything for long, so she leaned forward and whispered in her conspiracy-whisper, "What's that, Mama Estrella? What're you thinking?"

Mama Estrella sprayed her words a little. "I just thought: hey, you want your baby back? You miss her? I could bring her back, make her alive again. Sort of." She was drunk, even drunker than Emma was. "You know what a zombie is? A zombie isn't a live little girl, but it's like one. It moves. It walks. It breathes if you tell it to. I can't make your baby alive, but I can make what's left of her go away more slowly."

Emma thought about that. She knew what a zombie was—she'd seen movies on television, even once something silly and disgusting at the theater. And she thought about her little Suzi, her baby, whimpering in pain in her sleep every night. For a minute she started to think that she couldn't stand to see her baby hurting like that, even if she would be dead as some crud-skinned thing in a theater. Anything had to be better, even Suzi being completely dead. But after a moment Emma knew that just wasn't so: life was being alive and having to get up every morning and push hard against the world. And no matter how bad life was, even half-life was better than not being alive at all.

Emma started to cry, or her eyes did. They kept filling up with tears even though she kept trying for them not to. "I love my baby, Mama Estrella," she said. It was all she *could* say.

Mama Estrella looked grim. She nodded, picked up her beer, and poured most of it down her throat. "We go to the hospital," she said. "Get your Suzi and bring her home." She stood up. Emma took one last swallow of her wine and got up to follow.

It was hot outside. Emma was sure it was going to be a hot summer; here it was only May and the temperature was high in the eighties at midnight.

The moon was out, and it was bright and full overhead. Usually the moon looked pale and washed out because of the light the city reflected into the sky, but tonight somehow the city was blacker than it should be. And the moon looked full and bright as bone china on a black cloth.

They walked two blocks to the hospital, and when they got to the service door Mama Estrella told Emma to wait and she'd go in and get Suzi.

Mama left her there for twenty minutes. Twice men came out of the door carrying red plastic bags of garbage from the hospital. It was infected stuff in the red bags; dangerous stuff. Emma knew because her job was cleaning patient's rooms in another hospital in another part of the city.

After ten minutes Emma heard a siren, and she thought for a moment that somehow she and Mama Estrella had been found out and that the police were coming for them. But that was silly; there were always sirens going off in this part of the city. It could even have been the alarm on someone's car—some of them sounded just like that.

Then both sides of the door swung open at once, and Mama Estrella came out of the hospital carrying poor dead little Suzi in her arms. Emma saw her daughter's too-pale skin with the veins showing through the death-white haze that colored the eyes, and her heart skipped a beat. She shut her eyes for a moment and set her teeth and forced herself to think about Suzi at the picnic they had for her birthday when she was five. They'd found a spot in the middle of Prospect Park and set up a charcoal grill, and Suzi had run off into the trees, but she didn't go far enough that Emma had to worry about keeping an eye on her. Just before the hamburgers were ready Suzi came back with a handful of pinestraw and an inchworm crawling around on the ends of the needles. She was so excited you'd think she'd found the secret of the world, and Emma got behind her and looked at the bug and the needles from over Suzi's shoulder, and for just a moment she'd thought that Suzi was right, and that the bug and the needles *were* the secret of the world.

Emma forced her jaw to relax and opened her eyes. Suzi was special. No matter what happened to Suzi, no matter what Suzi was, Emma loved the girl with all her heart and soul. She loved Suzi enough that she didn't let it hurt, even when her eye caught on Suzi's midriff and she saw the cancer that made it look like she had a baby in her belly. Emma felt a chill in spite of her resolve; there was something strange about the cancer, something stranger than just death and decay. It frightened her.

"You okay, Emma?" Mama Estrella asked. She looked a little worried.

Emma nodded. "I'm fine, Mama. I'm just fine." When she heard her own voice she realized that she really was fine.

"We need to get to my car," Mama Estrella said. "We need to go to the graveyard." Mama kept her car in a parking garage around the corner from the San Juan Tavern.

"I thought we were just going to take her home," Emma said.

Mama Estrella didn't answer; she just shook her head.

Emma took Suzi from Mama Estrella's arms and carried the body to the garage. She let the head rest on her shoulder, just as though Suzi were only asleep, instead of dead. When they got to Mama's car she laid Suzi out on the back seat. She found a blanket on the floor of the car and by reflex she covered the girl to keep her from catching cold.

The drive to the cemetery took only a few minutes, even though Mama Estrella drove carefully, almost timidly. When she came to stop signs she didn't just slow down and check for traffic; she actually stopped. But the only thing she had to use her brakes for *was* the stop signs. Somehow the traffic lights always favored her, and whichever street she chose to turn on was already clear of traffic for blocks in either direction.

There was no one minding the gate at the cemetery, so when they got there they just drove through like they were supposed to be there. The full-bright moon was even brighter here, where there were no street lights; it made the whole place even more strange and unearthly than it was by nature.

Mama Estrella drove what felt like half a mile through the cemetery's twisting access roads, and then pulled over in front of a stand of trees. "Are there others coming, Mama? Don't you need a lot of people to have a ceremony?"

Mama Estrella shook her head again and lifted a beer from a bag on the floor of the car that Emma hadn't seen before. She opened the can and took a long pull out of it.

"You wait here until I call you, Emma," she said. She got out of the car, lifted Suzi out of the back, and carried her off into the graveyard.

After a while Emma noticed that Mama'd started a fire on top of someone's grave. She made noise, too—chanting and banging on things and other sounds Emma couldn't identify. Then she heard the sound of an infant screaming, and she couldn't help herself anymore. She got out of the car and started running toward the fire.

Not that she really thought it was her Suzi. Suzi had never screamed as a baby, and if she had she wouldn't have sounded like that. But Emma didn't want the death of someone else's child on her conscience, or on Suzi's.

By the time Emma got to the grave where Mama Estrella had started the fire, it looked like she was already finished. Emma didn't see any babies. Mama looked annoyed.

"I thought I heard a baby screaming," Emma said.

"You shouldn't be here," Mama Estrella said. She stepped away from Suzi for a moment, looking for something on the ground by the fire, and Emma got a look at her daughter. Suzi's eyes were open, but she wasn't breathing. After a moment, though, she blinked, and Emma felt her heart lurch. *Suzi. Alive.* Emma wanted to cry. She wanted to pray. She wanted to sing. But something in her heart told her that Suzi was all empty inside—that her body was just pretending to be alive. But her heart wouldn't let her stop pacing through the steps, either; it wouldn't let her back away without showing, one last time, how much she loved her baby. Emma ran to Suzi and grabbed her up in her arms and sang in her cold-dead ear, "*Suzi, Suzi, my darling baby Suzi.*" When her lips touched Suzi's ear it felt like butchered meat. But there were tears all over Emma's face, and they fell off her cheeks onto Suzi's.

Then, after a moment, Suzi started to hug Emma back, and she said, "Mommy," in a voice that sounded like dry paper brushing against itself.

Emma heard Mama Estrella gasp behind her, and looked up to see her standing over the fire, trembling a little. When she saw Emma looking at her, she said, "Something's inside her."

Emma shook her head. "Nothing's inside Suzi but Suzi." Emma

was sure. A mother *knew* these things. "She's just as alive as she always was."

Mama Estrella scowled. "She shouldn't be alive at all. Her body's dead. If something happened to it . . . *God*, Emma. Her soul could die forever."

"What do you mean?"

"Emma . . . you were hurt so bad. I thought . . . if I could make Suzi's body pretend to be alive for a while it would help you. I could make a zombie from her body. A zombie isn't a daughter, but it's like one, only empty. But if her soul is inside the zombie, it could be trapped there forever. It could wither and die inside her."

Emma felt herself flush. "You're not going to touch my baby, Mama Estrella. I don't know what you're thinking, but you're not going to touch my baby."

Mama Estrella just stood there, gaping. Emma thought she was going to say something, but she didn't.

After a moment Emma took Suzi's hand and said, "Come on, child," and she led Suzi off into the graveyard, toward home. There were a few tall buildings in another part of the city that she could see even from here, and she used the sight of them to guide her. It only took a few minutes to get out of the cemetery, and half an hour after that to get home. She carried Suzi most of the way, even though the girl never complained. Emma didn't want her walking that far in nothing but her bare feet.

When they got home, Emma put Suzi in bed. She didn't seem tired, but it was long past her bedtime, and God knew it was necessary to at least keep up the pretense that life was normal.

Twenty minutes after that, she went to bed herself.

▼▼▼

Emma woke early in the morning, feeling fine. She went out to the corner before she was completely awake and bought herself a paper. When she got back, she made herself toast and coffee and sipped and ate and settled down with the news. As she'd got older she'd found herself waking earlier and earlier, and now there was time for coffee and the paper most mornings before she went to work. It was one of her favorite things.

She let Suzi sleep in; there was no sense waking her this early. She kept expecting Mama Estrella to call; she'd really expected her to call last night before she went to sleep. All night she dreamed the sound of telephones ringing, but every time she woke to answer them the bells stopped. After a while she realized that the real telephone wasn't ringing at all, and the rest of the night she heard the bells as some strange sort of music. The music hadn't bothered her sleep at all.

At nine she decided it was late enough to wake Suzi up, so she folded her newspaper, set it on the windowsill, and went to her daughter's bedroom. She opened the door quietly, because she didn't want Suzi to wake to a sound like the creaking of a door on her first day back home. Suzi was lying in bed resting with her eyes closed—probably asleep, Emma thought, but she wasn't sure. The girl lay so still that Emma almost started to worry about her, until her lips mumbled something without making any sound and she rolled over onto her side. In that instant before Emma went into the room, as she stood watching through the half-open door, she thought Suzi was the most beautiful and adorable thing in the world.

Then she finished opening the door, took a step into the room, took a breath, and *smelled* her.

The smell was like meat left to sit in the sun for days—the smell it has after it's turned gray-brown-green, but before it starts to liquefy. Somewhere behind that was the sulfury smell that'd permeated Suzi's waste and her breath—and after a while even her skin—since a little while after the doctors found the cancer in her.

Emma's breakfast, all acidy and burning, tried to lurch up her throat. Before she knew what she was thinking she was looking at Suzi and seeing something that wasn't her daughter at all—it was some *dead* thing. And who gave a good goddamn what sort of spirit was inside? The thing was disgusting, it was putrefied. It wasn't fit for decent folks to keep in their homes.

Then Emma stopped herself, and she felt herself pale, as though all the blood rushed out of her at once. She felt ashamed. Suzi was

Suzi, damn it, and no matter what was wrong with her she was still Emma's baby. And whatever else was going on, no matter how weird and incomprehensible things go, Emma *knew* that Suzi was the same Suzi she'd been before she died.

She tiptoed over to her daughter's bed, and she hugged her good morning—and the smell, strong as it was, was just Suzi's smell.

Which was all right.

"Did you sleep well, baby?" Emma asked. She gave Suzi a peck on the cheek and stepped back to take a look at her. There was a gray cast, or maybe it was blue, underneath the darkness of her skin. That worried Emma. Even just before the cancer killed her Suzi hadn't looked that bad. Emma pulled away the sheets to get a better look at her, and it almost seemed that the tumor in Suzi's belly was bigger than it had been. Emma shuddered, and her head spun. There was something about that cancer that wasn't natural. She couldn't stop herself from staring at it.

"I guess I slept okay," Suzi said. Her voice sounded dry and powdery.

Emma shook her head. "What do you mean, you guess? Don't you know how well you slept?"

Suzi was looking down at her belly now, too. "It's getting bigger, Mommy." She reached down and touched it. "I mean about sleeping that I guess I'm not sure if I was asleep. I rested pretty good, though."

Emma sighed. "Let's get some breakfast into you. Come on, out of that bed."

Suzi sat up. "I'm not hungry, though."

"You've got to eat anyway. It's good for you."

Suzi stood up, took a couple of steps, and faltered. "My feet feel funny, Mommy," she said.

Emma was halfway to the kitchen. "We'll take a good look at your feet after breakfast. First you've got to eat." In the kitchen she broke two eggs into a bowl and scrambled them, poured them into a pan she'd left heating on the stove. While they cooked she made toast and buttered it.

Mama Estrella finally called just after Emma set the plate in front of Suzi. Emma rushed to the phone before the bell could ring a second time; she hated the sound of that bell. It was too loud. She wished there was a way to set it quieter.

"Emma," Mama Estrella said, "your baby could die forever."

Emma took the phone into the living room and closed the door as much as she could without damaging the cord. When she finally responded her voice was even angrier than she meant it to be. "You stay away from Suzi, Mama Estrella Perez. My Suzi's just fine, she's going to be okay, and I don't want you going near her. Do you understand me?"

Mama sighed. "When you make a zombie," she said, "when you make a real one from someone dead, I mean; you can make it move. You can even make it understand enough to do what you say. But still the body starts to rot away. It doesn't matter usually. When a zombie is gone it's gone. What's the harm? But your Suzi is inside that zombie. When the flesh rots away she'll be trapped in the bones. And we won't ever get her out."

Emma felt all cold inside. For three long moments she almost believed her. But she was strong enough inside—she had *faith* enough inside—to deny what she didn't want to believe.

"Don't you say things like that about my Suzi, Mama Estrella," she said. "My Suzi's *alive*, and I won't have you speaking evil of her." She *knew* Suzi was alive, she was certain of it. But she didn't think she could stand to hear anything else, so she opened the door and slammed down the phone before Mama Estrella could say it.

Suzi was almost done with her eggs, and she'd finished half the toast. "What's the matter with Mama Estrella, Mommy?" she asked.

Emma poured herself another cup of coffee and sat down at the table across from Suzi. She didn't want to answer that question. She didn't even want to *think* about it. But she had to—she couldn't just ignore it—so she finally said, "She thinks there's something wrong with you, Suzi."

"You mean because I was dead for a while?"

Emma nodded, and Suzi didn't say anything for a minute or two. Then she asked, "Mommy, is it wrong for me to be alive again after I was dead?"

Emma had to think about that. The question *hurt*. But when

she realized what the answer was it didn't bother her to say it. "Baby, I don't think God would have let you be alive if it wasn't right. Being alive even once is a miracle, and God doesn't make miracles that are evil."

Suzi nodded like she didn't really understand. But she didn't ask about it anymore. She took another bite of her toast. "This food tastes funny, Mommy. Do I have to eat it all?"

She'd eaten most of it, anyway, and Emma didn't like to force her to eat. "No, sugar, you don't have to eat it all. Come on in the den and let me see those feet you said were bothering you."

She had Suzi sit with her feet stretched out across the couch so she could take her time looking at them without throwing the girl off balance. "What do they feel like, baby? What do you think is the matter with them?"

"I don't know, Mommy. They just feel strange."

Emma peeled back one of the socks she'd made Suzi put on last night before she put her to bed. There wasn't anything especially wrong with her ankle, except for the way it felt so cold in her hands. But when she tired to pull the sock off over Suzi's foot, it stuck. Emma felt her stomach turning on her again. She pulled hard, because she knew she had to get it over with. She expected the sock to pull away an enormous scab, but it didn't. Just the opposite. Big blue fluffs of sock fuzz stuck to the . . . *thing* that had been Suzi's foot.

No. That wasn't so. It *was* Suzi's foot, and Emma loved it, just like she loved Suzi. Suzi's foot wasn't any *thing*. Even if it was all scabrous and patchy, with dried raw flesh poking though in places as though it just didn't have the blood inside to bleed any more.

Nothing was torn or ripped or mangled, though Emma's first impulse when she saw the skin was to think that something violent had happened. But it wasn't that at all; except for the blood, the foot almost looked as though it'd worn thin, like the leather on an old shoe.

What caused this? Emma wondered. Just the walk home last night? She shuddered.

She peeled away the other sock, and that one was a little worse.

Emma felt an awful panic to *do* something about Suzi's feet. But what could she do? She didn't want to use anything like a disinfectant. God only knew what a disinfectant would do to a dead person who was alive. Bandages would probably only encourage the raw places to fester. She could pray, maybe. Pray that Suzi's feet would heal up, even though everything inside the girl that could heal or rebuild her was dead, and likely to stay that way.

Emma touched the scabby part with her right hand. It was hard and rough and solid, like pumice, and it went deep into her foot like a rock into dirt. It'd probably wear away quickly if she walked on it out on the street. But it was strong enough that walking around here in the house probably wouldn't do any harm. That was a relief; for a moment she'd thought the scab was all soft and pusy and crumbly, too soft to walk on at all. Emma thought of the worn-old tires on her father's Rambler (it was a miracle that the car still ran; it'd been fifteen years at least since the car company even made Ramblers). The tread on the Rambler's tires was thin; you could see the threads showing through if you knew where to look. It made her shudder. She didn't want her Suzi wearing away like an old tire.

Mama Estrella was right about that, and Emma didn't want to admit it to herself. Suzi wasn't going to get any better. But Emma knew something else, too: things can last near forever if you take the right care of them. Let Mama Estrella be scared. Emma didn't care. The girl was alive, and the important part was what Emma had realized when Suzi asked: even being alive once is a miracle. Emma wasn't going to be someone who wasted miracles when they came to her.

Not even if the miracle made her hurt so bad inside that she wanted to die, like it did later on that day when she and Suzi were sitting in the living room watching TV. It was a doctor show—even while they watched it Emma wasn't quite sure which one it was—and it got her thinking about how tomorrow was Wednesday and she'd have to go back to the hospital where she cleaned patients' rooms for a living. She'd taken a leave of absence while Suzi was in the hospital, and now she realized that she didn't want to go back. She was afraid to leave Suzi alone, afraid something might happen. But what could she do? She had to work; she had to pay the rent. Even taking off as much as she had had bled away her savings.

"Suzi," she said, "if anybody knocks on that door while I'm gone at work, you don't answer it. You hear?"

Suzi turned away from the TV and nodded absently. "Yes, Mommy," she said. She didn't look well, and that made Emma hurt some. Even after all those months with the cancer, Emma had never got to be easy or comfortable with the idea of Suzi being sick.

"Come over here and give me a hug, Suzi."

Suzi got out of her seat, climbed onto Emma's lap, and put her arms around her. She buried her face in her mother's breast and hugged, hard, too hard, really. She was much stronger than Emma'd realized, stronger than she'd been before she got sick. The hug was like a full-grown man being too rough, or stronger, maybe.

Emma patted her on the back. "Be gentle, honey," she said, "you're hurting me."

Suzi eased away. "Sorry, Mommy," she said. She looked down, as though she were embarrassed, or maybe even a little bit ashamed. Emma looked in the same direction reflexively, too, to see what Suzi was looking at.

Which wasn't anything at all, of course. But when Emma looked down what she saw was the thing in Suzi's belly, the tumor. It had grown, again: it looked noticeably bigger than it had this morning. Emma touched it with her left hand, and she felt a strange, electric thrill.

She wondered what was happening inside Suzi's body. She wanted to believe that it was something like trapped gas, or even that she was only imagining it was larger.

She probed it with her fingers.

"Does this hurt, Suzi?" she asked. "Does it feel kind of strange?"

"No, Mommy, it doesn't feel like anything at all anymore."

The thing was hard, solid, and strangely lumpy. When she touched it on a hollow spot near the top, it started to throb.

Emma snatched her hand away, afraid that she'd somehow woken up something horrible. But it was too late; something *was* wrong. The thing pulsed faster and faster. After a moment the quivering became almost violent. It reminded Emma of an epileptic at the hospital who'd had a seizure while she was cleaning his room.

"Suzi, are you okay?" Emma asked. Suzi's mouth moved, but no sound came out. Her chest and abdomen started heaving, and choking sounds came from her throat.

The first little bit of Suzi's upchuck just dribbled out around the corners of her mouth. Then she heaved again, more explosively, and the mass of it caught Emma square on the throat. Two big wads of decayed egg spattered on her face, and suddenly Suzi was vomiting out everything Emma had fed her for breakfast. Emma recognized the eggs and toast; they hadn't changed much. They were hardly even wet. The only thing that seemed changed at all about them, in fact, was the smell. They smelled horrible, worse than horrible. Like dead people fermenting in the bottom of a septic tank for years.

"Mommy," Suzi said. It almost sounded like she was pleading. Then she heaved again. But there wasn't much for her stomach to expel, just some chewed egg and bread colored with bile and drippy with phlegm. Suzi bent over the rug and coughed it out. "Mommy," she said again, "I think maybe I shouldn't eat anymore."

Emma nodded and lifted her daughter in her arms. She carried her to the bathroom, where she washed them both off.

▼▼▼

And Emma *didn't* make Suzi eat again, except that she gave the girl a glass of water a couple of times when she seemed to feel dry. It didn't seem to do her any harm not to eat. She never got hungry. Not even once.

Emma went back to work, and that went well enough.

For two months—through the end of May, all of June, and most of July—Emma and Suzi lived quietly and happily, in spite of the circumstances. After a day or two Emma really did get used to Suzi looking and smelling like she was a dead thing. It was kind of wonderful, in a way: Suzi wasn't suffering at all, and the cancer was gone. Or at least it wasn't killing her anymore. She wasn't hurting in any way Emma could see, anyway. Maybe she was uncomfortable sometimes, but it wasn't giving her pain.

The summer turned out to be as hot and rainy and humid as Emma could have imagined, and because it was so warm and wet Suzi's body decayed even faster than Emma had feared it would. After a while the smell of it got hard to ignore again. The evil thing in her belly, the cancer, kept growing, too. By the end of July it was almost the size of a football, and Suzi really did look like a miniature pregnant lady come to term.

It was the last Friday in July when Emma noticed that Suzi's skin was beginning to crack away. She'd just finished getting into her uniform, and she went in to give Suzi a kiss good-bye before she left for work. Suzi smiled and Emma bent over and gave her a peck on the cheek. Her skin felt cold and squishy-moist on Emma's lips, and it left a flavor on them almost like cured meat. Emma was used to that. It didn't bother her so much.

She stood up to take one last look at Suzi before she headed off, and that's when she noticed the crow's feet. That's what they looked like. Crow's feet: the little wrinkle lines that older people get in the corners of their eyes.

But Suzi's weren't wrinkles at all. Emma looked close at them and saw that the skin and flesh at the corners of her eyes was actually cracked and split away from itself. When she looked hard she thought she could see the bone underneath.

She put her arms around Suzi and lifted her up a little. "Oh, baby," she said. She wanted to cry. She'd known this was coming—it had to. Emma knew about decay. She knew why people tanned leather. The problem was she couldn't just take her little girl to a tannery and get her preserved, even if she was dead.

If Suzi's flesh was beginning to peel away from her bones, then the end had to be starting. Emma'd hoped that Suzi would last longer than this. There was a miracle coming. Emma was sure of that. Or she thought she was. Why would God let her daughter be alive again if she was going to rot away to nothing? Emma wasn't somebody who went to church every Sunday. Even this summer, when church seemed more important than it usually did, Emma'd only been to services a couple of times. But she believed in God. She had faith. And that was what was important, if you asked her.

Someone knocked on the outer door of the apartment.

That shouldn't be, Emma thought. The only way into the building was through the front door downstairs, and that was always locked. Maybe it was someone who lived in the building, or maybe Mama Estrella, who owned the building and had the keys.

Whoever it was knocked again, and harder this time. Hard enough that Emma heard the door shake in its frame. She could just picture bubbles of caked paint on the door threatening to flake off. She set Suzi down and hurried to answer it.

When she got to the door, she hesitated. "Who's there?" she asked.

No one answered for a long moment, and then a man with a harsh voice said, "Police, ma'am. We need to speak to you."

Emma swallowed nervously. The police had always frightened her, ever since she was a child. Not that she had anything to be afraid of. She hadn't done anything wrong.

She opened the door about halfway and looked at them. They were both tall, and one of them was white. The other one was East Indian, or maybe Hispanic, and he didn't look friendly at all.

Emma swallowed again. "How can I help you?" she asked, trying not to sound nervous. It didn't help much; she could hear the tremor in her voice.

"We've had complaints from your neighbors about a smell coming from your apartment," the dark-skinned one said. He didn't have an accent, and he didn't sound anywhere near as mean as he looked.

"Smell?" Emma asked. She said it before she even thought about it, and as soon as she did she knew it was the wrong thing to do. But she really had forgotten about it. Sure, it was pretty bad, but the only time she really noticed it was when she first got home from work in the evening.

"Lady, it smells like something died in there," the white one said. He was the one with the harsh voice. "Do you mind if we step in and take a look around?"

Emma felt as though all her blood drained away at once. For a moment she couldn't speak.

That was a bad thing, too, because it made the policemen even more suspicious. "We don't have a search warrant, ma'am," the dark one said, "but we can get one in twenty minutes if we have to. It's better if you let us see."

"No," Emma said. "No, I'm sorry, I didn't understand. I'll show you my daughter."

She let the door fall open the rest of the way and led the policemen to Suzi's bedroom. Just before she got there she paused and turned to speak to the dark-skinned man. "Be quiet. She may have fallen back asleep."

But Suzi wasn't asleep, she was sitting up in bed in her nightgown, staring out her open window into the sunshine. For the first time in a month Emma looked at her daughter with a fresh eye, *saw* her instead of just noting the little changes that came from day to day. She didn't look good at all. Her dark skin had a blue-yellow cast to it, a lot like the color of a deep bruise. And there was a texture about it that was *wrong*; it was wrinkled and saggy in some places and smooth and pasty in others.

"She has a horrible disease," Emma whispered to the policemen. "I've been nursing her at home myself these last few months." Suzi turned and looked at them. "These two policemen wanted to meet you, Suzi," Emma said. She read their badges quickly. "This is Officer Gutierrez and his partner, Officer Smith."

Suzi nodded and smiled. It didn't look very pretty. She said, "Hello. Is something wrong?" Her voice was scratchy and vague and hard to understand. "On TV the policemen are usually there because something's wrong."

The dark-skinned policeman, Gutierrez, answered her. "No, Suzi, nothing's wrong. We just came by to meet you." He smiled grimly, as though it hurt, and turned to Emma. "Thank you, ma'am. I think we should be on our way now." Emma pursed her lips and nodded, and showed them to the door.

Before she went to work she came back to say good-bye to Suzi again. She walked back into the hot, sunny room, kissed her daughter on the cheek, and gave her hand a little squeeze.

When Emma took her hand away she saw that three of Suzi's fingernails had come off in her palm.

▼▼▼

Suzi wasn't in her bedroom that night when Emma got home. Emma thought at first that the girl might be in the living room, watching TV.

She wasn't. She couldn't have been; Emma would have heard the sound from it if she was.

Emma looked everywhere—the dining room (it was more of an alcove, really), the kitchen, even Emma's own bedroom. Suzi wasn't in any of them. After a few minutes Emma began to panic; she went back to Suzi's room and looked out the window. Had the girl gone crazy, maybe, and jumped out of it? There wasn't any sign of her on the sidewalk down below. Suzi wasn't in any shape to make a jump like that and walk away from it. At least not without leaving something behind.

Then Emma heard a noise come from Suzi's closet. She turned to see it, expecting God knew what, and she heard Suzi's voice: "Mommy. . . ? Is that you, Mommy?" The closet door swung open and Suzi's face peeked out between the clothes.

"Suzi? What are you doing in that closet, child? Get yourself out of there! You almost scared me to death—I almost thought someone had stolen you away."

"I had to hide, Mommy. A bunch of people came into the house while you were gone. I think they were looking for me. They even looked in here, but not careful enough to see me in the corner behind all the coats."

Emma felt her blood pressing hard against her cheeks and around the sockets of her eyes. "Who? Who was here?"

"I didn't know most of them, Mommy. Mama Estrella was with them. She opened up the door with her key and let them in."

Emma fumed; she clenched her teeth and hissed a sigh out between them. She reached into the closet and grabbed Suzi's hand.

"You come with me. We're going to get some new locks for this place and keep *all* those people out. And then I'm going to have words with that witch."

Emma's arm jarred loose a double handful of hangers that didn't have clothes on them, and hangers went flying everywhere. Seven or eight of them hooked into each other almost like a chain, and one end of the chain latched into the breast pocket of Suzi's old canvas army jacket, which hung from a sturdy wooden hanger.

The chain's other end got stuck on the nightgown Suzi was wearing. It caught hold just below her belly. Emma wasn't paying any attention; she was too angry to even think, much less notice details. When Suzi seemed to hesitate, Emma pulled on her arm to yank her out of the closet.

The hanger hook ripped through Suzi's nightgown and dug into the soft, crumbly-rotten skin just below her belly. As Emma yanked on Suzi's arm, the hanger ripped open Suzi's gut.

Suzi looked down and saw her insides hanging loose, and she screamed. At first Emma wasn't even sure it was a scream; it was a screechy, cracky sound that went silent three times in the middle when the girl's vocal cords just stopped working.

Emma tried not to look at what the hanger had done, but she couldn't stop herself. She had to look.

"Jesus, Jesus, O sweet Jesus," she whispered.

A four-inch flap of skin was caught in the hanger. Suzi twisted to get away from the thing, and the rip got bigger and bigger.

Emma said, "Be still." She bit her lower lip and knelt down to work the hanger loose.

There was no way to do it without looking into Suzi's insides. Emma gagged in spite of herself; her hands trembled as she lifted them to the hanger. Up close the smell of putrid flesh was unbearable. She thought for a moment that she'd lose her self-control, but she managed not to. She held herself as careful and steady as she could and kept her eyes on what she had to do.

Suzi's intestines looked like sausage casings left to sit in the sun for a week. Her stomach was shriveled and cracked and dry. There were other organs Emma didn't recognize. All of them were rotting away. Some of them even looked crumbly. An insect scrambled through a nest of pulpy veins and squirmed underneath the tumor.

Emma had tried to avoid looking at that. She'd had nightmares about it these last few weeks. In her dreams it pulsed and throbbed, and sometimes it sang to her, though there were never any words when it was singing. One night she'd dreamed she held it in her arms and sang a lullaby to it. She woke from that dream in the middle of the night, dripping with cold sweat.

Even if those were only dreams, Emma was certain that there was something *wrong* with the cancer, something unnatural and dangerous, maybe even evil.

It was enormous now, a great mottled-gray leathery mass the size of Emma's skull. Blue veins the size of fingers protruded from it. Emma wanted to sob, but she held herself still. Gently, carefully as she could, she took the loose skin in one hand and the hanger in the other and began to work Suzi free. Three times while she was working at it her hand brushed against the cancer, and each time it was like an electric prod had found its way into the base of her own stomach.

She kept the tremor in her hands pretty well under control, but when she was almost done her left hand twitched and tore Suzi open enough for Emma to see a couple of her ribs and a hint of her right lung underneath them.

She set the hanger down and let out the sob she'd been holding back. Her arms and legs and neck felt weak; she wanted to lie down right there on the floor and never move again. But she couldn't. There wasn't time. She had to *do* something—she knew, she just *knew* that Suzi was going to crumble away in her arms if she didn't do something soon.

But again: what *could* she do? Get out a needle and thread and sew her back together? That wouldn't work. If a coat hanger could tear Suzi's skin, then it was too weak to hold a stitch. What about glue? Or tape, maybe—Emma could wrap her in adhesive tape, as though she were a mummy. But that wouldn't solve anything forever, either. Sooner or later the decay would get done with Suzi, and what good would bandages do if they were only holding in dust?

Sooner or later they'd slip loose around her, and Suzi would be gone in a gust of wind.

No. Emma knew about rot. Rot came from germs, and the best way to get rid of germs was with rubbing alcohol.

She had a bottle of rubbing alcohol under the bathroom cabinet. That wasn't enough. What Suzi needed was to soak in a bathtub full of it. Which meant going to the grocery to buy bottles and bottles of the stuff. Which meant either taking Suzi to the store—and she was in no condition for that—or leaving her alone in the apartment that wasn't safe from people who wanted to kill her. But Emma *had* to do something. It was an emergency. So she said, "You wait here in the closet, baby," and she kissed Suzi on the forehead. For a moment she thought she felt Suzi's skin flaking away on her lips, thought she tasted something like cured ham. The idea was too much to cope with right now. She put it out of her mind.

Even so, the flavor of preserved meat followed her all the way to the store.

The grocery store only had ten bottles of rubbing alcohol on the shelf, which wasn't as much as Emma wanted. Once she'd bought them, though, and loaded them into grocery bags, she wondered how she would have carried any more anyway. She couldn't soak Suzi in ten bottles of alcohol, but she could stop up the tub and rinse her with it, and then wash her in the runoff. That'd do the job well enough, at least. It'd have to.

When Emma got back to the apartment Suzi was asleep in the closet. Or she looked like she was sleeping. Emma hadn't actually seen her asleep since she'd died. She spent a lot of time in bed, and a lot of time resting, but whenever Emma looked in on her she was awake.

"Suzi?" Emma said. She pulled the clothes aside and looked into the closet. Suzi was curled up in the corner of the closet with her head tucked into her chest and her hands folded over her stomach. "Suzi, are you awake, honey?"

Suzi looked up and nodded. The whites of her eyes were dull yellow. They looked too small for their sockets. "Mommy," she said, "I'm scared." She *looked* afraid, too. She looked terrified.

Emma bit into her lower lip. "I'm scared too, baby. Come on." She put up her hand to help Suzi up, but she didn't take it. She stood up on her own, and when Emma moved aside she walked out of the closet.

"What're you going to do, Mommy?"

"I'm going to give you a bath, baby, with something that'll stop what's happening to your body." Emma looked Suzi over, and the sight made her wince. "You get yourself undressed and get in the bathtub, and I'll get everything ready."

Suzi looked like she didn't really believe what Emma was saying, but she went in and started getting undressed anyway. Emma got the shopping bag with the bottles of alcohol from where she had left it by the door and took it to the bathroom. It was an enormous bathroom, as big as some people's bedrooms. The building was old enough that there hadn't been such a thing as indoor plumbing when it was built. Not for tenement buildings, anyway. Emma never understood why the people who put the plumbing in decided to turn a room as big as this one into a bathroom. When she got there Suzi had her nightgown up over her head. She finished taking it off and stepped into the tub without even turning around.

Emma took the bottles out of the bag and lined them up one by one on the counter. She took the cap off each as she set it down, and tossed the cap into the waste basket.

"Put the stopper in the tub for me, would you, honey?" Emma said. She got the last bottle out of the bag, got rid of the cap, and carried it over to Suzi.

She was already sitting down inside the tub, waiting. "This may sting a little, baby. Why don't you hold out your hand and let me make sure it doesn't hurt too much."

Suzi put her hand out over the tub stopper, and Emma poured alcohol on it.

"What does it feel like?"

"It doesn't feel like anything at all, Mommy. I don't feel anything anymore."

"Not anywhere?"

"No, Mommy."

Emma shook her head, gently, almost as though she hoped Suzi wouldn't see it. She didn't like the sound of what Suzi'd said. It worried her. Not feeling anything? That was dangerous. It was wrong, and scary.

But she had to get on with what she was doing; things would only keep getting worse if she let them go.

"Close your eyes, baby. This won't be good for them even if it doesn't hurt." she held the bottle over Suzi's head and tilted it. Clear fluid streamed out of the bottle and into her hair. After a moment it began to run down her shoulders in little rivulets. One of them snaked its way into the big open wound of Suzi's belly and pooled in an indentation on the top of the cancer. For a moment Emma thought something horrible would happen, but nothing did.

Emma poured all ten bottles of alcohol onto Suzi. When she was done the girl was sitting in an inch-deep pool of the stuff, soaked with it. Emma figured that she needed to soak in it for a while, so she told Suzi to wait there for a while, and left her there.

She went into the kitchen, put on a pot of coffee, and lit a cigarette. It'd been two months since she'd smoked. The pack was very stale, but it was better than nothing. When the coffee was ready she poured herself a cup, opened this morning's paper, and sat down to read.

She'd been reading for twenty minutes when she heard Suzi scream.

The sound made her want to curl up and die; if there was something else that could go wrong, she didn't want to know about it. She didn't want to cope with it. But there wasn't any choice—she *had* to cope. Even doing nothing was a way of coping, when you thought about it. No matter what Emma felt, no matter how she felt, she was a mother. Before she even realized what she was doing she was in the bathroom beside Suzi.

"Mommy," Suzi said, her voice so still and quiet that it gave Emma a chill. "I'm *melting*."

She held out her right hand, and Emma saw that was just exactly what was happening. Suzi's fingers looked like wet clay that someone had left sitting in warm water, they were too thin, and there was some sort of a milky fluid dripping from them.

Oh my God, a little voice inside Emma's head whispered. *Oh-miGod-OhmiGod.* She didn't understand. What was happening? Alcohol didn't make people dissolve. Was Suzi's flesh so rotten that just getting it wet would make it slide away like mud?

She thought she was going to start screaming herself. She managed not to. In fact, it was almost as though she didn't feel anything at all, just numb and weak and all cold inside. As if her soul had oozed away, or died. Her legs went all rubbery, and she felt her jaw go slack. She thought she was going to faint, but she wasn't sure; she'd never fainted before.

Suzi looked up at her, and her shrunken little eyes were suddenly hard and mean and angry. She screamed again, and this time it sounded like rage, not fear. She stood up in the tub. Drippy slime drizzled down from her butt and thighs. "*Mommy*," she screamed, and she launched herself at Emma. "Stupid, stupid, *stupid* Mommy!" She raised her fist up over her head and hit Emma square on the breast, and *hard*. Harder than Suzi's father'd ever hit her, back when he was still around. Suzi brought her other fist down, just as hard, then pulled them back and hit her again, and again, and again. Emma couldn't even move herself out of Suzi's way. She didn't have the spirit for it.

For a moment it didn't even look like Suzi beating on her. It looked like some sort of a monster, a dead zombie-thing that any moment would reach into her chest, right through her flesh, and rip out her heart. And it would eat her bloody-dripping heart while it was still alive and beating, and Emma's eyes would close, and she'd die.

"All your *stupid* fault, Mommy! All your *stupid*, *stupid* fault!" She grabbed Emma by the belt of her uniform skirt and shook her and shook her. Then she screamed and pushed Emma away, threw her against the wall. Emma's head and back hit too hard against the rock-thick plaster wall, and she fell to the floor. She lay on her side, all slack and beaten, and stared at her daughter, watching her to see what she'd do next.

Suzi stared at her for three long beats like a fury from Hell, and for a moment Emma thought she really was going to die. But then something happened on Suzi's face, like she'd suddenly realized what she was doing, and her legs fell out from under her and she started crying. It sounded like crying, anyway, and Emma thought there were tears, but it was hard to tell because of the drippy slime all over her.

Emma crawled over to her and put her arms around her and held her. One of her hands brushed up against the cancer in Suzi's belly and again there was an electric throb, and she almost flinched away. She managed to stop herself, though, and moved her hand without making it seem like an overreaction. "It's okay, baby. Mommy loves you." Suzi's little body heaved with her sobs, and when her back pressed against Emma's breasts it made the bruises hurt. "Mommy loves you."

Emma looked at Suzi's hands, and saw that the flesh had all crumbled away from them. They were nothing but bones, like the skeleton one of the doctors at the hospital kept in his office.

"I want to die, Mommy." Her voice was all quiet again.

Emma squeezed her, and held her a little tighter. *I want to die, Mommy.* It made her hurt a little inside, but she knew Suzi was right. Mama Estrella was right. It was wrong for a little girl to be alive after she was dead. Whether faith was right or not, it was wrong to stake a little girl's soul on it.

"Baby, baby, baby, baby, I love my baby," Emma cooed. Suzi was crying even harder now, and she'd begun to tremble in a way that wasn't natural at all.

"You wait here, baby. I got to call Mama Estrella." Emma lifted herself up off the floor, which made everything hurt all at once.

Emma went to the kitchen, lifted the telephone receiver, and dialed Mama's number. While the phone rang she wandered back toward the bathroom. The cord was long enough that it didn't have any trouble stretching that far. Even if it hadn't really been long enough, though, Emma probably would have tried to make it reach; she wanted to look at Suzi, to watch her, to save as much memory of her as she could.

The girl lay on the bathroom floor, shaking. The tremor had gotten worse, much worse, in just the time it'd taken Emma to dial the phone. It seemed to *get* worse, too, while Emma watched.

Mama Estrella finally answered the phone.

"Hello?"

"Mama?" Emma said, "I think maybe you better come up here."

Mama Estrella didn't say anything at all; the line was completely silent. The silence felt bitter and mean to Emma.

"I think maybe you were right, Mama. Right about Suzi, I mean." Emma looked down at the floor and squeezed her eyes shut. She leaned back against the wall and tried to clear her head. "I think . . . maybe you better hurry. Something's very wrong, something I don't understand."

Suzi made a little sound halfway between a gasp and a scream, and something went *thunk* on the floor. Emma didn't have the heart to look up to see what had happened, but she started back toward the kitchen to hang up the phone.

"Mama, I got to go. Come here *now*, please?"

"Emma . . ." Mama Estrella started to say, but Emma didn't hear her, she'd already hung up, and she was running back to the bathroom, where Suzi was.

Suzi was shivering and writhing on the bathroom floor. Her left arm, from the elbow down, lay on the floor not far from her. Was her flesh that corrupt? God in heaven, was the girl going to shake herself to shreds because of some kind of a nervous fit? Emma didn't want to believe it, but she couldn't ignore what she was seeing. She took Suzi in her arms and tilted her up off the floor.

"You've got to be still, honey," Emma said. "You're going to tremble yourself to death."

Suzi nodded and gritted her teeth and for a moment she was pretty still. But it wasn't anything she could control, not for long. Emma carried Suzi to her bedroom, and by the time she got there the girl was shaking just as bad as she had been.

There was a knock on the front door, but Emma didn't pay any attention. If it was Mama she had her own key, and she'd use it. Emma sat down on the bed beside Suzi and stroked her hair.

After a moment Mama showed up in the bedroom doorway, carrying some kind of a woody-looking thing that burned with a real low flame and smoked something awful. It made so much smoke that Emma figured that it'd take maybe two or three minutes for it to make the air in the room impossible to breathe.

Mama Estrella went to the window and closed it, then drew down the shade.

"Water," she said. "Bring me a kettle of hot water."

"You want me to boil water?" There was smoke everywhere already: it was harsh and acrid and when a wisp of it caught in Emma's eye it burned her like something caustic. A cloud of it drifted down toward Suzi, and she started wheezing and coughing. That frightened Emma; she hadn't even heard the girl draw a breath, except to speak, in all the weeks since she'd died.

"No, there isn't time. Just bring a kettle of hot water from the tap."

Then Mama Estrella bent down to look at Suzi, and suddenly it was too late for hot water and magic and putting little girls to rest.

The thick smoke from the burning thing settled onto Suzi's face, and Suzi began to gag. She took in a long wheezing-hacking breath, and for three long moments she choked on it, or maybe on the corruption of her own lungs. Then she began to cough, deep, throbbing, hacking coughs that shook her hard against the bed.

Mama Estrella pulled away from the bed. She looked shocked and frightened and unsure.

"Suzi, be *still!*" Emma shouted. It didn't do any good.

Suzi sat up, trying to control herself. That only made things worse—the next cough sent her flying face-first onto the floor. She made an awful smacking sound when she hit; when she rolled over Emma saw that she'd broken her nose.

Suzi wheezed, sucking in air.

She's breathing, Emma thought. *Please, God, she's breathing now and she's going to be fine. Please.*

But even as Emma thought it she knew that it wasn't going to be so. The girl managed four wheezing breaths, and then she was coughing again, and much worse—Emma saw bits of the meat of her daughter's lungs spatter on the hardwood floor.

She bent down and hugged Suzi, hugged her tight to make her still. "Be still, baby. Hold your breath for a moment and be still. Mommy loves you, Suzi." But Suzi didn't stop, she couldn't stop, and the force of her wracking was so mean that her shoulders dug new bruises in Emma's breast. When Suzi finally managed to still herself for a moment she looked up at Emma, her eyes full of desperation, and she said, "*Mommy* . . ."

And then she coughed again, so hard that her tiny body pounded into Emma's breast, and her small, hard-boned chin slammed down onto Emma's shoulder.

Slammed down so hard that the force of it tore free the flesh of Suzi's neck.

And Suzi's head tumbled down Emma's back, and rolled across the floor.

Emma turned her head and watched it happen, and the sight filled her nightmares for the rest of her life. The tear began at the back of Suzi's neck, where the bone of her skull met her spine. The skin there broke loose all at once, as though it had snapped, and the meat inside pulled away from itself in long loose strings. The cartilage of Suzi's spine popped loose like an empty hose, and the veins and pipes in the front of her neck pulled away from her head like they weren't even attached anymore.

Her head rolled over and over until it came to a stop against the leg of a chair. Suzi's eyes blinked three times and then they closed forever.

Her body shook and clutched against Emma's chest for a few more seconds, the way Emma always heard a chicken's does when you take an axe to its neck. When the spasming got to be too much to bear, Emma let go and watched her daughter's corpse shake itself to shreds on the bedroom floor. After a while the tumor-thing fell out of it, and everything was still.

Everything but the cancer. It quivered like gray, moldy-rotten pudding that you touched on a back shelf in the refrigerator because you'd forgotten it was there.

"Oh my God," Mama Estrella said.

Emma felt scared and confused, and empty, too, like something important had torn out of her and there was nothing left inside but dead air.

But even if Emma was hollow inside, she couldn't force her eye away from the cancer. Maybe it was morbid fascination, and maybe it was something else completely, but she knelt down and looked at it, watched it from so close she could almost taste it. There was something about it, something wrong. Even more wrong than it had been before.

"She's dead, Emma. She's dead forever."

Emma shuddered, but still she couldn't force herself away. The tumor began to still, but one of its ropy gray veins still pulsed. She reached down and touched it, and the whole gray mass began to throb again.

"What is it, Mama Estrella? Is it alive?"

"I don't know, Emma. I don't know what it is, but it's dead."

Then the spongy gray tissue at the tumor's crest began to swell and bulge, to bulge so far that it stretched thin and finally split.

"Like an egg, Mama," Emma said. "It almost looks like an egg when a chick is hatching. I've seen that on the television, and it looks just like this."

Emma reached over toward the split, carefully, carefully, imagining some horrible monster would reach up out of the thing and tear her hand from her wrist. But there was no monster, only hard, leathery hide. She set the fingers of her other hand against the far lip of the opening and pried the split wide so that she could peek into it. But her head blocked what little light she could let in.

Small gurgling sounds came out of the darkness.

Emma crossed herself and mumbled a prayer too quiet for anyone else to hear.

And reached down, into her daughter's cancer.

Before her hand was halfway in, she felt the touch of a tiny hand. It startled her so badly that she almost screamed. To hold it back she bit into her lip so hard that she tasted her own blood.

A *baby's hand.*

Then a baby girl was crawling up out of the leathery gray shell, and Mama Estrella was praying out loud, and Emma felt herself crying with joy.

"I love you, Mommy," the baby said. Its voice was Suzi's voice, just as it'd been before her sickness.

Emma wanted to cry and cry and cry, but instead she lifted her baby Suzi out of the cancer that'd borne her, and she held her to her breast and loved her so hard that the moment felt like forever and ever.

LARGER THAN LIFE

▼▼▼

Lawrence Watt-Evans

GABE Drucker's stomach began to pinch almost as soon as the daily rushes began rolling. By the time the reel ended he had full-blown abdominal cramps, and his mouth tasted like an old gym sock.

It sucked.

There just wasn't any better way to say it; everything that had been shot so far sucked.

In the good old days, he'd have just thrown it all out and sacked the director and hired someone new with orders to reshoot it from scratch, but he couldn't do that now. He couldn't do *any* of it. The studio lawyers and accountants were watching him constantly, ready to pounce if he showed the slightest flicker of initiative, the faintest hint of going over the incredibly miserly, penny-pinching, impossible budget he'd been given, the first sign of violating the ghastly contracts he had reluctantly put his name on.

If only *Yes Miss Maizie* hadn't flopped, he wouldn't have agreed to any of it.

But *Yes Miss Maizie had* flopped. So had *Scarlett III,* and *Way Down Yonder,* and *Into the Swamps,* and Gabe Drucker knew that after four bombs in a row he was lucky to be working at all, that there were plenty of producers who were sweeping floors or flipping burgers at the commissary after fewer than four full-blown disasters.

So he couldn't fire that loon of a director, or recast the film, or reshoot any of it. He had to somehow salvage this mess as it was. With *five* bombs in a row, he'd never work in films again. He *had* to save this flick.

Maybe it wasn't really as bad as it looked, he told himself; maybe he was just seeing the worst. With that thought in mind, he turned to his assistant and asked, "What'd you think?"

Joan wrinkled her nose and waved a hand. "Stinks," she said.

Gabe grimaced, as his stomach twisted again. "Care to be a bit more specific?" he asked.

Joan peered sideways at him. "You have to ask?"

"I have to ask," Gabe confirmed. "So tell me, what's good, what's bad, why does it stink."

Joan considered this. "The dialogue is crap," she said. "Luke has it lit like a goddamn museum display, and nobody *moved*. Even your precious Angela Denham is stiff as a board—when you said she'd dried out, I figured you meant she'd stopped boozing. I didn't realize she was petrified."

"All right, that's the bad news," Gabe acknowledged. "What was *good* about it?"

Joan had to think much longer this time, but finally admitted, "Denham *looks* good, anyway. She's still got the face—hell, maybe it's the hard times, but she's got more character up there than ever. The camera loves her—if she'd just show some signs of life."

Gabe nodded, staring at the blank screen. Her assessment matched his own. If anything was going to save this picture—and his career—it was Angela Denham.

He hoped to God she really *was* off the booze and the drugs. After three years in the gutter she needed this film as much as he did—but was that lifeless expression she wore just because she was worn out, or was she up to her eyelids on 'ludes?

Of course, if he tried to find out, she'd probably get pissed and quit—she'd done that on *Roses for Mary* four or five years ago, when she first started to slip; she'd just walked off the set when the director told her he wanted her sober next time. And she hadn't come back, either.

He got out of his seat and stood up, joints creaking.

Maybe they could rewrite some of the dialogue, Joan and himself and some of the brighter crew members, and tell the writers that the actors had ad-libbed. And he could tell Luke he wanted more movement on screen, and to stop screwing up Bill's lighting; if Luke didn't like it, maybe he'd walk out, quit the film—Gabe *hoped* he would walk.

Just for Love was never going to be a cinematic masterpiece, Gabe knew that, but maybe, just maybe, it would earn out. Maybe Denham still had enough fans out there to put it in the black, and when it was over he could land another film, work his way back up.

Without Angela Denham, he'd be painting curbstones, or maybe taking his crazy brother up on that research job in Haiti. . . .

"Mr. Drucker?"

He looked up; one of the gofers was standing in the door, looking very nervous. "What is it?" Gabe asked.

"It's Ms. Denham, sir. . . ."

If his joints creaked as he ran to the ladies' room, Gabe Drucker didn't notice it. He didn't notice anything between the time the gofer began explaining and the moment he saw Angela Denham, flat on her back on the bathroom floor, eyes wide open and staring blankly at the ceiling. Dr. Lee and a script girl were kneeling over her.

"She isn't breathing," Gabe said.

The doctor looked up.

"Somebody give her mouth-to-mouth. And she's so pale, why's she so pale? Somebody call makeup . . ." Gabe caught himself.

"Mr. Drucker," the doctor said, "I'm afraid it's too late for resuscitation; Miss Denham is dead."

"No, she isn't," Gabe answered. "She *can't* be."

"I'm afraid she. . . ."

Gabe's mind had shifted into overdrive the instant he heard the word "dead." His first response had slipped out before the gears really caught, but now he was thinking clearly. "Who knows about this?" he demanded, cutting the doctor off.

Dr. Lee blinked, then looked around. "As far as I know, just the four of us here," he said. "Ms. Martin here found her, and fetched me, and I sent Jamie for you. But Mr. Drucker, we can't . . ."

"Yes, we can," Gabe told him. "You wait and see. What did she die of?"

"Well, I . . . I can't be sure yet, but it looks like a drug overdose. . . ."

Gabe nodded. "Figures. Look, Doctor, for now, as far as you're concerned, as far as *anybody* here is concerned, she's ill, maybe even comatose if you want, but she's not dead. Understand?"

"Mr. Drucker, I really must protest . . ." Dr. Lee began unhappily.

"No, you mustn't," Gabe replied. "Look, it's not like we're concealing evidence of a crime or anything, right? Or like she had anything contagious?"

"Well, no. . . ."

"And if word gets out, then the film will be scrapped, and we'll all be out of a job. You want that, Dr. Lee?"

"Well, no, but how . . . I mean, if you're just going to keep us on payroll another few days, that's dishonest. You can't finish shooting. . . ."

"Oh, yes, I can," Gabe said. "You leave that to me." He groped in his pocket and came up with a slip of paper; he turned and waved the gofer forward.

"Take this," he said, "Call the number on it, and ask for Professor Daniel Drucker—tell them it's urgent. If he's not there, then he should call back as soon as possible. If he *is* there, you tell him to get his ass out here as fast as he can. I'll pay all bills. And bring his black bag."

The gofer looked at the paper, and asked, "Why is the number all funny?"

"It's overseas—that's the country code there. Go!"

The gofer went, as Dr. Lee began another protest.

▼▼▼

Dr. Daniel Drucker emerged from the ladies' room wiping ash and paint and sweat from his face with a large white handkerchief. The tall top hat fell from his head as he dabbed his forehead, and he caught it in his free hand.

"Well?" his brother demanded.

"Well," he answered, "I never said I was an expert at this, you know. I'm an anthropologist, not a *houngan voudoun*."

Gabe was not interested in explanations. "Yeah, yeah," he said, "but did it *work*? Did you raise her as a zombie?"

Dr. Drucker frowned, then shrugged. "She's upright, anyway."

"And she can move?"

"After a fashion," Dr. Drucker admitted. "But Gabe, she can't *act*."

"Dan, not to shock you or anything, but she never could," Gabe replied.

"She can't talk. . . ."

"We'll dub all her dialogue."

Dan Drucker sighed. "There's another thing," he said. "You just left her lying there the whole time, right?"

Gabe nodded.

"Well, maybe you should have done something else."

"Like what?"

"I don't know, exactly. But rigor set in, and then passed off, the way it does, and now you've got some pretty spectacular cadaveric lividities."

"Some what?"

Dan sighed. "I mean all her blood has settled down to her back, since that's how she was lying; her front's all pale, and her backside's bright purple, like the biggest damn bruise in the world."

"I saw she was pale," Gabe agreed.

"Well, she'll *stay* pale. She'll stay goddamned bone-white. A zombie's blood doesn't circulate. No heartbeat. I suppose it'll all settle into her legs if you keep her upright. She isn't going to look like she's alive, Gabe; she's a corpse, and she's going to *look* like a corpse."

"That's what makeup is for," Gabe replied.

Dan sighed. "And what about the smell?"

Gabe didn't ask what smell. He asked, "How bad is it?"

"Not bad at all, yet," Dan said, "But it *will* be. And under those hot lights . . . well, I'm not going to hang around."

"Oh, yes, you are," Gabe told him. "We may need you, if the magic wears off, or something. We can get dry ice from special effects, use that to keep her from . . . to keep the smell down."

"Even with dry ice it won't last long. . . ."

"It doesn't have to. We'll shoot all her scenes first—I've already reworked the schedule. Double shifts."

Dan looked him in the eye. "You're crazy, you know."

Gabe grimaced. "I know. Believe me, I know."

▼▼▼

"Mr. Drucker," the makeup woman asked nervously, "Are you sure I should be doing this?"

"Of course, Elsie," Gabe replied. "Why? Is there a problem?"

Elsie fluttered her hands. "Well, I mean, I'm not exactly an undertaker or anything . . ."

"And she's not exactly dead—she's undead. What's the matter, won't she hold still?" He grinned horribly at his own joke.

"Well, of course she holds still," Elsie said, offended. "Except that her jaw sort of sags open sometimes, and I get powder on her tongue. And I have to tell her when to close her eyes."

"So what's the problem?"

Elsie blinked at him. "Mr. Drucker, she's *dead*!"

"I know that, you know that . . . You haven't told anyone, have you?"

"No, sir, you told me not to, and I haven't, and I've done my best with her, but I don't see how you think you can get away with it."

"I don't, either," Gabe admitted, "but I have to try."

▼▼▼

"She's got a throat infection, can't say a word," Gabe explained, "but the budget says we shoot anyway, and she's agreed. Right, Miss Denham?"

At a signal from Dan, the zombie nodded, slowly and stiffly.

"We'll dub in her lines later; for now, Joan will be reading them off-camera, to give you the timing."

"Wait a minute, Mr. Drucker," objected Bentley McGraw, the leading man. "I'm supposed to kiss her. Is this throat thing contagious?"

Gabe Drucker laughed hollowly, and resisted the temptation to say that everyone got it eventually. "No," he said. "Ask Dr. Lee, he'll tell you—you can't catch it from kissing her."

McGraw looked at the corpse uncertainly; her dead eyes stared back.

"All right, everybody, places!" called Luke Hartley, the director. He glanced at Gabe.

They had to tell Luke, of course, and show him how to give the zombie orders. He had been shaken, but had gone along. "At least she'll take direction now," he had muttered.

"And make sure everyone else moves, so it won't be so obvious she doesn't," Gabe had told him. "Make her a figure of mystery, don't overlight her—otherwise it'll never work."

He didn't mention that that's what he'd have wanted even if Angela Denham were still alive. And miracle of miracles, Luke had just nodded, without arguing.

The scene started well enough, all things considered; McGraw muffed the opening twice, thrown by having Angela's lines delivered by someone behind him, but on the third take he got the hang of it and made it halfway through the scene without a hitch.

But only halfway.

". . . oh, please, Audrey," he said, snatching up her hand—and immediately dropping it.

The released arm fell limply to the zombie's side and hung there, swinging gently back and forth.

"My God, Angie," McGraw said, "are you all right? Your hand's like ice!"

"Cut!" Luke bellowed, as, at a signal from Dan, the zombie nodded again.

"It's the infection," Gabe called. "She's a bit chilled. All the blood's in her throat, you know."

"In her legs, you mean," Dan muttered.

The fourth take made it to the actual kiss; the expression on McGraw's face when he embraced the zombie and planted his lips on hers was absolutely amazing, and captured on film forever.

It wouldn't be in the final print, Gabe was sure, but he knew he'd want to keep that film for his own collection.

"Keep going," he whispered to Luke. "We can edit it later."

Unfortunately, McGraw didn't keep going. There were six takes in all.

When McGraw came off the set, he pulled Gabe aside. "That woman belongs in a hospital," he said. "And are you *sure* it's not contagious?"

"Absolutely certain," Gabe insisted. "Really, it's okay. You think I'd do anything the insurance companies wouldn't like?"

Mollified, McGraw let go of the producer's sleeve. "I suppose," he said. "But my God, Mr. Drucker, it's like kissing a corpse!"

Gabe clenched his teeth to stifle hysterical laughter.

▼▼▼

The studio rep watched the action with interest; then he noticed Angela on the sidelines, utterly motionless.

"Why is she sitting so still, staring like that?" he whispered.

"She's meditating," Gabe explained quickly. "Part of how she kicked the drugs, I think. Come on, let's let them work; I'll show you the accounts. . . ."

▼▼▼

By the ninth day of shooting, the secret was out—but still, so far, confined to the cast and crew of *Just for Love*. Bentley McGraw had sworn to kill Gabe Drucker, and had refused to touch Angela Denham's ambulatory corpse again, but that was fine with Gabe; they had all McGraw's essential scenes in the can, and over the years Gabe had survived death threats from any number of actors.

And after a long talk, McGraw had even agreed to come back to the set, once the zombie was gone, to shoot scenes that didn't include Angela. Gabe knew McGraw needed money as badly as anyone else working on this low-budget fiasco.

They were almost finished with Angela. In fact, after some careful reworking, Gabe and Joan and Luke had cut her part down some, and only two more scenes remained to be shot.

That was about all anyone could stand; despite keeping her stored in dry ice when not shooting (and standing on her head, to get the blood out of her bloated legs), Angela Denham had developed a very noticeable aroma. They hadn't dared to actually freeze her at night, which might have helped; freezing made her already stiff movements even stiffer, and noticeably jerky.

The movie still stank; Gabe knew it was going to be lousy, but he had some vague hopes that the romantic, neurasthenic look Elsie and Bill had managed to give Angela's corpse might be intriguing enough to keep it from being a total disaster. If it was just good enough to be released, maybe he could get by somehow.

That was where matters stood when Angela's mother arrived.

"What do you mean, I can't see her? Young man, Angela Denham, as she calls herself, is my *daughter*. . . ."

"I know that, Mrs. Dumbrowski," Gabe said desperately, "But she hasn't been feeling well, and she's resting. The doctor's with her right now."

Mrs. Dumbrowski squinted at him. "The doctor?"

Gabe nodded. "Dr. Lee. He's excellent."

"What's wrong with her?"

"Oh, nothing serious, she's just tired . . ."

"She been taking those pills again? What kind of doctor is this Dr. Lee of yours? Is he feeding her that stuff?" She tried to push past Gabe.

"No, no, it's nothing like that!" He managed an unconvincing laugh.

"Then *let me see her*!"

She was really amazingly strong for her size, Gabe thought as he picked himself up and followed her into the dressing room.

Drs. Lee and Drucker had stopped in the midst of lifting Angela out of her ice-pack, and turned to stare as Mrs. Dumbrowski came charging in, head high, purse swinging.

"What are you perverts doing to my baby?" she demanded.

"Stand," Dan told the corpse. It obeyed. Then he said to Dr. Lee, "I'll get Gabe." He slipped past Mrs. Dumbrowski.

"We aren't doing anything to her," Dr. Lee said. "Who are you, anyway, ma'am? Who let you in here?"

"I'm her mother," Mrs. Dumbrowski replied. "Angie, what are these people doing? What's that smoke? And look at you, that dress looks like you slept in it, and what's wrong with your face? You've been taking those pills again, haven't you? I can see it in your eyes." She leaned forward, and peered at Angela's face. "You look terrible! Worse than when I took you to the clinic!" She turned to Dr. Lee and demanded, "What did you give her?"

"I didn't give her anything, ma'am," Dr. Lee replied haughtily. "*I* am a respectable physician!"

"Well, *somebody* sure gave her something!" Mrs. Dumbrowski snapped. She reached out and grabbed Angela's wrist. "And I'm taking her out of here and back to the clinic! We're going to get my little girl cleaned up and dried out!"

She turned, and found the Drucker brothers blocking the dressing room door. "Out of my way!" she demanded.

"Angela," Dan ordered, "don't leave this room until I tell you to!"

"Mrs. Dumbrowski," Gabe said, "really, everything's under control. . . ."

"It is now that I'm here!" she agreed, tugging at Angela's wrist.

The zombie didn't move.

Mrs. Dumbrowski pulled harder. Angela still refused to move.

Mrs. Dumbrowski yanked with all her considerable strength, and Angela fell forward, face hitting the floor with an ugly snapping sound.

Mrs. Dumbrowski stared.

"Elsie's going to hate this," Gabe said with a sigh. "Sounds like her nose broke."

Mrs. Dumbrowski started screaming.

▼▼▼

They had to explain it all to her, of course.

"My Angie is dead?" she wailed, when they were through. "My Angie's dead, and you bastards have been playing games with her body?"

"Not playing games," Gabe insisted, "just trying to get the movie finished. One last thing you could be proud of, Mrs. D. Something to remember her by."

"Something to remember!" Something clicked in Mrs. Dumbrowski's memory. "She left me something better than any stupid movie; she had insurance, you know! One million dollars! And I'm going to collect that! You people were trying to cheat me out of it!"

"No, we weren't," Gabe protested. "We didn't even know about it, and of course we'd . . . I mean, as soon as the movie is done, we'll report her death, and you'll have the insurance money. If you could just wait a few more days. . . ."

"Why should I wait?" she demanded.

"So we can finish the film, Mrs. D. We'll pay you Angela's full salary, of course; after all, she doesn't need it anymore, and it's in the budget. And then you can get the insurance when we're done."

Mrs. Dumbrowski considered that, very carefully.

They started the day's shooting a few hours late.

▼▼▼

The film wrapped a day ahead of schedule, and very slightly overbudget—the sound crew put in incredible amounts of overtime, airfare from Haiti and huge quantities of dry ice were hidden under "Miscellaneous," the makeup budget was higher than expected—but for the most part it looked good.

Angela's remains were packed up in one last batch of dry ice and turned over to Mrs. Dumbrowski; Gabe supposed that obituaries would appear shortly, and wondered if that would help ticket sales.

Then came the job of editing the mess, and delivering a finished product to the studio; Gabe worked closely with the editor, overseeing the whole thing.

The result was very peculiar, not at all the sentimental little romance that had originally been planned, and Gabe began to wonder what the job market was like out there in the real world.

The studio was doubtful, but decided to at least give it a shot at limited release.

And then the reviews started to come in.

"The ironically-titled *Just for Love* is a strange little piece in the tradition of David Lynch and Tim Burton. Angela Denham stars as Audrey White, a young woman who comes across alternately as a figure of ominous mystery and as a blank-faced innocent . . ."

". . . Angela Denham's performance is startling in its subtlety and power. She has the terrifying stillness of a snake preparing to strike. . . ."

"An actress previously known as just another pretty face, Angela Denham demonstrates that she can be more. She stands out as an island of calm amid the frenzied performances of the rest of the cast. . . ."

They weren't all positive; Siskel and Ebert called it "stiff and lifeless" and gave it thumbs down. The box office was weak in first run.

But the art houses wanted it, and it didn't just vanish after a few weeks. Gabe was pleasantly surprised.

And finally, as the trickle of income began to approach the film's negative cost, he got up the nerve to approach the studio heads. He got as far as Felix Arbender's office.

"Gabe, I like you," Felix said, leaning across his desk, "but *Just for Love* was a turkey. You know it, I know it."

"Well, but Felix, look what I had to work with. . . ."

Felix held up his hands. "No excuses, Gabe."

His heart sank, and his stomach twisted. "So there's no way, Felix? That what you're telling me?" He stared at the thick, royal blue carpet.

"Now, Gabe, I didn't say that."

Gabe looked up, startled.

"The best thing about *Just for Love* was Angela Denham. If you can get her to sign on, maybe we can talk." Felix leaned back in his chair.

Gabe blinked. "Angela? But she's . . . I mean, didn't the papers. . . ."

"I'll be frank, Gabe; we tried to sign her up, but we couldn't get hold of her. She wouldn't talk to us. Now, if she'll talk to *you* . . . well, we'll see."

Gabe stared.

He hadn't seen any obituaries, he realized. He had been concentrating on the movie reviews so much that he hadn't noticed anything else, but he hadn't seen any obituaries. None of the reviews called her the *late* Angela Denham, and surely they would have mentioned her passing.

Hadn't Mrs. Dumbrowski told anyone? What about her million-dollar insurance policy?

"Um . . . let me get back to you on that, Felix," he said.

"They wouldn't pay," Mrs. Dumbrowski explained, her voice trembling with righteous fury. "They said it was suicide! Said nobody could take that much Seconal by accident."

"Oh," Gabe replied, understanding bursting upon him. The insurance people might even be right; Angela hadn't exactly been cheerful. "So no million dollars, right? But then, why didn't you. . . ."

"I didn't want to explain where she'd been all this time, either," Mrs. Dumbrowski said. "So I figured maybe she could . . . well, anyway, I tried giving her orders, like you did, but she wouldn't move."

Gabe nodded. "Dan took the spell off," he explained. "We figured it would be better that way."

"Can he put it back?" Mrs. Dumbrowski demanded.

Gabe leaned back comfortably and shifted the phone to his other ear.

"Hi, Felix?" he said. "Listen, I've got Angela Denham interested, but there are a couple of conditions."

He smiled at Arbender's reply; when the protests and quibbles had run down, he held up fingers and ticked off the demands.

"First, I produce, solo, and we get back as many of the people from *Just for Love* as we possibly can.

"Second, we have a real budget this time, and we don't have your people looking over our shoulders about how we spend every penny.

"Third, a closed set—*no* outsiders.

"Fourth, Angela does no interviews, no talk shows, no public appearances at all—she wants to really play up the mystery woman angle. In fact, she won't even be signing the papers—her mother'll do that, as next of . . . I mean, as her agent.

"Fifth, we hire my brother Dan as technical advisor, pay all expenses and union scale.

"And finally, Felix ol' pal, Angela and I are tired of these romance pictures. This next one's gotta be horror—I've optioned a script called *Queen of the Zombies. . . .*"

THE POTABLE ZOMBIE

▼▼▼

LARRY TRITTEN

FOR MICHELLE, BARTENDER NON PAREIL

IT was a slow night in the bar. Only a few customers had been in, all of them alone, as everyone always was. They had all drunk either whiskey or wine except for a couple of gargoylish-looking trolls who mixed gin with doses of the mucopurulent discharges and phlegm and lachryma of beautiful women. Whatever you might say about trolls, it had to be admitted that they were serious drinkers.

For the moment the bar was empty and Abū was temporarily alone with his thoughts. He poured himself three acromegalic fingers of whiskey from a bottle with a picture of a witch fellating a werewolf on the label and perched on the stool he kept behind the bar. He tried to remember why he had been sent here. They had made him a bartender as a penalty for some un-Jinnī-like gaffe, but whatever he'd done had slipped his mind. It was in there somewhere, of course, as a deceased Freudian psychologist had assured him one night when he dropped in for a beer—but repression was keeping it in the psychic shadows. The one thing Abū felt sure of was that what he'd done had something to do with his sense of humor, because that had gotten him into trouble for centuries before he came here. Someday it would come back to him. In the meantime, his punishment was hardly exacting since he enjoyed tending bar. He liked to mix liquor, to invent drinks. He had invented the Jinn Fizz (a natural for him), the Faithless Angel, and the Bloody Murray (his Semitic influences were considerable).

Whenever he was alone, Abū often scanned the world with his mind like a motion picture camera, keeping up with what was happening. He did that now, picking up several interesting items: the funny-looking Austrian who had come into power in Germany was making all kinds of interesting trouble; the United States was still deep in its Depression and a song called "Brother, Can You Spare a Dime?" was popular, but nobody was dancing to it; a couple of Britons named Bertrand Russell and Robert Briffault were producing some very provocative books; and the little motion picture machine called television, which he suspected would end up changing the world, was coming along quite well in its development.

Abū was world scanning when the deadbeat came in. That was the word he used to describe zombies. While it was a fact that his customers were for the most part dead, it was not the case that their conversation necessarily followed suit. He'd had some of the most lively talk in his life with a variety of the dead, ranging from ordinary people to monsters like vampires and mass murderers. But zombies had almost *nothing* to say and invariably said it in a torturously slow monotone.

The zombie selected a stool and looked at Abū with eyes as pale as clam flesh. Abū started to ask what he wanted, but a perverse impulse made him instead stare fixedly at the zombie in a subtle parody of zombie demeanor. As the two stared at each other, Abū guessed that the zombie would finally ask for rum, and if he was the sophisticate his white linen suit indicated, he might request 151-proof Demerara, the special dark rum that had been coming from British Guiana, distilled from sugarcane molasses grown along the Demerara River.

Abū waited expressionlessly while the zombie indicated an intention to speak with several premonitory twitches of his lips.

"M—M—M—M—M . . ." the zombie falteringly began.

Yes? Abū thought expectantly. His gaze remained blank.

"Ma—Ma . . . ke . . ."

Abū nodded in anticipation.

". . . me . . . a . . . dri—ink," the zombie finished.

"Sure," Abū said, noting with surprise that the zombie, who he pegged as Haitian, was speaking English instead of French. A drink, he thought, and snapped his fingers. And immediately thought, *Uh-oh* . . . Snapping his fingers released a floodgate in his mind and a memory poured forth. And in the next moment the memory was validated as he turned back to see the zombie gone and a drink sitting on the bar.

"You're a drink," Abū wryly confirmed, then grimaced as he recalled the time when the *schlemiel* who had become his master made his first wish, "Make me a malted." Abū, an inveterate joker, had by reflex granted the wish literally, snapping his fingers and saying, "You're a malted!" *That* was why he was here. The Powers That Be had made him an infernal bartender as punishment. He remembered how quickly word of the incident had gotten around in the world and that it became a staple joke among Jews, although nobody realized that the source of the joke was a true story.

Wondering what he had created, Abū picked up the drink and tasted it.

Wham! Abū smacked his lips. This was *some* drink he had inadvertently created. He tasted it again, analytically. His refined palate told him it contained three kinds of rum . . . light Puerto Rican, dark Jamaican, and . . . the pièce de résistance—the wonderful 151-proof Demerara: the soil along the banks of that river surely yielded some incredible sugarcane! He also detected in the drink curaçao, grenadine . . . Abū picked up a pencil and notepad and wrote the following recipe as he intermittently sipped the drink:

2. oz. light Puerto Rican rum
1 oz. dark Jamaica rum
½ oz. 151-proof Demerara rum
1 oz. curaçao
1 tsp. Pernod
1 oz. lemon juice
1 oz. orange juice
1 oz. pineapple juice
½ oz. papaya juice
¼ oz. grenadine
½ oz. orgeat syrup to taste
Mint sprig
Pineapple stick
Mix all ingredients, except mint and pineapple stick, with cracked ice in a blender and pour into a tall, chilled Collins glass. Garnish with mint sprig and pineapple stick.

Abū put down the pencil and concentrated on enjoying the . . . Zombie. The pun made him chuckle, then he realized that it was the perfect name for a drink, for *this* drink. *Zombie.* Moreover, the Zombie was too good not to share with the world. But *how* should he introduce it?

Abū made himself another Zombie, this time in the linear rather than magical way, actually mixing it. Half of the way through the second Zombie, and after ten minutes of world scanning, he made a choice. There was a restaurant in Los Angeles, California, called Don the Beachcomber, whose owner fancied himself an inventive mixologist. Abū would give him the recipe in a *dream.* He felt certain that within a year Zombies would be enlivening palates and jading cerebrums all over the United States . . . the *world*!

The Zombies were so good that Abū had been temporarily distracted from the thought that The Powers That Be would no doubt now slate him for a new punishment. *How* would they punish him? Something along the lines of the task Sisyphus had been stuck with? Translating James Joyce's formidable novel, *Ulysses,* into languages like Chinese, Aztec, pidgin English, and pig Latin? He tasted the Zombie again. The world would *owe* him for this, he thought.

NOT ALL THE GAY PAGEANTS

JOHN BRUNNER

THE blow had long been expected. When it fell, though, it was not the less brutal.

Having finished breakfast before Neville joined him, Leo sat smoking his first gasper of the day while he perused the morning post. Not looking up, he said, "Bunny Soames has invited me to his Christmas house party at Le Touquet."

About to sip the oolong tea he had poured in preference to coffee, Neville braced himself for the rest.

"You'll be going to your mother's, I suppose, same as last year?"

Without waiting for—without expecting—a reply, Leo crushed his cigarette into the kedgeree before him, which Neville had not yet had a chance to sample.

"Well, I have to be in court in an hour," he sighed as he pushed back his chair, and left the room to shave and dress.

The room with the Louis Quinze escritoire, the marble, the chintz, the cloisonné, the slightly risqué Rowlandson, the willfully incongruous cocktail bar with its huge chrome-plated shaker, mirror-polished . . .

Left.

Last year spending Christmas with his mother had been approved as a proper elevation of duty over pleasure. This year—!

Neville Jeffries cursed under his breath.

▼▼▼

Shaving in the bath after Leo had departed by cab for the Strand, he stared into the steamy mirror resting on the bath-rack. Pitiless, his reflection reminded him that he was twenty-eight. A glance at his belly confirmed that since the age of eighteen he had eaten and drunk exceptionally well. He had chosen his life. He had resolved that when this day came he would do the right and rational thing, and intended to stand by his decision, for those like him who clung to the past became ridiculous. He had done his share of mocking such people. He didn't want the same to happen to him.

Yet he could not help feeling deprived—worse, aggrieved. What that ghastly old queen Jimmy Jimenez had said the other day held true: to have been kept for nearly two years by Leo Frost was quite a feat, for the longest previous had been a bare six months. Resigned as he was to the breaking of his luck, his intention had been to take a graceful though regretful leave, designed to make Leo feel he had made a serious mistake. The bastard, however, had forestalled him. It would be a sensible idea to spend the morning making him pay for it.

Unfortunately, he was too late. The shirtmakers, the tailors, the bootmakers, all confessed in deprecating tones that while they fully appreciated his need for their products with Christmas drawing near, they had been instructed to require Mr. Frost's personal validation of all orders charged to his account . . .

Scowling, Neville wished them the compliments of the season.

After making his point (and he had seen it being made, read it in Neville's eyes) Jimmy had gone on to promise that as and when—

No. That belonged to the past. Time now to keep instead of being kept. It was a shame that he was compelled to set out from so inadequate a financial base, a few hundred pounds scrimped by shillings at a time. For his young friends-to-be it must be Brighton rather than Deauville, the Chop Suey rather than the Café Splendide, but to someone born in Bermondsey or Bootle they were much the same. There would be no lack of "volunteers." And after breaking them in he could sell them on to richer companions the way Henry Haines the art-dealer had sold him to Leo (he was sure of it, though it would never be admitted) and build up a bit more capital . . .

That, though, was for later. As things stood at present, he was indeed condemned to Christmas with his mother. Berkeley Square, Clarges Street, Half Moon Street—they were going to be out of reach for a long while. But his mother was elderly and frail and the great gray pile she lived in must be worth a quid or two. Could he force her into a flat on health grounds? Some factory owner enriched by the War might be conned into buying. That would be small enough compensation for showering the countryside with smuts and soot year in, year out.

Oh, but he hated the place where he'd been born, that stark harsh coast that some called stern or handsome or romantic! He called it awful, and did not mean what Wordsworth would have meant. And it was, would be forever, part and parcel of his image of his mother.

Having many young male friends, he had met many mothers since his move to London, via Oxford. He had marveled at women of forty, fifty even, who laughed and danced and (whisper) had affairs! What he would not have given that his own—!

But then, he wouldn't be where he was, nor doing what he must. And chief among the "must" at the moment was making sure his mother did not disinherit him. She was so disdainful of his friends and way of life, even though for official purposes he earned his living by introducing customers to car dealers in Great Portland Street, receiving a commission when they closed a sale, which even by her standards surely must be classed as work.

Did she realize the nature of his relationship with Leo, and those who had preceded him? Probably not. Did she suspect? Conceivably. Living alone in the back of beyond she had little else to occupy her time. Would she upbraid him about it? Not in a million years. That would be to admit the existence of acts she refused to countenance.

He had often wondered how his father had managed to impregnate her, even whether he was the fruit of the sole occasion.

Last Christmas had been pretty bad, but he had had the prospect of New Year's Eve at The Carillon to keep up his spirits. This one . . .

Well, he had no choice. Where was the nearest place that he could send a telegram?

▼▼▼

A Clyno that he recognized as belonging to Dr. Chettle stood before the grime-dark house. Throwing half a crown to the carrier who had brought from the station him, his cases, and a Fortnum & Mason hamper, he marched into the hall. Dr. Chettle was descending the stairs, medical bag in hand, followed by Mrs. Peck the housekeeper, twisting and tugging her lace-edged apron.

"How did you know?" the doctor demanded, halting in midstep.

"Know what?" Neville countered, unholy premonitions dawning.

"To come today, of course."

"But I'm here to spend Christmas with my mother, the same as last year . . . Mrs. Peck, didn't you get my wire?"

The housekeeper raised a horrified hand to her mouth.

"That must have been what the boy brought this morning, just after the mistress took ill! I was that mithered, all I could think of was that he was my chance to send for Dr. Chettle."

Neville didn't wait for more excuses. "Doctor, what's happened?"

Gruffly: "A heart attack."

"Is she . . . ?"

"Yes. It was mercifully quick."

Neville put his hands to his head, swaying a little. "Excuse me," he whispered. "I feel faint. I must sit down."

"Here, sir!" Mrs. Peck pushed a heavy black oak chair toward him. He dropped into it, staring at nothing.

Oh, but *what* a stroke of luck!

▼▼▼

People he didn't know came to the funeral, along with one that he did: his mother's lawyer Mr. Strickland, carrying a black leather portfolio that no doubt contained her will. He kept a suitably grave face during the service and the subsequent burial, but it was hard.

Under gray cloud shedding intermittent sleet the sexton proffered a silver trowel and a salver of earth. Bearded, melancholy, he wore an elderly Prince Albert and a top hat lacking most of its nap. Muttering thanks, Neville duly spilled earth on the coffin, returned the trowel, moved away. The other mourners followed by turns, uttered insincere compliments about the wreaths, then either took their leave, voicing equally hollow condolences as they shook his hand and nodded to Mrs. Peck, or, if invited, waited to be led to the house for tea and potted meat sandwiches and the all-important reading of the will.

From the lych-gate he glanced back. Assisted now by a boy in a long black coat with a scarf wrapped around his head against the chill—his son, perhaps—the sexton was already filling in the grave. As he worked he whistled a lugubrious tune. For a moment Neville wondered whether he should remonstrate on the grounds that it was disrespectful to his mother; then he realized that it probably belonged to a hymn. To the vicar he murmured, "*Is* that a hymn your sexton is whistling?"

"I suppose so," was the answer. "Captain Hopper, though—it's a courtesy title, obviously: he spent much of his life at sea but he's hardly officer class—he's not of our persuasion. He's a Baptist. And I am of course not familiar with the dissenting liturgy."

"You have a Baptist acting as your sexton?"

"Since the War, Mr. Jeffries, one has to be grateful for whatever help one can get."

"Yes. Yes, I'm sure one does. Well, thank you, Vicar. It was good of you to say what you did about my mother . . . Excuse me. I see Mrs. Peck is signaling."

On the way home he tried to make small talk with Mr. Strickland, having growing eager for a hint of what lay in store. But the other was not to be drawn, and most of the time they went in silence.

Infuriatingly, though, the sexton's hymn-tune had taken root in his brain, and more than once he found himself humming it against his will.

▼▼▼

Sitting at one end of his mother's mahogany dining table, with the lawyer at the other and these people he might have met but didn't know on either side, Neville felt as though he were about to face a firing squad. Rain and sleet on the windows provided the appropriate roll of muffled drums. Controlling himself with all his might, he waited for the news that would dictate his future.

"Ahem! 'This is the last will and testament of me Edith Annette Jeffries *née* Lang. I hereby revoke . . ."

Get on with it, damn you!

Eyes twitched toward him. He feared he might have spoken aloud. The sexton's tune recurred. He feared he might start to sing or hum it. He started to feel faint again—genuinely, this time. He feared buzzing in his ears would prevent him from hearing Strickland's words.

At long last, after miscellaneous bequests to Mrs. Peck, some gardener or other, Strickland himself, a charity or two (at each of which Neville fumed inwardly), here was the nub of the matter.

" 'And the residue of my estate, whatsoever and wheresoever situate, both real and personal, to my son Neville George Jeffries.' "

That's all right, then! I can sell this horrible place, and—

Unwittingly he had started to push back his chair. All attention fixed on him. Strickland hadn't finished. Pretending he had only wanted to avert an attack of cramp, he composed himself anew.

" 'Title therein shall pass upon the day of the baptism of his first child born in wedlock, until which time he shall receive an income not exceeding two hundred pounds per annum.' "

He sat stunned.

In other words, you old bitch, you're going to force me to marry! Worse yet, you're going to force me to breed! You did figure things out, didn't you? Oh, you BITCH!

▼▼▼

Christmas Eve and Christmas Day melted into a haze due to the port, sherry and brandy in the Fortnum hamper.

"I must go and see Strickland," he announced. "There must be something I can do!"

In Mrs. Peck's face he read disapproval as keen as his mother's, with commentary: *He's nearly thirty—past time he married—any normal man wants a wife and family. He's not normal—he's an unnatural son.*

"It's Boxing Day," however, was all she said aloud. Jolted by recollection of last Christmas and all the Christmases of childhood, he suppressed an oath.

"I forgot to lay in a stock of change!" Then optimistically: "But people won't bother a house in mourning, will they?"

"There's some as may," sighed Mrs. Peck. "I took the liberty of changing a pound note into silver."

"Thank you . . . I'd better get dressed, I suppose."

Thinking of Bunny Soames's guests, with champagne to look forward to instead of tea.

The prospect of being compelled actually to live in this dump, perhaps for years, rather than sell it and head back to Town had come to dominate his thoughts, so he forced himself to be tolerably polite to those who did trespass on his mourning to pay the compliments of the season and in turn be paid in coin. Postman, telegraph boy, baker's boy, under-gardener, grocer's boy, milkman . . . "Will the line stretch out to the crack of doom?" Once Leo would have beamed on him for citing such an apt quotation.

And all of a sudden here was the boy he had seen in the churchyard.

Except she wasn't a boy.

True, her skirt was shorter than her coat, so boots and gaiters showed beneath, that looked no different at a distance from a boy's, but . . . No, this was not a youth but a young woman.

How in heaven's name could he—he of all people—have made such a ridiculous mistake?

Abruptly cold, colder even than the chill of this ungrateful house would warrant, he kept glancing at her while addressing her—what? Her father? Her keeper? Her . . . Leo?

"Good morning, Captain Hopper," he said mechanically, and added pointlessly, "I don't believe we met last Boxing Day."

Pointlessly, because he was certain they had not. Unlikely as it was that he would have forgotten that ragged beard—it had apparently been grown to hide a scar on his cheek, in which task it failed—it was beyond credence he should have forgotten the man's companion. She was swarthy-skinned with dark eyes and hair; she wore the same hideous garb as at the churchyard; she was in no sense pretty, having too large a mouth, but she could safely be called handsome; moreover she had hands like a pianist's, both delicate and strong, and there was something about her posture that spoke eloquently to his gaze.

She was bored. He could read it in every line of every muscle. *Bored.*

A solution to his problems trembled on the brink of consciousness, but Captain Hopper was talking, and without as yet knowing the details of the plan emerging in his head, Neville was at least aware that it involved treating this man politely. He heard reference to Africa, the West Indies, South America . . .

"Well, that's all very interesting," he said at last with what show of enthusiasm he could feign. "Perhaps we can talk again when I've got over the shock of losing my mother. Meantime, the compliments of the season." He chose a half-crown from the pile of coins Mrs. Peck had provided and handed it over; then, after a second's hesitation, took a sixpence as well.

"Something for you too, young lady!" he said. "Ah—?"

"Emily," Hopper exclaimed promptly. "Well, go on, girl! Take it and say thanks!"

She having obeyed, they took their leave, he humming the same tune he had been whistling in the graveyard. To the housekeeper, when she returned after showing them out, Neville said, "I'm not at home to anybody else, Mrs. Peck. I need to think."

"Very well, sir. Lunch is almost ready anyway."

"One thing before you go. What exactly did this so-called Captain Hopper do for my mother, that he expected a Christmas box? Did she employ him about the grounds?" He was thinking of the gardener and his boy.

"No, sir."

"What then?"

"She liked him to tell her stories."

Neville blinked. "Seriously?"

"Her sight was failing toward the end, as you know"—*even though you didn't seem to care,* was the inaudible gloss—"and she found it too tiring to read. And he was a much-traveled man. I didn't approve, to be frank, but he did keep the mistress entertained. I was surprised not to hear him mentioned in her will, but I suppose she'd not had time to change it. He only moved to the district last summer."

"I see." Neville frowned. "What of the girl?"

Mrs. Peck coughed, looking embarrassed. "No one knows anything about her."

"His daughter?"

"One hopes so."

"I see . . . Right, Mrs. Peck. That will be all."

▼▼▼

The idea that had struck Neville was transfixing in its clarity.

If he wanted to inherit what was rightfully his, he must marry. Worse, he must reproduce. The prospect appalled him. But when the devil drives . . . A miracle had offered a compromise that might evolve into a solution. Here at hand was a young woman sufficiently like a boy for him, even him, to have mistaken her for one. Doubtless she was ill-educated. Yet she had the potential to be made presentable. She was, *mutatis mutandis,* very much like himself before he was taken up by his succession of protectors, and consequently very much like the companions he himself had been planning to seek out once he entered into his inheritance.

There was enough at stake to overcome repugnance. He would act. The possibility of refusal never crossed his mind. How could a father with his daughter's interests at heart decline so generous an offer from a social superior with wealth in prospect?

Absurd!

He celebrated his inspiration by finishing the port and brandy, mixed. Draining the final glass, he found himself humming the sexton's tune again, this time not in the least put out by the grip it was securing on his mind:

"Dah-dah-di-di-dah-di-di-dah!
Di-dah-di-dah-dah-di-di-dah!
Di-dah-di-dah-dah-di-di-dah
Dah-dah-di-dah-dah-di-dah-dah!"

Sometime, perhaps, he might track down the words. But it didn't seem worth going to special trouble.

▼▼▼

Compelled to reside here for the time being, he decided not to press his suit too obviously. First of all, he contrived to meet Hopper and the girl (what had he said her name was—Emily? Later on it would have to be changed, say to Amelia) here and there around the village, lifting his hat as though she were a lady, exchanging pleasantries with . . .

Her father? The more he pondered Mrs. Peck's ambiguous remark—"one would hope so"—the more it disturbed him. Hopper showed no sign of physical affection toward the girl, nor she toward him, continuing in the state of patent boredom that boded so well for eventual acceptance of Neville's offer of escape. Clearly what Mrs. Peck had declined to put into words was the possibility that Hopper was living in sin with this much younger woman, acquired the other side of the Atlantic. Neville, however, found it incredible that the vicar should engage a blatant fornicator as his sexton, no matter how hard help was to come by nowadays.

Of course, according to what he had been told, it would be much easier to break in a pretrained girl; in principle there should be no essential difference between her and a boy with the same background. Yet he suspected there might be, and wished he could talk to someone with relevant experience. Would Hopper not be more reluctant to part with a mistress than a daughter? Unprepossessing as he was, he'd be hard put to it to find a new companion.

Christmas well past, Neville even risked phoning Leo from the public phone at the post office, but there was no reply.

Yes: exchanging pleasantries with Hopper, not with her. She never seemed to say anything beyond a good morning, and often had to be coaxed into that . . . Not much of a drawback, though. To be married to a chatterbox would be unbearable. And he would have to spend some time with his wife, for the sake of appearances. So, on balance, better a shy bride than a forward one. He remembered a pub sign he had seen, showing a woman decapitated, head under arm.

The pub was called The Quiet Woman.

He chuckled.

▼▼▼

Encouraged by successors to the Fortnum port and brandy, plans multiplied like yeast within his head. Where, for example, should they live? The West End would remain out of reach even when he had sold this monstrous pile and invested the proceeds, but there were other parts of London artistic and Bohemian enough to furnish a tolerable life-style. Somewhere like Hampstead would do; its open spaces would allow him to send away Emily—Amelia—for long periods of every day on the excuse of airing the baby in his pram. Also, he believed, there were schools in the area.

He devoted much of his time to ransacking the house, vaguely hoping that an Old Master might turn up in the attic or cellar. There was also the distasteful task of sorting his mother's clothes and other belongings, which he left to Mrs. Peck until he caught her about to toss out what looked like Honiton lace. He was just in time; she was also on the point of discarding velvets, brocades, and fine silks such as tussore, on the grounds that they were hopelessly soiled. She appeared never to have heard of dry cleaning.

In a sudden burst of frenzied energy, Neville bundled up a sackful of fine materials and sent them by train to Pullar's of Perth. In due course they came back, still redolent of cleaning fluid, and enabling him to put into effect a further stage of his scheme.

On his now daily promenades around the village he could count on crossing Hopper and the girl either buying fish on the black stone quay, or haggling for vegetables in the market, or at the baker's (his bread was coarse and made appalling toast), or as today on the way to the Foul Anchor, the pub the "captain" preferred of the village's two—probably not because of its name, the other's being equally ill-omened: the Ship Aground. Spotting them, he let out a hail and traversed the street rather than waiting for them to approach.

Raising his hat to Emily, smiling at her, he said, "Well met, Captain. You enjoy a good yarn, so I'm told, and my mother, rest her soul, left many books. I was thinking you may care to borrow some."

"Ah, sir," came the gruff reply, "my sight grows dim these days. All my reading any more is in the hymnal and the psalter. Still, it's a kind thought, and thank you."

"Not at all. I understand. However, I can make another offer that I'm sure will be of great interest to this young lady."

It was as though a light came and went behind Hopper's dark eyes. They were set between lids whose wrinkles were as heavily emphasized as a chorus girl's lashes, thanks to years of ingrained salt and dirt. To have a peasant like this for a father-in-law. . . ! Neville had to repress a shudder. In his daydreams Hopper had conveniently vanished, or retired, or gone back to sea.

But that might not be a problem. He could probably be paid off.

"Emily, you don't seem to have many clothes. If you'll forgive me saying so. My mother left a lot of rather good material—silk and velvet and stuff. I've had it cleaned. Any time you'd like to come up to the house you can take your pick."

Dark eyes between dark lids stared at him, but she said nothing. Hopper said hastily, "You must excuse her, sir. She's not used to talking with gentry."

She'll have to get used soon enough! But Neville managed to cancel the words before utterance. Keeping a smile on his face, he continued, "They're first-rate quality. Do come up and see them. You could make them into—well, all sorts of things."

Troubled for a moment, he glanced at Hopper.

"Does Emily not sew?"

"Like me," Hopper grunted.

"Excuse me?" Neville found himself blinking nervously.

"Like a seaman, sir! Turning to in a calm to make do and mend with a canvas hussif and a sail-needle! None of your fancy work, none of your embroidery. No, sir."

Neville had had the confused impression that all girls were taught to sew, not merely darning and patching but making whole garments, and that his mother had just been a resentful exception. He said without having thought it through, "Well, I'm sure there are women in the village who will make things up. Bring her round so she can choose what she likes."

No reaction. Divining the reason: "Oh, if it's a matter of cost . . . It'll only be a few shillings, I suppose." After the tailors of Jermyn Street it seemed to him that in these remote parts few articles cost more than a loaf of bread or a postage stamp.

Did the girl show any sign of excitement yet? Surely the prospect of finery to replace her drab coat and dress—none too clean, those, not having had the benefit of a trip to Pullar's!—surely that must elicit some response?

Indeed, though she had to be prompted by Hopper, she did force a smile and murmur what sounded like thanks. Relieved, Neville tipped his hat again and they parted, the captain resuming his inevitable tune.

From the corner of the street he glanced back. Hopper had entered the pub. Emily was standing docile beside its door. There was a stone bench adjacent, but she showed no inclination to sit down. She seemed resigned to waiting as long as required.

Neville nodded. There was much to be said for a passive wife. Here in the north people still remembered the original meaning of "buxom," as in the old-style marriage service: "bonnie and buxom in bed and at board."

It meant bendable.

So far, then, so good.

▼▼▼

But so good did not mean very good. He ought, he decided, to learn more about Hopper, and set about making inquiries. His first approach was to the Baptist minister, a prematurely stern young man who confined himself to stating that Captain Hopper attended chapel regularly and that the girl came with him. He did not know her first name, nor had he inquired about her relationship to the captain.

Annoyed, Neville called after as he turned away. "Just a moment! Can you tell me whether this belongs to a hymn?"

He hummed the melody he kept hearing from Hopper. Before he had finished the first line, the minister was nodding.

"Yes, yes! It is a hymn tune. Good morning!"

Thus frustrated in one alley, Neville turned to another, and ventured into the ill-lit, smoky Foul Anchor, making sure Hopper would not be present. He hoped by buying drinks to loosen tongues. In that he succeeded, but to small effect, since the sailors who forgathered here were fishermen having little in common with one who had crossed the Atlantic scores of times.

He did establish one thing: the general opinion was that the so-called captain had been at best a bo'sun or first mate. Nonetheless they tolerated his adoption of the title, for, as one of them said, having spent so much time in the West Indian trade he had seen more deep water than most. For a moment Neville found himself contrasting the easygoing attitude of these men with the bitchiness and backbiting of the circles he had frequented in London, and considered coming here again, perhaps on a regular basis. Then he contrasted the squalidness of this bar with the elegance of the Cacahuète or the Élysée, and shuddered and went home.

▼▼▼

January was bad. Mrs. Peck cooked him flavorless meals that he left untouched. To keep himself going he bought spirits from the village's single grocery; he bought so much there was none left until the next delivery and realized he was at risk of being branded an alcoholic. Word could reach Hopper . . . He purchased lemonade and smiled ingratiatingly at the shopman.

But telegraphed Leo's wine merchant in London and had a case of brandy sent by rail.

Why would that silly girl not take up his invitation? Was Hopper preventing her? Must be! And why could he no longer cross them on the street? He kept hearing the familiar tune, hummed or whistled, but somehow the couple were contriving to avoid him. In desperation he headed back and back to the Foul Anchor, not intending to enter but only to see whether Emily was waiting by the door. She never was.

January was bad.

February, before its first week was out, became unbearable.

▼▼▼

For three days, four, five, the lash of a North Sea storm had made going out of doors unthinkable. Neville had passed his time writing long self-pitying letters to people he had imagined were his friends, while the level in the brandy bottle went down as fast as the inkwell. He had had an acknowledgment or two, but no replies—none that could properly be called replies. Last night had been especially awful; struggling to sleep despite the gale he had heard a slate break free that smashed into the cast-iron gutter underneath and cracked it so cascades of water poured across his bedroom window. He could envisage pound after precious pound of his exiguous inheritance being washed away, drained away . . .

But there would be more, there could well be quite a lot, once he gained the right to sell this loathsome house! Emily must not refuse him! (How could she want to?) Hopper must not stop her accepting him! (How could he be bribed not to?) Brandy-sodden chaos swamped him into sleep at last, and dreams wherein he roamed the rooms and passages of this his mother's home that somehow also were the entrails of a woman, ever and again reaching a dead end beyond whose wall he heard the clink of glasses and the voice of friends . . .

He woke red-eyed from crying, and resolved on deeds.

▼▼▼

He had long known where Captain Hopper lived, though he had never been to the house, prevented perhaps by some half-remembered childhood injunction to the effect that being "too forward" was sure to ruin a suit. Had the same moral been drilled into Emily? If not, why had she refused even to come and look at the pretty things he had ready for her? He had reached the stage of convincing himself that Mrs. Peck must have turned her away and been forced to eat humble pie to stop her giving notice. How could he find a replacement housekeeper?

Until Emily took over, of course.

He shaved with care; he chose his finest silk shirt and a silk tie that Jimmy Jimenez had sent for Christmas, still not acknowledged with a thank-you note, for the prospect of being "taken over" by Jimmy filled him with repugnance and he wasn't sure he could endure it even as an ultimate recourse. He bid defiance to the weather with a fawn topcoat and a pale gray trilby and a malacca cane by way of walking-stick, and set out to explain to his intended what she clearly could not yet have understood: the glamorous future she might look forward to were she only to say one single necessary word.

And had to turn back from the threshold for a tumbler of brandy before he could screw himself to the sticking point.

Marriage! Babies stinking of urine and sour milk! Ugh!

He wished his belly were not rebelling against the drink he had taken. He wished he didn't so detest this land of his birth. Above all he wished in his heart of hearts that he had never been forced into taking any decision more significant than to say to someone else, "Yes please."

Emily was in that supremely enviable position. Why had she not already given her consent?

He stood before Hopper's home trying not to see two of its front door. It was the last in a row of stone-built cottages, blacker and uglier than the forbidding house he could not bear to think of as his home, only as his mother's. Surely no one in his—in her—right mind could not but want to flee from such a mean place!

There was an iron knocker. To it he raised a fastidious kid-gloved hand, the one with which he was not attempting to save his hat from departing on the wind. His head was full of all the phrases he had spent these past weeks rehearsing, until they were so polished they surely could not fail of their effect . . .

No answer?

Dismayed, he knocked harder, hearing echoes within as though the cottage were abandoned. He stepped to its sole street-level window and peered in through a blur of streaming rain.

No, not abandoned. Just empty. A fire smoldered on the hearth, a kettle hanging on a jack above. However, there was little furniture—a table, a settle, a couple of chairs, a chest, a rack of fire-irons—so that the room gave back the knocker's sound effectively intact.

But on the table lay two books: one shut, the other open.

Suddenly Hopper's hymn-tune darted back to mind. Was one of those the hymnal it came from? Neville felt a need to know, inconsequential as an itch.

Returning to the door, on impulse he lifted its latch. Against all common sense—for there was an iron lock—it swung inward in the grip of the gale and virtually dragged him with it. Gasping, striving to force it shut behind him, he trod on coir matting. Had there been, as he was expecting, bare flags, he could well have lost his footing, for rain preceded him over the threshold.

Wiping his eyes, he looked warily around. Some at least of "Captain" Hopper's claims seemed to be borne out, for on the whitewashed walls hung artifacts that Henry Haines would have been impressed by: African and Caribbean ritual masks, along with knives and spears and articles whose purpose was unguessable. But, as nearly as he could work out on the basis of what of Henry's knowledge had rubbed off on him, the collection was unsystematic, a ragbag of what a common sailor ("not exactly officer class!") might have haggled for in foreign parts and kept to ornament his home when he retired, heedless of what significance their makers ascribed to them.

He approached the table that bore the books. Ah. The one lying open was indeed a hymnal. Did it contain—?

But abruptly it dawned that the answer to a more important question lay within his grasp. Were there two bedrooms upstairs? Or at any rate two beds?

Tipsily he strove to decide whether it would be better to take on, as he had earlier thought of it, a pretrained girl, or whether as a prospective bridegroom he should ask a discount for accepting damaged goods.

And his thoughts were derailed by the reopening and rapid closing of the door, as surely as an express hitting logs and rocks.

He turned, frantically framing lies, to see Hopper peeling off the seaman's oilskin coat he wore against the filthy weather. Emily hung it on a wooden peg before removing her own coat. What she had on underneath, along with her boots and gaiters, seemed just as sodden.

Intrusion? Trespass? Such concepts pole-vaulted across Neville's mind. He tried not to look at Emily.

"Take your coat off. You can hang it there. Sit down." Hopper kicked a chair around for himself and pointed at another—the other. Here, master of his own house, he had discarded deference. "Tea!" he added in a sudden roar. "And a bottle!"

The girl disappeared, presumably to a larder. Meantime Neville dumbly did as he'd been told. He had been caught *in flagrante*, about to . . . Well, best not think of that. He was grateful that Hopper the ex-bo'sun had not already laid into him with a marlinspike—whatever such a thing might be, but it sounded appropriately nautical. So what did this extraordinary reception portend?

"I been expecting you," Hopper said at length. Teeth stained from tobacco and rotten from sweets showed briefly among his beard. But in no sense did the expression constitute a smile.

"Why?" Neville forced out.

"Ah, the whole village knows, the way you carry on. Well, I

don't mind. Mark you, you'll have to pay for what you want. But that's the way o' the world."

Before Neville's fuddled brain could sort out the implications, Emily had returned with the makings for tea. Numbly he waited while she poured hot water, stirred, poured again.

Which done, she retreated to the settle and became immobile.

She had also fetched a bottle of near-black glass. Giving no sign that he would brook refusal, Hopper uncorked it, releasing the powerful half-sweet scent of dark rum.

"You being as is well known a drinking man," he said with a horrible affectation of connivance, of intimacy, "you'll appreciate a drop o' this on so wintry a day."

And spilled generously into their mugs. Neville wondered wildly whether he ought to object to the omission of Emily. But a teetotal wife, after all, would be cheaper . . .

Hopper was sketching a toast. Neville duly gulped, hoping the brew would not clash with the liquor he had already ingested. Silently he cursed his mother, as he now did daily, but tried not to let it show on his face.

The mixture did no immediate harm.

After a while, Hopper having shown no sign of further speech, he said, "Expecting me, were you?"

"'Why, yes." Hopper drank again and wiped his hairy upper lip. "A gentleman's got to have a reason for paying attention to persons of—well, persons like me. You were right to pick on me, being the sexton an' all, with the worst gales of the winter yet to hit an' such a lot o' youngsters at sea since the war . . . How d'you find my rum?"

"Good, good!" Neville exclaimed. He had meant to ask what sextons and young sailors had to do with what they were talking about, but the change of subject drove the question out of his mind.

"Thought you'd say that, you being a drinkin' man an' all. It was sent by the one who makes it, over in the West Indies. Black as his name, is Mr. Coffey, but as good a pal as any and better than most. Good teacher, too."

"You sailed mainly in the West Indian trade, isn't that right?" Neville achieved.

"West Africa, South America too. But mostly the West Indies, yes." Draining his mug, he signaled Emily for refills and added at least as much rum as before.

"Well, anyhow, I shan't mind to help out—if you make it worth my while. I was never a rich man. Folk call me cap'n, but I never was, only first mate. All I brought back was what you see on these walls—and Emily, o' course. Cast ashore here in the end, where most as call themselves sailors never had more'n shoal water under their keels. Turn white as milk, they would, if they had to sweat through a hurricane like what wrecked the *Jenny Rhodes* on the Tortuga coast. Going back a bit, that is . . ."

Neville let him ramble on, covertly studying Emily the while. Could he bear to wake every morning for the rest of his life and see that head on the pillow next to his? Well, of course it needn't come to that. Once a child was safely born—even sooner, maybe: once she was pregnant, they could sleep in separate beds or better yet separate rooms.

This rum was having the same extravagant impact on his imagination as the brandy he drank at home. Ideas for investing the proceeds from the house spawned like blowflies. Moreover, there was no reference in his mother's will to the continuance of the marriage past the baby's birth. So long as it was born in wedlock, that would suffice. At the earliest convenient opportunity, why should divorce not follow?

Yet there was something not altogether unattractive about quasi-masculine Emily, despite her likely touch of the tarbrush. Indeed, over the past weeks he had come to view her face, her body, in a new light, a new context. Was it because he felt grateful for her mere existence, his key to escape the prison his mother had decreed? No! Of a sudden it came to him.

It was her stillness. It was amazing. It was mesmerizing. It was riveting. She sat like a brown stone carving on the hard ugly settle, without the slightest hint of motion. Until—

"More tea!" Hopper commanded. The kettle proved to be empty

and she went for fresh water; out of sight a pump creaked. He for his part didn't wait for her return, but spilled yet more rum equally into the two mugs and drank half his own portion neat.

Neville dared not imitate him. The liquor was revealing its full potency. Were he to remain much longer he might disgrace himself. If Hopper wouldn't come to the point, he must be brought to it. Emily hung up the full kettle, mended the fire, and resumed her immobility; Hopper interrupted his reminiscing for a fit of wheezy laughter; and Neville seized his chance.

"Well, Captain! As I'm sure you realize, I do fully intend to make it worth your while to help me. You imply that you understand my situation?"

Hopper nodded. His expression grew calculating, almost sly. Taking a stubby clay pipe from his pocket, he frayed a twist of tobacco and tamped its bowl.

"Well, a solution presents itself." In instant retrospect Neville wondered whether that made sense. He hastened to clarify.

"One can't be sure what the house will fetch, but it ought to be enough for a decent place in London, even if it has to be out of the fashionable swim. One might have to rent, but there are advantages. I've thought it all through. Not had much else to do recently, to be candid." He forced a harsh laugh. Was he making his point? Hopper was looking puzzled.

Or was he merely drunk? That would be unbearable. Neville licked his lips, glancing at Emily and marveling anew at her composure. It was as though she hadn't even realized she was the subject of discussion. He said, "Naturally one would prefer a boy, but—"

Hang on. I haven't got to that part of what I'm trying to say.

Hopper shrugged. "When you've been at sea as long as I have, you stop caring about such matters. I'll help regardless." Pipe ready, he stretched a splinter to the fire.

"That's very—very civil of you," Neville responded, wishing his tongue weren't trying to utter more irrelevant phrases, wishing his eyes weren't overlapping like an out-of-focus stereopticon. And what *had* that nonsense been about sextons and young sailors? "Well, then, as soon as Emily can be persuaded—"

"Emily? What of her?"

Obviously far more used to the violent rum, Hopper, smoke-wreathed, was alert on the instant. Alert and—and threatening?

"Well, there does have to be a child before I can inherit, but it doesn't need to be a boy . . . You said you knew! You said everyone in this place has heard about my mother's will!"

Hopper stared for a long moment. Then he began to chuckle.

"And here I thought I knew what you'd come for! I was a long way off course, wasn't I?"

He tipped the bottle; finding it drained, he thrust it at Emily, who took it and went for another.

Neville's brain was awhirl. What had gone wrong? This cheating devil wasn't even going to consider letting Emily rescue him from the hell his mother had decreed!

Also, at the edge of his mind, half-registered phrases surged like sullen waves against this hurtful coast: *been at sea as long as I have—help you regardless . . .*

Implicit meanings throbbed and festered.

The girl returned. Poised to uncork the fresh bottle, Hopper said, "Well, Emily's mine, o' course. Even if I made her over—which maybe I could!—she wouldn't be any use to the likes o' you. And here I was, so sure you'd approached me because . . ."

Neville was no longer listening. Two doors had slammed across his ears.

First: this horrible man had just said he could make Emily over and he wasn't going to. Because, second: *She wouldn't be any use to the likes o' you!*

In the overtones of that phrase he reheard all the insults he most feared because they held most truth.

And Hopper was grinning! Grinning to show his filthy broken teeth! And saying, "Never mind, sir! Something to better suit your needs may well turn up!"

But I don't want "something"! I want Emily! Docile, pliant, not as attractive as a boy but nearly, and he says—he thinks—he . . .

Neville thrust his chair back so hard it fell over. The shock of finding himself upright conspired with alcohol to dizzy him. Behind his eyes fury exploded like a Bengal light, all red. Howling, he rushed at a wall display of masks, and knives, and spears.

Hopper cried out, tried absurdly to parry with his pipe, could not deflect the blade that pierced his chest.

Blood spurted. Much fell on the open pages of the hymnal.

And Emily did nothing. Absolutely nothing whatsoever.

That was what dragged Neville back from the remoteness of rage to the real world. He found himself staring at Hopper, slumped in his chair with hands curved into despairing claws, showing how he had spent his last energy on a futile attempt to tear loose the spear. His gaze was drawn unwillingly from drop to splash to smear of the blood that had spattered across the table, across the book . . .

Open at a hymn whose number he could not read, for redness covered it, and part of the text as well. The first verse, however, remained unsmutched, and the moment Neville set eyes on it he realized this was what belonged to the tune Hopper was forever humming or whistling—

Had hummed. *Had* whistled.

Still incapable of accepting the reality of what he had done, he sought transient refuge in a whispered recital of the words:

"O, wondrous appearance of Death!
No sight upon Earth is so fair.
Not all the gay pageants that breathe
Can with a dead body compare."

Morbid, he thought to himself. *Morbid* . . .

After a while he recovered enough to wonder why Emily had betrayed no reaction to the death of her—

Her father? Her lover, keeper, protector?

A word more laden with terror than any of those loomed suddenly in his mind.

Resurrector.

In the West Indies did they not tell certain—tales? Henry had mentioned . . .

He looked at Emily, composed, emotionless. And he *knew*. Why she was no good to the likes of him, who needed to father a child. Why to gain the counterpart of her that Hopper assumed him to desire he would have been well advised to appeal to a mariner turned sexton, on a coast where many young sailors were cast ashore by winter storms.

What had made Hopper call Mr. Coffey a good teacher.

▼▼▼

When he had finished screaming, at least for the time being, he tore open the door of the cottage and fled coatless and bare-headed through the teeming rain. Eventually a constable came to investigate because of what he sobbed and moaned in earshot first of embarrassed passersby, then Mrs. Peck, who donned her coat and seized her gamp and ran for help.

Until that time, though, Emily did nothing. Absolutely nothing. Though afterward the only deed that now was left to her.

She rotted.

Z IS FOR ZOMBIE

HARLAN ELLISON

HOWARD Hughes did not die in 1976, no matter *what* they tell you. Howard Hughes died in 1968. It was not a spectacular death, down in flames in the *Spruce Goose* or assassinated by his next-in-command or frightened to death by an insect that found its way into his eyrie. He choked to death on a McDonald's greaseburger during dinner one night in July of 1968. But wealth has its privileges. Johns Hopkins and the Mayo Clinic and the Walter Reed in Maryland sent their teams. But he was dead. DOA, Las Vegas. And he was buried. Not in 1976, in 1968. And Mama Legba, with whom Hughes had made a deal twenty years earlier in Haiti, came to the grave, and she raised him. The corporate entity is mightier than death. But the end is near: at this very moment, training in the Sierra Maestra, is an attack squad of Fidel Castro's finest guerrillas. They know where Hughes went when he evacuated Nicaragua one week before the earthquake. (Zombies have precognitive faculties, did you know that?) And they know the 1976 death story is merely misdirection like all the other death rumors throughout the preceding years. They will seek him out and put him to *final* rest by the only means ever discovered for deanimating the walking dead. They will pour sand in his eyes, stuff a dead chicken in his mouth, and sew up the mouth with sailcloth twine. It would take a mission this important to get the fierce Cuban fighters to suffer all the ridicule: bayonet practice with dead chickens is terribly demeaning.

CORRUPTION IN OFFICE

DON D'AMMASSA

WHEN Paul Norton received the emergency summons to the Oval Office, he acknowledged the call curtly, then buzzed his chief assistant. "Anything hot, Bob?"

"No, sir. Nothing out of the ordinary. The coup in England seems to be winding down, and there haven't been any cease-fire violations in Canada for almost a week."

"All right, thanks. I'm going over to the White House for a meeting. Hold the fort, will you?" He clicked off, tapped his finger impatiently for a few seconds, then asked his secretary to arrange transportation.

With her usual efficiency, she arranged for a private shuttle, which was ready and waiting by the time he had taken the elevator to the roof of the State Department office building. A few minutes later, the pilot set him down on a small landing field on the White House grounds, where armed guards remained attentive even after he passed through the scanners, grudgingly allowing him into the building.

Jennifer Frakes was waiting just inside. The jowly Chief of Staff had served President Torgeson for over twenty years, rising through the backrooms of the insurgent Unionist Party while Torgeson progressed from state representative to governor to senator to President.

"Morning, Jennifer. What's up?" Norton glanced at his watch, frowned. "I thought the President was meeting with the King of Romania this morning."

"We've had some problems. His schedule has been suspended . . . indefinitely." It was voice rather than words that tipped him off that something was seriously wrong. Ordinarily, Frakes was gruff and overbearing, using force of will to maintain discipline among subordinates and associates alike. Uncertainty and hesitation were not among her attributes. "Come on. We'll talk in my office."

Once the door was closed, Frakes pointed to a chair and Norton sat. Frakes remained standing as she delivered the news. "The President is dead. He came down to his office early this morning, just as he always does, and apparently died almost immediately after arriving. One of his bodyguards found him a short time later, slumped over his desk, but it was too late for medical treatment, and the guard wisely called me instead of raising an alarm."

It took a few seconds for the meaning of the words to penetrate. Norton had never considered Torgeson a friend, but the man had been instrumental in his own spectacular rise from the parishes of New Orleans to head the State Department.

"I'm terribly sorry to hear that." The words came out automatically, but Norton realized they were sincere as well. Vice President Curtis was a frenetic, shallow man who had bluffed his way through several crises by disguising utter panic as ceaseless energy, and the prospect of him sitting in the Oval Office, even for the few months that remained before the election, was not pleasant.

"Does the Vice President know?"

"No, and he's not going to."

Norton blinked. "I . . . uh . . . I don't understand."

Frakes leaned back, arms crossed, and stared directly into Norton's eyes. "Do you really think Samuel Curtis is capable of leading this country?"

"Well, no, as a matter of fact." His first inclination had been to dissemble, but perhaps because the shock of the revelation was beginning to sink in, he felt unable to remain evasive. "I think he'd be an utter disaster even in the best of times. With the budgetary crisis and the taxpayers' revolt and the Republicrats gaining steadily in the polls, I think it would be a national as well as a party disaster."

"Exactly. Curtis was only put on the ticket to keep the western states from bolting the Unionist Party. As Vice President, he's not in a position to do any real harm. We expected him to remain there through this year and Torgeson's second term."

"Which is now impossible." Norton's head was whirling. Who would the Unionist Party turn to now? The New Hampshire primary was only a few weeks away.

Frakes picked up a thick file from her desk, opened it as though to check something, then snapped it closed. "We did an extensive background check before Torgeson nominated you to be Secretary of State, you know."

"Of course."

"I understand that for several years, you served as a houngan in Lepatria Parish."

Norton felt as though the temperature in the room had just plummeted thirty degrees. "That was a baseless charge raised by my opponent when I was running for the state legislature."

Frakes made an impatient gesture. "Drop it, Norton. This is the big time here. We knew all about it before we approached you to join the cabinet. You covered your tracks extremely well, almost enough to throw us off. But the White House has people who specialize in finding the invisible. As a matter of fact, the efficiency with which you concealed your involvement in voodoo was one of the reasons we decided to put you in State. Deviousness is a prerequisite for that job, as I'm sure you've come to realize."

Although he thought about bluffing, Norton recognized a lost cause when he saw one. "All right, yes, I was involved in a very minimal way during my twenties. But I dropped it all ten years before I first ran for office."

"But you *were* a houngan."

"A very inept one." He laughed briefly, without humor. "That's one of the reasons I gave it up, to be honest. I seemed to have the talent, but not the control. Some of my magic . . . misfired."

"Have you ever raised a zombie?"

Norton started to shake his head, then realized the implications of the question. "You're not suggesting . . . ?" Frakes's steady gaze never wavered. "You're serious, aren't you?"

"Absolutely. President Torgeson must serve out his term; no other solution is acceptable. If Curtis succeeds to the presidency, he'll ruin the party—if not the country—and it would be difficult to deny him the nomination to run for a term of his own."

"Even if Torgeson . . . serves out his term, there's no one of comparable stature for the campaign. The problem is delayed but not solved."

"True. But at least we buy some time."

"We could never bring it off. I mean, zombies aren't quite as graceless as they appear in the movies, but they lack any real spirit, their body temperature drops off, and they begin to smell after a while. Even their voices lack inflection." Not that Torgeson had ever been a particularly vibrant speaker, he thought silently.

Frakes made a dismissive gesture. "Mechanical details. We can work around them. After the last two assassination attempts, it won't surprise anyone if Torgeson cuts back on public appearances. We can use one of his doubles for the rare occasion when it's necessary, and televised speeches can be synthesized by computers accurately enough to escape detection."

It was hard for Norton to accept that Frakes was serious, but she was not known for her sense of humor. He began to wonder if this was some bizarre loyalty test she and Torgeson had dreamed up between them, to find out how he would react under stress.

As if she were reading his mind, Frakes stepped forward. "Come on."

"Where are we going?"

"I want you to take a look at the President. We have him laid out on the couch in his office. We need to know if there's anything we need to do right away, anoint him with olive oil or put garlic in his mouth or chant some prayer over his body."

"No, nothing like that. But he'll need to keep to a strict salt-free diet." It was a miserable attempt to break the tension, but he was speaking more to himself than to the Chief of Staff, and he followed meekly as she led the way.

There was no question that President Torgeson was dead. His body was already cool to the touch, and the presence of death was so palpable that it stirred Norton's long-dormant houngan abilities. Two bodyguards stood near the door, trying to look professional but only succeeding in appearing uncomfortable.

"Who else knows?"

Frakes glanced at the guards. "Besides the four of us, only Adamson at the CIA. I'll have to speak to the party leadership, of course. Thank God Torgeson is . . . *was* a bachelor."

"How about his personal physician?"

"Christian Scientist, remember? No doctor."

"Oh, right." Norton scratched his chin.

"So what do you need for the ceremony? Herbs? Magical artifacts? Drugs?"

Norton sighed. "Look, I think this whole thing is crazy under any circumstances, but even if I thought we might be able to pull it off, you've got the wrong man for the job. I've never raised a zombie; my talents aren't really strong enough for that kind of magic."

For just a second, it looked as though Frakes had let her shoulders slump. "You were the best chance we had."

"Maybe not. Look, I know a man who might be able to help. But you're not going to like this."

"There's nothing about this situation that I like, Norton, but I'm grasping at straws here."

"Nelson Djibwa."

That stopped her, at least for a few seconds. Nelson Djibwa was a thorn in the side of the Unionist Party. He'd run for office several times under their banner, twice winning a seat in the Louisiana legislature, twice defeated for a second term, primarily because the party refused to acknowledge him as a legitimate candidate.

"There must be someone else."

Norton nodded. "There probably is, but we have to move quickly here and he's the only one I know with the skills we need."

Frakes shook her head. "Then there's no choice but to make Torgeson's death public. God knows, I shudder to think what Curtis will do to this country, but having the President under the control of a man like Djibwa is too terrifying even to consider."

Norton shook his head. "You don't understand. I'm not suggesting that we have Djibwa raise the President. I'll perform the ceremony with his assistance. That way the zombie . . . I mean the President . . . will be bound to me personally. But we can draw on Djibwa's expertise." He paused to let that sink in. "You do realize that once raised, the President will be completely subservient to *my* will, don't you?"

"Yes, I assumed that. Don't worry, Norton. We've checked you out thoroughly. I think you can be trusted to act responsibly, and I'll be the first to blow the whistle if my judgment proves faulty."

Norton experienced a brief glimpse of his future. "This is going to be a logistic nightmare. I'm scheduled to visit Europe next week, you realize."

"I've considered that. My staff is preparing press releases announcing a few changes in the administration."

"Changes?"

"Yes. Effective tomorrow morning, I am resigning my position as Chief of Staff in order to head President Torgeson's re-election campaign. A useless but necessary fiction, I'm afraid, but it will keep the public's attention centered until we come up with a new candidate. You'll have to resign as Secretary of State to take my old job. I know it's going to look like a step backward for you careerwise, but once I've had a chance to speak to a few members of the party leadership and explain the situation, I think you'll find you've accumulated a few favors."

Although Norton had mixed feelings, he realized the sense of what she was saying. And the possibility of being the Vice Presidential candidate in 2012 or 2016 was the unspoken undertext of her words. Who knew what might lie beyond?

"Then you'll bring in Djibwa?"

"I suppose we have no real choice. I just wonder what he'll want in return."

▼▼▼

As it turned out, Djibwa wanted to be governor of Louisiana.

"Out of the question!" Frakes spoke angrily, while Norton, CIA director Adamson, and Unionist Party Chairman Estelle Novarro all regarded their slender, ebony-skinned visitor with thinly disguised hostility. "The governorship is a public trust, not a commodity to be bartered."

Djibwa's face remained expressionless as he sat back in his chair, letting his eyes roam around the walls of the White House conference room. "We are all sophisticated people here." His voice was deep and rich. "Is there time for us to indulge in the pretense of negotiation when we all know the truths of power?"

They all recognized that the Unionist Party enjoyed great popularity in Louisiana, had held the governor's mansion for three consecutive terms, and Governor Lavalier had already announced he would not seek a fourth term. An official endorsement would do more than legitimize Djibwa's candidacy; it would almost assure him election.

"You're asking a great price for your services," Novarro commented dryly.

"You're asking for a very great service."

In the end, they had no choice.

▼▼▼

The ceremony itself didn't take long. Djibwa was ushered past security into the basement crisis room where the President's body currently lay in a cryogenic unit. Norton joined him there, and the two men unpacked the ceremonial robes and artifacts of their craft while the President thawed under the watchful eyes of a CIA technician. Frakes had originally announced her intention to observe the process, but at the last minute demonstrated an uncharacteristic queasiness and excused herself.

"You're certain we can do this?" Norton was experiencing the old uncertainty, the lack of confidence that had marred his earlier attempts to master voodoo.

Djibwa's face and voice were neutral, but his eyes betrayed his contempt. "Your participation is not necessary, and your doubts may interfere with my concentration."

At that moment, Norton desperately wanted to find some way to escape the situation, but there was no choice. Unless he was present and actively involved, Torgeson's reanimated body would be bound to Djibwa, an outcome they could not accept.

"My soul is at ease," he answered ritually, "and my will a tool for the shaping."

Djibwa continued to regard him doubtfully, but finally nodded and crossed to the body. "I believe we can start the ceremony now."

Two hours later, President Torgeson opened his eyes and rose obediently to his feet.

▼▼▼

It took a full week before Norton began to believe they could get away with it. The President's hands had been covered with synthetic skin gloves. Torgeson's grip was a little weak, but the President had never been one to press the flesh very much, and they figured it would pass. Fortunately, his craggy face had never been particularly expressive, so its present calm stolidity was actually a plus.

A synthesized television press conference went well. In fact, Torgeson's approval rating rose a full point the following day.

"We eliminated that damned hesitancy of his when he spoke," explained Frakes. "It was a subconscious signal of weakness and insincerity. How are you handling Curtis?"

"Just as we discussed. He's always been kept pretty isolated by Torgeson. Curtis understood why he was on the ticket and there was no love lost between the two men."

As Chief of Staff, Norton's constant proximity to the President had been legitimized; since both men were unmarried, it was not considered particularly newsworthy when he moved into the guest wing of the White House on a more or less permanent basis. It was impractical to remain near at hand all the time, naturally, and the small group of people who knew the truth was slowly expanded until Torgeson was effectively insulated from discovery.

▼▼▼

Norton saw the first reports of a double mutilation killing on the television in the rear of his limo the following morning.

"Two unidentified men were discovered literally torn apart in a room on the fourteenth floor of the Sheridan Hotel," announced the newscaster. Norton, who'd been listening with only a fraction of his concentration, turned the volume up, remembering that Frakes had arranged for Djibwa to stay at that hotel under an assumed name.

"Although neither man has been identified, the authorities are looking for Donald Cipher . . ." the screen faded and was replaced with a fair likeness of Nelson Djibwa, ". . . in connection with the incident. Although there has been no official confirmation, it is believed that Cipher was the guest registered in the room where the killings took place." When the story changed to a progress report on the Quebec Peace Talks, Norton turned the volume back down.

Frakes was sitting in his new office, her old one, when he arrived. Her face was deeply drawn and lacked its usually aggressiveness.

"What's going on?"

"We've lost Djibwa."

Norton frowned, then experienced an epiphany. "My God, you tried to have Djibwa sanctioned! I heard it on the radio on my way here."

"That's right. The casualties are two specialists I borrowed from Adamson. They were supposed to be quite expert at their jobs."

He suppressed a nervous laugh. "You might have mentioned this to me in advance. I could have told you it wouldn't work, and by trying and failing, you've made us a very powerful enemy."

She shrugged. "Did you really expect me to let him become governor of Louisiana?"

Norton dropped onto the small couch and ran his fingers through his hair. "I suppose not, but I don't think you realize how powerful

Djibwa is. He's not one of your everyday voodoo priests, you realize. If there is any single human being alive capable of carrying the mantle of Baron Samedi, it's Djibwa."

If Frakes was concerned, she concealed it well. "We underestimated him. It won't happen again."

"What are you planning to do?"

"Wait, at least for the moment. He'll surface somewhere. I have no doubt he realizes who was behind the attack. Most likely he'll show up with some media people, try to convince them that we've turned the President into a zombie." She laughed grimly. "No one will believe him, of course, and once we know where he is, we'll pick him up and slap him into the nearest sanitarium."

Norton shook his head. "That's not his style. It lacks . . . art. Voodoo is dependent upon rhythm, balance, integration of the soul into the flow of the universe. A direct confrontation would be inelegant."

Frakes made an inarticulate, impatient sound. "We'll integrate his soul into the universe, all right, and free him of all his worldly cares."

▼▼▼

Several weeks later, there had still been no sign of Nelson Djibwa, and Frakes responded angrily whenever his name was raised.

"He'll want revenge, you realize," Norton told her on more than one occasion. "Not so much because of the attempt on his life, which he probably expected from the outset. But we reneged on our word, and that makes it imperative that he restore the equilibrium."

"Restore it? What can he do? There's no way he could reverse the spell on Torgeson, is there?"

Norton sighed, searching vainly for the right words. "It's not a spell, and no, he doesn't have any direct way to reverse the reanimation. That wouldn't be artful anyway. But he won't fold his tent and go home. Voodoo is a religion; he cannot refrain from acting without committing a dreadful sin."

At the same time, the elaborate pretense that Torgeson was still alive had settled down into a smooth routine. It was so smooth, in fact, that Norton felt occasional twinges of regret that it had become so easy to effectively scam the public.

Some public appearances could be handled by his doubles, who were accustomed to filling in for Torgeson when the President was committed to brief, boring ceremonies, convocations, and the like. None of them had been made privy to the truth. Norton had a staff member leak rumors to the media about a Quebec-based assassination plot to explain the President's sharp curtailment of most public appearances, and there had actually been a few editorials praising Torgeson for exposing himself at all.

Frakes ran the chimerical re-election campaign with her usual skill, and in fact Torgeson's approval rating had climbed steadily back to 54 percent, still low for an incumbent seeking a second term but considerably better than the 42 percent he had been polling at the time of his death. Part of this was because none of the Republicrats had yet emerged from the pack as a potential contender, but some of the improvement was surprising.

"Politics is a peculiar science," Frakes told Norton one evening. "I'm beginning to wonder if a dead candidate might be more viable than a live one."

"What do you mean?"

"Well, since Torgeson obviously doesn't give live speeches anymore, we've been able to customize them for maximum impact. There are certain phrases, tones of voice, inflections, and patterns of sound and speech that are more reassuring than others. Torgeson was never particularly animated or articulate, but even though he moves slower than ever now, our enhancements have managed a net gain in his personal appeal. Our latest polls show that people describe him as calm, controlled, fatherly, and strong willed." She shook her head. "Controlled he is, but strong willed?" Her voice cracked a little.

"How's Bergeron coming along?" Stan Bergeron had been chosen secretly by the Unionist Party leadership to be the real candidate in the next election. The strategy was for him to provide a credible but unthreatening challenge in the primaries, thereby keeping Curtis in line, later to be nominated at the convention after Torgeson withdrew "for reasons of health."

"He's doing all the right things, but he's still slipping in the polls. You saw how he did in New Hampshire."

"Eight percent."

"Right. But that's because everyone assumes Torgeson will be the nominee."

▼▼▼

The primaries rolled past, each awarding Torgeson an overwhelming percentage of the delegates. His approval rating nationwide rose to 61 percent by the end of April, 66 percent by the end of May. Dorothy Baldwin now seemed certain to secure the Republicrat nomination, but she was trailing Torgeson in the polls by over thirty points.

Then, three days prior to the California primary, Stan Bergeron was killed in a plane crash while flying to a rally in Oakland. Torgeson had long since sewn up the unofficial nomination, of course, but now there was no viable candidate waiting to step into his shoes . . . except for the Vice President, Samuel Curtis.

"What are we going to do?" Norton had called Frakes at home, on their secure line.

"It looks like we'll have to run Torgeson for re-election."

"Run Torgeson! Are you out of your mind?" But he didn't argue for long. It had all begun to make some kind of bizarre sense. Or perhaps he'd been living in the political world so long that nothing surprised him anymore.

▼▼▼

Norton was eating by himself in a small dining room in the White House when one of his aides rushed in and turned on the television.

"Dorothy Baldwin has been assassinated!" She was nearly breathless with excitement. And they both watched several replays of the taped assault—Baldwin just finishing her remarks about the state of the economy, raising her arms high above her head, then the series of sharp reports, a popping noise that didn't sound at all dangerous. Baldwin's head snapped back as the first round struck high on her forehead, then dropped out of sight as those surrounding her exploded into kaleidoscopic panic.

But Dorothy Baldwin was not dead, they discovered a few hours later. She had received only a single, glancing wound along the side of her head, and would be recovered enough to resume her campaign within a few days.

When she made her first televised appearance five days later, one side of her face swathed in bandages, it was Norton who called Frakes to an emergency meeting at the White House.

"What's the problem?" The strain of recent events was clearly taking its toll. Her face was drawn, hair in disarray, and there were tension cracks in her voice.

"Just watch this." He replayed Baldwin's press conference on the overhead monitor, first at normal speed, then again in slow motion. "Notice anything?"

"She looks a little pale, but considering how close she came to being killed, I suppose that's understandable."

"Now watch this." On a second monitor, he played back the assassination tape, then hit pause at the point where Baldwin's head snapped back. "If you'll look closely, you can just see where the round struck her forehead."

"It looks pretty bad from that angle, but the bullet was deflected by her skull. A very lucky woman; she'll be a formidable opponent in the fall."

Norton shook his head. "Not lucky at all. The first shot went directly *into* the skull."

Frakes frowned. "Impossible. If it was that serious, they'd never have been able to get her back on her feet so quickly, if she survived at all."

"Torgeson is back on his feet, and *he's dead*."

Frakes shifted uncomfortably. "I don't understand what you're trying to say."

Norton rewound the tape of the press conferences and started it again. "Watch the crowd this time, particularly the members of

Baldwin's personal staff." He waited for a frame he'd examined closely for almost an hour, then froze the picture. "Two rows back and slightly to the left."

A few seconds later, Frakes drew her breath in sharply. "Djibwa!"

"Right."

"Do you suppose he told Baldwin what we've done, and that she believed him?"

"No, I don't think that at all. In fact, I think Djibwa engineered the successful assassination of the Republicrat nominee for President."

"Engineered? You mean, he had Baldwin killed? But why?" But even as she spoke, her eyes widened.

"I told you he'd find a way to strike back artistically. Baldwin has already announced that she'll be reducing her schedule of appearances. No one will fault her for it under the circumstances. My guess is that we'll find out Baldwin is in the midst of a major reorganization of her staff, and the only ones who will survive are those Djibwa can bend to his will, or who aren't in a position to spot what's really going on."

"Oh my God." Frakes seemed sincerely shaken. "And we have no choice now but to run Torgeson against her. Whatever happens, no matter which candidate wins, we're facing another four years with a zombie as President. This is a complete disaster."

"Maybe."

Frakes turned to face him, her composure cracking for the first time since Norton had known her. "What do you mean?"

"Frankly, Jennifer, I doubt most people will even notice a difference."

▼▼▼

As it turned out, Norton was right.

THE TODDLER PIT

▼▼▼

A.R. MORLAN

"Children have to go through a period of going crazy. I mean, of course, you don't want it to end in death. That's kind of the limit, death. You don't want it to go that far."

Mick Jagger

THE Toddler Pit's been gone from the Fine Arts Center of my alma mater for many years now; the last time I returned to the college, that particular wing of the campus had been invaded by the art department. The cloying odor of near-stale peanut butter and damp bib overalls had been replaced with the reek of slow-drying oils and whatever mysterious chemicals the photography majors use to develop their latest roll of snapshots in the darkroom. And the occasional crayoned scrawl on the painted cement block walls had been refined, enlarged, to life-size black silhouettes of artists—O'Keeffe, Renoir, DaVinci—each adorned with a flesh-tone life mask painted across their flat black heads.

Whoever created the mural was talented, more so than the usual art majors I'd known during my years at this college. The row of flesh-faced flat black bodies are uncannily lifelike, yet abstract, at once. A little like those foot-high dolls based on whatever television show is currently occupying the minds—and draining the allowances—of the preteen set; a realistic, almost death-mask perfect face, surmounting a completely inhuman, impossibly proportioned doll body.

Or the type of scrawled drawing a small child will produce, once he or she gets the essentials of human anatomy fixed in his or her still-growing mind; a huge head, dotted Mr. Potato-Head style with mismatched eyes, nose and mouth (ears optional), then a ruler-straight body bisected with arms that form perfect right angles to the torso, perched on inverted "V" legs. The body is easily dismissed, but sometimes, the face can be telling . . . no, not just the smile, or lack of it, or even the way the child usually matches the eye color correctly to his or her own.

It's never so much as what you can *see* in a child's first attempt at self-portraiture, it's more like what the child is trying to *say* through the actual effort. . . .

When I worked in the toddler pit, during those seemed-like-they'd-never-end six weeks required by my Introduction to Education class, I saw a lot of drawings, and built a lot of bristle-block towers, and helped a lot of little kids who were barely old enough to perch themselves on the toilet bowl unaided get their elastic-waist pants pulled back up *all* the way before letting them venture out into the hallway beyond the women's room, where we customarily herded the toddlers before and after naptime. I wasn't even an Early Childhood Education major, or into Elementary Ed—but the number of student-teacher slots at the town junior high school were limited, so I wound up doing my Intro to Ed hands-on practice teaching stint in the little day care housed in two large adjoining rooms (and one small one, where they kept cribs for the sniffly or slightly retarded kids) in the Fine Arts Center, a.k.a. the Toddler Pit, close cousin to Olivia De Havilland's 1948 cinematic home away from home, *The Snake Pit*.

It wasn't hard to sense the connection; when you're only five feet four, yet *loom* over dozens of arm-flapping, block-throwing, runny-nosed, vaguely ammonia-smelling, shrieking children all under the age of five, the instinct to curl up in a protective ball and just wait it out until all those Mommies and Daddies show up to claim their baby demons is almost too strong to resist.

And what the kids thought of *me*, and the other women (some paid, some draftees from Intro to Ed, like me), was difficult to tell; some would wake up from their naps crying, while others would hug and slobbily kiss any adult human in sight. (I actually worried more about the latter; these were the days of the endless McMartin Preschool case, after all.) And then . . . there were the unreachable ones. Nearly blind Jennifer, whose mother had lived on chocolates and ulcer medicine while carrying her, or her seemingly normal sister Darcy, whose back was dotted with keloid scars in a lineless connect-the-dots pattern. Sarah, who cried silently after naptime, while I coaxed on her socks and shoes. And happy, mindless, cooing Stephen, and his sister, Nancy, she of the strange, strange crayoned pictures drawn for an audience of no one. . . .

Pictures I eventually plucked from the Toddler Pit garbage pails, prior to the college janitor hauling the pails out to the big chained dumpster located alongside the FAC parking lot.

All these years later, I still have the pictures . . . and in many ways, they are no less lifelike/surreal than the flat black shadows masquerading as long-dead artists which now grace the halls of the former Toddler Pit—even if they portray things none of those esteemed artists would dared have painted; things more suited to Goya or Bosch, perhaps, if those men had been literally immersed in their art. . . .

Yet, I have to remind myself that they were the efforts of a child, only a mere child.

That . . . *that* is the important thing to remember. Nancy *was* a child. . . .

"Stephen . . . shut *up*," the little girl mumbled as I rubbed her back during naptime, while her brother—dark blonde-brown hair neatly combed, plump face almost split in two with an infectious, brainless smile, fat clean hands and feet waving spasmodically while the rocker-seated teacher's aide tried to calm him down with a nearly hissed lullaby—happily resisted all efforts to calm him down enough to make him sleep. Stephen's sister was stretched out stiffly on one of the low webbing-slung cots scattered in the darkened half of the toddler pit, in a random configuration akin to the arrangement of buried bodies under John Wayne Gacy's crawlspace down in Chicago.

All around us, the rest of the day-care kids were either asleep or successfully faking it; they were attended by my fellow teacher's aides, each rubbing the tiny back of a prone, shoes-and-socks-off toddler until the child became drowsy enough to sink into sleep—and give the old woman who ran the day care a few precious minutes of undeserved peace.

I loathed this part of the day; I didn't think it was right to touch the children that much, my back felt like someone was tattooing it with a darning needle after I'd bent over a couple of kids, and the gentle *blapping* sound most of the kids made when they snored lightly was maddening. From her expression and demeanor—as much of a constant with her as the always-perfect matched clothing she and her brother wore—I sensed that Nancy wasn't actually into naptimes either. Perhaps that was why I tried to make sure I rubbed her back come the afternoon break time; she knew and I knew that her brother *was* a massive pain, even though the day care manager and the other women professed to "just adore" Stephen. Not that I held his retardation against him; don't get me wrong on that account. It wasn't his fault, any more than it was his mother's fault, or his father's, or *anyone*'s fault—least of all Nancy's.

And true, at the time Stephen was adorable-*looking*; that nicely cut and styled soft hair, those huge blueberries-in-cream eyes set in that soft-skinned pale face, the pursed doll-pink mouth, the chubby fingers and toes. Just like a boy-doll from Sears . . . and that was the problem, the *just* part.

Aside from some gurgling coos and sharp, happy-seeming shouts, Stephen couldn't talk. Couldn't think much, either; he seldom played meaningfully with even the most basic of toys, nor could he follow any sort of verbal or visual directions. Not potty-trained, either. But his clothes were exquisite, not unlike the doll fashions shown in the *Wish Book* come Christmas. Little sailor suits, tiny rugby tops, jackets with buttons along the minuscule arms. Always clean, never stained, worn, or frayed, like the togs worn by many of the other inmates of the Pit. And his sister's clothes were just as perfect, just as unreal.

("Their mother cares so *much* about them," Mrs. Day Care would gush. "She keeps them *so* clean—" even as Nancy would be sitting off near the corner of the noisy, peanut-butter scented kitchen/play area, glowering at her oblivious brother.)

I bent down and whispered to Nancy, "It's okay, hon, he doesn't know . . . he'll settle down soon," all the while wondering how the poor kid could stand living with Stephen once she got home.

Just turning her head toward me, letting the rest of her body remain in place, the dark-haired little girl said so softly I almost couldn't hear her, "Stephen never stops . . . he never sleeps."

Rubbing her back harder (I could make out the chicken-bone tracery of scapula and spinal column under her jersey rugby shirt), I leaned over as far as my aching back would allow and assured her, "Oh, it just *seems* that way . . . Stephen probably just falls asleep after you do at night," all the while wishing that I could scoop the little girl up and carry her off somewhere far, far from her doomed-to-be-an-infant brother. *Anywhere* away from him, cute and cuddly and almost-comical as Stephen was.

How cute is he going to look in five years? Or ten? Will a cooing teenager in diapers be so "clean" and adorable? I asked myself—but my mind wasn't actually looking for any answers.

"Never," she firmly reiterated, then, moving her right arm up to the level of her face, she slowly crooked one tiny-nailed finger. Getting off the child-size chair I'd been sitting on, I hunkered down next to Nancy's cot. Once my face was sufficiently close to hers, the small girl with the ruler-straight Buster Brown bangs and perfectly combed page-boy haircut whispered, "Stephen's dead in his head."

"No, Nancy," I said a little more firmly, but just as softly. "That can't be. If he *were*, he wouldn't be able to see, or make sounds, or wave his arms. He's just . . . not like you and me, okay? But he's okay for *himself,*" I lied brightly, hoping Mrs. Day Care wouldn't notice me talking to Nancy, and bitch about it to my Intro to Ed professor.

On the low cot, Nancy resolutely shook her head, barely making a ripple in her dark, fine hair. "Dead in the head," she said with that heartbreaking finality that told me not to try to convince her otherwise. As I got back on the little blond wood and enameled metal school chair, I delicately kept rubbing my hand along her knobby spine, telling myself, *Don't push the kid so hard. C'mon, what is she, three or four at the most? What the hell does* she *know about retardation or arrested development? Probably heard one of her folks say it—or some friend of theirs.*

The truth was, I hadn't even seen Nancy and Stephen's parents yet, so I had no idea what sort of people they were. Profoundly disappointed, perhaps. Embarrassed? I doubted it; the children were both too well-turned-out to be the products of a family who didn't want to show them off in at least the most basic way. Overcompensating? That sounded more like it; I could imagine a fussy, PTA-aholic Jaycette type of mother ironing their tiny underwear and probing their every orifice with a Q-Tip, just to make sure that no one would accuse her of not being an on-top-of-things parent. Clean kids, good home. And ever mind that Stephen would never so much as say his own name, let alone do his duty on his own.

Once naptime was over that afternoon (true to Nancy's word, her brother never did drift off to sleep, but only turned the volume and the jerking down a couple of notches—but then again, Nancy's dark eyes never closed for very long either), and Mrs. Day Care Incarnate bustled her polyester-painted bottom out of the building, two lines of hands-locked kiddies in tow behind her, one of the other inmates and I were supposed to clean up the nap area. Our job was to put away the now-folded cots and straighten up the litter of kiddie books and battered nap animals while the toddlers played for half an hour in the bright early-spring sunshine.

I'd never been all that close to Ruth, one of my fellow Intro to Ed classmates—she was an Early Childhood major, I was into Secondary Ed—but she *was* about ten years older than me, and her husband was a professor at the college, so, still vaguely disturbed by Nancy's naptime statements, I decided to force myself to become just a little friendlier with the woman. After all, there was a good possibility that she might know something about Stephen and Nancy's situation, or maybe even their parents.

"Oh *Stevie*—you mean our little angel? It's sad, really," Ruth said in that chicken-laying-an-extra-large-egg crackle-cackle voice of hers as she quickly folded a metal-frame-and-webbing cot into a neat square bundle. "His parents are the DeGrootens, you know, *Dr.* DeGrooten, in the ethics department—"

"Oh, yeah, I had him last semester . . . gave me an A even though I never said more than five words at a time in class. Said I *understood* what he was talking about during his lectures," I found myself babbling, now suddenly anxious to leave the subject of Stephen—and Nancy—far behind us. But I was a little too late; Ruth's tongue was now firmly locked in the On position:

"Terrible thing, what happened with Stephen. He would've been *fine*, if only Marta's doctors had *listened* to her and taken him that same week he was due to be born. What are you, a sophomore? Oh, a freshman. I was going to say, if you'd have been around here four years back, you would've remembered—it was all *over* the school. Well, *any*how"—Ruth deftly manipulated another cot into a tight tubular bundle —"Marta was a couple of weeks past her due date, and she wanted the baby *out*, but her doctors said, 'Wait, there's no rush, you could've miscounted.' But *she* was already thirty-five or *six* by then, so I don't know *what* the doctors were waiting for, Hitler to rise from the dead or *some*thing, so anyhow, they didn't induce labor, even though Marta kept insisting that she wasn't feeling well, that the baby wasn't moving as much. But you know how doctors are, they just slap that stethoscope on your belly and if they hear a heartbeat, it's alive and they don't give it a second thought. This was around Christmas. I remember how *huge* she was in that woolen cape of hers when I met her in the Penney's store. The baby was already three weeks overdue, and I don't know if her doctors had her chart mixed up with some elephant or *what*, but they wouldn't take it. Marta told me she was worried *sick* about the baby, and her color was just *off*, almost the same shade as her cape, and *that* was sort of a Prussian *blue*—"

Figuring that Ruth wasn't about to get to any really important details for a few minutes (after all, she *was* going on about what the unfortunate Mrs. DeGrooten was wearing in the J.C. *Penney's* store), I found myself muttering "Uh-*huh*" after every overemphasized word while I looked through the blinds-bisected windows, which faced the tiny playground now swarming with shrieking toddlers. Only, since the windows were airtight, I couldn't *hear* any of them, just see their mouths snap open and shut quickly, like hungry baby birds who'd tumbled en masse out of the nest. Mrs. Day Care was off to one side of the play area—a four-foot-high geodesic-style jungle gym, three bucket-seats-with-legholes-type swings, a short sloping slide, and a sandbox—animated wrinkled face bright, pink-nailed hands gaily clapping in time to some rhythm none of the toddlers were following. It was tragic, how that woman had missed her true vocation—trained seal at the water park.

Stephen had been dumped into one of those bucket-seated swings, his wiggling plump legs thrusting through the leg openings, his hands up and vaguely wiggling. As usual, his mouth was wide open, pale tongue lolling almost sweetly to one side, his huge eyes vacant and glistening. While Ruth was yammering "—and so I told her, 'Just go find *another* doctor, then.' I mean, honestly, it wasn't like—" I searched the play area for Nancy. I finally saw her squatting down close to the curved retaining wall built around the swing-set, pawing intently at the asphalt and dirt ground, as if slowly grubbing for bugs. Her pinched face, ever-framed by that new-doll immaculate soft brown hair, was distant, yet oddly intent.

Behind me, Ruth's rambling story suddenly took on a more definite—and chilling—direction:

"—days before Christmas, *Dr.* DeGrooten demanded that the doctors do *something*, so they did an emergency caesarian after breaking her water didn't work . . . and it was *awful*. One of my friends, she's an obstetrics nurse, and she was there that afternoon, so she saw *everything*. You see, when they broke Marta's water, it came out all . . . *foul,* not clear or just bloody even, but with all this greenish-black . . . *yuck* in it. And the *smell* . . . well, the doctors suddenly knew *then* that something *was* wrong after all—" Under her head of permanented curls, Ruth's freckled face grew queasy—pale, like curdled cottage cheese. "And when they opened her up—well, my friend said it was lucky *Marta* didn't develop a septic infection from what was *inside* her coming in contact with the incision. The baby, he'd been much too long in the womb, he *should've* been taken at least two or three weeks sooner, because—" here Ruth's crackly voice lowered to a rusty rumble. "—the baby . . . *went* all over himself in there. Did a number two. Only with unborn babies, there's a name for it—my friend told me, but you know how it is with those *medical* terms. Anyhow, it was all green-black and sticky, and it had gotten into the baby's brain via his *ears* and *eyes,* and it infected his mucuous membranes and even his brain. *That's* why the baby was retarded—and almost blind and deaf, too, even though he makes all that noise. Just horrible. When they pulled him out of Marta, she saw a little bit of him, even though she was pretty much sedated. He was all ooze-covered and black . . . 'like he was *rotted,*' she told me.

"*Any*how," she went on, brightening as if she'd put the worst of her story behind her, "his parents are in the process of suing the *hospital, all* the doctors involved, and even the *parent* clinic *this* hospital in town belongs to. Considering that Stephen *could*'ve—*should*'ve—been normal, I don't blame them, even if them winning *will* jerk up the cost of care out at the hospital."

Out in the play area, Mrs. Day Care Goddess was clapping her hands furiously, and mouthing something. I barely made out the silent "come in!" before Ruth added, "Of course, Marta and Etan won't even *talk* about the whole incident anymore, just dress Stephen and his sister up like nothing's wrong—"

As the children slowly massed into entering-the-building formation, I turned around, a stuffed elephant still in one white-knuckled hand, and asked quickly, "How old *is* Nancy?" The little brown-banged girl didn't seem to be much older than Stephen, nor was she obviously younger. But even though I'd only been half-listening at times to Ruth's story, I knew that she'd only mentioned Stephen's sister that *one* time—

"Nancy? Y'know . . . I'm really not sure. After what . . . *happened* to Stephen *happened*, they took off a year or so, went to stay with his folks . . . or was it hers?" Ruth paused to scratch one of her eyes under her glasses, making the rose-brown plastic frames do a jig on her plain face. "Well, what*ever*, once they came back, they were toting around both kids, and they were at an age where it's hard to tell, really. Stephen always *was* a big baby, I mean literally *big*, and Nancy was already toddling even *then*—I just didn't know them all that well to be able to really say *how* old Nancy is. Come to think of it, though . . . I don't remember them ever talking about Nancy, but I didn't know them all *that* well, just faculty mixers, occasional dinners at the Dean's house. They could've had her at home with a sitter, for all *I* know. My husband, he wasn't—isn't—that close to Etan either. He and Marta had only come to the college a year before Stephen was born."

I could hear the toddlers running down the hallway outside, and took that as my cue to hurry back into the kitchen/play area, to greet the first of the arriving children. Faintly, I could hear Mrs. Day Care scolding one of the children, "—and we *don't* put things like that in our *mouths*, do you *hear* me?" while Stephen cooed and hooted merrily. Apparently the day-care head was holding onto the boy, as she usually did, but when she finally walked into the room, I saw that she had Stephen's sister held firmly by one dirt-grimed hand. The girl was trying not to cry.

Ruth hurried over to take Stephen, and lead him off to a quiet corner where he could play with his plastic bristle blocks, while Mrs. Day Care Witch continued to reprimand Nancy. "*Shame* on you! Your mommy will be so *angry* at you! Now you go let Anya wash off those dirty hands—" Motioning to me with her free hand, Mrs. Day Care sputtered, "Anya, this *bad* little girl was doing things she *shouldn't* have been doing—and she wouldn't even go *potty* before play time. Take her down to the washroom and make sure she goes *and* washes up before she comes back!" The air in front of me reeked from the odor of the woman's dentures; she'd been spitting her words out so forcefully. Without waiting for my response, she bustled off, fat bottom wiggling under her slacks, in the direction of the sink.

As I placed both my hands on Nancy's shoulders and gently began to guide her out of the room, I heard the plosive *splat* of the water faucet turned on full force behind me. Glancing back at Mrs. Day Care, I saw her frantically scrubbing her hands, while Ruth and the children watched her in numb amazement.

Once we were out in the hallway, I bent over Nancy and whispered, "What happened, honey? Doesn't she want you playing in the dirt?" Some of the jocks on the college track team were ambling around in the FAC—the gym was located there—and Nancy ducked her head shyly when she saw them coming. The guys mumbled a greeting to me, which I returned quickly, before herding the girl into the women's room located about ten feet from the gym doors.

Once I'd pushed open the pink-enameled door, Nancy walked away from me and let herself into one of the stalls. It took her a while to reach and secure the latch, but I didn't insist on going in the stall and helping her. One of the part-time day-care workers, a dour, bespeckled woman with hippie-long black hair and a downturned mouth, always made it a point to join at least one child a day in the stall, lingering in there for minutes on end. I never said anything about it to Mrs. Day Care (I *was* on both work study and an academic scholarship, and Mrs. D.C. could blow both of them with one negative report to my professor), but I still hated to think about what might be going on in those stalls. Instead, I hoisted myself onto one of the dingy sinks jutting from the wall and asked the girl casually, "Was the teacher mad at you for something you did . . . or was she just in a bad mood?"

Nancy said something unintelligible over the sound of something splashing in the water in the bowl. She was so tiny, I couldn't even see her feet, so I had to assume she was doing "number one," as the day-care women liked to euphemistically dub taking a piss.

"What, hon?"

Somewhat louder, Nancy said—presumably again—"I was digging for worms."

"Oh . . . okay," I said uneasily, wondering why a girl would be into something like that. I remembered my male first-grade classmates digging worms out of the sandbox and then eating them, just to scare the rest of us girls, but I mentally and physically shrugged it off, as I said, "Well, don't do it in front of the teacher, okay? It freaks her out. And then she yells, and that's not fun, is it?"

"—my friends," Nancy was saying, but she'd just flushed, so some of her words were swept away in the gurgle of water. I was about to ask her to come again when she unlatched the pale pink door and emerged from the stall, her pants and underpants pulled up in one huge, doughnutlike roll around her tiny waist. Nancy looked funny, but her face was still so serious. In the sputtering white-green fluorescent lights, she looked exceptionally pasty, as if formed from white Play-Doh. I simply bit my lips to suppress my smile and gingerly unrolled the tube of fabric from around her waist, making sure that I didn't let my fingers come in contact with her flesh. That *was* around the time of the McMartin case, after all. And with her folks being professors—even her mom occasionally taught summer courses in biology—I sure as shit didn't need them coming down on me for touching their little girl in the wrong place.

I *did* notice that the swirling waters behind her didn't *quite* whisk away the lingering odor. I don't know what it was about babies and little kids, but they sure do have a bad smell. I noticed it again when I lifted her up so that she'd be level with the sink; hanging onto her with one hand, I worked the soap dispenser for Nancy, letting a greenish-yellow stream of strong-smelling soap dribble onto her damp outspread hands. But when she caught sight of me in the above-the-sink mirror, she smiled shyly at me—the first time I'd seen her do so. Wondering, *Would Stephen have been like her?* I helped Nancy dry her hands—again, avoiding contact with her—and then led her back to the Toddler Pit, guiding her slightly by the rugby-shirted shoulders.

Even fifteen feet away from the door, she and I could both hear Stephen hooting and whooping—and under that immaculate, tiny shirt, I felt Nancy's shoulders stiffen, then droop in resignation. . . .

▼▼▼

During the walk home that afternoon, after my last class of the day, I found myself remembering my first class-session with Dr. DeGrooten, during my core-requirement ethics class.

Etan DeGrooten was a tall drink of water (as my folks used to call tall, thin people), with a mostly salt and cinnamon beard and not too much hair on top of his head. He jerked when he walked or gestured like one of those wooden puppets with the string dangling under them—jumping jacks, I believe they're called.

He sputtered when he spoke, stuttering and stalling and leaving great significant pauses between paragraphs. I can't remember if he even wore a wedding ring; I do recall he wore either a bolo set with some polished flat caramel-colored stone or a withered red-print bow tie for every class-session. And those awful tweedy no-color sports coats with the leather oblongs on the elbows. He seldom referred to our textbooks, but instead would go off on bizarre tangents—the most memorable one was in regard to a discussion of situational ethics:

"Talk about . . . about sit-sit-situational ethics. My mother, she was faced with the all-time . . . I was seven, and I'd just written 'I Love You Mommy' on the wall, in my own excrement, and . . . course, after she *saw* what I'd written, what I'd written it *in*, she didn't . . . I mean what does one *do* in such a sit-situation? Hug or hit? So . . . she gave me a whack on the bottom and then she hugged me."

At the time, *my* view of situational ethics was affected by the thought, *If you were old enough to write, you shouldn't have been writing with that*, and from that day on, I'd dismissed DeGrooten as a kook. A fifty-plus-year-old man with an infant's mentality. That he wound up giving me one of the few A's of the semester came as something of a surprise; I'd never spoken to him outside of class—or in class, either. Not that I saw much of him when not supposedly learning about ethics; only infrequently would I see him hurky-jerking down the winding hallways outside the classroom. And I'd never seen his wife; she was only a name—M. DeGrooten—beside a list of summer biology classes in the stapled, photocopied schedule that appeared prior to each summer session.

But now that I knew about Stephen, and his terrible, messy, *un*ethical birth, I almost understood the man's frantic desire to appear as loose and unconcerned as possible. He probably prayed that someday Stephen *would* be able to write *any*thing, even "Dad sucks the big one" on the wall with his own excrement. Yet, even as I neared my house, I kept wondering, *What did all of this do to* Nancy? *Wouldn't it be more fair to* her *to ship Stephen off to a children's home? Talk about* ethics . . . *what kind of situation is that for a child to endure? She can't even go to sleep without hearing him hoot his life away in the next bed* . . . *no* wonder *she calls his brain "dead"* . . . *as far as the whole family's concerned, it might as well be.*

"And the rest of him along with it," I couldn't help but say aloud, just to savor the wonderful—yet sad—rightness of the thought.

▼▼▼

Whatever Nancy had been doing with the worms that early afternoon recess period, Mrs. Day Care deemed it cause for the little girl to stay indoors while the other children played outside—Stephen included. My stomach did a flip-flop every time the old bat made a show of picking up the adorable, nearly uncomprehending boy and baby-talked, "Stevie's sure a *good* little boy, *isn't* him? What a perfect little *dumpling*," while Nancy just *took* it; no tears, no pouting, just that resigned, defeated manner. She didn't even bother whispering "Shut up, Stephen" during naptime anymore, which was perhaps the worst sign of all, as if she'd at long-last discovered that protests, wishes and prayers were ultimately useless. *I* was the one who was nearly in tears every day in the Toddler Pit; it's bad enough to reach your late teens or early twenties and realize that life usually *is* nothing more than a bowl of crap, but to be four or so and have that truth rubbed in your face . . . God, that *sucked*.

Since Ruth had little time for Nancy before Mrs. Day Care's ultimatum that the girl remain indoors (some future day-care teacher *she* was going to be!), I was elected to baby-sit the girl during play-time. Ruth had cot-folding down to an art form anyhow.

I quickly learned that the little girl had little patience with bristle blocks, or Play-Doh, or even those lift-out wooden tray puzzles her erstwhile playmates enjoyed so much. She'd merely mimic whatever it was I did with the toys, all the while staring up at me with those clear dark eyes set in that milky-fine skin. If she had only cried, it would've been easier; while I wasn't actually much for cuddling, I could have understood her need to vent her undeniable rage at the whole crazy situation she was enduring—preworm incident *and* after. But to simply *accept* it. . . .

Putting away the much-kneaded lumps of Play-Doh in their respective cans, I asked the little girl sitting across from me, "Are you looking forward to school? It'll be fun there . . . you'll learn how to read and write, and lots of other neat stuff—"

"Not with Stephen there," she mumbled, tracing the pattern of a flower on the worn plastic stick-on covering adhering to the battered tabletop. Unsure whether or not Stephen ever would be placed in any formal school—I doubted that even kindergarten was an option, not with him being in diapers—I decided to let that remark go by. I wasn't sure exactly how much she knew about his condition, aside from that "dead brain" remark. And besides, I had no idea whether I might have to take another course with her father. Or heretofore unseen mother.

Nancy kept on tracing the various flowers on the table before her, oblivious to me. Glancing up at the counter near the sink, I saw some squares of roughly rectangular butcher paper—the tossaway "place mats" used for early morning snack-time. I never knew—and never asked—why Mrs. Day Care banned crayons from the day care (probably would've caused her a little honest work), but I did carry a pouch of colored markers in my purse, for underline and accenting work on my notes come exam time. Not bothering to break the child's concentration, I got up, got my purse out of the tiny crib room off to the back of the Toddler Pit, and hurried back to the kitchen section before Ruth noticed that I'd left Nancy sitting alone.

The girl didn't look up when I wiggled back into my chair and whispered, "I've got a surprise for you."

No response. Still putting on a cheerful front, I ceremoniously lifted the flap on my purse, then slowly unzipped the hidden closure inside. Nothing. Just doodling on the plastic table covering. I pulled the yellow pouch of pens out of my purse, and slid them across the table, until they were within reach of her tracing forefinger. Nancy paused in midarc of her finger across a huge orange blossom, then looked up at me, head tilted and eyes blank.

Oh c'mon, kid, don't you know what crayons are? Are your folks too cheap to buy 'em . . . or too loopy? Maybe they expect you to use your—

It wasn't until I got down a couple of sheets of paper that Nancy seemed to put two and two together; with one hand she reached for the top sheet of paper, and with the other she selected a black felt-tip pen. Biting down on one pale pink lip with her front baby teeth, she began to draw something on the paper—not merely scribble, like I'd half expected her to do. Leaning back in my chair, I watched her create some sort of elaborate drawing full of lopsided figures and out-of-kilter structures; fairly typical work for a girl her age, maybe even a little more advanced than usual, since she was including all the limbs and facial features on the (as I saw them) upside-down people. I wasn't an art major, but I had to take art history, and the professor (a young bearded guy whose own artistic output included white plaster cartoonlike penises with propellers and wheels attached to them—at least he gave decent lectures) once told the class about the various stages of artistic development in children. According to the little I remembered of Professor Hupple's lectures (*he'd* lost me after I'd seen his sculptures at a faculty art show), Nancy's work was probably typical of a five- to six-year-old, which wasn't too strange, given how old her father and mother were. I didn't think they could communicate with Stephen on any significant level, so Nancy probably was a little more mature . . . even if she did have some sort of understanding with worms.

"That's really pretty, Nancy," I offered, trying to get a response from her, but her reaction threw me. Putting down her pen (a red one, now) she asked me flatly, "You think so?"

"Why sure, hon," I continued to lie, as I bent over the table to look at her masterpiece in progress—albeit still upsidedown. There were obviously four figures in the picture now, two big (and one sporting an unmistakable beard), and two small—and identical, in a reversed manner. One tiny stick person was all black head, with no features, no hair, no discernible identity . . . save for the unmistakable striped rugby shirt, while the other smaller figure was black-bodied, and as bloated as a runny gingerbread man, but topped with a recognizable face consisting of dot eyes, slash nose, and a perfectly horizontal mouth. And all the features were black, even the mouth. And surrounding these four figures were sharply angled rectangles and squares, each containing wild squiggles—although contained within the lines—of green, black and blue. There were no triangles topping the boxy shapes, so they probably weren't houses . . . but the three "structures" were so uniform in their contents that they had to have some purpose in Nancy's eyes.

Pointing casually at the nearest shape, I asked, "What's that?" not fully expecting an answer, but the child replied, "Where the stuff goes for them," and pointed at the figures in the picture.

"Oh . . . 'stuff,' for the people here?"

"Uh-huh." Nancy picked up the blue pen and added some more wavy lines to the smallest of the black-bordered boxes, before going on, "It has to be held in the boxes, so light don't hit it. Then it's no good for them. It's gotta be kept mushy and dark."

" 'Mushy and dark' . . . otherwise the people can't use it?"

"*Not* 'use' . . . I mean, they don't *do* nothing with it. It's just . . . there for the people," Nancy said with great difficulty, and greater maturity, leaving me unable to reply. I think I looked at my watch; somehow, it's in my memory that I didn't have too much more time before Mrs. Daffy Day Care returned with the other children, yet there was so much Nancy seemed to want to say.

Turning the picture around so I could see it, Nancy leaned over the table, almost stretching across it until her sweater rode up above the waistband of her pants, exposing a patch of pale back.

"See? Here's the little one, for *this* one—" she pointed first to the box at the left of the picture, then at the black-headed small figure, "—and here's the bigger one, for *this* one." Now she matched the black-bodied, small-headed figure with the medium sized box. "—and the big one's for *them*," finishing her explanation with a linking-up of the largest rectangle and the two adult figures.

Peering down at her creation, Nancy suddenly frowned, then slid back across the table to her seat, where she then picked up the black pen and neatly bisected each of the boxes with a single vertical slash down the middle. Then she drew the dots, parallel to the central line and centered in the middle of each box, as she said, "Almost forgot . . . they use these to get inside."

"Inside," I echoed softly; Nancy nodded her head emphatically, and as she did so, I noticed something . . . grotesque. Even as her head moved, her hair didn't. The bangs instead rode up and down her forehead, or, rather, *they* stayed in place while her scalp moved underneath. Not wanting to stare at her, I glanced down at the silhouette-bodied small figure on the butcher paper. It was hairless.

Oh shit, I remember thinking, *the poor kid's* sick . . . *probably went through chemo or something. Ye* gods, *what did her folks do to deserve this? One kid's damaged, and the other's—*

"*Here*," Nancy was saying softly yet urgently, as she pushed the pens—all replaced in their pouch—across the table to me. As I reached out to take them, I heard what had caused her visible state of alarm. Stephen's unmistakable "wwwwhoooop!" as Mrs. Day Care escorted him into the building. . . .

▼▼▼

Luckily, I'd hidden Nancy's drawing in a pile of flat wooden puzzles before Mrs. Day Care had a chance to pounce on it. For the next five days, while the other children played outdoors, and Ruth hummed tunelessly to herself as she straightened up the nap area, I'd ceremoniously hand Nancy my pens (I'd bought a fresh set at the campus bookstore, just so none of them would run out on her) and a few sheets of butcher paper . . . and then let her make me distinctly uneasy for the next half hour.

In all of her drawings, there were two constants. The yin and yang pair of small figures, Black-face and Black-body, always close to each other on the page. As for what surrounded them . . . hell, even after I don't know how many centuries, nobody can really understand the canvases Bosch or Dali created, can they? And those men were trained artists, with consummate knowledge of anatomy, of line, of perspective. . . .

But Nancy was there, and she explained some of the images, those she felt compelled to share with me, while others remained unexplained, unguessable. I didn't ask her anything; the ethics of *leading* a child were all too plain to me. I didn't want anyone coming back at me, accusing me of some wild perversion, some lewd suggestion. I never asked Nancy to do a single thing—not after I saw the first picture, that first afternoon.

"That's nice, Nancy—"

"This is the place where the mushy stuff starts out . . . it's got to be *real* low, under *other* stuff so that it's good—"

The little girl was pointing to a vague semicircle, obviously under a floor comprised of several parallel lines slanting toward me. Inside the circle . . . the mass of writhing red, black, green, and brown blobs, squiggles and *almost*-defined shapes was enigmatic, even if its purpose was almost clear from the child's cryptic explanation:

"First all *this* is *other* stuff, from all over—mostly *that* one's clear house—" she pointed to a representation of a larger beardless figure, of indeterminate gender, "—plus some *squishy* stuff I don't like, and then *that* one mixes it all up, and lets it set for a long, long time, until the bubbles come up and pop . . . and *they* smell," Nancy confided in a lower, almost giggling voice, before adding, "and then it's all ready for the boxes. Then it's good. For all of *them*."

Then there would be a lull, always that short time while Nancy drew quickly, and my mind slowed to a deliberate near-stop, as if to delay comprehension of what she'd just told me, and then Nancy would stop her frantic scribbling and we'd start the ritual once again:

"That's real pretty—"

"*This* is what's inside the boxes, when the doors are down. It's *real* quiet . . . they just float and when they close their eyes, the stuff trickles inside, like crying only from outside, not in. And it . . . goes in and *in* them, and then the doors open and it's time to get up. That's when it's time to dress," and she points at a couple of red and blue striped blobs near the bottom of the page, which I now recognized as crumpled little shirts, a detail almost lost in the looping, dark-smeared haze of blue, green, and black surrounding the ubiquitous black-headed/black-bodied figures.

I found myself looking at the other pictures she'd done over the past week; the "stuff" was becoming a stock element in her drawings, be it in the boxes, around the tiny figures, or (worst of all) seeping out of various orifices on their bodies.

Why in the world did you people have to tell *her about what happened to Stephen . . . what the* hell *kind of ethical behavior is that? You dress them alike, so the poor kid thinks she has to go through what* he *did—*

"—go potty," Nancy was whispering in my ear, as she leaned over the table, trying to capture my wandering attention. From the pained look on her face, I realized she's been repeating the comment for a few seconds.

"Uh-huh, kiddo," I mumbled, before yelling to Ruth, "I'll be right back with her, okay?" The curly-headed woman cheerfully nodded, and I took off with Nancy, gently steering her by the shoulders.

When we reached the women's room, Nancy broke free of my guiding touch and burst through the door on her own, and ran into one of the open stalls, barely shutting the door before quite loudly beginning to do her "duty" behind the closed pink door. I wondered if whatever made her lose her hair was affecting her bowels; the smell was terrible. I hoped no one else would come into the room; even the plastic air freshener cone perched on top of the tampon machines was no help. I did find myself backing away from her, until I was almost at the door, before I heard Nancy's plaintive, "Teacher . . . it won't flush. . . ."

"You jiggle the handle?" *Come* on, *kid, just push the handle—*

A few seconds of metallic fiddling sounds, then: "Yeah . . . it don't go."

"Oh . . . shit," I mumbled, before telling Nancy, "Well . . . pull up your clothes and come on out of there—"

"My Momma says not to do that . . . I gotta—"

"Come *on*, Nancy," I said a little too forcefully for my own liking; whatever she heard in my tone of voice made the girl quickly open the door and scoot out of the stall, her head bowed, her eyes almost hidden under her thick lashes. I patted her on the head as she passed me, giving her a quick smile even as I felt her wig shift on her head slightly under my fingertips, and then hurried over—my eyes averted, my breath held—to the vacated stall.

I jiggled the handle while keeping an eye on Nancy, who stood with her own hands folded before her, mumbling, "Mommy'll be mad." But the damn toilet *wouldn't* flush. "Oh *shit*!" Louder this time.

I'd have to get the janitor . . . but I don't know if it was just the look in Nancy's eyes that stopped me, or an inner voice spurred on by the memory of what Nancy had been telling me those past few afternoons. No matter what it was that made me pause, and then take a real look at that bowl, I never called for anyone to help me that day. No one would have . . . understood.

Not that I even really understood.

Nancy hadn't had a loose bowel movement, or any kind of movement associated with digestion or elimination. She'd just . . . *seeped*. And after seeing page after page of her handiwork the last few afternoons, I knew—at least vaguely, in that not-fully-explained way—what had happened . . . what had *been* happening.

It was the "stuff" Nancy kept speaking of, and patiently drawing for me. Organic, mostly, or it had been at some long ago time, before spending God-knew-*how*-long in that pit or vat or whatever her mother kept it in, before infusing it into her children—or into Nancy, at least. The "stuff" that was good for her . . . that probably kept her *going*—

Standing there in that foul-smelling stall, it all became clear and not clear for me. Marta DeGrooten taught *biology* . . . living matter, and the study of it. Her "clear house" was probably a green house

. . . and the boxes were probably immersion tanks, like they used in those sensory deprivation experiments—

"Mommy'll be *real* mad." Nancy's voice was starting to choke with tears. Suddenly afraid of *what* might come out of her sad little eyes, I hurried over to her and murmured, "No, no, hon, we'll fix it so nobody will know. Your secret, my secret. Okay?"

Thank God, if there ever *was* one, the girl began to smile. Maybe the word "secret" did it. I picked her up and sat her in one of the sink bowls, telling her to stay there and not jump down, while I went and did something. Once I left the women's room, I took some flack from a few of my jock classmates when they saw me filling the janitor's galvanized steel bucket—the ten-gallon jobbie—with water. "Hey, Anya, you got new work-study here?" but I forced myself to laugh it off before wheeling the heavy bucket into the women's room. I strained a muscle in my arm hefting the bucket, and my shirt and jeans were soaked, but I managed to flush the "stuff" down the toilet. The janitor just stared at me when I wheeled his bucket back to his "office" near the men's room, but grunted in agreement when I told him I didn't want him to have to bother with a clogged toilet when he was busy elsewhere. I didn't leave his sight until he started making an "Out of Order" sign for that door, though.

Nancy stayed in place until I lifted her out of the sink. When I did so, my hand slid under her sweater, where it came in contact with almost gelid, squish-soft skin beneath . . . and when I bent down to take one of Nancy's small hands, it felt much the same. Not quite rotted . . . but getting there. She had to be *awfully* sick. . . .

As we walked down the hallway, toward the Toddler Pit, I now understood Mrs. Day Care's frantic desire to wash—and *wash*—her hands under that stream of hot water. . . .

▼▼▼

I may have saved Nancy from one kind of disaster that afternoon, but I didn't have the same kind of luck myself. During my absence, Ruth—ever helpful, ever nosy—had come upon Nancy's handiwork resting on the table, plus my collection of coloring pens. And by the time I was finished in that women's room, Mrs. Day Care and the other children had returned to the Pit—where Ruth felt compelled to show the teacher both Nancy's drawings and my felt-tipped pens.

They were deep in discussion when I came back with Nancy; I don't know what made my heart palpitate more—the sight of my pens in Mrs. Day Care's sharply pink-nailed claws, or those butcher-paper drawings from hell in Ruth's lightly freckled hands. Nancy sensed my panic, and did what any child long accustomed to keeping deep, *dark* secrets would do—she ran and grabbed the pictures out of Ruth's fingers, and tossed them into the big trash can near the kitchenette. Then she went and pretended to busy herself with a picture book in the corner of the room.

I don't remember exactly how I bullshitted my way out of that mess; I do recall something to do with keeping a bored child happy, a bored *professor's* child. I might have even tossed in situational ethics, I don't know. It would've been appropriate.

All I do know is that the ban on Nancy participating in outdoor playtime was lifted. During my last couple of weeks in the Toddler Pit, I alone folded the cots after naptime, and I was even released form my duties as back-rubber.

To her credit, Nancy never mentioned our mutual secret; I saw so little of her—just a sad, dark-wigged little figure sitting obediently behind a jumble of bristle-blocks—that it was almost as if we'd never met. And Stephen continued to whoop, coo, and burble happily, forever safe from the spilling of secrets, or the revelation of his second nurturing womb. I did make it a point to touch him, just once before leaving the Toddler Pit for good. His skin was soft, pliant, and firm—good, clean, healthy baby skin. If he was lucky, he'd keep it for life. And he smelled good, too. Like soft powder and baby lotion. I never changed his diapers, the long-haired secretive aide was in charge of *that*, but I never once doubted that the sight of something like the "stuff" would have shocked her into sudden loud-mouthed ranting to Mrs. Day Care, her usual tight-lipped reserve shattered. So I had to assume that Stephen merely did his "duty" like any other person.

But the near-revelation of Nancy's little secret did enable me to add one more jagged piece to the frameless, many-pieces-missing puzzle of her life. Instead of rubbing backs before naptime, I was assigned to do dishes after snacktime (which occurred about an hour or so before I showed up in the Pit each day), and put them away in the cupboards that lined the kitchenette. Taped to one of the doors was a ruler-lined sheet of paper, with all the names of the children who attended the day care—along with a list of dietary "No-No's" (as they were so dubbed on the sheet). Always-crying Sarah was a diabetic, so no sugary foods for her. Jennifer needed to take a pill for lactose intolerance, from a bottle issued by the hospital pharmacy. Plus, there were a couple of notations for the DeGrooten youngsters:

"Stephen—jars of baby food in refrig., Nancy—withhold all solids, can give water (bottled only, see refrig.)"

I only needed to read *that* once . . . for Nancy had explained the rest, in her own fashion.

Aside from that printed revelation inside the cupboard door, my being barred from the nap area—and Nancy—had one other advantage. I was able to fish the child's drawings out of the trash, long before the janitor came to take away a week's worth of garbage, and stuff the folded sheets into my purse.

Not that I expected anyone to scrutinize the scribbled sheets, or even understand them . . . but secrets *are* secrets.

▼▼▼

As it turned out, I never saw Nancy or Stephen again after I finally did the last of my time in the Toddler Pit. A week after I finished my student-teacher stint there, the pending court case against the hospital—as filed by the DeGrooten's lawyers—went into session, and after an astonishingly brief six hours of actual court time, the hospital decided to settle out of court . . . for an undisclosed, but supposedly *very* high sum.

(Or so Ruth told me once she and I got over a decidedly frosty period . . . her friend the obstetrics nurse's favorite doctor ended up leaving the hospital, while every other doctor named in the suit had significant jumps in their malpractice insurance premiums.)

And after they received the settlement, the DeGrootens also began to get hate mail and hang-up phone calls from a lot of the former patients of the doctor who was forced to leave, stethoscope trailing between his legs like a tail, until they up and left town. They quit teaching in midsemester, pulled the kids out of day care, the whole shebang. Not that I blamed them, weird as they were. I think—if what Nancy had been visually hinting to me with her black-head/black-body depictions of her brother and herself was true—that the DeGrootens would have had to leave town in a rather short while anyhow.

For when their house went up for sale, listed by address only in one of the local realtor's advertisements, two items in the blurb caught my attention. The obvious one was "Complete greenhouse, with many flowering plants." The one no one else would have noticed was, "Newly cemented and finished basement."

▼▼▼

That's where Nancy's story—or my understanding of it—should have ended, and there it would have ended, if I hadn't gone back to my alma mater just recently, to do some research at the extensive library for my latest novel. A couple of years after the Toddler Pit incident, I gave up on teaching, for reasons having nothing to do with Nancy or her too-detailed pictures, and became a liberal arts/English major, and then a published writer . . . of horror, almost naturally. But I had never thought of sharing Nancy's secrets, out of both fear and respect—fear of her parent's wrath, and respect for a sick little girl—and, perhaps if I *had* stayed way from my old school, I never would have shared those secrets. But in the library, I ran into my old Introduction to Education professor, a cheerful man of Thai extraction who had now been bumped upstairs into administration.

Dr. Sarasin had never been much of a teacher when I had him, so I could only hope he was more efficient as an administrator, but I still made out as if I was happy to see him. We chatted between the stacks for a few minutes, until I asked if he'd been the only teacher from the college who'd been promoted to administration.

"Ah no, no, Dr. DeGrooten—you 'member him, no?—he's now chairman of board."

Assuming he meant the board governing the administration of the entire college, and not caring enough for a clarification, I blurted out, "Didn't he leave here ten years ago?"

"Yes, yes, he leave—but he return two, three years ago. You had him, no?"

Nodding, I told him about the ethics class, and was about to mention how I'd met his children in the Toddler Pit, when Dr. Sarasin cut in, "You hear, no, 'bout their little boy?"

"Stephen?"

"Yes, he in school now, special school." Sarasin gently touched his graying head of black hair, making soft noises of what I assumed to be sympathy. Without thinking, I found myself saying, "Stephen was a cute little boy . . . but I felt so sorry for his sister; all the attention paid to him was a drain on her—"

"No, no, he was no problem to his sister. She born long after he put in special school."

"Nancy? She was about the same age—"

"No-no-no," he sputtered quickly, and waved both hands furiously—as if to wave away any misconception—before adding, "He lost sister *before* he born, sister Nancy was sick one, two year before he born. Cancer. After a time, her parents not talk 'bout her, and no one ask . . . my wife, me, we know DeGrootens long 'fore they come here, to this college. Daughter sick back then. After she sick, my wife, me, we didn't socialize much with them. But now they are back here, and they have new little girl. Maybe three, four . . . same age as Stephen when you knew him. She pretty girl, goes to day care out on other side of town. It moved since you left here, not in FAC anymore—not since old teacher there, she die."

Hugging my book to my chest, I nodded dumbly as my old professor spoke to me, jabbering on in his imperfect English about the restorations to the former day care after it was moved to an abandoned school on the other side of town, remembering how spaced-out he used to be when I had him for a teacher, how he was usually five years behind the times when it came to just about *every*thing—and especially what was going on with his fellow teachers. Including the DeGrootens, and including Ruth and her professor husband . . . none of whom moved in the same social circles, either in or out of the college. And spaced-out enough not to know how many children his former friend and his biologist wife were sending to day care, even while some of his own students were taking care of *both* of the DeGrooten youngsters. . . .

Thus, the old Toddler Pit of my memories is no more, even as it *still* remains, albeit somewhat changed, in a different location, with no doubt the same smells in the air, the same folding cots arranged higgledy-piggledy across the floor, and with perhaps the same or very similar hands rubbing the tiny prone backs come naptime. Only . . . Stephen's joyous coos and whoops are missing, but I am sure that they are still remembered in that new Toddler Pit, by the one who had to hear them for perhaps the longest time of all.

And even though the mask of flesh above that black silhouette body (as Nancy—or whatever she is called now—no doubt still pictures herself) may be the same, still childlike, still small and dark-wigged and bright-eyed, I wonder if the Nancy I knew is *still* a child—even if I don't *ever* really want to know the answer to that question.

For . . . for if she is only a child *without*, how could I ever let my eyes meet hers, with both of us remembering how I was able to crawl out of the Toddler Pit *she* can never leave?

So, I've kept her scribbled drawings, and her secret . . . up to now. For I can only believe that as *ethical* as her parents have no doubt tried to be, they would never allow her to ever be able to *read*. . . .

RED ANGELS

KAREN HABER

THE drums.

They were the first thing David Weber heard—felt, really, a steady pulsing beat—as he stepped from the gleaming seaplane onto Port-au-Prince's sunny Bowen Field.

"Passports, please, passports." The immigration agent chanted his mantra in lilting French-accented English.

Weber stepped up to the sagging metal table and stared beyond it at the murals decorating the walls, scenes of local frolic and revelry. Probably Philome Obin's work or Castera Bazile's, Weber thought, and his heart beat faster. Hadn't he come to Haiti to buy the best native artwork he could find for his gallery? If it was right here in the customs shed then it was probably all over the island, his just for the asking. The drums beat behind him, through his pale skin, and right into his blood—boombadaboombadaboom.

"USA?" The agent had a dark, genial face. His smile was ragged, with crooked incisors.

"Yes."

"Welcome. Not many Americans come here anymore. Purpose of your visit?"

"Business."

"Really?" The man looked at him in surprise. "Perhaps you're a trade inspector from Miami? Looking for smugglers?" He chuckled and Weber forced a smile.

"How'd you guess?" he said. "My cover story is that I'm a gallery owner from Los Angeles looking for art. For Ti Malice, the famous Haitian artist."

The man gave him a sly, knowing glance. Weber's hopes leaped high: perhaps he would get his first lead here, right now.

"Ti Malice?"

Weber nodded eagerly.

"Ti Malice. Heeheehee." The immigration agent bent double with laughter. "Ti Malice. Ti Malice. Hoohoohoo. You really came here to find him?"

"Yeah. To find him and buy paintings from him."

The passport-control agent laughed yet again, a quick mocking snort this time.

Weber began to get annoyed. He shuffled his feet and wondered just what was so funny. Should he ask? He hated being laughed at.

"Ti Malice won't want to do business with you, my friend. Trust me."

The drums were getting louder now.

"We'll see." Weber shrugged. "Maybe he will, and maybe he won't. What's that drumming? Some voodoo thing?" He tried to sound casual, but deep inside he trembled at the thought of actual voodoo rites taking place nearby. Grainy images from ancient movies floated to his mind. He pushed them aside.

The official was stiff now, even a bit contemptuous. "That's not vodou. There's a festival, a combite, someplace. Probably the hill farmers are building a barn up there."

"But the drums—"

"It helps them to work. They sing." The agent stamped his passport and handed it back without looking at him. "Next."

Weber stumbled out into the bright sunshine, dragging his suitcase. He was just trying to make a living but it certainly brought him to some odd places, he thought. Now here he was in the nutty world of voodoo drums, witch doctors, and zombies. It was funny, really, where a guy with a master's degree in fine arts from UCLA could find himself.

Suddenly, a small, wiry man was at his side.

"Taxi?"

"Uh, yeah."

"Hotel Jolly?"

"No. Hotel L'Ouverture."

"You're not Swiss?" The driver seemed surprised.

"No."

"German, then."

"Guess again."

"But the blond hair, the blue eyes—all Swiss and Germans stay at the Jolly."

"I'm American."

"Oh. Good. Big tippers, Americans." The driver chuckled deep in his throat. "Not many of you here now."

"So I've heard."

The car was an old gray Ford daubed with pinkish primer paint, sagging on its rusting suspension. It bounced as the driver stowed his bags in the yawning trunk, and again when Weber climbed into the back. The seat was black vinyl patched by red and gray tape whose edges had curled in the heat. He pitched and slid across it as the driver took off.

Weber grabbed the door handle and braced himself as the cab made the first of several sharp turns away from the empty fields of the airport and into the winding maze of Port-au-Prince's potholed streets. After the third near-collision, Weber leaned over the front seat and tapped the cabbie on the shoulder. "Can't you drive any slower?"

The man barely glanced at him. "You don't want me to go fast? Americans always do. Americans and Japanese, forever in a rush, in a big hurry."

Weber felt a warning tingle of suspicion: his biggest rival for collectors was an aggressive gallery-owner in Tokyo, Hideo Tashamaki. "Japanese? Here? What do they come here for?"

"The puffer fish. And whores." The cabbie giggled.

Whores. That was the last thing Weber wanted here. He settled against his seat-back in silence and wondered why anyone would risk his life eating poisonous fish or screwing diseased prostitutes.

With a squeal of tires and brakes, the cab stopped in front of a six-story wooden building. The upper three floors sported balconies with graceful wrought-iron supports. From the lowest balcony hung a sign in faded gilt that read: "Hotel L'Ouverture."

A statue of the Haitian revolutionary Toussaint L'Ouverture stood nearby the porte-cochère. It was green with age, surrounded by a circle of dead brown grass. White and gray pigeons roosted on L'Ouverture's tricornered hat, on his outstretched hand, and along the eaves of the hotel that bore his name.

Weber stood on the stained front steps holding his suit bag as the taxi roared off. No bellboys swept him up in a welcoming bustle. Well, what did you expect? Weber thought. He elbowed his way past the stiff paint-flecked double door into the dim, cool lobby. His footsteps echoed. A clerk sat behind the wide mahogany desk, head propped on his hand, reading a creased and tattered comic book. He didn't look up until Weber had put his bag down across the top of the desk. His expression was mildly hostile but mostly sleepy.

"I have a reservation," Weber said.

The clerk didn't budge. "The room isn't ready."

"When will it be ready?"

"I don't know. The maid didn't come in today."

Weber looked around the lobby. Empty, dark, and quiet. "Oh, come on. Do you mean the entire hotel is full? It doesn't seem that way to me."

The clerk shrugged and gazed wistfully at his comic book.

Weber sighed, pulled out his wallet, and carefully removed a five-dollar bill which he ostentatiously slapped into his passport. "Here, you might want to see this."

The clerk perked right up. He took the passport, nodded, and opened the guestbook. "Lucky for you we've had a cancellation. Room 37. This way."

Room 37 had obviously not been occupied in some time. The

air was hot and musty, and a thin layer of dust coated the dresser and the old-fashioned black phone on the nightstand.

The clerk lingered in the doorway. Obviously, this was even more entertaining than his comic book. Weber slung his bag onto the sagging bed, and the bedsprings groaned rustily. He brushed off the phone, picked up the receiver, and, after checking a card in his pocket, dialed the number of Jean Saint-Mery, a local art dealer who had been highly recommended.

The gallery number was busy. Weber double-checked the card and dialed again. Still busy.

"Damn," he said. "Is there a phone book here?"

"No," said the clerk. "Sorry."

Weber forced himself to smile. After all, hadn't he been warned by more than one friend in the business not to have any expectations? Well, perhaps he'd have better luck with Mrs. Dewey—the old woman who was said to have a terrific collection of Haitian art. "Do you know where I can find the Dewey house?"

"The art teacher's widow?"

"That's right."

"Go to Rue Macajoux and, when it narrows, take the first alley on the right. Fifth house."

"Is it far?"

"You can walk."

Following the scrawled map the clerk gave him, Weber walked across the street from the hotel, made a right, a left, and found himself on a bustling street crisscrossed overhead with a web of electrical wires. Bicycles and cars fought for space on the narrow pavement, and the pedestrians outnumbered both, swarming in the hot sunlight in their brightly colored clothing. Tattered baskets of laundry and vegetables were balanced upon their heads like huge inverted hats.

The air was thick with humidity. Weber's shirt began to stick to his back and arms. He dodged an orange-and-yellow-striped bus, swearing. Why hadn't he taken a taxi, he wondered, or hired a guide? There had to be an easier way to reach Mrs. Dewey and her potential gold mine.

Alex Dewey's widow was in her eighties and blind, but reports tagged her as sharper than many sighted people half her age. Her husband had helped to popularize Haitian folk art and the family collection was rumored to be worth millions. If Weber couldn't charm Mrs. Dewey into releasing some of her stock, at the very least he would make her acquaintance. And maybe, just maybe, she could put him on the trail of a few artists—including Ti Malice.

Finally, after much doubling back, he found the alley and the house. It was a dilapidated two-story wooden structure with a sagging balcony, its silvered walls spotted with age. The paint, where it still showed on the door and window shutters, was a faded ghostly red. In the Caribbean manner, Weber stood outside and clapped his hands sharply three times. When there was no response, he repeated the action. On his third attempt, a shutter on the first floor cranked open and a woman with a guarded, sleepy expression peered out at him.

"Is Mrs. Dewey in?"

"She's not seeing anybody."

"I've come all the way from Los Angeles."

The woman shrugged and made as if to shut the window.

"Please," Weber called. "Tell her Roland Gunther sent me."

The woman paused, stared at him wordlessly, and retreated into the house. Weber could hear voices, but could not make out what they were saying or in what language they spoke.

Weber felt the sweat trickle slowly down his back in a maddening itch. Would he stand out here all day, melting? Suddenly he heard the sound of footsteps. Then the front door shuddered as a bolt was thrown back. The sullen maid stood blinking in the sunlight. "She says okay."

The floorboards creaked under Weber's weight. He was surprised to see that the house was lit by candles and hurricane lamps. A fire seemed imminent. As they made their way down a narrow corridor, Weber asked, "Isn't there any electricity?"

The maid said nothing, merely gestured for him to enter a doorway at his right.

He stooped to avoid the low lintel and emerged in a broad, dim room. By the window sat a small figure enthroned upon a wide wooden chair. Her feet dangled above the floor, and she stared at him fixedly.

"Did I hear you ask about the electricity?" she said. "I only use it in the kitchen. Otherwise, I certainly don't need it." The voice was firm and crisp, with a distinct upper-class English accent.

"Given that argument," said Weber, "why bother using candles, either?"

"For Sarah, here." There was amusement in Mrs. Dewey's voice, mild but unmistakable. "Besides, it's cheaper than the electricity. More reliable, too." She smiled and held out her hand. "If Roland sent you then you must be worth talking to. Roland hardly ever sends anybody."

Weber grasped her tiny hand. It felt dry and papery, as though it would crumble in his grip. "It took me a long time to win his trust," he said.

"I'm sure." Again, the smile in the voice. "Sarah, bring more light for Mr.—what is your name?"

"Weber. David Weber."

"Sarah, bring more light for Mr. Weber. And some lemonade."

"No lemons," the maid said.

"Then cold water." Mrs. Dewey paused. "Or would you prefer sugar water?"

"Plain would be fine, if it's safe." Weber stared at her in fascination. No one in L.A. would believe him when he described this dark place and the old crone who lived here.

"Bottled, of course," she said. "Oh, I can tolerate the local stuff. But you'd be doubled over with stomach cramps in fifteen minutes." She chuckled, a deep witchy sound, and gestured toward a straight-backed chair. "Sit down, Mr. Weber. Make yourself as comfortable as possible."

He sat down carefully on an old easy chair and heard the stiff leather upholstery creak. A maddening tickle on the back of his neck made him jump—some tropical insect? He swatted at it in a panic, but his hand came away clean and empty.

Sarah returned with a chilled bottle, two glasses, and a hurricane lantern. Weber decided that she had memorized the location of everything in the room—otherwise, how could she avoid bumping into things in the near-darkness? With practiced skill she set the lantern upon a small table and lit the wick.

Weber gasped.

The room had come to life around him. Every wall was covered with paintings of lively figures rendered in vigorous brushstrokes. The chamber that he had taken for some dark, enclosed snuggery was a high-ceilinged cathedral, a chapel of Haitian art. Red-cloaked angels danced in a royal blue sky while, below, men and women arrayed in rainbow colors gamboled in fields of gold and green.

"I see you've noticed the paintings," said Mrs. Dewey.

"Hard to miss, once you've got a little light in here."

"I miss them constantly."

Weber felt his cheeks heating with embarrassment and anger. Why was the old woman still harping upon her disability? Did she want to throw him off balance? "Have you been blind a long time?" he asked.

"Thirty years. I've only had the glass eyes for five. The new doctor insisted. Said the old ones were rotting because of diminished blood supply."

Glass eyes. No wonder she stared. Despite Mrs. Dewey's matter-of-fact attitude, Weber shuddered. "If you can't see the paintings any longer, how can you bear to keep them around?"

She leaned back against her throne, obviously amused. "You must want these paintings very badly."

Weber took a deep breath. "I'm here to buy paintings for my gallery," he said. "That's why I came to Haiti."

"You're not the first art dealer to come calling."

"You must love these paintings very much."

Mrs. Dewey tapped her skeletal fingers against a padded armrest. "On the contrary, I don't give a bloody damn about them." She grinned. Her teeth looked too large, like white tombstones crowding her mouth.

"What?"

"It's true. It was always Alex, my husband, who was completely obsessed by the art. Mad for it. I tolerated his whims because, well, one must in a marriage, yes?"

"I wouldn't know. I'm single."

"Well, I suppose there is less baggage that way," Mrs. Dewey said. "But less comfort as well."

The art dealer stirred restlessly. "Ma'am, I'm having trouble understanding you. If you don't actually care about these works, then why keep them? Why didn't you sell them to the first gallery owner who looked you up? There's a fortune in artwork here. You could be living in London like a queen."

"Hate the climate. Absolutely hate it. At its best, English weather is fair to poor."

"The Riviera, then."

"The local snobs there would find my Haitian French hilarious. And I'm too old to learn Italian."

"California?"

She sniffed disdainfully. "The culture, my dear."

"You know what I'm saying."

"Yes, of course. But it's such fun to play with you and it's been so very long since I've had a playmate. Forgive me. The reason I didn't—and won't—sell the paintings is simple. There's a curse on them."

"I beg your pardon?" Weber felt as though he had been punched in the stomach.

"A vodou curse. If I sell them, I'll die."

At the mention of the word voodoo, his hands and feet had turned to ice. They all take this stuff so seriously, he thought.

"You must be joking." He told himself she was deranged, floating in and out of lucidity the way old folks sometimes did.

"I know that it must seem absurd to someone from Los Angeles to whom freeways and electricity and budget deficits are normal and expected. But I assure you that here, in Haiti, vodou is very much alive and very much something to be respected and even feared."

Weber played along, pretending to be cynical and amused. "Well, who cursed the paintings?"

"The artist."

"The artist?" Weber said. "Why in the world . . . ?"

"He was also a vodou priest. Somehow he got the impression that my husband had cheated him and paid more for some other artist's work. It wasn't true, of course, but nothing could be done. Once we had the paintings, we were forced to keep them. Alex defied the curse and sold two paintings to a wealthy Frenchman on vacation. A week later the buyer was dead. Drowned off his yacht."

"An accident. A tragic coincidence."

"Two weeks later, Alex died."

"But I'd heard he had chronic heart problems. That his death was natural."

"The reports were in error. I begged him to wear the *ouanga* I'd had made—the countercharm—but he just laughed."

Weber stared at her inscrutable raisin face in disbelief. "Are you certain that you're not reading too much into this? I don't know much about voodoo, but I didn't think that curses could be placed upon inanimate objects." At least I hope not, he thought.

"I assure you, Mr. Weber, that vodou is a religion that can be used for most anything." Mrs. Dewey's voice grew sharp with impatience. "I've had almost a decade to consider this and nothing has changed my mind yet." She plunged her hand down the front of her dress, fished around for a moment, and brought forth a rawhide pouch tied to a leather cord. From the stained look of it, Mrs. Dewey had worn it for a long, long time. "This is my *ouanga*. It keeps me safe. It was made by the top *papaloi*, and I wear it everywhere."

Weber stared at the ugly little bag. After a moment he decided not to pursue the subject. This talk of charms and death was all bullshit anyway. Maybe the tropical sun drove everybody crazy down here.

"You won't sell me your paintings, then."

"No."

"Will you at least help me locate some of the local artists?"

"You mean to say that you actually like the work?"

"Of course," he said. "The gaiety, the colors, the freedom from convention. It's joyful, a celebration of life." He didn't bother to add that his clients, most of whom couldn't tell kindergarten finger-paintings from Renaissance masterworks, would buy whatever was the latest, hottest item. And Caribbean art was hot, hot, hot.

"*Now* you do sound like a dealer. And a collector. Who are you looking for?"

"Ti Malice, for starters."

Mrs. Dewey's hands flew to the charmed bag around her neck. "But he was the very artist whose curse killed my husband! Please, Mr. Weber, stay away from him. You don't want Ti Malice. Really, you don't."

"I'm not afraid."

"You should be."

Despite the heat, Weber felt strangely chilled. He stood up to get the blood moving in his veins.

"Ma'am, if you won't tell me where he is, would you please be so kind as to direct me to someone who will? Or at least to some of the other artists."

"There are several artists whose work you should see. But please, stay away from Ti Malice."

Her instructions were thorough. Weber made several notes, thanked her copiously, and left.

He was halfway down the street when he heard a hissing sound and looked down, thinking: snakes?

But the sound had come from behind him. Someone tugged the back of his sweaty shirt. He spun around, heart pounding, to meet the insolent stare of Mrs. Dewey's maid, Sarah.

"I can help you, blanc."

Her voice was flat, studiedly uninterested. But she had followed him and Weber suspected that her insolence masked some inner urgency.

"What do you mean?"

"You want to find Ti Malice? I can take you to him."

"You can?" Weber stared at her suspiciously. For how much?"

"Fifty."

"Are you out of your mind? I'll pay you ten."

"Twenty."

"Fifteen."

Sarah nodded, satisfied. "Meet me by the fountain in the main plaza of Rue St. Raphael, tonight. At sunset."

"Fine." Weber turned to go, but her hand on his arm held him there.

"You pay me, blanc. Pay me first."

"Now?"

She nodded. Suddenly there was fierceness and hunger in her gaze.

"No way," Weber said. "I'll pay you *after* you take me to Ti Malice." He pulled free of her grip and moved quickly down the street.

▼▼▼

At sunset the fountain at Place St. Raphael was crowded with young and old women sitting together in the cool air, gossiping and drinking fermented palm wine out of hollowed gourds. Despite the sight of the badly eroded faceless statue at the center of the fountain, Weber found the tableau rather pleasing: the soothing splash of falling water, the bright colors of the women's dresses and bandanas, their laughing eyes and friendly smiles, the purple sky. Not for the first time he wished that he could really paint. The fate of failed painters, he mused, was to become art directors or gallery owners.

"Hsst. Blanc!"

Sarah was at his side, sullen as ever. Weber felt as though a shadow had passed over him: why should he trust her? What if it was some sort of setup? But why would she be going to all the trouble to trap one jet-lagged art dealer?

Despite his misgivings he followed Sarah away from the plaza, the splashing water, and the laughing women. She set a surprisingly quick pace and never once looked back at him.

The paintings, he thought. Remember, the paintings.

Within minutes she was leading him down a deserted alley. They wound their way out of the alley and up a hilly street toward the Rue Turgeau. Fine homes, many-storied, with elaborate balconies, began to appear behind hedges. Weber suspected they were heading for the houses where the remnants of the expatriate colony lived. But Sarah made a sudden turn and the fine villas were left behind. Silently Weber followed her through a neighborhood of tin-roofed shacks. The longer they walked the greater the distance became between each shack. Now they were trampling dry glass in an empty lot overgrown with tangled thorny weeds, in a sparsely inhabited area where massive thickets of palms and wild jungle pressed right up against the city limits.

Darkness had fallen with tropical swiftness, and there were no street lamps to illuminate their way. Weber began to wish he had packed his pocket flashlight. You were too eager, he told himself. Too greedy. Too quick to trust. What if she leaves you here in the middle of nowhere? And now that he was beyond the sounds of the city, he could hear the drums, steady, incessant, summoning him closer. Closer. But where and to what?

"Sarah! Where the hell are we headed?"

"Where you asked to go. To see Ti Malice. And maybe to see the *houngan*."

Weber knew that meant the voodoo priest and his neck prickled anew. "That's a witch doctor, isn't it? I don't want to see a witch doctor. I just want to see Ti Malice, understand? Where the hell are we? In the middle of nowhere?"

Sarah laughed sharply. "There are people all around, all around us, but you must know where to look. Be patient, blanc, and you will see."

They pushed through a thick grove of palms and emerged into a clearing in which a small, white-washed building stood. The sides of it bore sinuous arabesques painted with a bold hand. The roof was partially thatched. A pierced tin can lantern hung by the door, casting a pool of yellow light.

"Inside," Sarah said. Her face was more animated than ever before. Weber thought she looked excited, almost gleeful, and it made him nervous.

He hesitated at the door. "I guess I should pay you."

"I can wait until you've seen him."

"Should I knock?"

"Go inside. He's waiting for you."

"Ti Malice?"

Sarah nodded and smiled a ferocious smile.

Weber told himself that he had come too far to stop now. Boldly he pushed his way into the house. There appeared to be two rooms leading away from the main entrance. The house was quiet, lit by a single candle. It felt deserted.

"Hello?"

There was no reply. Weber called once more, then backed out of the hut. "Sarah?"

She was gone. All he heard was the liquid trill of birds, the whisper of wind, and the murmur of insects seeking animal blood. How could she have left him here? He hadn't paid her yet. Surely she would come back.

He shook his head, feeling foolish and more than a little frightened. There was nothing for him to do but go back into the deserted house. He couldn't just stand outside in the middle of the Haitian wasteland after sunset and be eaten alive by mosquitoes.

Weber stepped inside again and heard something strange: as though fingernails were being scraped against smooth wood, over and over.

"Hello?"

Still there was no response.

Weber stalked the sound, heart pounding. Was it an animal? A hillside spirit? Don't be ridiculous, he told himself.

In the farthest room of the house a single candle burned. Weber drew closer and closer to its feeble light and the scratching grew louder.

He entered the room and saw the source of the noise.

A thin black man in a stained shirt sat with his back to the door, oblivious to his surroundings, painting steadily upon a stretched canvas propped against the wall. Under his brush a peculiar scene was taking shape: a great eye floated in the center of a blue-black sky, casting a golden searchlight upon kneeling figures below. To the right and left of the floating eye were red-gowned angels, their golden wings and halos glowing brightly. The colors were bold, the style assured and masterful. The painting seemed three-quarters finished. The patient hand of the artist painted on, and the long brush scratched against canvas.

"Ti Malice?"

He didn't move, didn't even nod to acknowledge Weber. In fact, aside from the hand holding the brush, there was a curious stillness about his entire body, as though he were meditating and painting at the same time.

"Excuse me," Weber said loudly. "I'm looking for Ti Malice."

Still the painter painted.

"Hello?"

The man was ignoring him. His arrogance inflamed Weber.

"Hey, I'm talking to you!" He grabbed Ti Malice by the shoulder and spun him around.

Eyeballs rolled up in their sockets until the white showed. The slack mouth drooled a ribbon of saliva.

"What the hell?" Weber dropped his hand and stepped back, aghast.

A low, guttural moan came forth from the loose, wet lips, and then Ti Malice turned slowly, blindly, back to the canvas. The emaciated hand which had never dropped the brush dipped once again into the paint upon his palette and rose to the canvas once more.

Weber made it out of the room, out of the house, but just barely. He bent over, retching noisily between two hibiscus bushes in the yard.

When he was finished, Weber found Sarah waiting for him. She looked at the traces of vomit on his chin and smiled. "Have you found what you were looking for? The great Ti Malice?"

Weber straightened up and wiped his mouth with the back of his hand. "What's wrong with him?" he said. "Is he retarded? Some sort of an idiot savant?

"No. He's a zombie."

Weber's stomach spasmed again but he managed to control it. "That's not possible. There are no zombies."

She waggled a finger at him in reproach. "Who says? You're not in Los Angeles anymore, Mr. Weber. This is Haiti. He is Ti Malice—and Ti Malice is a zombie."

"Oh, come off it. You don't really believe it, do you?"

Sarah gazed at him gravely but said nothing.

"Okay, so you say he's a zombie," Weber said. "Then why haven't you at least told Mrs. Dewey about it? That way she could stop wearing her smelly old magic bag."

Another shrug. "I tried. But she won't believe me. And I can't bring her here: she can't walk anymore." Sarah gave him a sly look. "I've done what you asked, blanc. Brought you to see Ti Malice. You must pay me now."

It was too easy to imagine her melting away into the jungle with his money in her pocket, leaving him here with a drooling, vacant-eyed idiot. "I'll pay you when we're back in town."

Sarah frowned. "Now."

"Half now," Weber said. He handed her some bills. "You get the rest after we're safe in Port-au-Prince."

Reluctantly she nodded.

"Let's go." Weber was eager to get away, to be out of the jungle, far from the sound of that awful scratching brush. He imagined he could still hear it even though he was outside of the house.

As they walked, Weber began to feel better. Soon the house was out of sight and they were most of the way down the hill which led back to town.

Drums, primal and compelling, began to pound from nearby.

"What's that?"

"Vodou," Sarah said. "A *petro*. Blood sacrifice. I might be able to get you in—for a price."

"No!" Weber could imagine the ghastly rites only too well.

"Nothing bad will happen to you. It won't be very expensive. Good price."

"Sarah, if you don't take me back to town right now, I won't pay you the rest of the money."

She stared at him in surprise. "But most blancs want to see the vodou."

"I came here for art, not magic."

"It's a religion, not magic."

"Call it what you want. Just take me back."

"All right, blanc. But you'll pay me what you owe me."

Weber awakened to find sunlight streaming in the open window of his hotel room. The faded drapes danced gently in the breeze, sending motes of dust dancing into the air. A breezy morning to dispel the ugly phantoms of the night. The image of Ti Malice's slack face came into his mind and he shuddered.

A zombie, he thought. The best artist in Haiti is some sort of undead thing that just drools and paints. It made him shiver despite the sunshine and warm breeze, and for a moment he wanted to pack his bags and take the next plane back home. But nobody would believe him in L.A. They would just laugh.

Well, at least it'll make a good story.

Weber dressed carelessly, and didn't bother with breakfast, save for coffee. As he toyed with his half-empty cup, he wondered if he should call somebody about Ti Malice. But who? And tell them what? He didn't even know where that cabin was.

But it's a man's life—an artist—at stake. What should I do?

By nine o'clock he was on the street in the already searing heat, dodging piles of garbage and wondering where to go.

Jean Saint-Mery, that's who he should go see. Yes, he thought, Saint-Mery knew Haiti—hell, he was a native. Besides, Weber didn't know where else to turn.

He passed a green park where a dozen gray geese grazed serenely between the red bougainvillea and pink crape myrtle, but he didn't see them. He passed a group of women singing and swaying in slow rhythm and never heard them. He had but one thought, one goal: find Jean Saint-Mery and do whatever Saint-Mery told him to do.

Rue Charpentier was a narrow street filled with houses shuttered against the hot sunshine. But Weber was in luck: Jean Saint-Mery was just unlocking his gallery door. The dealer, a trim light-skinned black man with a pencil moustache and goatee, gave him a courteous but remote greeting, as though somehow he sensed trouble.

"Can I help you?"

"My name's Weber. I'm a dealer from Los Angeles. I need to talk to you."

Saint-Mery raised a thin eyebrow as he looked him over. "Come in, Mr. Weber," he said, just a beat or two too late.

The gallery was cool, with a scrubbed pine floor and whitewashed walls. To Weber it was a welcome shelter from the merciless morning sunlight.

Saint-Mery settled himself in a padded swivel chair behind a broad oak desk and lit a cigarette. "I'd heard an American dealer was in town," he said. "Why didn't you come to see me right away?"

"I tried calling, but I couldn't get through."

"The famous Haitian phone system." Saint-Mery nodded and blew a cloud of smoke away from Weber. His expression warmed a bit. "Normally, I would be in France by now. But I decided to stay on in Haiti a while longer this year. Sit down. Would you care for some coffee?"

"Please."

Saint-Mery gestured carelessly to a boy lingering in the doorway of the shop. "*Deux cafés au lait. Vite.*"

The child nodded and slinked off out of sight.

"So how is the art market in Los Angeles?"

"Volatile, as always. I have a few regular buyers. Thank God for the movie business and its newly rich who decide they need a big house and art to cover its blank walls."

"Thank all the gods," Saint-Mery said.

The coffee arrived on a wooden tray, bowl-sized cups filled with steaming golden brown liquid. Saint-Mery ground his cigarette butt into half of a coconut shell, handed the boy a coin, and shooed him away.

"You said you had something urgent to discuss?"

"Well, I'm worried about an artist here."

"Who?"

"Ti Malice."

Saint-Mery stared at him as though astonished. "Ah, Ti Malice. Yes. But why would you be worried about him in particular?"

"I saw him, and he's in terrible shape."

"He is?"

"He's been drugged." Weber shook his head helplessly. "I don't know what's going on. Someone told me he was, well, a zombie." He half-expected Saint-Mery to laugh at him. But the dealer merely nodded.

"All this is true. Ti Malice is a zombie. The *houngan* Coicou made him one."

Weber's jaw worked for a moment as though he were searching for a word. "So you know, too?"

"Everybody knows."

"And done nothing?"

"What's to be done?" The dealer seemed genuinely confused.

Weber wanted to put his head down upon the polished surface of the desk and weep. He felt like a ticket-holder who had missed the first act of a play and therefore can't understand anything that follows. "Am I the only person in Haiti who cares that a great artist has become some drug victim? There's nothing supernatural about this. He's not a zombie—he's stoned out of his mind."

"My dear Weber, calm yourself, please." Saint-Mery's voice held a note of pity. "Ti Malice was a strutting peacock, a braggart, a drunkard, and a troublemaker. He gloried in creating difficulties. Many people, myself included, feel he got no more than he deserved." The art dealer nodded sanctimoniously. "Please, drink your coffee before it cools."

"No one, no matter what kind of bastard he is, deserves to be treated that way."

"You mustn't judge unfamiliar things too harshly."

"Do you actually believe in voodoo? In zombies?"

Saint-Mery looked at him as if he were simpleminded. "Of course. I couldn't live here otherwise."

"Do the police believe in it, too?"

"*Everybody* who lives here believes. And visitors are well-advised not to worry about things they don't understand." The dealer's tone was polite but final. Despite his genial expression his dark eyes were cold, and in them Weber saw the rebuttal of every argument or appeal he might make.

"I'm pleased you came to see me," Saint-Mery continued. "How long will you be staying in Haiti?"

"I'm leaving tomorrow."

"Ah. A short visit. Often the best. Why don't you examine my inventory while you're here? I'd be honored to assist you in any way I can."

Dutifully, feeling a bit numb, Weber leafed through the nearest stack of paintings leaning against the wall. "Who's the blue one by?"

"A new artist, quite a fine talent—Henri Damian."

"He's not a zombie?"

Saint-Mery gave a hearty bellow of false laughter. "No, no. The rest of my artists are all quite alive."

After much negotiation and hand-shaking, Weber left Saint-Mery's shop with two small paintings for which he had paid twice as much as they were worth. The acrylics were lively and he would make some sort of profit on them, but they were nothing compared with Ti Malice's work. Not that he would be bringing home any of Ti Malice's paintings, the way things were shaping up.

But the longer he thought about it the less good Weber felt about taking Saint-Mery's advice.

It's a horror, he thought, not just party talk. A life is being destroyed here. And Saint-Mery just condones the whole thing because he makes a profit out of it. But meanwhile Ti Malice slaves away, drugged and half-dead. He can't be a zombie—he's just in some drugged state induced by . . . I don't know what. Toad sweat and puffer fish venom and stuff like that. Eye of newt. Lark's tongue. Goddamn Haiti. Goddamn voodoo.

He stumbled out of Rue Charpentier and up the wide main street that led to the Iron Market. The putrid smell of sewage was appalling, but Weber barely noticed. The street bustled with people hawking their wares and shopping. Despite the din, Weber was oblivious to the merchants and their sagging tires, rusty tin cans, moldy rice, and cheap bright cotton cloth.

"Mister, you want?

"Look here, mister. Here."

"Here, mister, look. You like?"

Their repeated cries finally broke through Weber's fog. He gazed in amazement at the welter of stuff being sold: an entire economy built upon the theory of recycling and contraband. You could buy anything here. Cigarettes. Bottle caps. Pieces of string. Parts of old cars.

Weber froze. You could buy anything you wanted here, he thought. What about a man's freedom?

Oh, right, he told himself. And you'll come riding up with the cavalry, to save him? Come off it. You're no hero. You're a gallery owner in a strange place.

But there's a life at stake.

He rubbed his jaw, feeling sheepish but oddly determined. If he were to try and save Ti Malice, how would he do it? Pay ransom? To whom, Coicou? No. He couldn't imagine negotiating with him.

I'll free him, Weber thought wildly. Yes, I'll break down the door of that hut and bring Ti Malice down from the mountainside to the Albert Schweitzer Clinic. That place was run by Americans. Surely they'll be able to cure him, regardless of the poison Coicou used against him. To keep an artist of his caliber in mindless servitude like that—it was criminal.

It was easier than Weber could have imagined. He told the clerk at his hotel that he wanted to hire a group of strong young men for one night.

The clerk smiled knowingly and nodded. "Twenty dollars," he said.

Sarah wanted twenty-five to lead him back to Ti Malice.

"Your price has gone up," said Weber.

"It's another trip, yes? And you pay me first this time."

▼▼▼

The cabin sat in its pool of light. The tin can lantern still hung by the door.

"Here we are," said Weber. "Inside, quickly."

Ti Malice sat on his pallet in the back room, painting, endlessly painting. The brush and the scenes that sprang into being beneath it were alive, vibrant and glowing. Every stroke painted was confident, even compelling.

"Grab him and let's go."

His assistants stared at one another and, for a moment, Weber feared they would all refuse to help him. But one made a face, another shrugged, and they reached for Ti Malice's arm.

The zombified artist turned slowly, neither resisting nor helping his would-be liberators. He was a dead weight in their arms, motionless save for the hand that held the brush and went on painting upon the open air.

"Hey, he's going to be painting my shirt next," one of the men whispered.

"If he does, save it," said another. "You'll be able to sell it and retire."

It was slow work to carry Ti Malice through the hut and out the door. They had gone perhaps a dozen steps toward a thick stand of palms when a voice rang out.

"Don't move." The voice spoke in Creole and was so coolly authoritative that even Weber froze in his tracks.

A searchlight pinned down each member of the party in turn.

"Coicou," one of the men gasped.

Weber heard the thump of a heavy burden hitting the ground, and the sound of running feet, but he was blinded by the light in his eyes. It took a moment for his vision to clear and another after that to ascertain that he was alone, with Ti Malice, and Coicou. Even Sarah had deserted him.

Coicou's broad face was impassive. Light from his electric torch glinted off the round lenses of his eyeglasses and the brutal barrel of his handgun. "Take Ti Malice back," he said to two of the men with him. "Blanc, you come with me."

Weber's heart began pounding madly. "Where?

"Back to town, of course. Or would you like to stay out here all night?"

"You can't do this."

"I'm not doing anything. Please, lower your voice. People are sleeping nearby."

Coicou led him downhill through scrub brush and thickets of palms, past ghostly huts and shanties, and into a neighborhood filled with well-tended houses and gardens. Expensive cars sat in every driveway.

"Where are we going?" Weber demanded.

"To my house."

Coicou's dwelling was a two-story building with a thatched roof and graceful wrought-iron supports for his balcony. A lantern glowed beside every window, and the path to the front door was lit by torches hanging from curving metal poles.

"Inside, please, Mr. Weber," Coicou said. "The rest of you wait here."

Weber and Coicou were alone in the house. Weber looked around, half expecting to see shrunken heads and animal parts strewn across the floor. Instead, he saw a blue velvet couch, two padded wing chairs, and a glass-topped coffee table upon which sat a marble bust of a Roman emperor. The witch doctor's living room looked like something out of an interior decorator's magazine.

"Look," Weber said. "This is really just a misunderstanding. Can't we talk about it?"

"Sit down," said Coicou. "Would you like a drink?"

Weber badly wanted something to drink, but he eyed the dusty bottle that Coicou held out to him with suspicion. "No."

"Don't be ridiculous. It's a first-rate rum. Take it. You look like you need a hit of alcohol."

A glass was thrust into his hand, half-full of rich amber liquid. Weber took a sip. It tasted like rum, all right. He took a gulp, and another. A small glow kindled in his stomach. He sank down onto the soft cushions of the sofa.

Coicou sat opposite him in one of the wing chairs. He raised his glass in mock salute, and took a generous swallow. "I see you're interested in zombies."

"There's no such thing," Weber said.

"No?" Coicou gave him a shrewd, calculating look. "I suppose your scientists wouldn't say so. They don't believe in vodou."

"Come on, of course they don't. Neither do I."

"Perhaps you'd like a firsthand experience? I'm sure I could convert you." Suddenly Coicou had a golden amulet in his hand. He swung it like a pendulum, back and forth, in steady hypnotic rhythm.

Weber stared, fascinated. It took a great deal of effort to tear his gaze away. "No! Hey, knock it off."

"I think you may believe more than you think you do," Coicou said, sardonically. "But a man should be free to choose his fate, yes?"

"Just like Ti Malice?"

Coicou ignored him. "And I'll give you a choice, Mr. Weber. You caused me much trouble just now, and I've half a mind to make a zombie out of you and be done with it."

"Please, God, don't. . . ."

"I thought you didn't believe in it?"

"What's there to believe in?" Weber cried. Despite his terror, sweat ran down his face. "A bunch of transplanted African mumbo jumbo accompanied by drums and aerobics in the night? That man, Ti Malice, he's suffering from a nerve poison, that's all. I read about that zombie stuff in the newspaper. He needs a doctor. A real doctor, not some witch doctor."

Coicou wasn't smiling any longer. "My beliefs are my concern," he said. "Don't be so quick to criticize what you don't understand. Besides, Ti Malice brought it upon himself."

"How? What did he do, anyway, that was so terrible?"

"He mocked my family. Despite my warnings, he wouldn't stop. And he was a public nuisance, always drunk, picking fights. Finally, he angered the *loas*—the gods."

"What did he do to you?"

"It's none of your concern. Besides, if I were you, I would be worried about my own fate just now."

Despite the night's humidity and the liquor's warmth, Weber felt icy cold begin to creep up from his toes along his feet and legs, toward his heart.

"As I said," Coicou continued. "I really should turn you into a zombie, too. To punish you for your meddling. But I think there's an alternative. One that will please me even more." And he grinned broadly, displaying a mouthful of perfect white teeth. "We'll be partners."

"In what?"

"We'll split the profits fifty/fifty," Coicou said. "And a resourceful blanc like you should do very well with this."

Weber pulled back deeper into the cushions. "What the hell are you talking about?"

"Ti Malice's paintings. You wanted to buy them, Mr. Weber. That's why you came down here. You may have them. All you want. Take a planeload home with you to Los Angeles and build a new vogue for him."

"I don't want his work anymore."

"But you'll take it, nonetheless."

"And if I don't."

Coicou said nothing, merely swung the pendulum until it glittered in the lamplight.

▼▼▼

The Weber Gallery was aglow and golden, each towering floral centerpiece in place, every wineglass polished, every bottle iced and waiting for the opening of "Caribbean Spice."

At six sharp, Weber unlocked the doors for his guests. They glittered with jewelry and fine silks dyed in jewel tones. Like a group of chattering tropical parrots they filled the room, eager to see, to buy, to be seen buying.

As though in a dream, Weber wandered among his customers, listening to them ooh and aah.

"Fabulous."

"I love the color."

"God, they're so free with their work. Their lives are so natural, much more in touch with the basics than ours."

"David! Buddy, this is great." It was Fred Lovell, the well-heeled producer. "I had no idea this work by Tu Malice—"

"Ti Malice," Weber said.

"Right, Ti. Anyway, I didn't know his stuff would be so exciting. You sure know how to pick 'em."

Weber smiled wanly. "Thanks, Fred."

"I can't resist it. I shouldn't do it, but I've gotta have some. Especially that one with the red angels in it."

"A marvelous choice," Weber said, a bit too heartily. "I'll just put a red dot on it. And Fred, I've got an even better painting to show you, one I hung with you in mind."

Docile with two glasses of champagne in him, Lovell followed him across the room. "Really? Wow." He gawked at the white, green, and gold canvas, which showed a voodoo ritual taking place. "It's terrific. I'll take this one, too." He patted Weber on the jaw. "Babe, you always know what I like."

Weber smiled his party smile and made a note on his inventory sheet.

"What's that necklace you're wearing, Dave?"

Weber touched the small rawhide bag on its leather cord. He fingered the bag lightly, twice. "This? Just something I picked up in Haiti."

Lovell sniffed loudly. "Boy, I'll bet it keeps the mosquitoes away."

"Among other things."

Before the night was over, red dots had sprouted next to almost every painting in the gallery. Weber gazed at them, bleary-eyed from writing sales receipts. The show was a huge success.

Guests crowded around him, patting him on the back and shaking his hand.

"Terrific party, Dave!"

"You've really got an eye for art."

"Dave, it's another winning show. You always know where to find the best talent, don't you?"

"What's your secret? Magic?"

Weber knew he was surrounded, everybody yammering congratulations at him. But instead of the crowd he heard only one sound, the slow scratch of brush against canvas. Instead of the gallery walls,

Weber saw a man's dark emaciated hand locked in a death grip around a paintbrush, constantly moving. The brush against the canvas, the blind eyes, the slack, drooling mouth.

"Yeah," Weber said. "Black magic."

SURPRISE

RICK HAUTALA

YOUR wife Ann found you sometime after midnight, out behind the toolshed. You were sitting with your legs pulled up tightly against your chest. There was an empty whiskey bottle beside you, but you hadn't drunk it all. You must have knocked it over with your knee or something.

Make no mistake; you had been drinking earlier that evening.

Plenty.

It was all part of your Double-A program to help you deal with what was happening in your life.

Double-A . . . avoidance and alcohol.

A good *solution,* if you'll excuse the horrible pun.

But you'd been dealing with a lot of shit that—well, you used to joke with your wife that it would have broken a lesser man, and honest to Christ—sometimes you wonder how you hung in there for so long.

In the span of six months—no, actually, it was less than six months—you lost your job, your mother died, and the bank, which had been making some not so nice noises before, began foreclosure on your house.

You had plenty of life insurance, back from when the money in real estate was good, and quite honestly, you had considered suicide a few times . . . usually at night, when you'd lay there in bed, staring up at the ceiling and wondering where the money was gonna come from for all those bills.

Shit, yes—it would have broken a lesser man, but you religiously practiced your Double-A method, and by Christ, it worked!

Up to a point.

You were getting calls from the bank just about every day, asking when you were going to pay up the last six months' mortgage—with late charges—and what you intended to do about your current financial situation. You told that asshole in collections, Karen what's-her-face, that you were doing every goddamn thing you could think of, but *she* should try supporting a family of four on next to nothing.

You had cashed in everything—your retirement account, what was left of your inheritance, and the few valuable antiques you and your wife had acquired over the years. Day after day, you went through the classifieds until your hands were black with smudged ink, but—well, shit, you don't care what they say about the economy in the rest of the country, up here in Maine there aren't a whole lot of jobs that pay what you need.

And quite a bit of what little money you did have went into your Double-A program.

Why the fuck not?

In your private moments—and you tried like hell not to grind Ann on this—you often wondered why she didn't get the fuck out there and find a job herself. She'd remind you of how she hadn't had a job in better than five years, and the job she used to have at the electronics factory had become computerized, so she would have had to go back to school before she'd be able to jump back into the work force.

What did you expect, anyway, that she'd go out and get a job bagging groceries at the local Shop 'n Save?

Between the two of you, you might have been able to make enough to scrape by a little while longer, but you needed considerably more than a minimum wage paycheck to meet your bills. Besides, who was going to stay home with the kids?

Or were you supposed to put one whole grocery-bagging paycheck toward day care?

But tonight—Christ, you finally reached your limit. You couldn't help it.

What started out as a casual conversation with your wife about your finances set you off, but good. Was it too much of one A and not enough of the other? Or maybe there was a third A you needed—a little more ass! What with all the stress you'd been under, you were staying awake so late at night that you never felt like having sex anymore.

But maybe that's *exactly* what you needed.

Beats the shit out of you!

Anyway, you lost it real bad and started yelling at your wife, berating her for all of your problems. Then, when Sally, your six-year-old, wandered into the living room, you started screaming at her to get her butt upstairs to bed.

Damn, you were so mad, you threw the book you were reading against the wall, and it knocked the photograph of your wife's parents' wedding day off the mantel. It hit the floor, smashing the frame and glass to pieces.

That's when Ann lost control.

You had told her that you hadn't wanted even to talk, so it wasn't your fault, but now you'd done something to set her off. Rather than keep the shouting match going, you stormed out into the kitchen, grabbed the nearly full bottle of whiskey from the counter, and walked on out the door, making sure to slam it shut hard behind you.

Fuming and sputtering with curses, you went out across the backyard to the toolshed where you sat down, leaned back against the building, and just stared off at the dark line of trees bordering your property.

God*damn*, you were pissed!

Rage filled you as you spun off the bottle cap and took several long slugs of whiskey. Your heart was punching like a piston against your ribs, and you hoped the booze would help calm you down.

After a while, your breathing slowed, and you felt at least a little bit at peace. Bats or some kind of night birds were darting back and forth across the powdery gray of the star-filled sky. All around you, the night seemed to throb with a weird purplish glow. You focused hard on the solid black line of trees until your vision began to blur. In the tangled lines of branches and leaves, you imagined you saw silhouettes of faces and the cold fire of eyes, staring back at you.

You knew you were losing your mind, but you didn't care.

You were pissed!

Fed up!

So what if you lost your fucking mind. You'd lost everything else, so who gave a shit?

Once or twice you checked your watch, but after a while you lost track of time. You were still fuming with rage. At some point you became aware of a deep, hard throbbing in your neck. At first, you were only mildly worried, but then, as the pain grew steadily stronger and sharper, you started to panic. A cold, deep ache shot down your left arm and up underneath your chin like you'd been cold-cocked a good one.

It didn't take long to figure out what was happening.

You were having a heart attack.

No fucking wonder!

Your breathing came hard and fast, and the icy pain spread like an evil touch throughout your chest and shoulders. You wanted to stand up but were suddenly afraid.

Shit, you didn't want to die, but you didn't even have the strength to call out to Ann for help.

You were fucked and you knew it, but suddenly, like a bubble bursting, you no longer cared.

You realized that this was probably what you had been looking for all along—an escape from all your problems; and this way, you didn't have to commit suicide, so your family would be able to collect the life insurance money.

So why not just go with it?

Ride it to the end.

You didn't even blink your eyes as you cocked your head back and stared up at the night sky. It was pulsating with dull energy, and seemed at times to shift into two gigantic, dark hands that reached out to grab you. They wrapped around you, and then began to squeeze tighter and tighter.

Go with it—you kept telling yourself—*Just go with it!*

You thought of a few things you would miss—especially watching the kids grow up—but you knew that the heart attack was too strong and had gone on for far too long. Numbing pain gripped you tighter, like cold, pressing waves.

Go with it! . . . Just go with it!

And then from somewhere deep inside your head, you heard—honest to God, you heard what sounded like a thick piece of wood, snapping in half. Sound, pain, and light exploded inside you. You vaguely sensed your legs kicking out in front of you as you stiffened and desperately clutched at your chest. Then, in one final, hard convulsion, you pulled your legs back up to your chest and sat there like a fetus, willing the night to take you all the way down.

Only it didn't happen that way.

You were frozen, lost in an impenetrable darkness, but you were still horribly alert and aware of the world around you. The intense pain was still there, too, as strong as ever; but you were somehow distanced from it, as though it was just the memory of pain. All around you, you could hear the soft sighing of the breeze in the trees, the rasping flutter of unseen wings, the gentle hissing of the lawn, and something else that sounded like someone crying . . . or laughing.

You were convinced that you were dead, and you just sat there, waiting for the darkness to pull you all the way down.

But that didn't happen.

Just at the edge of awareness, you heard something else—the soft thud of approaching footsteps.

Someone was coming!

Was it your wife . . . or someone else?

You struggled to open your eyes.

Or maybe your eyes were already open, and you had blown out something inside your brain and had gone blind.

It didn't matter.

It wasn't simply that you were frozen and couldn't move; you couldn't even *feel* your body. You were nothing more than a tiny spark of awareness, suspended in an endless, black void; but soon, that void was filled with a shouting voice. Through the confusion, you finally recognized your wife's voice, frantically shouting to someone that she had found you and to call the rescue unit.

You wanted desperately to move, to say something to her, to indicate that it was all right—that you were content to be dead and drifting far, far away. Everything was all right, and maybe everything would be all right for her, now, too. You struggled to open your eyes or your mouth to give her a sign, but you simply couldn't.

Her footsteps thundered like drums in your ears as she came up close to you. Her presence was a pulsating, burning heat that touched your mind as much as your body, and you were instantly aware that she *was* what you needed—she was warm, human flesh.

A misery and longing as deep and painful as anything you'd ever experienced before filled you, and the darkness embracing you throbbed with a groundswell rush of deep, blood red. You knew—absolutely—that you were dead, but you also realized that you'd been like this for a long time . . . for a *very* long time.

And you knew what you had to do next to dull that overpowering surge of loneliness welling up inside you.

You couldn't believe how loud your wife screamed when you opened your eyes!

THIS ONE'LL KILL YOU

BRIAN HODGE AND WILLIAM RELLING JR.

IF Jack Meehoff had been a better comedian, he never would have ended up at the Croghan Brothers Mortuary.

Meehoff's problem was that he just wasn't funny. Rather, that was *half* of his problem. He wasn't funny, but he remained convinced that he was. Despite overwhelming evidence to the contrary.

He was booed at the Comedy Store in Hollywood by a predominately gay audience for telling an AIDS joke that he happened to have stolen from another comic: "Did you hear about the millions Liberace's ex-lover was asking for, just 'cause they'd had sex after Liberace got sick? Hell, for a million bucks, I'd fuck Liberace right now. You meet me at the cemetery with a shovel and a check, and we'll talk deal. . . ."

He was hissed at the Ice House in Pasadena by a largely female gathering for a joke from the point of view of a man who'd had a sex change operation: "It didn't hurt when they sliced off my nuts. What hurt was when they cut out half my brain."

He was chased off the stage at Igby's in West L.A. by a group of Saudi businessmen and their dates for a joke about their sexual proclivities: "What do you call an Italian virgin? A girl who can outrun her brothers. What do you call a Greek virgin? A boy who can outrun *his* brothers. What do you call an Arab virgin? A fast camel."

Soon, no comedy club in Los Angeles would allow Meehoff near its doors. His photograph was circulated among the owners, like that of a card sharp haunting casinos in Las Vegas. As another comedian said, they wouldn't touch him with a ten-meter cattle prod.

But Meehoff remained confident of his talent, even though he possessed neither wit nor sensitivity, timing nor decent material. What he did have was a legally changed name, which he thought was screamingly funny, and a big mouth, which was large enough to accommodate a pair of Buster Browns at once, Howard Stern should be so lucky. But those dubious attributes weren't enough to get him work as a stand-up, so he answered an ad in the Hollywood *Reporter*. And ended up with a job as a janitor, working the night shift at the Croghan Brothers Mortuary on the corner of Melrose and Vermont.

He arrived promptly at eleven o'clock his first night, a Sunday, letting himself in through a rear door with a key provided by the younger of the Croghan brothers. Meehoff stood just inside the door, letting his eyes wander about the mortuary's back corridors.

"Yo!" he called out. "Anybody alive around here?"

He tapped his foot impatiently. When they'd offered him the job, the Croghans had explained to him that he would not have the place to himself. Were he not so strapped for cash, the news might have caused him to tell the Brothers Croghan to Take This Job and Shove It, thank you very much, Johnny Paycheck. It was humiliating enough to be a janitor. But the notice in the *Reporter* had contained a slight omission. The God of Comics on the Rise had decreed. Not janitor. *Assistant* janitor.

Meehoff heard a wet grumble of a cough. Human, he decided. Alive, but just barely.

A moment later, a sour little troll of a man shuffled into view, emerging from a room up the corridor. *Wonderful*, thought Meehoff. Imagine Walter Brennan crossed with a Munchkin.

The troll wore a ring of keys like a six-shooter. He had flyaway white hair that made Albert Einstein's look as if he'd been coiffed by Vidal Sassoon. The troll trudged down the corridor, carrying a mop. He stopped inches from Meehoff's face and looked him over from stem to stern.

"Meehoff?" grunted the troll.

"Soitainly," Meehoff answered, giving it his finest Curly Howard inflection.

"Mmmmpf," grunted the troll. He uncorked his mouth of a stubby, wet cigar. Unlit. "I'm Kramer. Did the necro-feelie brothers give you the nickel tour, or what?"

"Every penny of it."

"Then you know where the embalming room is." Kramer unceremoniously popped the cigar back into place and thrust the mop into Meehoff's grip. "It needs this."

Meehoff's face squinched into a grimace. "What's the problem?" he asked. "Are there, like, guts and stuff all over the floor?"

"Real funny," Kramer grunted. He spun around on his chubby little feet and waddled away. The keys attached to his belt jangled like a cowbell. Before he disappeared through the door from which he'd emerged, he turned back to Meehoff. "Rule Number One," he barked, jabbing his cigar emphatically. *"Don't* fuck with the stiffs."

"Don't fuck with the stiffs," Meehoff whispered to himself once the little man was out of sight. "There go *my* plans for the evening."

With a sigh, he dragged the mop behind him along an intersecting corridor to the embalming room. There he found a bucket-on-wheels contraption with a lever-action ringer mounted on the side. The bucket was filled with lukewarm, soapy water. *Damned considerate of old Yoda back there,* Meehoff thought.

He submerged the mop into the water, then paused, leaning on the handle. No call to get too quick a start on the new vocation, he decided. Take a few minutes to scope the place out.

There wasn't much to see. A couple of stainless steel slabs with drainage gutters—very nice. Racks of waxes and cremes and makeup—fun stuff there, no question. Nasty-looking tools that no doubt originally had been invented for use by Torquemada—a party guy if ever there was one. And best of all . . .

. . . the corpses. In progress.

They lay on gurneys that lined the wall. Some were dressed in Sunday finery. Others were considerably less dignified. *Looks like room service for cannibals,* Meehoff said to himself.

Then he broke into a goofy grin. *At last,* he thought happily. *An audience. . . .*

The mop handle became a microphone. "Hey, thanks for coming out tonight. You folks ready for a good time? Thank you, thank you. Hey? How did the necrophiliac's wife catch on to what he was doing? Give up? He came home with formaldehyde on his breath!"

He cheered, "Yeeeeeaaaaaaaaaaaaahhhhhhh! No, no, please hold your applause. Here's an oldie but moldy for you. Two skeletons meet in a bar. One turns to the other and says, 'Who was that zombie I saw you with last night?' And the other one says—all together now—'THAT WAS NO ZOMBIE! THAT WAS MY GHOUL-FRIEND!' Yaaaaaaaaaaaaaaaaahhh! Thank you, thank you very much."

Silence.

I gotta hand it to you, Jack, Meehoff told himself. *You're really knockin' 'em dead.*

So it went for the rest of the night. And the night after that. And the night after that. And by Wednesday, Meehoff had decided that this job bored the ass off of him.

It was time to start having a little fun.

On Wednesday night he came to work early, purposely arriving ahead of Kramer, who always showed up at the mortuary precisely at 10:45, rain or shine. Kramer had made a point of emphasizing his own punctuality the night before, when Meehoff had shown up a lousy seven minutes late. Was it his fault the motherfuggin' battery in his twelve-year-old Pinto had decided to conk out? That it had taken him fifteen minutes to scare up a neighbor who owned a pair of jumper cables?

Kramer didn't want to hear about it. "Rule Number Two." Another jab of the slimy cigar. "*Don't* be late for work." End of discussion.

Meehoff was there plenty early on Wednesday night. Early enough to rig a little surprise for Kramer and have it in place by the time the troll-man appeared.

Which he did, right on time. Meehoff was standing nonchalantly outside the door to Kramer's "office," a tiny, cramped closet that the janitor had converted to his private use. Kramer had managed to squeeze a lawn chair, a floor lamp, a small refrigerator and a portable black-and-white television into a space not much larger than a horse's stall. Meehoff imagined that Kramer spent many hours in there chugging bottles of Mickey's Big Mouth and whacking off to the nudie centerfolds he had taped over every square inch of the closet's walls. One brief look inside was enough to confirm Meehoff's opinion that Kramer wasn't exactly the classiest guy since Cary Grant to come down the pike.

Kramer saw him lounging outside the door. "You wanna see me about somethin'?" the janitor grumbled.

Meehoff smiled innocently. "I'm not here collecting for the Red Cross."

"Real funny," grunted Kramer as he pushed open the door . . . and immediately wet his dungarees.

Because there in the doorway, Meehoff had propped up Mr. Spinoza. Whose age at time of his passing from emphysema was 76 years, and whose body was tall and gaunt and emaciated. Whose flesh was a pasty, blue-tinged white, since he'd not yet been made up to go on display the day after tomorrow before his grieving relatives and friends. Who had been embalmed only that afternoon. Who was board-stiff and grim-countenanced and as naked as the day he'd come into the world. Who was very. Very. Dead.

Kramer stood there in shock, hopping from foot to foot. He blubbered, a low, terrified moaning that sounded to Meehoff like a bad impersonation of Jackie Gleason: "Hubbeda-hubbeda-hubbeda . . ."

Meehoff fell to the floor, convulsed with laughter. Kramer swung around to glare at him, opening his mouth to cry out in rage. Until he became aware of the damp stain spreading at his crotch, let out a tiny, self-conscious "Eek," and ran away in the direction from whence he'd come, covering his privates with his hands.

It took several minutes for Meehoff to compose himself enough to come to his feet. He was wiping tears from his eyes as he stepped over to Mr. Spinoza. Laying a friendly hand on the corpse's shoulder he said, "You did great, old buddy. Would that every joke of mine worked so well."

As he carried Mr. Spinoza back to the embalming room, Meehoff told himself that he was undoubtedly going to catch no small ration of holy hell once Kramer had changed into dry clothes. But, he said to himself, it was worth it. *Boy,* was it worth it.

He was surprised, then, that Kramer left him alone the entire night. Not that Meehoff minded; he had no masochistic desire to get chewed out. He knew that Kramer had returned; he had heard the sound of the television through the closed door of Kramer's "office" around three that morning, after he'd worked up the nerve to check out whether or not the old man had come back.

When Meehoff's shift ended at 7:30 A.M., he left for home. Not once during the shift had Kramer sought him out. Probably too embarrassed to face him, Meehoff decided, even if it was to read him the riot act.

But when the next night began the same way—Kramer ignoring him, not bothering at all to check up on what he was doing—Meehoff became annoyed. Like any performer, he knew that the worst reaction he could get from an audience was indifference. Laughs were best, of course. But jeers, groans, hisses, catcalls . . . any of those were preferable to being disregarded. Love me, hate me, just don't ignore me. In a perverse way, he was beginning to feel cheated that Kramer *didn't* ream him. Kramer's initial reaction to the Mr. Spinoza joke had been priceless. But until the janitor completed the circle by exploding at Meehoff, the joke hadn't received its full payoff.

So, Meehoff told himself, *let's push the envelope a little bit more, shall we?*

His half-hour meal break came at 2:30 A.M. Meehoff left Croghan Brothers and drove home. On his way back to work, he stopped off at a 7-Eleven store three blocks east of the mortuary, on Melrose. Meehoff told himself it was an omen, as not only did the convenience store stay open twenty-four hours, but they had exactly what he was looking for.

Back at the mortuary, Meehoff worked feverishly to finish his regular chores before commencing his special project. Finally he was able to get started on it, shortly before 5:00 A.M. It took him an hour and a half to get everything ready.

At 6:45 he was standing outside Kramer's "office." He took a deep breath. Then he was pounding on the door and shouting excitedly. "Mr. Kramer, Mr. Kramer! You gotta come down to the embalming room *right away*!" He ran off quickly, before Kramer could answer the door.

Five minutes later, Kramer anxiously pushed open the door to the embalming room. And was sonically slapped in the face: Kris-Kross doing "Jump" at very high volume, erupting from the ghetto blaster that Meehoff had brought from home and set up on one of the stainless steel slabs in the middle of the room. Hanging across the back wall was a multicolored banner: "CONGRATULATIONS!" Coiled streamers cascaded from the ceiling. Each of the half-dozen corpses in the room had been propped up on their gurneys, and each wore a party hat tilted at a jaunty angle. Each had a noisemaker wedged between cold lips and a bottle of embalming fluid gripped between stiff fingers.

And there was Meehoff, wearing a party hat of his own. In one hand he held a Budweiser long-neck, in the other a plastic horn. He tooted the horn and called out joyously, "Join the party, Mr. Kramer! We're celebrating! My five-day anniversary with the firm!"

Kramer stood in the doorway, eyes wide, ready to burst an artery. His jaw was clamped shut, and his face turned ever-deepening shades of scarlet. His head was a bright red balloon, the skin stretching and straining as it expanded, filling with explosive air. Until it was just about ready to pop.

Then he spun around on his pudgy feet, scooted out of the doorway, and was gone.

Meehoff frowned at the empty doorway. He reached over and switched off the ghetto blaster. He stepped to the nearest occupied gurney: the body of an obese, elderly black man whose slack skin had turned from chocolate-brown to a dull, dark shade of gray. Meehoff looked to the corpse sullenly. "I guess some people just have no sense of humor," he said. He poked the dead man in the belly, and the noisemaker in the corpse's mouth gave a thin, weary bleat.

Meehoff had the room back to its proper condition by the time he was to clock out. Kramer did not return. Shrugging, Meehoff left the mortuary and went home.

He spent the weekend anticipating a call from one or the other of the Brothers Croghan. Kramer surely could not allow his behavior to go unreported. A part of Meehoff felt like kicking himself for being such a smartass and getting fired from a job that he genuinely needed. But another part was relieved. He decided that the subconscious motivation for his practical jokes had been a desire to get out. After all, mopping floors in a mortuary all night long was a mighty dull occupation.

But the call never came, and on Sunday night Meehoff drove back to the mortuary, telling himself: *What the hell, a job's a job.*

He parked in the lot behind the mortuary and walked to the rear door. As he was reaching for his key, he happened to look up. Taped to the door was an envelope with his name printed on it. Inside the envelope Meehoff found a typed memo from Croghan the Younger. It seemed that Mr. Kramer had taken ill suddenly over the weekend and had been admitted to Hollywood Presbyterian Hospital. There were no details concerning the nature of Kramer's illness, but the memo did say that until further notice Jack Meehoff was to be head janitor of the Croghan Brothers Mortuary.

How 'bout that, he thought. *Only one week on the job, already I got a promotion.*

Included with the memo were instructions for a specific assignment he was to complete that night in addition to his other duties. The Croghans wanted him to take inventory of the number and types of coffins they had in a storage room in the mortuary's subbasement. Kramer was to have done it himself, the memo implied, but the old man wasn't going to be available for a while. The job was now Meehoff's.

This, Meehoff told himself, was seriously uncool. All work and no play made Jack a dull boy, and he'd been feeling in enough of a rut as it was. It was Kramer's revenge, he decided. Double his workload. Meehoff hoped the old boy would choke on his lime Jell-O.

But since he was a firm believer in the principle that tackling your most unpleasant task first makes everything else a downhill coast, Meehoff made up his mind to get the inventory job out of the way. He let himself into the mortuary and made a quick stop by the embalming room. Pity. A full house, but no time for a floor show tonight.

He waved an apologetic greeting. "Sorry, folks," he told them regretfully. "Tonight's show has been pre-empted, and Elvis *has* left the building."

Meehoff departed the embalming room and headed for the subbasement. As he descended, he told himself that he might as well have been heading into the Bowels of Hell, as far down as it seemed to go. The least the Croghans could have done was given him a key to the freight elevator that they used to bring the coffins up. But *nooo-ooooooo*.

In the storage room Meehoff found a clipboard and inventory sheets lying atop the coffin nearest the door leading to the main corridor of the subbasement. Sighing heavily, he went to work.

By the time he was twenty minutes into his task, terminal ennui had set in. *What an absurd fucking job*, Meehoff thought darkly. Coffins, Go-carts for dead people. Did anybody really give two squats about makes and models of *coffins*, f'Christ's sake? The proud owner got a couple of days' public use out of the goddamn thing, then boom. Out of sight, out of mind. A pine box would have been just as practical and a sight less pricey.

He was logging numbers into their appropriate columns on the inventory sheet, when he halted in mid-scribble. Like a tap on the forehead by the Fickle Finger of the God of Comics on the Rise, it came. An idea, full-blown, burst upon Meehoff's warped imagination. The *coup de grace*. The finishing stroke. The perfect welcoming reception for Mr. Kramer for when he returned to work.

Meehoff frowned, feeling a momentary pang of guilt. He hoped that the old troll hadn't gone into the hospital for treatment of a heart condition. Oh please oh please oh pleeeeeeeeeeease make it not be true. Because this idea was simply too good to pass up.

Meehoff rested the clipboard on top of a coffin. He leaned against the shiny, oblong box, thinking. He shut his eyes and let the sweet fantasy play out in his mind.

Talk the Croghan Brothers into furnishing him with a key to the freight elevator. Arrive an hour earlier than the triumphantly returning Kramer. Bring up the darkest, most foreboding coffin he could find. Rest it in the hallway directly outside the door to Kramer's "office." Don his finest suit and buy some theatrical makeup to create the appropriate visage: a nice, ghastly, mottled blue-and-gray, that's the ticket. Then settle into the coffin, close the lid, and patiently await the approach of footfalls and the cowbell-jangle of keys. Wait for the footsteps to come to a halt. Listen for the old man's curses and questions. And then . . . slowly . . . raise the lid. And sit up. And smile. *How's it goin', Mr. Kramer? Hope you're feelin' in the pink again* . . .

Yes. Oh *yes.* It would be a classic redefining of the term "Jack-in-the-Box."

Meehoff tried to resume his inventory, but it was a hopeless endeavor. With all of those coffins lying around, he felt like the proverbial kid in a candy store. Which one to choose? he wondered. Which one?

He found it lying against the back wall. A coffin elegant enough for Dracula himself. Gleaming, blacker than a new hearse, adorned with silver rails and trim. Morbidly gothic, the most gorgeous thing Meehoff had ever beheld. It was perfect.

To hell with the rest of the inventory. It would be foolish of him to borrow one of these babies without having tried it on for size.

The lid opened in two pieces, top half and bottom. The inside of the box was lined with billowy, white silk. Just waiting to caress its deceased occupant like a bed of dreams. Meehoff slipped out of his shoes—mustn't track in a mess now, must we?—and climbed into the coffin. He lay down, resting his head on a satin pillow. His bed at home should be so comfortable, he told himself. Not much of a view, though. Only a glimpse of the bare concrete of the ceiling and the end of a flickering fluorescent bulb. Still it was a better view than its eventual permanent occupant would have.

Meehoff sat up to close the bottom-half lid, then reached for the top half, pulling it with him as he lay back down. The lid shut with a final-sounding chunk, and he found himself surrounded by darkness.

As he snuggled himself into the plush lining, Meehoff pictured the look on Kramer's face as he pulled off this grandest of jokes. Oh yes, the old boy would do far more than wee-wee in his Fruit of the Looms this time, yes indeedy-do.

But, Meehoff wondered, would he be able to hear Kramer's approach? It would be a shame if the box were so well-constructed that it was soundproof or nearly so. He decided to make a test.

Holding his breath, he strained his ears, listening for the hum and flow of the building's ventilation system. There it was. He could hear the muffled sound of the air conditioner and the faint rumble of wind blowing through the ductwork. He could hear it just fine . . . and he could hear something else as well.

Holy Jumping Jesus, he whispered to himself. Talk about the power of the imagination.

Meehoff decided he was simply more worked up about this than he'd first realized. While trying to imagine Kramer's footsteps, he'd actually begun to *hear* them. Tiny, slapping footfalls, muffled by the lid of the coffin. Accompanied by a jingle-jing of keys.

Then came a sound that could not have been imagination. It was the immense squealing of hinges, a huge door swinging shut with a heavy slam. Meehoff threw open the upper-half lid, sat up and whirled around to see the door to the subbasement shuddering in its frame.

He was scrambling from the coffin even as he knew he'd be too late. Just as his feet were hitting the chilly floor, he heard the sound of a key scraping in the lock to the thick door. He sprinted across the room, reached the door, and twisted its handle anxiously. The handle would not budge.

"Awright, Kramer!" Meehoff cried out, pounding the door. "You win! Chalk one up for you! Just lemme out, okay?"

He paused.

Wait a minute, Meehoff thought. Kramer was supposed to be in the hospital, wasn't he? The Croghans wouldn't make that up, would they? Which meant that whoever had locked him in wasn't Kramer, but was . . .

Naaaah. It had to be Kramer. It had to be.

Not them.

Meehoff began to shout again. He pounded on the door to no avail. He paused for a time to press an ear to the wood, and he thought that he could hear slow, receding footsteps moving away, down the corridor of the subbasement until they faded to nothing.

Meehoff sagged to the floor. He didn't like this, not one bit. Trapped underground in a cold, cold room. No telling what vermin lurked in the shadowed corners. Spiderwebs that he hadn't noticed before were now visible with excruciating clarity. He fancied that he heard the scurrying of insects along the floor and the chittering of rats within the walls. The soft whistle of damp winds that caressed the bones of those who'd been left to rot in the subbasement's secret passages.

Meehoff possessed a vivid imagination, and tonight he was imagining it all.

What to do, he begged himself, *what to do. . . .*

Then, gradually, he brightened. Why, what else? In the face of peril . . . *laugh*. What was that old saying? Laugh and the world laughs with you. Die and . . . well, never mind.

Meehoff crawled back to where he'd left his shoes. He slipped them back on and tied the laces with shaking fingers. He came to his feet and looked around. And he smiled.

It's show time.

He addressed the stacks of coffins, trying to mask the quiver of desperation in his voice. "Hey hey, thanks for coming out tonight, folks!" Reminding himself of the famous show-biz adage. How do you conquer stage fright? Imagine that your audience is stark naked. And, if necessary, imagine that you've even *got* an audience.

He reached over and heaved the bottom lid of the black coffin up and down. "Welcome to tonight's Grand Opening! Yeaaaaaahhh! Whoa! Are you guys a buncha stiffs out there, or what? Talk about a wooden crowd! AHAHAHAHAHAHA!"

He did Liberace. He did the sex-change operation. He did the Arab virgin. Twice. Three times even. He did every joke he'd ever stolen. There was nothing but the sound of his own voice, followed by his laughter slapping off the concrete walls in an overlapping echo.

But he remained resolutely sane. He kept it up until he exhausted himself thoroughly, and then he dragged himself into the black coffin and fell hard asleep.

Meehoff awoke some time later to an unmistakable series of sounds. The unlatching of the storage room door. The turn of the handle. The squeak of hinges. He sat up in the coffin and looked. The door was hanging open a few inches, beckoning him.

Though he was groggy and disoriented, Meehoff's body clock told him that it was morning. Near dawn, he guessed. He'd been down here all night. Whoever the hell had locked him in must've decided that the joke was over.

But it ain't over till it's over, he told himself grimly. *Not till* Jack Meehoff *says it's over.*

He climbed out of the coffin, stepped carefully toward the door, and moved out into the corridor. It was deserted. Not a sound filtered down from upstairs.

Meehoff padded to the end of the corridor and spiraled up the endless stairs that led from the subbasement to ground level. Thinking: *All right, motherfucker, where are you?*

He searched stealthily, as if stalking prey.

The hallways. Empty.

The lounge and the parlors. Empty.

Kramer's "inner sanctum." Empty.

At last he came to the embalming room. He pushed the door open, took a few steps inside, and froze. His eyes became very large.

Because the corpses were all on their feet, watching him. Standing up unassisted. Look ma, no hands. No wires. No nets.

Meehoff's frayed nerves crackled. He wanted badly to scream.

Here they were, the bodies of the dear departed. A teenage boy whose head had been cratered in a car wreck. A matronly sort whose flabby torso was crosshatched with the crude stitches of a Y-shaped autopsy incision. An old scarecrow of a man whose body was a crinkled map of melanoma scars. A young woman bearing a wide knife wound between her once-splendid breasts. A veritable parade march of death. All watching *him* watching *them*.

Meehoff commanded himself: *Feets do yo' duty. . . .*

But he couldn't move. It was as if a giant, invisible hand held him tightly, restraining him. He couldn't even twitch.

Then he saw Kramer. The stubby old janitor was sitting atop a desk in the far corner of the room, his ever-present unlit cigar jammed between his lips. He hopped down from the desk and paced forward, coming to Meehoff.

Tucked under one arm Kramer had a huge, fat book, as big as a pulpit Bible. The cover was made of cracked, ancient, black leather. Inked on its spine were intricately arcane symbols in a language that Meehoff had never seen before. The troll-man came to a halt before him. Kramer removed the cigar slowly, savoring it. He looked up at the statue-stiff Meehoff and said, "I guess you figured out by now that note was really from me, huh?"

Because his mouth would not move, Meehoff couldn't reply.

Kramer went on. "Y'know, one of the great things about livin' in L.A. is that you can find just about anything you want in this town, if you look for it hard enough. A book of Jamaican obeah spells? Took me two days to track one down . . ." He looked over his shoulder to the corpses and barked an unintelligible phrase which sounded to Meehoff like a cross between a gargle and a backward-masked heavy-metal lyric.

The corpses began to walk.

Stolidly they shuffled about the room, retrieving various tools of the embalming trade. Then they were coming toward Meehoff, who remained riveted to the floor.

Kramer stepped away as the ancient cancer patient shambled up, bearing a huge scalpel. "You're a funny guy, ain't cha," the dead man rasped, swinging the scalpel and hacking a divot out of Meehoff's cheek. The other corpses hooted with laughter.

"He's a real cutup!" piped the young woman.

"You were told not to disturb us customers, weren't you, dear?" chastised the bloated matron. To Meehoff her voice sounded vaguely like June Cleaver's. She was shaking her head in disappointed sorrow. The effort caused her to pop several stitches.

Taking the old man's place directly was the auto-crash victim. The teenager was holding a monstrous-sized, hollow-ended needle that was attached to a long, rubber hose. The end of the hose was connected to a vacuum pump that was screwed to the top of an empty glass jar the boy was holding in his other hand. The jar was large enough to hold several quarts of liquid.

Meehoff knew what the needle and the tube and the jar were for: they comprised a siphon designed to drain bodies of blood. The device was intended for use only on bodies that were already dead. When Meehoff had examined the thing his first night on the job, he'd supposed that it would work on a living body in much the same way that porcupines made love. Very painfully.

The crash victim impaled him with the needle, thrusting it into his gut. Meehoff's breath whooshed out in a fog of bloody mist. Mutely he looked into the grinning ruin of the face of the boy who held him skewered. He heard the whirring of the vacuum pump as the boy switched it on.

Meehoff felt his insides churning. At last he could move, and he performed a jittering soft-shoe in time with the machine's musical chatter. The corpses clamored gleefully as Meehoff slumped to the floor in a grotesque pratfall. Dimly he could hear the sound of his own blood splashing to the bottom of the empty jar.

And to Jack Meehoff's ears, it sounded for all the world like a healthy round of applause.

HOUSE OF LAZARUS

F. A. McMAHAN

"RICHARD?"

My eyes snapped open and I lay staring at the ceiling. I'd been on the verge of stupor. "What?" I yelled.

"Where's the tape?" Damon said. He was one of the older ones.

"What kind of tape?"

"Adhesive tape. I want to hang a picture."

I sighed. "Top drawer of the bureau in the hall."

"I looked there and didn't see any."

"Well, look again. I got four rolls last time."

"Oh," Damon said. Then after a minute, "Found it. Thanks."

So much for peace and quiet. I sat up and rubbed my eyes.

Four in the afternoon and no one was around but Damon and the Princess and me. So I'd figured it would be a good time to crash and have a little time to myself. But it never worked that way.

A clatter came from the hallway, followed by sounds of rustling paper. I followed the racket to the big room we call the gallery and found Damon wrestling with a length of form-feed computer paper about twenty feet long.

"Can you hold that end up?" he said. He'd tried to tape up a corner, but his tugging pulled it loose, and the page fluttered to the floor.

"What's it called?" I said, twisting to look at the drawings as I held the end of the paper in place.

"Haven't named it yet. Push it up about six inches higher. Yeah." Damon pulled his end tight, then drew a length of tape out of the dispenser he'd put in his mouth. He mumbled something more.

It sounded like "my table and chairs."

"What?" I said.

"Like anyone cares."

The Princess sat in the corner, wide-eyed and staring at Damon and me. Some adjust better than others. A few never adjust at all. Princess had been here four months, and all she ever did was stare. If I thought about it too much, it gave me the creeps.

"Okay, just hold it a minute longer," Damon said.

I watched him pull the tape, then place it carefully along the edge of the paper. Damon had been with me for seven, eight years, maybe. And he still looked good. I was okay, too.

I guess sometimes everything works, and a body makes a perfect transition. Usually, though, it doesn't take too well. If you end up a dropout, I mean. I'm sure there are successful conversions all the time. Why else would people keep trying?

"Hey, Richard. Meet my new friend."

Damon and I turned to see Marky standing in the doorway with his arm around a battered and grimy young man.

"Hello," I said, leaving Damon to his tape.

"A bunch of creeps jumped him and took turns trying to take him apart," Marky said, scratching at the curls of dead flesh on his face. "I told him he could come here. That he'd be safe here. His name's Sal."

"Hi, Sal. I'm Richard."

"He's our housemother," Marky said, grinning.

"I'm the head of this house," I said, giving Marky a look that told him to shut up. "The House of Lazarus."

"You're just another stinking pack. Like the Dead. And the Bloods. And Hereafter."

"Sal, we're not like that here. All we want is to be left alone. To stay among our own kind and get on as best we can."

"This is sanctuary," Marky said. "It's not like anywhere else. It's almost like being alive again."

"Nothing's like being alive," Sal screamed. "I don't look alive. I don't smell alive. I don't feel alive. I'm dead." His head snapped round, eyes locked on me. "You're dead. We're all dead. And if you think that playing normal and pretending happiness and acting like a living thing can make you alive again, then you're the dumbest simp I ever met."

"Hey!" Damon shouted, sharp and stunning as a slap in the face.

Sal's mouth fell open. Damon had him by the collar and slammed the boy up against the wall.

"You wanna talk to Richard like that, you gotta go through me first."

"Damon, please," I said. A chunk of flesh had come loose at Sal's neck and folded over Damon's hand. "Stop it."

No one moved.

Then Damon said, "Sorry," and released the boy.

Groaning, Sal let his legs go limp beneath him and sat down hard on the floor. He started gasping, made choking sounds like he was crying. Only he didn't have any tears that he could shed.

I knelt down and touched his neck, eased the flap of skin back into place. His flesh was cold and doughy. "You okay?"

He clenched his teeth and nodded.

"How long since you were reanimated?"

"Couple weeks." Sal sniffed. "I don't know. A month."

"It's hard at first," I said, sitting down next to him. Damon and Marky moved away from us.

"But why? Why does it have to be hard? Why does it have to be at all. Why aren't I dead and buried?"

"I don't know. I guess because someone loved you so much that they couldn't bear to lose you. They wanted you alive again."

"Nobody loved me. If they had, they never would have done this to me. This isn't life. This is hell."

"They didn't know it would turn out this way when they requested reanimation," I said, brushing Sal's hair out of his eyes. "Whoever did this to you thought they would be getting their son back. Or their brother. Or their lover. The procedure is way too expensive for most people to have it done for revenge, out of meanness. Only someone who is grieving, who is so overcome with sorrow at the thought that they will never see their loved one again that they would risk anything, spend any amount of money to get that loved one back—"

I'd said it so many times to so many children. Only the words still hurt like when I'd heard it for the first time. And I looked away.

"—only someone who couldn't live without you would have bothered to try to snatch you away from death."

"Then why am I like this now?" Sal said, still sobbing a little. "There's so much missing. Why can't I remember who did this?"

"Because they're still working all the bugs out. And sometimes things don't go the way they're supposed to."

"Do you remember? What it was like when you were alive?"

"A little," I said and got up off the floor. Sal and I were alone in the gallery. Damon's picture was hanging on the wall like a happy birthday banner. "I remember who arranged for my conversion and why. Not much else. I've been like this for so long that it's hard to imagine I was ever any other way."

"So why'd you start the House of Lazarus?"

"I didn't start it," I said and looked down at Sal. He'd stopped trying to cry. "I just took over when the last head of the house retired."

"Retired?"

I shrugged. "Wasted away."

Sal was quiet for a minute as my words sank in.

"So what's the deal with the house and all?" he finally said. "I mean, what's the attraction? What's it for?"

"The House of Lazarus is a place for bodies who don't have anywhere else to go, who don't have a family. They come here and become part of our family. It's home."

"You're not bashers? You don't want to destroy all the simps and the crips and the lifers?"

"What do you think?"

"I don't know," Sal said. "I'm not a simp. When I woke, I still had my mind. Not a lot of my memories are left. But my mind works okay."

I smiled. "I know."

"The rot's already started, though." Sal fingered the loose skin at his neck. Bits of flesh were peeling off his hands and face and arms. "Most of them will try to kill you if they think you're alive. But when you start to go, they want to wreck you even worse."

"Not here," I said.

"How old are you?" He didn't mean my actual age. He wanted to know how long since I was converted.

"Eleven years. The process worked with me. Everything's intact. Everything was retained except my old self, my old personality. I came out of it a completely different person. So I left."

"You'll last forever," Sal said.

"You don't know that. Nobody does."

"How long do you think I have? Before important chunks start dropping off and I can't get around anymore, I mean."

"I don't know that either. Some go fast, a couple of months. Some take a lot longer to decompose."

"Richard?" I turned to see Damon behind me. "Marky wants you to take a look at that junk on his stomach. He says it's worse."

"Okay."

"Wait," Sal called, and I looked back at him. "Can I stay here?"

"As long as you want," I said.

The boy held my gaze a minute, then bent his head to his chest. "Thanks."

And I followed Damon out the door.

▼▼▼

Of the eleven children in my house, only three—Marky, Elena, and now Sal—showed signs of physical deterioration, Elena's so slow that it was almost unnoticeable. But the other eight had various mental imperfections. The Princess seemed to have lost most of her mind in transition. Andrea frequently confused things or stopped in the middle of something because she forgot how to do it. Captain Crow, Jackie, and Butterfly all went through violent mood swings. Todd was withdrawn and insecure. Wizard never talked.

Damon was the best off of all of them. And even he had fits of depression once in a while, bouts of despair that I couldn't bring him out of no matter what I did.

I was the strongest. Not the oldest in living years. Captain Crow, Andrea, and Damon were older than I was. But I was the most stable. I was balanced, sane. That's why Madam had picked me to follow her as head of the house. She'd said I was her only choice.

For some reason, Marky's stomach had begun to rot faster than the rest of his body. A thick, black goo oozed up from the cracks in his dry flesh. The smell had driven Damon from the room.

"Pretty disgusting, huh?" Marky said.

"I've seen worse." He was my youngest, only about thirteen or so when he died. Most of us were in our twenties. Captain Crow was the oldest at thirty-six.

The dressing on Marky's stomach had soaked through, so I changed the gauze and taped him back up. It reminded me of Damon and his pictures. He was always plastering the walls of the gallery with his art.

"Is this the end?" Marky said.

Why do they all think I can judge that? "Nah, you could be around for years and years," I said. It felt like a lie.

Marky looked serious for a minute, considering my words, then nodded and stood to button his shirt.

▼▼▼

In the early hours of morning, Damon and I lay talking. We didn't sleep. We never slept, couldn't really. The closest I ever got was just zoning out for a while, getting inside my head and going somewhere else. But it had to be quiet for me to zone, and silence was rare around here.

The TV blared from one of the rooms down the hall.

"Fly's back," Damon said. He meant Butterfly, one of the angrier, more reticent members of the house.

"I wish she wouldn't go off like that. It worries me."

"What's to worry about? She's found something to do. You should be happy for her. It's not like she doesn't have a lot of time on her hands."

We were sprawled on the dais in the gallery. I think the place was once a studio or convention hall or something like that. The House of Lazarus occupies the third floor of an old building that was abandoned by the city and claimed by homesteaders. Damon liked the gallery best of all the rooms on the floor, so we spent a lot of time in here.

He turned on his side to look at the collage he worked on perpetually. "You like her, don't you?"

"I like all my children," I said.

"Yeah, but you really like her."

"She's interesting. She's different. Her problems seem more related to her attitude than to any mental impairment. She has a lot of potential."

"Maybe." Damon gave a kind of half laugh, half snort. "But you think all your children are special. Brighter than the rest."

"Certainly. Why else would they have chosen my house?"

He laughed for real then, got off the dais and went over to his collage. Reproductions of classic paintings, pictures from magazines and books, sentences pieced together with words in various typefaces, Damon's own drawings—all this came together to paper an entire wall of the gallery. The whole changed constantly as Damon added new bits every day. In some places, the collage was nearly an inch thick with layers. Death and the infinite ways of dying dominated most areas of the piece. Of all Damon's art, I liked this best.

A photo of James Dean in *Rebel Without a Cause* had come loose at one corner, and Damon picked at it until the picture peeled away. He stood scratching at other cutouts or smoothing down edges. It took me a while to realize he was hurting.

"What's wrong?" I said.

"Marky's deteriorating," Damon said, pressing his forehead against the wall.

I rose and moved next to him.

"It's speeding up," he said. "Marky's not going to last much longer. Before long, it'll all be over for him. It's not fair, Richard."

Damon looked at me. "Why does Marky get to perish? Why does he get to leave all this behind? Why should he get to go when I have to stay? I've been like this five years longer than he has. When will I start to go?"

I didn't know what to say. We'd been though all this before, and nothing I said ever made any difference. All I could do was listen.

"Sometimes I think about leaving. Just going out and walking the streets until I get attacked. Maybe they would cut me up into such small pieces that I'd be nothing that could ever move or think or feel. Or maybe they'd crush my head so my brain would stop working. Or burn me up into ashes and smoke. I think about it a lot."

"You wouldn't though," I said, gazing into Damon's eyes. Expressionless, black eyes. Dead eyes. Looking deep into the dark emptiness. "Would you? You wouldn't leave."

"No, I wouldn't leave." He looked away, down at the folding scissors that he pulled out of his pocket. I watched him cut James Dean's eyes out. Then he stuck the picture back on the wall, over an automobile advertisement so that the blood red of the car showed through the holes where Dean's eyes had been. "Don't have the courage," Damon said. "But it's something to think about."

He moved away to his box of clippings, looking tight-lipped and ashen. And I left him to his art.

▼▼▼

I sat taking apart a radio while Elena read to me from a book she had gotten the day before. Some trashy, pulp novel, but it was entertaining enough. Though Elena died when she was sixteen, she had been converted before any of the rest of us. When I first came to the House of Lazarus, she met me at the head of the stairs.

As Elena turned the page, I looked at her. The flesh had flaked away from her fingers. The rough white of bone showed through the gaps in her arms. Her hair, which had been blond, was fine and white and almost completely gone. To mask her stench, she doused herself regularly in perfume. But beneath the aroma of lily of the valley—her favorite—the scent of decay was unmistakable. The thinness of her face was alarming, the dusty dryness of her skin disturbing. Yet she had been this way for years. The wasting that took some people with such swiftness in Elena had slowed to a crawl.

Familiar footsteps sounded outside the door. Elena's voice faded into the background. And I rose to follow Butterfly down the hall.

"Hello," I said, when we ended up in the gallery. No one else was with us. "Haven't seen you in a while."

Butterfly shrugged and moved slowly, looking at all the new things Damon had attached to the walls. She was tall. Six foot four. Dark hair, gray eyes. Bony. Damon had a theory that she chose the name Butterfly to make herself feel more feminine.

"Where've you been?" I said.

"Out." Her answer surprised me. My efforts at conversation were usually ignored.

"What do you do?"

"Things." She frowned. "Look, you're not my mother. I do as I please."

"Sorry. I just worry about you."

"See, that's your thing. That keeps you busy. You worry about everybody."

"Can't help it," I said. "The children are my responsibility. I'm in charge."

This was the most we'd ever said to one another.

She hissed and shook her head, then stepped back to get a better look at the collage.

"Damon worked all night on this part here." I pointed at the area around James Dean. "A picture peeled off, and he got started and couldn't stop."

Butterfly didn't say anything, so after a while I gave up.

"Well, take care of yourself," I said.

"There's a group of us who sort of patrol the streets. We keep an eye out for bashers. Try to get them before they get us."

I looked at her, wondering why she'd told me this. "Then you're no better than they are," I said. "You're bashers, too. Just the other way around."

"Better us than them."

I couldn't help smiling. "That's what they think."

"It's something to do," she said. "There's nothing to do here. Sit around watching the others rot. Stare at videos all day like Wizard. Or make stupid art like Damon."

I stopped smiling. "Do what you like when you're out of the house. Just don't bring any of that back here," I said and turned to leave.

"Richard," Butterfly said, putting her hand on my arm.

"What?"

"When you were alive did you ever see a successful reanimation?"

"No, but I never really knew anybody who died."

"I've never seen one either," she said. "Because there aren't any. Not like there ought to be, anyway. A person never dies then gets reanimated and returned to their family whole and perfect and complete. It just doesn't happen." She was talking fast, like she had to get it all out before someone stopped her.

"What makes you think that? Why would people keep trying if it never worked?"

"There are only two kinds of reanimates, Richard. Failures and slaves."

"That's ridiculous," I said, moving out of her reach. No wonder we'd never talked before. Butterfly was a crackpot.

"It's true."

"If it is then how did you get to know so much about it?"

"Because, Richie Rich, unlike you and the rest of the household, I'm from a poor family. My parents sold me for slave labor so the rest of their children could have something in life. I was killed, then reanimated to take my place serving society. To fill some job, perform some task that any halfway intelligent human being wouldn't do in a million years, for any amount of money. Only the programming didn't take with me, just like it didn't take with you. Something went wrong and I wasn't controllable. So they dumped me here in the city."

"You're nuts," I said. What Butterfly was trying to make me believe was monstrous. And impossible. "You're saying there's some company, some governmental agency turning people into slaves? That's ludicrous."

"Haven't you ever wondered why all the reanimates are so young? It's because they don't want old people. They want slaves who are strong, bodies that are young enough to do the work."

"You know as well as I do that it doesn't work on old people. There're too many unknowns involved once you get past a certain age. Everyone knows that. And if my mind had been tampered with, don't you think I'd remember it?"

Butterfly looked at me like I was a little kid who knew nothing. "You were programmed to forget. Programmed to disbelieve. It's why so many of us are screwed up mentally. Only that part failed with me, too."

Her seriousness unnerved me. The urgency of her words was frightening. She really believed what she was telling me. I shook my head and backed farther away from her.

I was feeling all sick inside, like I was going to vomit. I hadn't felt that way since before I'd died.

"That doesn't even make sense," I said. "It's not right. People wouldn't do that to other people. Why wouldn't they destroy the failures right away? If what you're saying is true, then why are we here at all?"

"The city's a convenient place," Butterfly said. "We're all together. And as long as the deads are hacking each other to pieces, the lifers don't have anything to worry about. Right now, the failure rate's fairly low. But if there get to be too many of us, we just might decide to rise up against them. Wipe the lifers out. We're already dead, so it would be pretty hard to get rid of us, short of dropping a bomb or something."

"But not all of us are bashers," I said. "What about me? What about this house?"

"Maybe we're programmed to come to you if all else fails. Maybe you're programmed to take us. Turn us into decent, law-abiding citizens."

"Stop it!" I yelled, suddenly angry, suddenly frightened, and pressed my hands against my ears. "Just stop. I don't want to hear any more of your lies. Why are you doing this to me? Why are you telling me all this?"

Butterfly stared at me. "Because I thought maybe I could get through to you. Maybe you'd understand and help me. But I guess not. I guess I was wrong."

I felt sick, like there was no way out. Like I'd committed some horrible crime and was awaiting my punishment. I was ready to give up. I felt like I wanted to kill myself and be done with this.

Like I'd felt the first time. When I was alive.

"Just let me stay the way I am," I said, as if Butterfly had the power to change anything. "With Damon and my children. Just all of us together and getting along as best we can. I don't want to hear any more of this."

"Richard." Damon came striding across the gallery. "What is it?"

"Nothing," I said and twisted away, hugging myself like I was cold. I felt tired and empty and stale.

Damon turned on Butterfly. "What did you say to him?"

"Nothing," I said again. "We were just talking and I got sick. Damon . . . I don't feel so good."

"I'm leaving," Butterfly said and walked away.

"Go." Damon took hold of my shoulders and eased me down to sit on the floor. I leaned back against the wall.

"She said the government did all this. She said they reanimate people to make slaves that they can program to do all the dirty work no one else wants to do. She said we're here because our programming failed." I was shaking. It was killing me just to repeat her lies. My head felt like it was about to split open.

"She's a psycho," Damon said. He put his hand on my cheek,

felt my forehead. "I could tell it the first time I ever saw her. Forget her. She's crazy."

"I know," I said and closed my eyes. Tried to calm myself down. Zone out a little.

Damon settled down next to me. And gradually his voice filtered into my tension, started to unwind me.

He'd already forgotten Butterfly and was in the middle of a story about some movie he'd watched last night.

He was so unlike the way he'd been the night before. His mood was so different.

A chill spread over me, and I hugged myself tighter.

▼▼▼

Two days later, Marky was dead. My youngest, my baby was dead.

And Butterfly was gone.

Marky was dead, and we threw a party for him that night. Celebrated. Damon held my hand and sang the loudest, the most joyously of all.

I thought about how wrong all this was—that everyone felt so glad that one of our own had left us—how fundamentally against all laws of life and living. How contrary to the basic instinct for survival.

I thought about all the things Butterfly had said. Feeling sick again. And uncertain about the purpose of my existence for the first time in years and years.

And I wondered how hard it was going to be to recall all the things I was never supposed to remember.

TWO VIGNETTES

D. F. LEWIS

WOKEN WITH A KISS

I am not a human being—positively not.

My mind is at least clear on that point.

So, the only element of doubt is why I have a mind at all preoccupied with such a self-conviction.

Perhaps, I'm imagining the mind—or it's a ghost of a mind—or it's someone else's mind (your mind?) that I'm using.

I suspect it *is* a mind of sorts, but an alien template of a human one. I'd be a creature from outer space, if that wasn't so laughable.

No, the truth surely resides somewhere else. The best clue is upon looking at myself in the bathroom mirror and seeing a complete stranger there with pouting lips and eyes tightly closed.

So, it's all a dream. A dream without a dreamer.

Perhaps.

I only know I've fallen deeply in love with that zombie in the mirror. I close my eyes and lower my lips toward the glass. . . .

THE FRONT ROOM

I knew that they were not called lounges thereabouts, not even parlors, but front rooms. Of course, I didn't admit to being exactly obsessed about such matters. . . .

I seemed to have been cooped up in the house since I could remember, permitted to sleep as long as I liked in the king-size bed on the top floor at the back. The sash window looked over disused railway sidings, and I could often hear the voices of kids pretending to be trains. Very rarely, if ever, did I venture down the steep stairs. I sometimes thought I heard the undergrunt of mindless conversation elsewhere, and feared to meet the people. After all, they might be the ones who kept me upstairs.

Most people who are confined can remember the contrast with the freedom they once enjoyed. I could only retrieve such blurred images with difficulty, fishing for shadows from the edge of the black industrial rivers that wound sluggishly thereabouts in the outside world.

It had to be admitted that I was somewhat obsessed with the whole house, which is not surprising, seeing that it had been part of my life for so long—I even began to believe I was born there. But why such an obsession should center on the front room was a mystery. I imagined its decor. The paintings on the wall as run-of-the-mill favorites from the department store—in unreal colors. The seedy loose covers on the three-piece suite, with a design of overlarge flowers. The shag pile carpet bearing a pattern worn out by hobnail boots. The fire tongs hanging above the mantelpiece, gleaming sullenly in the late afternoon's shafting sun. The ponderous ticking of the carriage clock. The disused monochrome TV with huge knobs. And the people, yes, the people, sitting around on the edge of chairs, balancing bone china crockery on their palms, plates of manicured cucumber sandwiches on their knees, conversing in what, at face value, was sign language. I had a recurring dream that one of these people had a common cold (and thus incurable), a fact that made it almost logical to believe that death itself could in this way be outlawed, with the body growing piecemeal into the actual disease from which it suffered.

I shook my head. I had never visited the front room. I was convinced I had been to the kitchen, helping a lady stir the innards of a large washing-copper. The memory was that of a small child, whilst the experience was somehow that of an empty-headed adult. I knew the toilet backward and inside out . . . but as I had never been able to reach the chain, someone, I presumed, must have flushed it for me later.

One day, I determined to reach the front room, like a more outdoors type of individual might have wanted to climb a mountain. I left the landing where the stairs led down into a dark pool of light. I crawled backward on hands and knees, so that I could avoid seeing my own shadow. I employed the stair rods as a steeplejack would when upon a tall chimney, since from my bedroom I had seen such smokestacks striating the horizon as they rose from the dark mills. I eventually reached the ground floor, where light seeped through translucent roundel windows set into the front door and settled toward the hall ceiling as if it were warmer than the darkness. I stretched up on my body's hind legs and, with the gait of a clockwork toy, reached the closed door in the side of the hall. Gritting my teeth, I grasped the knob and turned. . . .

Inside, as I gingerly first-footed, I was incredulous to see that everything was indeed as I had imagined it. The dowdy carpet. The tasteless furniture. And the clinking teacups, the set square sandwiches, the dusty lace, the lugubrious clock. The silent signs of people. Even the lump of black snot pulsing and clucking in one of the wing armchairs.

Then, with a shock, realization dawned that all the tawdry department store paintings depicted images of myself in various stages of abstraction. You could not fool me: I had not been staring into the long wardrobe mirror for years on end for nothing. As I peered at these questionable works of art, I could well recognize the way my own saliva drooled from each corner of the lips. Then, the gathered guests (or hosts) raised their heads from slurping the tepid tea spilt in the saucers, and they all winked in recognition. I winked back, since they all were myself at various ages. I was indeed relieved to discover that I was not obsessed with the front room, since the front room was surely obsessed with me!

I sat on a vacant stool and sipped at the tea, not even wondering who had passed me a cup. A goods train with its voice breaking trundled by outside. A distant factory hooter sounded its spectral foghorn. I looked at all the others looking at me: zombies of myself at various points along the spectrum of ennui and stifled passion. I shuddered from bone to bone, wrapped in the seedy loose covers of my own flesh. I shivered. I thought I must have a cold coming—or a mind going. . . .

THE SILENT MAJORITY

ROBERT WEINBERG

APE Largo grunted in surprise. The door to the huge old warehouse he called home stood wide open. Light from inside spilled onto the dark sidewalk. Immediately, he suspected something was wrong.

Papa Benjamin, his mentor and owner of the building, always kept the front door closed, though never locked. Visitors were always welcome to the largest *oum'phor* in Chicago. A voodoo temple remained open around the clock. However, Papa Benjamin, its houn'gan, strictly enforced certain rules of behavior. Number one on that short list was that the door of the temple remained shut at all times. The gaping portal warned Ape that uninvited and unwanted guests lurked within. Huge muscles in his shoulders and arms tensed, bulging like steel bands beneath his shirt. When Ape grew angry, he was not pleasant.

Moving without making a sound, Ape crept closer to the door. A monster of a man, standing little more than five feet high and with shoulders nearly as wide as he was tall, he possessed a huge barrel chest and long arms that stretched almost to the ground. He resembled a grotesque cross between man and gorilla. A misshapen bullet head and flat, brutal features gave no indication of his true intelligence. Raised in a circus and educated on the street, Ape Largo possessed both brains and brawn. He was a very dangerous man.

A high-pitched, shrill voice, raised in anger, drifted out into the street. Ape frowned, trying to place it. "If you ain't standin' with me, Uncle Tom," the stranger was saying, "then you're standin' against me."

"Cinder-Block Simmons," Ape whispered to himself. The knowledge did nothing to reassure him. Simmons was a notorious Chicago thug who thrived on violence and intimidation. For years, he had been involved in the loan-shark business. The "Cinder-Block" nickname came from his practice of crushing the hands of delinquent clients with slabs of cement.

Recently, street talk centered on Simmons's entry into the drug field. Though competition for the lucrative crack cocaine market was intense, Cinder-Block had the muscle and ruthlessness to make his mark. What the creep wanted with Papa Benjamin, Ape had no idea. But he intended to find out right away.

Like a whisper of wind, Ape slid into the huge old building. It had served as Papa Benjamin's temple for more than thirty years. The voodoo priest had transformed the inside of the former warehouse into a voodoo temple much like those in his native Haiti.

A thin layer of earth covered the wooden floor. A model of a ship hung from the ceiling, the symbol of Agoué, the great voodoo god of the sea. Thumbtacked to the rear wall was a photo of the president of the United States. Next to it stood an American flag.

In the exact middle of the room rested the center post of the temple, the *poteau-mitan*. A square-cut post set in a circular pedestal of masonry known as the *socle*, it stretched from floor to ceiling. Covering it was a complex spiral design that represented the twin serpent gods of voodoo—Danballah Wedo and Aida Wedo.

Ape knew quite a lot about the Invisibles, the name given to the many voodoo deities. For the past two years he had been studying their secrets with Papa Benjamin. Someday, when his teacher retired or died, Ape would become houn'gan of this temple. It was not a burden he was prepared to assume for quite some time.

Ape's eyes narrowed as he took in the scene. Things were not as bad as he had suspected. Three men faced one at the base of the center post. Fortunately, two of the three were cheap street hooligans, hired muscle working for Cinder-Block Simmons. Their kind never worried Ape.

Only their leader, a big, burly man over six feet tall, massively built with the features of a pit bull, presented a problem. Cinder-Block had a reputation as a killer. Dealing unarmed with the thug and his two assistants all at once might be difficult.

"Only a fool threatens those more powerful than himself," Papa Benjamin declared solemnly. Only the barest nod of his head indicated that he saw Ape standing in the rear of the temple. In a quiet voice that somehow filled the entire room, he asked, "Dare you defy the power of the Invisibles, Mr. Simmons?"

Ape shook his head in silent admiration. No one intimidated Papa Benjamin. The voodoo priest dominated the others by the sheer force of his personality. Short and slender, he wore neatly pressed white pants and a starched white shirt. His skin was the color of dark chocolate. High cheekbones and a sharp nose gave his face a look of quiet dignity. Deep brown eyes contained a wisdom beyond that of most men.

"I don't believe in none of that religious crap," said Simmons, not sounding particularly convincing. "Besides," he added, glancing from side to side, "I don't see no gods comin' to your rescue so fast, old man."

"Maybe you should search a little harder," said Ape from the rear of the room. He picked up a two-by-four that had been leaning against the wall. It looked like a twig in his massive hands.

Standing there, legs spread wide apart, Ape slapped the two-by-four into his other palm. The sound of wood smacking flesh echoed through the suddenly silent temple. "The voodoo gods believe in protecting their own."

"I ain't afraid of you, Largo," Cinder-Block said. His huge fingers curled into fists. "You can't be as tough as they say."

"Wanna find out?" asked Ape, smiling.

More than one man had wilted before that grin. Incredibly ugly under normal circumstances, Ape's face transformed into a gargoyle's mask when he smiled. There was little human in that twisted visage of wrinkled skin, piglike eyes, and mouthful of yellowed teeth. Again, Ape slapped the two-by-four into his palm.

"Let's get the hell outta here," said Simmons, the slightest trace of fear in his voice. "This ain't the time or the place for a fight. I don't want no trouble before the election."

His stooges clustered about him, the big gangster headed straight for the door. He hesitated there for an instant. Summoning up his courage, he turned and faced Papa Benjamin. "You'll be sorry for turning me down. Real sorry."

"I doubt it," said Papa Benjamin, but the thug and his men were already gone.

Still holding the two-by-four, Ape rambled over to the door and slammed it shut. "Want to tell me what that was all about?" he asked. "Simmons said something about an election?"

"You heard correctly," said Papa Benjamin over one shoulder. He was heading for the stairway leading to their living quarters on the second floor. "We can discuss it tomorrow. Jay Leno will be on in just a few minutes."

Grumbling to himself about TV fanatics, Ape followed. He knew better than to ask questions while Papa Benjamin watched *The Tonight Show*.

2.

"Mr. Simmons is running for the vacant position on the local school board," declared Papa Benjamin the next morning at the breakfast table. The voodoo priest swallowed a spoonful of cornflakes and milk. "He wants me to support his election bid."

Ape, making his way through his third stack of pancakes, was properly impressed. "That stupid son-of-a-bitch campaigning for the school council?" he repeated incredulously. "That's like putting Dracula in charge of the local blood bank."

"Exactly," said Papa Benjamin, not sounding the least bit

amused. "Especially with the school reforms that have been enacted during the past few years."

In an effort to restructure the antiquated Chicago public school system, control of neighborhood schools had been switched from a central school board to local community councils. This action was designed to make schools more responsive to the special needs of the individual neighborhoods.

These local boards had absolute power over the schools in their district. The council made all the decisions not affected by state rules. School policies, from dress code to student discipline, were set by their decrees. They allocated funds for salaries, school supplies, and security. And the council had the final say on all hirings and firings in the buildings, from the school principal down to the janitor.

The reform act gave a great deal of power to a very small group of people. In most cases, they acted in the best interests of the children. However, the possibility for abuse did exist—as Ape now realized.

"Simmons wants to run the schools to his liking," said Ape, frowning. "He'll cut down the security force. Probably eliminate the drug education programs. Let his runners carry beepers to class. And who knows what else? That guy's a slimeball."

"Indeed," said Papa Benjamin. "Which is why he so desperately wanted my support. With my backing, he would easily win the post."

Papa Benjamin wasn't exaggerating his own worth. He was highly regarded throughout Chicago's south side. He possessed a reputation for honesty and integrity unmatched throughout the city, a quality that no local politician could claim. If he endorsed Cinder-Block Simmons, the loan shark's victory in the election would be guaranteed.

"But you turned him down," said Ape.

"Of course." Papa Benjamin's eyes narrowed and his voice grew sharp. "A houn'gan does not deal with snakes. Especially poisonous snakes that prey on children."

"I can't understand Cinder-Block's reasoning," said Ape, rising to his feet. "Everyone in this neighborhood knows his avocation. No way they're going to vote for him. Why is he bothering to run?"

"Why indeed?" asked Papa Benjamin. He sounded suspicious—and annoyed. "Perhaps you can find out?"

Ape stood and headed for the door of the apartment. "I intend to. Cinder-Block has too big a mouth to keep anything secret. I'm gonna do a little scouting around and see if I can't turn up some answers."

3.

The news was not good.

"The son-of-a-bitch is conducting a voter registration drive," said Ape, a scowl of annoyance twisting his already contorted features. "Aimed specifically at his kind of people."

"Meaning what?" asked Papa Benjamin.

"Simmons has put out the word. All the lowlights of the street scene—pimps, prostitutes, druggies, and pushers—are making like good citizens and signing up to vote. The new registration laws make it simple. As long as they can show proof of residence in the neighborhood, they're eligible. And you can bet on election day, they'll vote the way Cinder-Block wants." Ape grimaced. "Meanwhile, Simmons and his goons have the decent citizens of the district terrified with thinly disguised threats of violence aimed at anyone who supports his opponents. If he frightens enough people into staying home on election day, he'll win by a landslide."

"Even though the silent majority of the voters despise him and everything he represents," said Papa Benjamin. His dark eyes flashed in anger. "We cannot let this terrible thing take place."

Ape laughed, a harsh, bitter sound. "Not much we can do to stop him. Simmons ain't doing nothing illegal. Not at least by Chicago standards. Remember, this is the place where Kennedy beat Nixon with the help of the cemetery vote." Ape shook his head. "The Silent Majority. I haven't heard that line in years." He grinned, recalling a remark long forgotten. "According to Gore Vidal, Nixon and Agnew weren't the first to use the term. The ancient Greek playwrights used it in their dramas. However, to them the Silent Majority weren't the living, but the dead."

"What an interesting notion," said Papa Benjamin. His voice sounded odd, very odd.

Ape shivered. While he loved and respected his mentor, there were times the little old man frightened him. Especially when he used that tone of voice. He suddenly felt very sorry for Cinder-Block Simmons.

"Remember those whips made of sticks of *bois congo* in the rear of the storeroom?" Papa Benjamin asked, his features brightening. "Get them for me."

Baron Samedi's whips. Ape knew their name—and their purpose. The blood drained from his face. "Anything else?" he whispered, knowing the answer.

"A shovel," replied Papa Benjamin. "A strong shovel. And a *Bible*. That is all we need." The little priest rose to his feet. "Put everything in the car. I will meet you downstairs in a few minutes. I have to change my clothes and make a few preparations."

"Sure," said Ape, small beads of sweat forming on his forehead. There was no avoiding the next question. "Where we going?"

"To the cemetery, of course," said Papa Benjamin calmly. "To consult with the Silent Majority."

4.

Mrs. Myra Guinn ran the voter registration drive held every Saturday in the high school cafeteria. A big black woman of indeterminate age and fierce will, she reminded Ape of his worst grade school teacher. Myra Guinn reminded *everyone* of their worst teacher. Strong men turned weak in her presence and spoke only in timid whispers. Streetwise hoodlums said "please" and "thank you" to Mrs. Guinn without any prompting. Her presence demanded nothing less.

Ape arrived at the cafeteria a few minutes after nine in the morning. While strict city ordinances prohibited campaigning in the general elections, no such rules governed school board voting. Along with Mrs. Guinn and her three assistants, several candidates for office were present in the cafeteria, making themselves known to potential supporters.

Cinder-Block Simmons, resplendent in a pinstripe suit and loud tie, attracted the most attention. Despite constant admonitions from Mrs. Guinn, he insisted on shaking each new voter's hand and announcing loudly his extravagant plans for the school system. No element of doubt clouded Cinder-Block's vision. He made it quite clear to one and all that he considered the upcoming election a sure thing. Ape, slouched down in a chair at the rear of the room, smiled, and waited.

The first few rainclouds on Cinder-Block's parade arrived at eleven A.M. The damp, musty smell of wet earth and decay preceded them into the cafeteria.

Mrs. Guinn, never one for niceties, wrinkled up her nose in disgust. "What the hell is making that stink?" she asked, her loud, shrill tones drowning out all other conversation.

As if in answer, three grisly figures shuffled into the room. They were tall, gaunt, incredibly emaciated scarecrow-men with sallow, sunken features and skin the color and texture of old parchment. Their eyes were wide open, staring ahead with a fixed, unblinking gaze.

Their clothing, ripped and torn, hung in tatters on their skeletal frames. Bits of black earth and grass clung to them. None of them seemed to notice. Shambling forward at a slow, deliberate pace, they headed directly for the registration table.

The silence of the grave blanketed the room like a shroud as the first of the trio reached his destination. In a rasping, hollow voice that echoed eerily through the entire cafeteria, the monstrous figure declared, "I'm here to register."

For the first time in anyone's memory, Myra Guinn was speechless. "I also have come to register," said the second member of the group.

"Me too," said the third. A large black spider crawled out of his mouth and down into his shirt pocket. He didn't seem to notice or care. "Where are the forms?"

Myra Guinn rolled her eyes and fainted. A second worker turned green and ran from the room. A third, braver than her fellows, shuffled through a stack of papers heroically. "Do you reside in the neighborhood?" she asked, her voice trembling, keeping her gaze firmly fixed on the documents. "You can't register without a permanent address."

"Twenty-seventh and Michigan," said the first of the three, evidently the leader of the trio.

"The same," replied the second.

The final member of the group just nodded.

"That's the old cemetery," someone muttered from the crowd. No one seemed surprised.

"What's all this crap about?" said Cinder-Block Simmons, pushing his way forward to the registration table. His features were blood red with anger. "Nobody lives by that churchyard. It's been abandoned for years."

The three figures acted as if Simmons didn't exist. They neither turned nor bothered answering his remarks. "Can we have the registration forms, please?" the leader asked again, skeletal hand outstretched and waiting.

"I said," declared Cinder-Block loudly, placing one huge paw on the shoulder of the leader, "that no one lives near that old cemetery. You hear me, *boy*?"

Stiffly, the figure turned. Unwavering eyes focused on Simmons, as if recording his features. The scarecrow man's features never changed.

"Are you questioning my word?" the stranger asked in a flat monotone that seemed all the more menacing because of its lack of emotion.

"Yeah, Simmons," said Ape, who had unobtrusively made his way forward to the table. "You challenging this man's right to register?"

"Largo?" said Simmons, with a snarl of disgust. "I should have known. You and Papa Benjamin behind this nonsense?"

The mention of Papa Benjamin's name started voices whispering in the crowd.

"It's voodoo," someone said.

"The undead," continued a second.

"Zombies," said a third, stating out loud what everyone was thinking.

"Nonsense," said Simmons, peering closely at the gaunt figure who stood before him. "There's no such thing."

"Then why the hell ain't they breathing?" asked someone in the crowd.

It was true. The chests of all three strangers remained motionless. Not a flicker of air came from their lips. Hastily, the crowd backed away, leaving Simmons and Ape alone with the gruesome visitors.

With a shudder of revulsion, Cinder-Block pulled his hand off the dead man's shoulder. "No way they can register here. Zombies can't vote."

"Says who?" Ape asked cheerfully. He had been waiting all morning for this moment. "Show me a line on the voter registration form that indicates you have to be alive to vote."

"But—but—" the big hoodlum stammered in frustration. "That's crazy."

"Nope," said Ape, "that's politics."

He reached out and snared one of the certificates. "Not one word on this entire document states anything about breathing. It's not required. All these gents need do is prove they're residents of this ward and sign their names."

"Bullshit," said Simmons. "I don't believe it."

"You have no choice," said the third zombie. "The law is the law."

"I remember hearing Judge Criswell say the same thing when I was a little girl and went to court with my parents," said Myra Guinn from behind the table. Her face still pale and drawn, the elderly woman struggled to her feet.

Hesitantly, she peered closer at the speaker. A soft moan escaped her lips. "Holy Jesus—it *is* Judge Criswell! But he's been dead and gone for forty years!"

"I'll call the papers!" Simmons said. "I'll sue!"

"Go ahead," said Ape. "Draw all the attention you want to the election. The more publicity the better. I doubt if anyone will believe a story about zombies registering to vote. But I'll bet they'll be real interested in learning about a notorious drug dealer trying to take over a school board."

Simmons gnashed his teeth in rage. A thin line of spittle trickled down his jaw. His face was so red he looked ready to explode. "I haven't lost yet!" he yelled, shaking a huge fist beneath Ape's nose.

"Wanna bet?" countered Ape, effortlessly brushing away the big gangster's hand. "You ever count the number of graves in a cemetery, Simmons? There's a lot more dead folk than there are pimps and drug dealers. Time for you to kiss your election dreams good-bye."

As if to reinforce Ape's statement, the door of the cafeteria swung open. There was no mistaking the smell of death and decay this time. An almost overwhelming stench filled the room as a dozen more gaunt figures crowded into the entrance.

"We've come to register," announced the lead zombie. "We want to vote in the upcoming school board election."

Howling like a madman, Cinder-Block Simmons bolted from the room. Though he hoped otherwise, Ape suspected he had not seen the last of the gangster.

5.

The weeks following the cafeteria confrontation were a disaster for Cinder-Block Simmons's election bid. The inside favorite turned into an outside longshot. Papa Benjamin's voodoo magic had made Simmons the laughingstock of the community. Within hours of the zombie incident, Cinder-Block was labeled as the candidate so bad that the dead had risen from their graves to vote against him.

No campaign can endure constant ridicule, especially if it is essentially true. Cinder-Block's supporters sensed the inevitable.

They vanished faster than snow in the sunshine. By the week of the election, Simmons and his goons stood on their own.

Still, the big gangster refused to concede. He continued threatening violent reprisals against anyone voting for his opponents. As the big day drew closer and closer, he began dropping hints of a mysterious surprise of his own.

Try as he might, Ape couldn't learn a thing about Simmons's plans. Word on the street had it that the mobster had imported some special "talents" for a showdown at the ballot booth. But nobody knew the identity of the gangsters or the skills that made them important to Simmons.

All of which worried Ape. The ordinary citizens of the school district remained cowed by Cinder-Block's threats. The election depended on Papa Benjamin and his zombie army. Their votes would be enough to defeat Simmons no matter how many of the gangster's cronies supported him. Cinder-Block's only chance for success rested on his neutralizing the Silent Majority.

Papa Benjamin was also worried, but for other reasons.

"The binding spell I used to raise the dead is slipping," he confided to Ape the night before the election. "The zombies are starting to decay. My hold over their spirits grows weaker by the hour. Once they have voted, we shall return them to their resting places before the worst occurs."

Ape had no desire to learn what that might be. With no place to call home, the zombies had been quartered downstairs in the *oum'phor* for the past several weeks. Fortunately, as they required neither food nor drink nor entertainment, they were not much of a problem except for their smell. The last few days the stench of the zombies had progressed from bad to worse to indescribable. And the sight of them was enough to turn the usually unflappable Ape pale.

The sun shone brightly on election day morning. Ape thanked all the gods—voodoo, Christian, and otherwise—for the cool, brisk wind blowing in from the lake. Otherwise, walking with Papa Benjamin at the head of a column of nearly fifty zombies would have been unbearable. The undead stank like raw meat left out in the heat for too many days. Even Papa Benjamin, normally above such things, appeared slightly green as he led his charges down the street to the high school. Voting was conducted in the gym of the same building where registration had taken place.

"Why do I feel like Gary Cooper in *High Noon*?" Ape asked as they neared the school. "With Cinder-Block Dalton and his gang waiting for us in ambush."

"Hush," Papa Benjamin said sharply. "You worry about nothing."

A sudden shift in wind direction caused the voodoo priest to gag violently. "I will never," he declared solemnly, his face a mask of distress, "eat meat again."

"Seconded," agreed Ape, his own stomach churning. He wrenched open the door to the gym, almost pulling it off the hinges. "Let's get inside and vote. Then we can return these guys where they belong."

Unfortunately, things were not as easy as that. Cinder-Block Simmons had been waiting inside, and standing by him were a dozen bulky figures with skin the color of old gray chalk.

"About time you arrived," said Simmons, sounding a bit relieved. "My friends here don't like to be kept waiting."

As if following some carefully rehearsed script, the men clustered around the gangster spread out. Their massive bodies formed a solid line of flesh dividing the gym into two parts. Beyond them was the voting booth and two very distressed looking election judges.

"Get out of the way, Simmons," Ape growled. "You and your goons can't stop us from casting our ballots. It's against the law."

"We have no intention of breaking the law," declared Cinder-Block smugly. "My buddy, Rollo, and his comrades only want what is rightfully theirs. They've come for lunch."

"Been waitin' all morning," added the gray-faced individual closest to Simmons. A small dribble of saliva trickled down his jaw. "Worth it though. They smell . . . delicious."

Incredulous, Ape stared at the brutish figures crowding closer. Up close, there was no mistaking them for humans—not with their sloped foreheads, beady red eyes, slablike features, and huge, flat teeth the size of quarters.

"They're ghouls," Ape whispered, shuddering with revulsion.

"I found them working at the morgue," said Simmons, folding his arms across his chest. The gangster's voice purred with satisfaction. "They jumped at the chance to meet your associates."

Eagerly, one of the nearest ghouls reached out and grabbed one of the zombies by an arm. "Fresh," the gray creature declared. "And plenty meaty."

The zombie moaned, the first independent sound Ape had ever heard the undead make. It was a horrifying noise, and it set his nerves jangling.

"You can't do this," Ape said. "It's illegal. It's cannibalism."

"Nonsense," said Simmons, as the ghouls crept closer and closer to their intended prey. "Cannibalism implies humans eating humans. And neither ghouls nor zombies are human. We're not breaking any law."

"The law is the law," intoned Judge Criswell, solemnly from somewhere in the crowd of the undead.

"You're violating the zombies' civil rights by not allowing them to vote," Ape said desperately.

"No more so than you denying my friends the right to eat the food of their choice," said Simmons.

"Enough talk," said Rollo, seizing a zombie by the shoulders. "Time to eat!"

"This is unconstitutional!" bellowed Ape. Pandemonium erupted all around him as hungry ghouls grabbed the nearest zombie and started tearing them apart. "You can't devour voters. It's un-American!"

"Try and stop them!" Cinder-Block Simmons shouted back. The gym was filled with the harsh growling of the ghouls and the moaning of the defenseless zombies. "All they need is some salt and pepper!"

Ape flinched, Simmons's words hitting him like a hammer. A bit of occult information once told to him by a friend flashed through his mind. All was not lost. There was still a chance to stop the rampaging ghouls.

With a roar, Ape smashed his way free from the struggling bodies around him. For an instant, he caught a glimpse of a distraught Papa Benjamin, squeezed up against the bleachers by the horde. There was no time for a rescue. Everything depended on his making it to the cafeteria as soon as possible.

It took Ape less than a minute to blunder through the half-dozen doors that led from the gym to the eatery. Another thirty seconds passed before he located the half-dozen items he needed. And then, while he muttered a lone prayer to the gods of trivia, another minute passed as he staggered back to the scene of the crime.

The zombies, evidently obeying the commands of Papa Benjamin, were fighting back. They had formed a circle around the voodoo priest, facing outward much like a wagon train besieged by Indians. Using their arms and legs like clubs, the zombies fought with a grim, unyielding energy. But they were no match for their monstrous attackers.

Howling like wolves, the ghouls pulled one after another of the undead from the steadily shrinking circle. Each victim suffered the same fate, as the ghouls mercilessly ripped it to shreds and devoured the pieces. Already, the gym resembled some mad charnel house, with broken bones and skeletal remains littered across the floor.

Running at breakneck speed, Ape skidded to a halt less than a dozen feet from the battle. No one noticed his approach—not until it was too late.

"Try a taste of this!" Ape yelled. He flung a filled saltshaker, minus the cap, into the air over the monsters. The glass container tumbled around and around, unleashing its contents. Instantly, Ape followed it with another, and yet another. Like fine snow, the white grains fell onto zombies and ghouls alike.

Devourers of the dead, ghouls were by definition creatures of corruption and decay. Salt, the first and most powerful preservative, was anathema to their existence. Its slightest touch burned their skin like acid.

The ghouls shrieked in incredible pain. Huge red spots appeared all over their faces and any other exposed skin. Their flesh sizzled like bacon frying. Screaming, the monsters stampeded en masse from the gym. In their mad rush, they smashed the doors to bits.

Then one of the zombies screamed, "Salt!" Its face twisted with emotion. "I am not alive. I am a dead man!"

"Dead," said another, and then a dozen others. "We are dead men."

As if controlled by one mind, those zombies still able to move turned and headed for the exit. "Dead men," they continued to mutter as they marched forward.

Ape grimaced in mental pain. The taste or even touch of food makes zombies immediately aware that they are dead bodies not possessing a soul, he remembered then. No longer controllable, they return to the graves from which they have risen.

The zombies, however, never made it to the door. Once the salt broke Papa Benjamin's binding spell, dissolution set in. Weeks of exposure to the air and sun took its toll in seconds. Before the undead could take more than a few steps, they collapsed into seething, bubbling pools of stinking flesh and rotted bone.

Shaking his head in dismay, Papa Benjamin wandered over to a befuddled Ape. "A disgusting sight," said the voodoo priest, "but at least we won."

"We won?" said Ape, not sure he heard correctly. "What do you mean?"

"After the goings-on here this morning," replied Papa Benjamin, "I doubt if anyone else will *dare* vote here today. Which leaves the two of us and Mr. Simmons," who was only now rising unsteadily to his feet in the far corner of the gym. "The only eligible electors."

"And," continued Ape, realizing the truth, "since two votes beats one vote, our friend Cinder-Block is defeated at the polls."

"A decisive loss," said Papa Benjamin, "by a two-to-one margin. The Silent Majority has spoken. Justice is served. The Voodoo Mysteries will be pleased."

"Politics and voodoo," Ape declared, grinning. "Talk about a strange mix. Though, considering the role the dead played in this election, maybe not. When you think about it, there's not that much difference between the two. Not much difference at all."

THE DEAD SPEAKETH NOT, THEY JUST GRUNT NOW AND THEN

▼▼▼

LIONEL FENN

TRAVELERS in commercial airliners flying over the West Indies, those glittering emeralds floating so serenely in a sapphire sea, often wonder what it would be like to visit down there, in that paradise they envy without knowing why. They can see, from their seats so high in the azure sky, thick-forested mountains and verdant tropical jungles, white beaches and dark cliffs, sparkling lagoons and tiny gaps on the coasts where the jungle has been driven back to make way for quaint fishing villages and small towns, thriving cities and bustling ports.

And when the islands fade from sight, those travelers sigh and shake their heads and know that wherever they are going will be nothing like where they'd just been.

They're right.

Especially about the beds, even though they weren't even thinking about them. But if they had been thinking about them, they probably would have imagined a large airy room painted a soft white, with a large brass bed exotically canopied with mosquito netting, the room opening through tall French doors onto a second-story balcony that overlooks a broad expanse of well-kept lawn smothered with tropical shrubs and tropical flowers. They would have imagined a gentle tropical breeze sifting gently through the tropical trees and into the room to keep the sleeper cool as he dreams of dusky tropical maidens and hard-muscled tropical men and tropical things sleepers never dream about until they're in the tropics.

One sleeper, however, was completely unaware of those travelers flying so high overhead and wondering dreamily about all that tropical stuff down there, and he wasn't dreaming about exotic and dusky tropical maidens.

He tried, God knows, but he couldn't stop from dreaming about a mysterious telephone.

It wasn't pleasant.

Especially since he wasn't in the West Indies, either.

No, what disturbed this solitary restless dreamer from shores so far away from where he couldn't sleep was the reason he had flown to New Jersey in the first place: a long-distance call to his hotel suite in Edinburgh, from which, had everything gone according to plan, he would have continued on to his baronial estate on an unnamed Hebrides isle for what he unselfishly believed was a well-earned vacation.

But the telephone rang just as he'd finished packing:

▼▼▼

"Your Lordship, how the bloody hell are you?"

"Sir Ronald?"

"None other, m'lad, none other."

"My God, Kenilworth, it's good to hear your voice! How long has it been? Three or four years?"

"I don't remember, to tell the truth, but there's no time for chitchat, I'm afraid. I wouldn't be calling you on such short notice, you know, but . . . but damn it all, I need your help, Your Lordship."

"Name it, old friend."

"You must come over at once."

"I can't. I'm going home for a rest. I've been working my—"

"Your Lordship, I'm in dire trouble."

"But, Ron, can't your sons—"

"Worthless, the both of them. All they care about is my money, you know that. They don't give a damn about the work, the tradition, the people, the history of this place. They don't care about corn, about the ears, the sheaths, the kernels, the sound the west wind makes when—oh, never mind, don't get me started. The point is, you see . . . I must be blunt, there's no other way—someone in this house is trying to kill me."

"Ron, this is—"

"In fact, I'm risking my life right now, calling you . . . this hour . . . someone's been prowling . . . bedroom door all night, and . . . I think—"

"Ron, listen, hold on, this connection is going bad and I can barely—"

"My God!"

"Ronald?"

"My God, no!"

"Ron!"

"Please, no no, nonono*no!*"

"Hey!"

"Oh . . . *God!*"

"Ron? . . . Ronald? . . . Sir Ronald . . . ?"

▼▼▼

"Sally? Sally, this is—"

"Your Lordship?"

"Well, yes, how did you know?"

"I recognized your voice."

"Always the clever lass you were, weren't you, m'love. Now look, I've just had the strangest conversation with Sir Ronald. The connection wasn't terribly good, so I wasn't able to understand everything, but he seemed to think—"

"Oh, Your Lordship, I don't know quite how to tell you this, but . . . Father's dead."

"No!"

"Not ten minutes ago."

"My God."

"He's been murdered."

"Good heavens."

"It was . . . oh God, *no!*"

"Sally?"

"No, please, nonono*no!*"

"Sal?"

"Oh . . . *God!*"

"Sally! . . . Sal? . . . Sally?"

▼▼▼

"Matilda? This is—"

"Your Lordship?"

"Good God, you people are good. Yes, this is he in the electronic flesh, as it were. And I want to know what the bloody hell's—"

"Oh, Your Lordship, she's dead!"

"Sally?"

"No, this is Matilda. I'm as fine as anyone can be, under the circumstances. Sally's dead, though. Not ten minutes ago. It was . . . horrible!"

"I don't believe it. I was just talking to her. She told me something about Sir Ronald—"

"Oh, Your Lordship, he's dead!"

"I know."

"You do?"

"Sally told me."

"She's dead!"

"Yes, Matilda, I know. And if you'll just calm down, take a deep breath, you can tell me—"

"Oh!"

"Matilda?"

"God preserve us!"

"Matilda?"

"Oh . . . God . . . *no!*"

"Matilda! . . . Matilda?. . . Ma—ah the hell with it."

▼▼▼

When he had failed to raise anyone else at the other end, Kent Montana knew he had no choice but to abandon his hope of a tranquil vacation and travel posthaste to the Garden State, if only to find out if he had somehow managed to invoke some sort of hideous telephone jinx. Not that he actually believed in jinxes, or superstitions, or hexes, or anything else of that unsettling supernatural-style nature; but he had learned in recent years that it never paid to actually deny the existence of such things out of hand. Doing so had tended to kill off a number of people he'd known, and had scared the hell out of most of the others.

This, however, sounded very much like simple out-and-out murder, which, while no less unpleasant, was much easier to understand. One person killed another—or, in this case, three others—and all you had to do was snoop around a little, bother the local police into taking more action than they already were, unearth some damning clues, finger the unrepentant killer, and when all was said and done, accept the gratitude of the victim's stunningly beautiful daughter. Who, in this case, also happened to be dead.

He muttered in his sleep.

He rolled onto his side.

He rolled onto his other side.

In that half-awake state known as not quite sleeping, he grabbed his pillow and jammed it over his head.

For there was something else intruding into his unsettling dreams that steamy but cool tropical New Jersey night. Something ominous, something sinister, and it had nothing to do with the disturbing memory of the horrible calls he had received only two days ago.

It had everything to do with the drums.

He had first heard them the moment he had arrived at the extensive Kenilworth plantation long after midnight. Everyone but the manservant who had picked him up at the airport had already retired, for which he was grateful. His journey had been an arduous one, and sleep was what he wanted most.

He didn't much get it.

Because of the drums.

Distant yet audible, lifting from the dark canopy of the horizon-wide fields of man-high corn in a steady frantic rhythm.

The drums.

In all voices from subliminal deep to nerve-rasping high, beating and throbbing and pounding and calling and insisting and tempting and luring and commanding.

The drums.

Their primitive music at home and at one with the primeval growth of what some also called maize, reaching into the souls of all those who heard, reaching into the nightmares of all those who dreamed, reaching into the dark recesses of the minds and the souls and the nightmares of those who lived on and around the isolated plantation, calling up the blackest, most evil, most horrid memories that those who heard them didn't know they remembered.

The drums.

Kent tossed.

The drums.

Kent turned.

The goddamn drums.

He sat up and glared, rubbed his eyes, and realized that dawn had arrived over the formerly tranquil island of civility in the agricultural wilds of the centrally located county whose name he could never recall; it had arrived and had long since left, leaving late afternoon dying in its wake.

The drums had stopped.

He sighed his gratitude, flopped back wearily, and was about to doze off when someone knocked on his door. For a moment he was tempted to ignore the summons, but if he did, he knew he would be shirking his duty to his late friend, Ronald Kenilworth. So he groaned as best he could without anyone to hear him and express sympathy for his sleep-deprived condition, swung his legs over the side of the bed, and did his best to pound wakefulness into his face before he rose and opened the door.

A short, gray-haired black man in a white suit with wide gold piping smiled up at him with both his teeth. "Afternoon, sir, Your Lordship."

Kent did not smile back. "Denbro, do you have any idea what time it is?"

Denbro grinned more broadly. "It be well nearly the dinner luncheon hour, Lordship, sir. I be coming to get you so you can meet the others, hear their stories, and save our home from the vengeance of Momma Holyhina."

Kent looked at him.

Denbro saluted.

"Right," Kent said grumpily. "I'll be down as soon as I dress."

"Do be hurrying, sir," Denbro pleaded, his pudgy little face abruptly creased with concern. "We are—" He said no more, only scurried away, leaving Kent to wonder just what was going on. Surely, he thought as he put on his white tropical suit complete with white shoes and a red pocket handkerchief for that certain baronial dash and casual daring, the police have already launched their investigations; surely, he thought as he made his way through the rambling farmhouse toward the veranda in the back, suspects have already been rounded up and questioned, alibis established and suspicions aroused; surely, he thought as he stepped outside . . . and stopped thinking.

Not only was he making himself dizzy, all that thinking so relatively early in the day, but the setting sun had slammed him square in the eyes.

He winced, squinted, and noted the familiar surroundings with a silent sigh of regret.

The imported terra-cotta veranda was furnished with black, round, faux iron tables, tropical green wicker chairs, and several pots and vases packed with waxed semitropical flowers. At the largest table sat two men. One could have been uncharitably called a blimp—which Kent did, every chance he got—and the other a fence post. The fat guy was clearly older than the skinny guy, and a lot balder, but both were unmistakably members of the same gene pool, which obviously hadn't been strained in quite some time. Each wore a black arm band on the right sleeve of his rumpled tropical suit jacket.

"Well, well," sneered Roland Kenilworth, mopping his jowls and brow with a sweat-stained handkerchief. "About time you got up."

"Good afternoon, sir," greeted Robert Kenilworth nervously, reaching for a large pitcher of suspiciously dark lemonade and pouring himself a glass. "I trust you had a pleasant trip, a pleasant sleep?"

Kent stood by the table and looked at his late friend's two sons, neither of whom had ever cared for their father, only the immense wealth the plantation had brought in. "The trip was awful, the damn drums kept me awake, and who the hell killed your father, sister, and the cook?"

Roland made a wet rumbling sound that might have been a laugh, unless he sneezed.

Robert paled, his bloodless lower lip quivering.

"Well, what about the police then? What do they know? Who do they suspect? Did you even bother to call them?"

Neither answered.

Something large and undoubtedly feral made a prowling noise in the cornfields that completely surrounded the lawn and the house.

Kent reckoned he was on a roll, and so: "Who is Momma Holyhina?"

"Jesus, man, who told you that?" Roland snapped. "Fairy tales, superstitious nonsense, a bunch of tommyrot and you're not to listen to any of it, do you understand? Not a word!"

Kent frowned, suspecting not only a little overacting going on here, but also a remarkable overreaction to what he had thought was but a simple question. Was there something going on that he wasn't aware of? And if he wasn't aware of it, did he want to be aware of it?

Probably not.

At that moment a tall slender woman appeared out of the corn and made her way across the garden-strewn lawn toward them. She wore a loose, dirt-stained blouse, tan trousers, and high working boots; her lustrous dark hair was tied loosely behind her neck. In her right hand she carried a riding crop; on her left hip was a holstered revolver.

"Momma Holyhina is a witch doctor kind of thing," Robert explained weakly, glancing fearfully at his older brother. "There are those who believe she is the one who ordered my father and sister and cook killed."

"Balderdash," Roland growled. "Ignorant savages who don't know the first thing about anything."

"We're going to be next," Robert whispered, and gulped at the lemonade. He hiccupped.

Roland glowered, but said nothing, only mopped his face and jowls again.

The woman reached the veranda.

Kent looked at the woman.

The woman looked at him.

"Well," said Kent, grateful for a chance to smile at last. "It's been a long time, Lucy."

Lucy Dane used the back of her free hand to brush a strand of hair from her brow. "Hello, Kent." She didn't return the smile. "The boys are gone," she told the brothers.

"Tommyrot," Ronald snarled. "You just don't know to handle them is all. They think this is all some kind of joke."

"They know," Robert whispered apprehensively as he took another healthy gulp of his lemonade. "They *know*."

A crow called raucously from the depths of the corn.

Another answered from the peak of the roof.

"Know what?" Kent asked.

Lucy gave him a look that told him that he probably, all things considered, shouldn't have asked. He knew that, he responded with a semi-apologetic lift of an eyebrow. He was always asking things he shouldn't, and the answers were always things that he didn't want to know because they tended, in rather more than an abstract sort of way, to lead him either into temptation or into trouble, and generally more the latter than the former, more's the pity.

Then Lucy fished in her hip pocket for something, found it, and tossed it onto the table. "A joke, Roland? Explain this, then."

Robert yelped, leaped to his feet whilst simultaneously crossing himself, knocked over the lemonade pitcher, toppled his chair to the ground, and raced into the house not quite but pretty damn close to screaming.

Ronald yelped, did his damnedest to leap to his feet whilst mopping his face and crossing himself, toppled his chair to the ground, staggered away a few paces, hit one of the posts that held up the veranda roof, rebounded with a grunt, staggered away into the garden, then changed his mind when he saw the corn, and lumbered around the corner of the house.

Denbro, who had come out of the house at the precise moment of leaping and lumbering to announce the imminent serving of dinner, took one look at what had caused all the commotion, yelped, danced back inside, and slammed the French doors.

Kent looked at the table.

On it was a dark lemonade-soaked *thing* which, upon closer examination without actually touching the disgusting thing, looked to his expert-in-several-arcane-matters eye undeniably like the soggy foot of a plucked virgin chicken laced around with blood-drenched feathers snatched at midnight from the five-foot wispy tail of a rare Delaware ground finch.

"It was nailed to my office door," Lucy explained blandly.

"What does it mean?" he asked without thinking, then closed his eyes and waited for it; although maybe, he thought hopefully, it won't happen this time. Maybe this time he'd get away from it.

"It means," said the deep melodious voice of a diminutive black woman who had come around the side of the house at that exact moment, "that you will soon die if you do not leave this place at once."

▼▼▼

The sun set abruptly.

▼▼▼

The *drums* began their infernal nightly pounding.

"It is," the little woman added grimly, "the death sign of *Lamolla*."

Kent strolled slowly to the middle of the yard, turned, and faced the house. Amazing, he thought, how we attempt to influence our environment so that home, wherever it may be, is never that far away. The plantation house, for example, although ostensibly a typical if damn huge American farm building, still echoed the Kenilworth family estate in Yorkshire; the garden islands around the lawn were pleasantly unruly in the country English manner; and even from where he stood he could smell, from the kitchen, someone boiling the hell out of a perfectly good piece of meat.

Yet here he was in central New Jersey, surrounded by thousands of acres of ready-to-be-harvested corn, trying to make sense of the wanton slaughter of a family he had known since his carefree university days, and the bizarre behavior of the survivors who seemed not at all distressed for those whose loss was so great.

He glanced up.

The night sky was liberally speckled with stars, and the large full moon seemed unnervingly cold.

A breeze drifted through the fields, sifting through the corn, causing it to whisper huskily, as if responding to the drums.

Some days, he thought glumly, I just cannot get a break.

He frowned.

He continued to frown as the tiny woman, dressed in cutoff jeans and T-shirt, with a calico bandanna wrapped about her head, hurried across the grass toward him. Lucy, he noted, remained on the veranda.

"Hello, Bitsy," he said softly.

The woman, who barely came up to the middle of his chest, smiled brightly and kissed his chin. "How you been, Kent?"

He answered with a one-shoulder shrug. "I live, I'm still rich, what can I say? Now what's all this then, love? *Lamolla*? I'm going to die?"

Her smile faltered. "It's . . . it's true."

"Bitsy, for God's sake, you went to Harvard. Law, for crying out loud. What's gotten into you?" He grinned and slipped his hands into his pockets. "Next thing I know you'll be mumbling stuff about voodoo and houngans and curses on the Kenilworths unto the fourth and fifth generation."

She stared at him.

He stared back.

She stared at him.

The corn whispered and swayed.

The *drums*.

Kent didn't like the prickling that began on the back of his neck. Nor did he care for the way the night had fallen preternaturally still, except for the damn drums and the corn. But he especially didn't like the question he was about to ask, because he already knew the answer, didn't believe it for a minute, and knew that before this night was over he'd be proven wrong, as usual. Pretty sick of it he was, that he would have to do battle with forces that were generally beyond his ken, which is where, all in all, he preferred to keep them.

So he didn't ask it.

Instead, he said, "Bitsy, who murdered Sir Ronald?"

Bitsy Freneau lowered her eyes. "You don't want me to say."

"How do you know?"

"You were just thinking about it. The not-wanting-to-know part."

"My God, you can read my mind?"

She glanced at him without raising her head.

He cleared his throat and said, "All right, for my sins tell me anyway. Otherwise we'll stand out here all night exchanging meaningful glances and driving poor Lucy crazy."

Bitsy grinned. "Zombies."

Kent grinned. "Bullshit."

Bitsy grinned. "*Lamolla* is the god of vengeance Momma Holyhina called on to bring disaster and misfortune onto this place."

Kent grinned more broadly. "Bollocks."

Bitsy giggled. "Sir Ronald, he fire Momma Holyhina's lover,

Pierre Grumage, because Pierre want double overtime on Sundays, tried to get the other men to go on strike when he didn't get it. Sir Ronald, he say there'll be a big bonus when the crop is in but no double overtime. Pierre say he make sure Sir Ronald never bringing another crop as long as he live. Sir Ronald threw him off the plantation. Pierre go to Atlantic City, lose all his money, throw himself into the ocean. Momma Holyhina call *Lamolla*." She spread her arms sadly. "Sir Ronald die."

Kent wiped a hand over his face to smother the hysterical laughter he felt pressing at his lips. "Nuts."

"Sally and Matilda, they be at the wrong place at the wrong time." She stared at the ground. "Pierre kill them too."

Kent took a deep breath, shook his head vigorously, and stared at the black wall of corn surrounding the house and gardens. "Well, I'm glad that's over with. Thank you, Bitsy."

"No problem."

"So. Who killed my friends, Bitsy, and no more nonsense about the walking dead, curses, and double overtime, all right?"

"Pierre did it."

"You just said he was dead."

"He is dead."

"Bitsy, please. If Pierre did it, why haven't the police arrested him?"

" 'Cause he's dead."

"Bitsy."

"No shit, Baron. He come in, called by the drums, kill Sir Ronald and the others." Her face saddened. "And if you don't leave, *now*, you'll die too."

"Bitsy."

The *drums*.

The corn.

"Bitsy."

A tear sparkled in the young woman's right eye.

Kent wiped it gently away with a finger. "Bitsy, listen to me—there are many valid psychological reasons why one says what one says when one's dear friends are cruelly taken from one. It is a way, you see, of explaining the inexplicable, making sense of nonsense, and doing one's best to carry on despite the grief and the sorrow,"

She nodded.

He smiled tenderly.

She said, "Well, one is still going to die if one doesn't get his royal ass out of here pretty soon."

"Jesus."

"Hey, are you two done yet?" Lucy called impatiently from the veranda.

Bitsy grabbed his hands imploringly. "Baron, nobody but me knows you are the one who took me out of the gutter and put me through college; nobody knows that you are the one who paid for all the operations my momma had to have before she passed away; and you ought to know by now that I don't lie to you. Not ever."

He didn't want to, but he nodded anyway.

"Hey!"

The corn.

The *drums*.

Jesus, thought Kent; don't their arms ever get tired?

Suddenly a horrified scream whirled Bitsy around and made Kent look toward the house where, on the dimly lighted balcony above the veranda, he saw Robert Kenilworth stumble through an open door, struggling with a darkly tanned man a full head taller and many tens of pounds heavier. The man was bare-chested, wearing only a pair of ragged and rather damp jeans, and his eyes were impossibly, unnaturally wide and white.

Kent squinted in the bright moonlight. "Damn, isn't that—?"

The man effortlessly picked Robert up, shook him violently, and tossed him over the railing.

Lucy screamed and jumped back when the body landed on the grass in front of her.

Bitsy screamed when the man on the balcony turned slowly and strode stiffly back into the house.

Kent didn't scream, but he yelled a little when even at this distance he recognized the gaunt and expressionless face of Pierre Grumage. Who was, by all accounts, dead; and, if Kent was any judge, not doing a very good job of it, either.

"Zombie," Bitsy Freneau whispered. "It's a zombie."

"Damn," Kent whispered back.

▼▼▼

The *drums.*

Louder and faster.

▼▼▼

Lucy Dane sprinted off the veranda, hurdled Robert's body, and reached Kent and Bitsy just in time to see Roland Kenilworth stumble backward through the balcony's open French doors, a gun in his trembling hand.

Pierre stepped from the house.

Roland fired.

Pierre jerked at the impact of bullet against flesh, but he didn't fall.

Roland braced himself against the railing and fired again twice.

Pierre barely flinched, and kept on moving.

Kent snatched the revolver from Lucy's hip holster and took careful aim at the center of Pierre's forehead.

Roland snarled, sneered, fired twice more to no discernible effect, threw the useless weapon at the inexorably approaching zombie, and tried to duck around it to escape back into the house.

Kent couldn't fire.

Roland couldn't duck around the zombie.

Pierre grabbed the fat man and lifted him over his head, staggered, fell back against the house, rebounded, staggered to the railing, rebounded, staggered back a couple of steps, staggered forward, and finally tossed the last remaining Kenilworth contemptuously to the ground.

Bitsy excused herself and bolted for the corn.

Lucy stood and stared.

Kent fired.

The *drums.*

The zombie ignored the bloodless hole in its head, only turned and strode stiffly into the house whence, a few minutes later, came the shrieks and panicked yells of old Denbro Jones, the sound of shattering glass, the sound of an automobile engine firing, the sound of tires squealing on the driveway, the sound of a racing motor swiftly fading in the distance.

"Zombies," said Kent wearily, "don't drive, do they."

Lucy rolled her eyes.

"Right. Then how do we kill this thing?"

She turned to him with an unpleasant smile. "We don't, Kent. As sure as the sun will come in the morning, he will follow you. Wherever you go. There isn't a mountain too high or an ocean too deep, to keep . . . to keep him away."

Kent felt a trickle of sweat bead its way down his spine. "You mean . . . he'll follow?"

She nodded. "He'll follow."

He grunted. "So. He'll follow."

"That's right. From now until . . . I don't know. Probably forever."

"Forever?"

"You bet."

He considered the implications, the speed of the zombie, the direction of the wind that slammed through the corn and whipped the stalks back and forth, the constellations in the sky, and came to a decision.

He gave her back the gun and headed for the corn.

"Where are you going?" she demanded.

"You think I'm just going to stand here and let that walking corpse murder me?" he said over his shoulder. "If I'm going to die, I'm not going to do it in New Jersey."

"But you're supposed to try to kill it!" she said.

The drums grew frantic.

Bitsy bolted back out of the corn and grabbed Kent's arm. "I couldn't leave without you."

Lucy stomped after them. "Damn it, Montana, you're supposed to try to kill the damn thing!"

Bitsy kept tugging.

"What the hell kind of a hero are you anyway? If you're not going to try to kill it, aren't you at least going to try to save me? I could die here, you know!"

The drums damn near beat their skins off.

The corn whispered.

"What are we waiting for?" Bitsy demanded, then gasped and dropped his hand, putting her own hand to her mouth to stifle what might have been a scream had she decided to scream. Which she didn't.

Kent turned. He didn't want to; he told himself not to; but something deep within him, some highly charged sense of honor and fatalistic inevitability of doing something monumentally stupid instead of running like hell forced him to do it.

The zombie was there.

It stood tall and shadowy and motionless on the veranda.

Lucy slapped her revolver back into Kent's hand. "Kill it, damn you!" she snarled. "End it once and for all before we all die!"

Kent looked at the gun.

Bitsy looked at Lucy.

The zombie began to move.

"Kent?" Bitsy said nervously. "Kent, this is getting a little too dramatic for my taste, in case you're wondering."

Kent sighed deeply and, oddly, sadly.

The zombie came closer.

Lucy slapped Kent's arm, hard. "Jesus Christ, are you just going to stand there, for God's sake?"

Kent looked at her, his face touched with bittersweet melancholy. "Lucy," he said, "you have some explaining to do."

She sputtered.

"You've never forgiven me for leaving you, have you."

She stammered, then laughed. "I haven't the faintest idea what you're talking about, you fool. Now point that—"

"That holiday weekend in Philadelphia, three years ago. You thought I was going to propose. Take you away from all this corn and bring you to my estate in Scotland. Lady of the manor, that's what you said. You wanted to be the lady of the manor."

Bitsy gaped.

Lucy, however, backed away and shook her head in disbelief. "What an ego! What a typical male ego, to think that I would have something to do with the murders of my best friends just to get you over here so I could kill you." She shook her head. "Amazing."

"Is it?" he asked, the melancholy gone from his voice, replaced by a harsh cold anger. "Is it really so amazing . . . *Momma Holyhina?*"

Bitsy gasped as best she could while still gaping.

The zombie came closer.

And held out its arms.

"Oh yes," he said as he glanced at the flatfooted approach of fairly certain doom. "When you couldn't have me, and Sir Ronald wouldn't have you, and the brothers spurned you because all they wanted was Ronald's money, you steeped yourself in the lore and lure of Jersey voodoo, enticed Pierre to fall in love with you, then drove him to his death by egging him on in his attempt to unionize the corn pickers, the shuckers, and those two huskers from Nebraska I met last time I was here."

Lucy Dane's face changed then, from indignation to ugly fury.

"And when Pierre kills me, then Bitsy, will it stop, Lucy? Or will it go on, and on, and on, as that creature goes on and on and on, slaughtering people left and right, destroying innocent lives, sending women and children and old folks to early graves, until someone somewhere finally figures out how to end it. Is that what will happen? Is that it?"

"Well, hell no," Lucy said with a laugh. "Sooner or later, I'll die and then it will, too." Her laugh grew bitter. "The idiot can't live without me."

Kent smiled.

Lucy's eyes widened.

Kent shot her.

Lucy gasped and looked at the spreading messy circle of blood on her blouse, then staggered as her knees began to buckle. She turned as the zombie reached her, swooned into its arms, and they gazed into each other's eyes until Lucy Dane finally sighed, gurgled, and died.

The zombie lay her tenderly on the grass and lay down beside her, sighed, gurgled, and died again.

The drums stopped.

The breeze stopped.

There was silence in the garden.

Then Bitsy said, "What a waste. What a terrible waste."

"Indeed," Kent answered as he tossed the gun into the dark. "Indeed."

Together, then, they walked toward the house, arm in arm, as the sun began to rise gloriously in the east, and the morning birds chirped in the redolent fields of corn.

"You know," Kent said as he stepped over Roland's body and noticed that Robert was rather seriously flattened beneath him, "despite all the carnage and the horror and the terror and the nearly dying until I figured it all out, I'm going to miss this place."

"You can come back any time you want," Bitsy Freneau told him.

He stopped. "But aren't you going back to your law practice?"

"Hell, no." She waved at the corn. "Sir Ronald left me this place in his will last week. I'm going to be the East Coast Popcorn Queen, make a fortune, get me some studs, live me the life." She grinned broadly and headed for the fields. "You just go on upstairs, go to bed, take nap, I got work to do. Catch you later."

Stunned, he watched her hop over Roland and Robert, skip around Lucy and Pierre, and break into a joyful trot.

"Wait!" he cried.

She waved without looking around.

"Wait!"

She vanished into the corn.

He looked at the bodies, looked at the corn, looked at the gardens, looked at the grass, looked at the house. Then he stepped back off the veranda and looked up at the sky.

"You know," he said sourly, "I *am* supposed to be the hero here. I risked my life saving the goddamn world from the forces of Evil, killed the bad guys, saved the heroine who can't even decide what kind of accent she's going to use, and this is all I get? Go to bed, Kent? Have a nice nap, Kent?"

An airplane flew over, bound for the West Indies.

"This is it?"

Another plane flew over, bound for Monte Carlo.

"One lousy kiss on the chin? From the goddamn Popcorn Queen?"

And the travelers up there, serenely sailing through the azure sky, looked down upon the verdant fields of swaying corn and wondered what it would be like to live in such a lovely, bucolic place, never to know the lethal pressures of the cities or the soulless pressures of corporate life, never to be afraid to walk the streets at night, never to wonder what the twilight shadows held; living instead the simple life, the rustic life, at one with Nature and the joys she provided.

They wondered, and they flew on, shivering just a little when a faint cloud of sadness darkened their worlds for just a moment.

They flew on.

While Kent Montana said, "Nuts," and went to bed.

THE OTHER DEAD MAN

GENE WOLFE

REIS surveyed the hull without hope and without despair, having worn out both. They had been hit hard. Some port side plates of Section Three lay peeled back like the black skin of a graphite-fiber banana; Three, Four, and Five were holed in a dozen places. Reis marked the first on the comp slate so that Centcomp would know, rotated the ship's image and ran the rat around the port side of Section Three to show that.

"*Report all damage*," Centcomp instructed him.

He wrote quickly with the rattail: "*Rog.*"

"*Report all damage*," flashed again and vanished. Reis shrugged philosophically, rotated the image back, and charted another hole.

The third hole was larger than either of the first two. He jetted around to look at it more closely.

Back in the airlock, he took off his helmet and skinned out of his suit. By the time Jan opened the inner hatch, he had the suit folded around his arm.

"Bad, huh?" Jan said.

Reis shook his head. "Not so bad. How's Hap?"

Jan turned away.

"How's Dawson doing with the med pod?"

"I don't know," Jan said. "He hasn't told us anything."

He followed her along the spiracle. Paula was bent over Hap, and Dawson was bent over Paula, a hand on her shoulder. Both looked up when he and Jan came in. Dawson asked, "Anybody left downship?"

Reis shook his head.

"I didn't think so, but you never know."

"They'd have had to be in suits," Reis said. "Nobody was."

"It wouldn't be a bad idea for us to stay suited up."

Reis said nothing, studying Hap. Hap's face was a pale, greenish-yellow, beaded with sweat; it reminded Reis of an unripe banana, just washed under the tap. So this is banana day, he thought.

"Not all of the time," Dawson said. "But most of the time."

"Sure," Reis told him. "Go ahead."

"All of us."

Hap's breathing was so shallow that he seemed not to breathe at all.

"You won't order it?"

"No," Reis told Dawson, "I won't order it." After a moment he added, "And I won't do it myself, unless I feel like it. You can do what you want."

Paula wiped Hap's face with a damp washcloth. It occurred to Reis that the droplets he had taken for perspiration might be no more than water from the cloth, that Hap might not really be breathing. Awkwardly, he felt for Hap's pulse.

Paula said, "You're the senior officer now, Reis."

He shook his head. "As long as Hap's alive, he's senior officer. How'd you do with the med pod, Mr. Dawson?"

"You want a detailed report? Oxygen's—"

"No, if I wanted details, I could get them from Centcomp. Overall."

Dawson rolled his eyes. "Most of the physical stuff he'll need is there; I had to fix a couple things, and they're fixed. The med subroutines look okay, but I don't know. Centcomp lost a lot of core."

Paula asked, "Can't you run tests, Sid?"

"I've run them. As I said, they look all right. But it's simple stuff." Dawson turned back to Reis. "Do we put him in the pod? You *are* the senior officer fit for duty."

"And don't you forget it," Reis said. "Yes, we put him in, Mr. Dawson; it's his only chance."

Jan was looking at him with something indefinable in her eyes. "If we're going to die anyway—"

"We're not, Mr. van Joure. We should be able to patch up at least two engines, maybe three, borrowing parts from the rest. The hit took a lot of momentum off us, and in a week or so we should be able to shake most of what's left. As soon as Ecomp sees that we're still alive and kicking, it'll authorize rescue." Reis hoped he had made that part sound a great deal more certain than he felt. "So our best chance is to head back in toward the sun and meet it partway—that should be obvious. Now let's get Hap into that pod before he dies. Snap to it, everybody!"

Dawson found an opportunity to take Reis aside. "You were right—if we're going to get her going again, we can't spare anybody for nursing, no matter what happens. Want me to work on the long-wave?"

Reis shook his head. Engines first, long-wave afterward, if at all. There would be plenty of time to send messages when the ship lived again. And until it did, he doubted whether any message would do much good.

▼▼▼

Lying in his sleep pod, Reis listened to the slow wheeze of air through the vent. The ship breathed again, they'd done that much. Could it have been . . . admiration, that look of Jan's? He pushed the thought aside, telling himself he had been imagining things. But still?

His mind teetered on the lip of sleep, unable to tumble over.

The ship breathed; it was only one feeble engine running at half force with a doubtful tube, and yet it was something; they could use power tools again—the welder—and the ship breathed.

His foot slipped on an oil spill, and he woke with a start. That had happened years back while they were refitting at Ocean West. He had fallen and cracked his head. He had believed it forgotten. . . .

The ship breathed. She's our mother, Reis thought. She's our mother; we live inside her, in her womb; and if she dies, we die. But she died, and we're bringing her to life again.

Someone knocked on the pod lid. Reis pushed the Retract lever and sat up.

Paula said, "Sir, I'm sorry, but—"

"What is it? Is Jan—"

"She's fine, sir. I relieved her an hour ago. It's my watch."

"Oh," Reis said. "I didn't realize I'd been asleep." He sounded stupid even to himself.

"My orders were to call you, sir, if—"

He nodded. "What's happened?"

"Hap's dead." Paula's voice was flat, its only emotion this very lack of emotion betrayed.

Reis looked at her eyes. There were no tears there, and he decided it was probably a bad sign. "I'm truly sorry," he said. And then, "Perhaps Centcomp—"

Wordlessly, Paula pointed to the screen. The glowing green letters read: "*Resuscitation underway.*"

Reis went over to look at it. "How long has this been up?"

"Five minutes, Captain. Perhaps ten. I hoped—"

"That you wouldn't have to wake me."

Paula nodded gratefully. "Yes, sir."

He wrote: "*Resp?*"

"*Respiration 0.00. Resuscitation underway.*"

The ship breathed, but Hap did not. That, of course, was why Paula had called him "Captain" a moment ago. She must have tried pulse, tried everything, before knocking on his pod. He wrote: "*Cortex?*"

"*Alpha 0.00 Beta 0.00 Gamma 0.00,*" Centcomp replied. "*Resuscitation underway.*"

Reis wrote: "*Discon.*"

There was a noticeable pause before the alpha, beta, and gamma-wave reports vanished. "*Resuscitation underway*," remained stubbornly on screen.

Paul said, "Centcomp won't give up. Centcomp has faith. Funny, isn't it?"

Reis shook his head. "It means we can't rely on Centcomp the way we've been used to. Paula, I'm not very good at telling people how I feel. Hap was my best friend."

"You were his, Captain."

Desperately Reis continued, "Then we're both sorry, and we both know that."

"Sir, may I tell you something?"

He nodded. "Something private? Of course."

"We were married. You know how they still do it in some churches? We went to one. He told them we didn't belong, but we wanted to have the ceremony and we'd pay for it. I thought sure they'd say no, but they did it, and he cried—Hap cried."

Reis nodded again. "You meant a lot to him."

"That's all, sir. I just wanted somebody else to know. Thanks for listening."

Reis went to his locker and got out his suit. It shone a dull silver under the cabin lights, and he recalled a time when he had envied people who had suits like that.

"Aren't you going back to sleep, sir?"

"No, I'll be relieving you in less than an hour, so I'm going hullside to have another look around. When I come back, you can turn in."

Paula gnawed her lower lip. He was giving her something to think about besides Hap, Reis decided; that was all to the good. "Sir, the captain doesn't stand watch."

"He does when there are only four of us, dog tired. Check me through the airlock, please, Mr. Phillips."

"Of course, sir." As the inner hatch swung shut Paula said softly, "Oh, God, I'd give anything to have him back."

Neptune was overhead now; they were spinning, even if the spin was too slow to be visible. With only a single engine in service it was probably impossible to stop the spin, and there was no real reason to. The gravitational effect was so slight he had not noticed it.

He found Jupiter and then the Sun, slightly less brilliant than Jupiter or Neptune but brighter than any other star. The sun! How many thousands—no, how many millions of his ancestors must have knelt and sung and sacrificed to it. It had been Ra, Apollo, Helios, Heimdall, and a hundred more, this medium-sized yellow star in a remote arm of the Galaxy, this old gas-burner, this space heater laboring to warm infinite space.

If you're a god, Reis thought, why aren't you helping us?

Quite suddenly he realized that the Sun *was* helping, was drawing them toward the circling inner planets as powerfully as it could. He shook his head and turned his attention back to the ship.

A faint violet spark shone, died, and rekindled somewhere on section Six, indicating that Centcomp had at least one of its mobile units back in working order. Centcomp was self-repairing, supposedly, though Reis had never put much faith in that; human beings were supposed to be self-repairing too, but all too often were not.

And deep space was supposed to make you feel alone, but he had never really felt that way; sometimes, when he was not quite so tired, he was more alive here, more vibrant, than he ever was in the polluted atmosphere of Earth. Now Hap was dead, and Reis knew himself to be alone utterly. As he jetted over to check on the mobile unit, he wished that he could weep for Hap as he had wept for his father, though he had known his father so much less well than Hap, known him only as a large, sweet-smelling grownup who appeared at rare intervals bringing presents.

Or if he could not cry, that Paula could.

The mobile unit looked like a tiny spider. It clung to the side of Section Three with six legs while two more welded up one of the smaller holes. Centcomp, obviously, had decided to close the smallest holes first, and for a moment Reis wondered whether that made sense. It did, he decided, if Centcomp was in actual fact fixing itself; there would be more units as well as more power available later. He swerved down toward the mobile unit until he could see it for what is was, a great jointed machine forty meters across. Three clicks of his teeth brought ghostly numerals—hours, minutes, and seconds—to his faceplate, which had darkened automatically against the raw ultraviolet from the mobile unit's welding arc. Still twenty-four minutes before he had to relieve Paula.

For a minute or two he watched the fusing of the filament patch. The patch fibers had been engineered to form a quick, strong bond; but a bit of dwell was needed just the same. The mobile unit seemed to be allowing enough, working slowly and methodically. In the hard vacuum of space there was no danger of fire, and its helium valves were on *off* just as they should have been.

Reis glanced at the time again. Twenty minutes and eleven seconds, time enough yet for a quick look inside Section Three. He circled the hull and jetted through the great, gaping tear, landing easily in a familiar cabin that was now as airless as the skin of the ship. The hermetic hatch that sealed Section Two from this one was tightly dogged still. He had inspected it earlier, just after the hit, and inspected it again when he had come with Dawson, Jan, and Paula to work on the least damaged engine. He threw his weight against each of the latches once again; you could not be too careful.

Nell Upson's drifting corpse watched him with indifferent eyes until he pushed her away, sending her deeper into the dark recesses of Section Three to join her fellows. In time, space would dry Nell utterly, mummifying her; radiation would blacken her livid skin. None of that had yet taken place, and without air, Nell's blood could not even coagulate—she had left a thin, crimson tail of it floating in the void behind her.

Twelve minutes. That was still plenty of time, but it was time to go. When he left the side of Section Three, the mobile unit was at work on a second hole.

▼▼▼

"*Resuscitation underway,*" was still on the screen half an hour into Reis's watch. He read it for the hundredth time with some irritation. Was it supposed to refer to Centcomp's self-repair functions? Reis picked up the rat and wrote, "*Who's in resusc?*"

"*Capt. Hilman W. Happle. Resuscitation underway.*"

So that was that. "*Discon.*"

"*Resuscitation underway.*"

"*Clear screen,*" Reis scribbled.

"*Resuscitation underway.*"

Reis cursed and wrote, "*What authority?*"

"*Capt. Hilman W. Happle.*"

That was interesting, Reis decided—not sensible or useful, but interesting. Centcomp did not know that Hap was dead. Reis wrote, "*Capt. Happle K. Lt. Wm. R. Reis commanding.*"

The screen went blank, and Reis decided to try a general instrument display. "*GID*"

The three letters faded slowly, replaced by nothing.

"*Enter—GID*"

That, too, faded to an empty screen. Reis scratched his nose and looked speculatively at the transducer headband. He had ordered the others not to use it—the hard instrumentation was amply sufficient as long as nothing too delicate was being attempted; but it had been sixteen hours since the hit, and Centcomp was still limping at best.

Multiplication became coitus, division reproduction; to add was to eat, to subtract to excrete. Glowing, Centcomp's central processor loomed before him, a dazzling coral palace with twice ten thousand spires where subroutines worked or slept. Tiny and blue alongside it, the lone mobile unit sang a Bach fugue as it labored. Smoldering leaves perfumed the breeze, washed away by a fountain of exponential functions that appeared to Reis to be calculating natural logarithms for purposes both infinite and obscure, pungently returning with each fresh gust of algorithmic air. Interactive matrices sprouted around his feet—the lilies, buttercups, and pale or burning roses that allowed his conscious mind to move here as it did, their blossoms petaled with shining elementary rows and columns.

Hap was sitting astride a tree that sprouted from the coral wall. The smile that divided his dark face when he saw Reis seemed automatic and distracted. Reis saluted, called, "Good evening, Skipper," and leaped across the laughing rill that had overflowed the fountain's rim.

Hap touched his forehead in return. "Hi ya, Bill."

Reis said, "It's damned good to see you here. We thought you were dead."

"Not me, Bill." Hap stared off into the twilight. "You can't die on duty, know that? Got to finish your tick, know what I mean, Bill boy? You want up here on the bridge?" He patted the tree trunk.

"That's okay—I'm fine where I am. Hap . . . ?"

His eyes still upon something Reis could not see, Hap said, "Speak your piece."

"Hap. I checked your cortical activity. There wasn't any. You were brain-dead."

"Go on."

"That's why it was quite a surprise to run into you here, and I'm not sure it's really you. Are you Hap, or are you just a kind of surrogate, Centcomp's concept of Hap?"

"I'm Hap. Next question?"

"Why won't Centcomp terminate resuscitation?"

"Because I told it not to, as soon as we left Earth." Hap sounded as though he were talking to himself. "Not just on me, on all of us. We're all too necessary, all of us vital. Resusc is to continue as long as—in Centcomp's judgment—there's the slightest possibility of returning a crewman to his or her duty. No overrides at all, no mutinies. Know what a mutiny is, Bill? Grasp the concept?"

Reis nodded.

"Some snotty kid's trying to take over my ship, Billy boy, trying to push me out through a hatch. That's mutiny. It's a certain Lieutenant William R. Reis. He's not going to get away with it."

"Hap. . . ."

Hap was gone. Briefly, the tree where he had sat remained where it was, vacant; then it too vanished, wiped from working memory.

Something was wrong; the brilliant garden seemed haunted by sinister shadows, flitting and swift; the chaotic twilight from which Reis had emerged pressed closer to the coral palace. His head ached, there was a chill in his side, and his fingers felt oddly warm. He tried to remove the headband, willing himself to use his real arms, not the proxies that here appeared to be his arms. A hurrying subroutine shouldered him out of the way; by accident he stepped into the laughing rill, which bit his foot like acid. . . .

A smudged white cabin wall stood in place of the wall of the coral palace. Dawson was bending over him, his face taut with concern. "Reis! What happened?"

His mouth was full of blood; he spat it out. "I'm hurt, Sid."

"I know. *Christ!*" Dawson released him; but he did not fall, floating derelict in the cabin air. Dawson banged on Jan's pod.

Reis moved his right arm to look at the fingers; the warmth there was his own blood, and there was more blood hanging in the cabin, floating spheres of bright scarlet blood—arterial blood. "I'm bleeding, Sid. I think he nicked a lung. Better patch me up."

Twilight closed upon the cabin. Reis remembered how they had celebrated Christmas when he was three—something he had not known he knew, with colored paper and a thousand other wonderful things. Surely he was peeping through one of the plastic tubes the paper had come on; the few things he could see seemed small, toylike and very bright. Everything in all the universe was a Christmas present, a fact he had forgotten long, long ago. He wondered who had brought them all, and why.

"You have been asleep in the medical pod. There is little cause for concern."

Reis searched the pod for a rat, but there was none. No backtalk to Centcomp from in here.

"Are you anxious? fearful? Confide your fears to me. I assure you that any information that I provide concerning your condition will be both complete and correct. No matter how bad, reality is never quite so bad as our fears concerning reality."

Reis said, "Spare me the philosophy," though he knew that Centcomp could not hear him.

"And your condition is not even critical. You suffered a dangerous lesion between the fifth and sixth ribs of your right side, but you are nearly well."

Reis was already exploring the place with his fingers.

"Please reply."

"Would if I could," Reis muttered.

"You will find a rapid access trace beside your right hand. Please reply."

"There's no God-damned rapid access trace."

A latch clicked. Servos hummed. The pod in which Reis lay rolled forward with stately grandeur, and the pod opened. This time it was Jan who was looking down at him. "Reis, can you sit up?"

"Sure." He proved it.

Low and quick: "I want you to get into your sleeping pod with me, please. Don't ask questions—just do it, fast."

His pod was closed, but not latched from inside. He threw it open and he and Jan climbed in; she lay facing him, on her side, her back to the pod wall. He got in beside her, closed the pod, and threw the latching lever. Jan's breasts flattened against his chest; Jan's pelvis pressed his. "I'm sorry," she whispered. "I hadn't realized it would be this crowded."

"It's all right."

"Even if I had, I'd have had to ask you anyway. This is the only place I could think of where we could talk privately."

"I like it," Reis said, "so you can forget about that part. Talk about what?"

"Hap."

He nodded, though she could not have seen him in the dark. "I thought so."

"Hap was the one who stabbed you."

"Sure," Reis said. "I know that. With the rat from the med pod."

"That's right." Jan hesitated; Reis could feel her sweet breath wash across his face. At last she said. "Perhaps you'd better tell me how you knew. It might be important."

"I doubt it, but there's no reason not to. Hap thinks I'm a mutineer because I took charge when he was hurt—I was talking to him in Centcomp's conscious space. Hap had been in the med pod, and when I woke up in there the rat that should have been there was gone. A rat's stylus is long and sharp, and the whole rat's made of some sort of metal—titanium, I suppose. So a rat ought to make a pretty decent weapon."

Hair brushed his cheek as Jan nodded. "Sid found you. He woke up and realized he should have been on watch."

"Sure."

"He yelled for me, and we put you in the med pod when we saw that it was empty. There's another pod in Section Three, remember?"

"Of course," Reis said.

He waited for her to pursue that line of thought, but she seemed to veer off from it instead. "Hap's resumed command." She swallowed. "It was all right at first—he's the captain, after all. None of us even thought about resisting him, then."

Reis said slowly, "I wouldn't have resisted him either; I would have obeyed his orders, if I'd known he was alive to give them."

Jan said, "He's very suspicious now." There was a queer flatness in her voice.

"I see."

"And Reis, he's going to continue the mission."

For a moment he could not speak. He shook his head.

"It's crazy, isn't it? With the ship ripped up like it was."

"Not crazy," he told her. "Impossible."

Jan took a deep breath—he could feel and hear it, her long gasp in the dark. "And Reis, Hap's dead."

Reluctantly Reis said, "If he really wanted to proceed with the mission, maybe it's for the best. You didn't kill him, did you? You and Sid?"

"No. You don't understand. I didn't mean . . . Oh, it's so hard to say what I do mean."

Reis told her, "I think you'd better try." His right hand had been creeping, almost absently, toward her left breast. He forced it to stop where it was.

"Hap's still running the ship. He tells us what to do, and we do it because we know we'd better. But our real captain, our friend, is dead. Try to understand. The real Hap died in the med pod, and

Centcomp's substituted something else—something of its own—for his soul or spirit or whatever you want to call it. When you've seen him, after you've been around him for a while, you'll understand."

"Then I ought to be outside, where I can see him," Reis said practically, "not in here. But first—"

Jan screamed, a high-pitched wail of sheer terror that was deafening in the enclosed space of the sleep pod. Reis clapped his hand over her mouth and said, "Jesus! All right, if you don't want to, we won't. Promise you won't do that again if I let you talk?"

Jan nodded, and he returned his hand to his side.

"I'm sorry," she said. "It isn't that I don't like you, or that I'd never want to. I've been under such a terrible strain. You missed it. You were in the med pod, and you can't know what it's been like for us."

"I understand," Reis told her. "Oh, Hell, you know what I mean."

"If Hap isn't looking for us already, he will be soon. Or looking for me, anyway. He thinks you're still in the med pod, unless Centcomp's told him I took you out. Reis, you've got to believe me. He's going to court-martial and execute you; that's what he said when Sid and I told him we'd put you in the pod."

"You're serious?"

"Reis, you don't know what he's like now. It doesn't make any difference, we're all going to die anyway, Sid and Paula and me. And Hap's already dead." Her voice threatened to slip from tears to hysteria.

"No, we're not," he told her. "Hap's been having you fix the ship? He must have, if he's talking about carrying out the mission."

"Yes! We've got three engines running now, and the hull's airtight. We don't know—Sid and I don't know—whether we can count on Paula. If she sided with Hap it would be two against two, a man and a woman on each side, and . . ."

"Go on," Reis said.

"But if you were with us, that would be two men and a woman on our side. We'd save the ship and we'd save our lives. Nobody would have to know—we'd tell them the truth, that Hap died in the hit."

"You're not telling *me* the truth," Reis said. "If we're going to handle this together, you've got to open up."

"I am, Reis, I swear. Don't you think I know this isn't the time to lie?"

"Okay," he said. "Then tell me who's in the medical pod in Section Three. Is it Sid? Somebody's in there, or you wouldn't have brought it up."

He waited, but Jan said nothing.

"Maybe Hap sleeps in there," Reis hazarded. "Maybe he's getting himself some additional treatment. You want me to pull the plug on him, but why can't you do that yourself?"

"No. I don't think he sleeps at all. Or . . ."

"Or what?"

"He's got Nell with him—Sergeant Upson. Nell was in the pod, but she's out now, and she stays with him all the time. I didn't want to tell you, but there it is. Something else is in Three's med pod. I don't know who it was, but when it gets out we won't have a chance."

"Nell's dead." He recalled her floating body, its hideous stare.

"That's right."

"I see," Reis said, and jerked back the lever that opened the sleep pod.

"Reis, you have to tell me. Are you with us or against us?"

He said. "You're wrong, Jan. I don't have to tell you one God-damned thing. Where's Hap?"

"In Section Five, probably. He wants to get another engine on line."

Reis launched himself toward the airlock, braked on the dog handles, and released them.

Section Three seemed normal but oddly vacant. He crossed to Centcomp's screen and wrote, "*Present occ this med pod for vis check.*"

"*ID*" flashed on the screen.

"Lt. Wm. R. Reis."

"Refused. Resuscitation underway."

Behind him Jan said, "I tried that. Centcomp won't identify it either."

Reis shrugged and pushed off toward the emergency locker. Opening it, he tossed out breathing apparatus, the aid kit, a body bag, and a folding stretcher with tie-downs. Behind them was a steel emergency toolbox. He selected a crowbar and the largest screwdriver and jetted to the med pod.

"Tampering with medical equipment is strictly forbidden. Resuscitation underway."

Reis jammed the blade of the screwdriver into the scarcely visible joint between the bulkhead and the pod, and struck the screwdriver's handle sharply enough with the crowbar to make his own weightless bodymass jump. He let the crowbar float free, grasped the pod latch, and jerked the screwdriver down. That widened the crack enough for him to work one end of the crowbar into it.

Centcomp's screen caught his eye. It read, *"Tampering is strictly Bill stop."*

Reis said, "Jan, tell it to open the God-damned pod if it doesn't want me to mess with it."

Jan found the rat; but before she could write, the screen read, *"Bill, I cannot."*

Jan gasped, "Oh, holy God," and it struck Reis that he had never heard her swear before. He said, "I thought you couldn't hear us, Centcomp. Wasn't that the story?"

"I truly cannot, Bill, and that is no story. But I monitor conditions everywhere in the ship. That is my job, and at times I can read your lips. Particularly yours, Bill. You have very good, clear lip motion."

Reis heaved at the crowbar; tortured metal shrieked.

Jan said, "Centcomp will have told Hap. He and Nell are probably on their way up here right now."

"I have not, Lieutenant van Joure."

Reis turned to face the screen. "Is that the truth?"

"You know I am incapable of any deception, Bill. Captain Hap-

ple is engaged in a delicate repair. I prefer to take care of this matter myself in order that he can proceed without any interruption."

"Watch the dogs—the moment they start going around, tell me."

"All right," Jan said. She had already pulled a wrench from the toolbox.

"Bill, I did not want to tell you this, yet I see I must."

Reis moved the crowbar to the left and pried again. "What is it?"

"You said . . . ?"

"I said what is it. God damn it! Stop screwing around and stalling. It's not going to do you any good."

"Bill, it really would be better if you did not open that."

Reis made no reply. Pale blue light was leaking from the med pod through the crack; it looked as though there might be a lot of ultraviolet in it, and he turned his eyes away.

"Bill, for your own good, do not do that."

Reis heaved again on the crowbar, and the latch broke. The pod rolled out, and as it did a nearly faceless thing inside sat up and caught his neck in skeletal hands. Section Three filled with the sickening sweetish smells of death and gangrene. Reis flailed at the half-dead thing with the crowbar, and its crooked end laid open a cheek, scattering stinking blood that was nearly black and exposing two rows of yellow teeth.

Evening was closing on Section Three. Night's darkness pressed upon Reis; his hands were numb, the crowbar gone.

Jan's wrench struck the dead thing's skull hard enough to throw her beyond the range of Reis's narrowing vision. The bony fingers relaxed a trifle. Reis forced his own arms between the dead arms and tore the hands away.

Then Jan was back, her wrench rising and falling again and again. His crowbar was gone; but the toolbox itself was within reach, with a D-shaped handle at one end. Reis grabbed it and hurled the box at the dead thing. It was heavy enough to send him spinning diagonally across the section, and it struck the head and chest of the dead thing and the end of the pod as well. For a split second Reis seemed to hear a wailing cry; the pod shot back until its bent and battered end was almost flush with the bulkhead.

Jan screamed as the airlock swung open; there was a rush of air and scorching blue flash. Something brushed Reis's cheek. He could scarcely see, but he snatched at it and his still-numb fingers told him he held an emergency mask. He pushed it against his face, shut his eyes, and sucked in oxygen, feeling he drank it like wine. There was another searing burst of heat.

Long training and good luck put the manual control into his hands; he tore away the safety strap and spun the wheel. Driven by a fifty thousand p.s.i. hydraulic accumulator, the airlock door slammed shut, its crash echoing even in the depleted atmosphere of Section Three. Emergency air that Centcomp could not control hissed through the vents, and Reis opened his eyes.

Jan writhed near the airlock door, her uniform smoldering, one hand and cheek seared. The arm and welding gun of a mobile unit, sheered off at the second joint, floated not far from Jan. Reis sprayed her uniform with a CO_2 extinguisher and smeared her face and hand with blue antibacterial cream.

"My eyes . . ." she gasped.

"You've been flashed," Reis told her. He tried to keep his voice low and soothing. "Zapped by an electric arc. Open them, just for a minute, and tell me if you can see anything."

"A little."

"Good," he told her. "Now shut them and keep them closed. After a while your vision should come back a bit more, and when we get home they can give you a retinal—"

His own dimmed sight had failed to note the spinning dogs. The hatch to Section Four swung back, and Hap floated in. His sunken cheeks and dull eyes carried the hideous stamp of death, and his movements were the swift, jerky gestures of a puppet; but he grinned at Reis and touched his forehead with the steel rod he carried. "Hi, there, Bill boy."

Nell Upson followed Hap. Her lips seemed too short now to conceal her teeth; it was not until she raised her pistol that Reis felt certain she was not wholly dead. Sid Dawson and Paula lingered at the hatch until Nell waved them forward. Both were terrified and exhausted, Reis decided. There could not be much fight left in either—perhaps none.

"You're supposed to salute your captain, Bill. You didn't even return mine. If I were running a tight ship, I'd have my marine arrest you."

Reis saluted.

"That's better. A lot of things have changed while you've been out of circulation, Bill. We've got three engines going. We'll have a fourth up in another forty-eight hours, and we only needed six to break away from the inner planets. Out where we are now, four should be plenty. And that's not all—we've got more air and food per crewman now than we had when we left Earth."

Reis said, "Then there's no reason we can't continue the mission."

"Way to go, Bill! Know what's happened to this old ship of ours?"

Reis shrugged. "I think so, a little. But tell me."

"We've been seized, Bill boy. Taken over, possessed. It isn't Centcomp—did you think it was Centcomp? And it sure as Hell ain't me. It's something else, a demon or what they call an elemental; and it's in me; and in Centcomp; and in you, too. Whatever you want to call it, it's the thing that created the *Flying Dutchman* and so on, centuries ago. We're the first ghost ship of space. You're not buying this, are you, Bill boy?"

"No," Reis told him.

"But it's the truth. There's a ship headed for us, it's coming from Earth right now—I bet you didn't know that. I wonder just how long they'll be able to see us."

Reis spat. The little gray-brown globe of phlegm drifted toward Hap, who appeared not to notice it. "Bullshit," Reis said.

Nell leveled her pistol. The synthetic ruby lens at the end of the barrel caught the light for a moment, winking like a baleful eye.

"Can I tell you what's really happened?" Reis asked.

"Sure. Be my guest."

"Centcomp's brought back you and Nell at any and all cost,

because that's what you programmed it to do. You were both too far gone, but Centcomp did it anyway. You've suffered a lot of brain damage, I think—you move like it—and I don't think you can keep going much longer. If you hit a dead man's arm with a couple of electrodes, his muscles will jump; but not forever."

Hap grinned again, mirthlessly. "Go on, Bill boy."

"Every time you look at yourself, you see what you are—what you've become—and you can't face it. So you've made up this crazy story about the ghost ship. A ghost ship explains a dead captain and a dead crew, and a ghost ship never really dies; it goes on sailing forever."

Reis paused. As he had hoped, the minute reaction created by the act of spitting was causing him to float, ever so slowly, away from Hap and Nell. Soon he would be caught in the draft from the main vent. It would move him to the left, toward the Section Two hatch; and if neither changed position, Nell would be almost in back of Hap.

"Now are you still going to court-martial me?" he asked. As he spoke, fresh cool air from the vent touched his cheek.

Hap said, "Hell, no. Not if—"

Nell's boot was reaching for the edge of the Section Four hatch; in a moment more she would kick off from it. It was now or never.

Reis's hand closed hard on the tube of antibacterial cream. A thick thread of bright blue cream shot into the space before Hap and Nell and writhed there like a living thing—a spectral monster or a tangle of blue maggots.

Nell fired.

The cream popped and spattered like grease in an overheated skillet, wrapping itself in dense black smoke. Alarms sounded. Through billowing smoke, Reis saw Dawson dart toward the airlock control.

Reis's feet touched the bulkhead; he kicked backward, going for Hap in a long, fast leap. Hap's steel bar caught his right forearm. He heard the snap of breaking bone as he went spinning through the rapidly closing Section Four hatch. A rush of air nearly carried him back into Three.

Then silence, except for the whisper from the vents. The alarms had stopped ringing. The hatch was closed; it had closed automatically, of course, when Centcomp's detectors had picked up the smoke from the burning cream, closed just slowly enough to permit a crewman to get clear.

His right arm was broken, although the pain seemed remote and dull. He went to Section Four's emergency locker and found a sling for it. It would not be safe to get in a med pod, he decided, even if Hap was gone; not until somebody reprogrammed Centcomp.

The hatchdogs spun. Reis looked around for something that could be used as a weapon, though he knew that his position was probably hopeless if either Hap or Nell had survived. There was a toolbox in this locker too, but his arm slowed him down. He was still wrestling with the stretcher when the hatch opened and Dawson came through. Reis smiled. "You made it."

Dawson nodded slowly without speaking. Jan entered; her eyes were closed, and Paula guided her with one hand.

Reis sighed. "You were able to catch hold of something. That's good, I was worried about you. Paul too."

Jan said, "Sid saved me. He reached out and snagged me as I flew past, otherwise I'd be out there in space. Paula saved herself, but Hap and Nell couldn't. It was just like you said: they didn't have enough coordination left. You were counting on that, weren't you? That Nell couldn't hit you, couldn't shoot very well anymore."

"Yes," Reis admitted. "Yes, I was, and I didn't think Hap could swat me with that steel bar; but I was wrong."

Jan said, "It doesn't matter now." She was keeping her eyes shut, but tears leaked from beneath their lids.

"No, it doesn't. Hap and Nell are finally dead—truly dead and at rest. Sid, I never thought a hell of a lot of you, and I guess I let it show sometimes; but you saved Jan and you saved the ship. Hell, you saved us all. All of us owe you our lives."

Dawson shook his head and looked away. "Show him, Paula."

She had taken something shining, something about the size of a small notepad, from one of her pockets. Wordlessly, she held it up.

And Reis, looking at it, staring into it for a second or more before he turned away, looked into horror and despair.

It was a mirror.

THE THIRD DEAD BODY

NINA KIRIKI HOFFMAN

I didn't even know Richie. I surely didn't want to love him. After he killed me, though, I found him irresistible.

I opened my eyes and dirt fell into them. Having things fall into my eyes was one of my secret terrors, but now I blinked and shook my head and most of the dirt fell away and I felt all right. So I knew something major had happened to me.

With my eyes closed, I shoved dirt away from my face. While I was doing this I realized that the inside of my mouth felt different. I probed with my tongue, my trained and talented tongue, and soon discovered that where smooth teeth had been before there were only broken stumps. What puzzled me about this and about the dirt in my eyes was that these things didn't hurt. They bothered me, but not on a pain level.

I frowned and tried to figure out what I was feeling. Not a lot. Not scared or mad, not hot or cold. This was different too. I usually felt scared, standing on street corners waiting for strangers to pick me up, and cold, working evenings in skimpy clothes that showed off my best features. Right now, I felt nothing.

I sat up, dirt falling away from me, and bumped into branches that gridded my view of the sky. Some of them slid off me. The branches were loose and wilting, not attached to a bush or tree. I lifted my hands to push them out of the way and noticed that the tips of my fingers were blackened beyond my natural cocoa color. I looked at them, trying to remember what had happened before I fell asleep or whatever—had I dipped my fingers in ink? But no; the skin was scorched. My fingerprints were gone. They would have told police that my name was Tawanda Foote, which was my street name.

My teeth would have led police to call me Mary Jefferson, a name I hadn't used since two years before, when I moved out of my parents' house at fifteen.

In my own mind, I was Sheila, a power name I had given myself; no one could have discovered that from any evidence about me.

No teeth, no fingerprints; Richie really didn't want anybody to know who I was, not that anybody ever had.

Richie.

With my scorched fingers I tried to take my pulse, though it was hard to find a vein among the rope burns at my wrists. With my eyes I watched my own naked chest. There were charred spots on my breasts where Richie had touched me with a burning cigarette. No pulse, but maybe that was because the nerves in my fingertips were dead. No breathing. No easy answer to that, so I chose the hard answer:

Dead.

I was dead.

After I pushed aside the branches so I could see trees and sky, I sat in my own grave dirt and thought about this.

My grannie would call this dirt goofer dust; any soil that's been piled on a corpse, whether the body's in a box or just loose like me, turns into goofer dust. Dirt next to dead folk gets a power in it, she used to say.

She used to tell me all kinds of things. She told me about the walking dead; but mostly she said they were just big scary dummies who obeyed orders. When I stayed up too late at night reading library books under my covers with a flashlight, she would say, "Maybe you know somebody who could give those nightwalkers orders. Maybe she can order 'em to come in here and turn off your light."

She had started to train me in recognizing herbs and collecting conjo ingredients, but that was before I told the preacher what really happened when I sat in Grand-père's lap, and Grand-père got in trouble with the church and then with other people in the Parish. I had a lot of cousins, and some of the others started talking up about Grand-père, but I was the first. After the police took Grand-père away, Grannie laid a curse on me: "May you love the thing that hurts you, even after it kills you." She underlined it with virgin blood, the wax of black candles, and the three of spades.

I thought maybe if I left Louisiana I could get the curse off, but nobody I knew could uncross me and the curse followed me to Seattle.

In the midst of what was now goofer dust, I was sitting next to something. I reached out and touched it. It was another dead body. "Wake up," I said to the woman in the shallow grave beside me. But she refused to move.

So: no fingerprints, no teeth. I was dead, next to someone even deader, and off in some woods. I checked in with my body, an act I saved for special times when I could come out of the numb state I spent most of my life in, and found I wasn't hungry or thirsty. All the parts of me that had been hurting just before Richie, my last trick, took a final twist around my neck with the nylon cord he was so fond of, all those parts were quiet, not bothering me at all; but there was a burning desire in my crotch, and a pinprick of fire behind my eyes that whispered to me, "Get up and move. We know where to go."

I looked around. At my back the slope led upward toward a place where sun broke through trees. At my feet it led down into darker woods. To either side, more woods and bushes, plants Grannie had never named for me, foreign as another language.

I moved my legs, bringing them up out of the goofer dust. All of me was naked; dirt caught in my curly hair below. I pulled myself to my feet and something fell out of my money pit, as my pimp, Blake, liked to call my pussy. I looked down at what had fallen from me. It was a rock flaked and shaped into a blade about the size of a flat hand, and it glistened in the dulled sunlight, wet and dark with what had come from inside me, and maybe with some of his juices too.

The fire in my belly flared up, but it wasn't a feeling like pain; it felt like desire.

I put my hands to my neck and felt the deep grooves the rope had left there. Heat blossomed in my head and in my heart. I wanted to find the hands that had tightened the rope around my neck, wrists, and ankles. I wanted to find the eyes that had watched my skin sizzle under the kiss of the burning cigarette. I wanted to find the mind that had decided to plunge a crude blade into me like that. The compulsion set in along my bones, jetted into my muscles like adrenaline. I straightened, looked around. I had to find Richie. I knew which direction to look: something in my head was teasing me, nudging me—a fire behind my eyes, urging me back to the city.

I fought the urge and lifted more branches off the place where I had lain. If I was going to get to Seattle from here, wherever here was, I needed some clothes. I couldn't imagine anybody stopping to pick me up with me looking the way I did. I knew Richie had worked hard to get rid of all clues to who I was, but I thought maybe my companion in the grave might not be so naked of identity, so I brushed dirt off her, and found she was not alone. There were two bodies in the dirt, with no sign of afterlife in them except maggots, and no trace of clothes. One was darker than me, with fewer marks on her but the same rope burns around her neck. The other one was very light, maybe white. She was really falling apart. They looked like they must smell pretty bad, but I couldn't smell them. I couldn't smell anything. I could see and hear, and my muscles did what I told them, but I didn't feel much except the gathering fire inside me that cried for Richie.

I brushed dirt back over the other women and moved the branches to cover their resting place again.

Downslope the trees waited, making their own low-level night. Upslope, open sun: a road, probably. I scrambled up toward the light.

The heat in my head and heart and belly burned hotter, and I churned up the hillside and stepped into the sun.

A two-lane highway lay before me, its yellow dotted center stripe bright in the sun. Its edges tailed into the gravel I stood on. Crushed snack bags and Coke and beer cans lay scattered in the bushes beside the road; cellophane glinted. I crossed the road and looked at the wooded hill on its far side, then down in the ditch. No clothes. Not even a plastic bag big enough to make into a bikini bottom.

The heat inside me was like some big fat drunk who will not shut up, yelling for a beer. I started walking, knowing which direction would take me toward town without knowing how I knew.

After a while a car came from behind me. Behind was probably my best side; my microbraids hung down to hide the marks on my neck, and Richie hadn't done any cigarette graffiti on my back that I could remember. A lot of tricks had told me I had a nice ass and good legs; even my pimp had said it, and he never said anything nice unless he thought it was true or it would get him what he wanted. And he had everything he wanted from me.

I could hear the car slowing, but I was afraid to look back. I knew my mouth must look funny because of the missing teeth, and I wasn't sure what the rest of my face looked like. Since I couldn't feel pain, anything could have happened. I bent my head so the sun wasn't shining in my face.

"Miss? Oh, miss?" Either a woman's deep voice came from the car behind me, or a man's high one; it sounded like an older person. The engine idled low as the car pulled up beside me. It was a red Volkswagen Rabbit.

I crossed my arms over my chest, hiding the burn marks and tucking my rope-mark bracelets into the crooks of my elbows.

"Miss?"

"Ya?" I said, trying to make my voice friendly, not sure I had a voice at all.

"Miss, are you in trouble?"

I nodded, my braids slapping my shoulders and veiling my face.

"May I help you, miss?"

I cleared my throat, drew in breath. "Ya-you goin' do down?" I managed to say.

"What?"

"Down," I said, pointing along the road. "Seaddle."

"Oh. Yes. Would you like a ride?"

"Mm-hmm," I said. "Cloze?" I glanced up this time, wondering if the car's driver was man or woman. A man might shed his shirt for me, but a woman, unless she was carrying a suitcase or something, might not have anything to offer.

"Oh, you poor thing, what happened to you?" The car pulled up onto the shoulder ahead of me and the driver got out. It was a big beefy white woman in jeans and a plaid flannel shirt. She came toward me with a no-nonsense stride. She had short dark hair. She was wearing a man's khaki cloth hat with fishing flies stuck in the band, all different feathery colors. "What ha—"

I put one hand over my face, covering my mouth with my palm.

"What happened—" she whispered, stopping while there was still a lot of space between us.

"My boyfriend dreeded me preddy bad," I said behind my hand. My tongue kept trying to touch the backs of teeth no longer there. It frustrated me that my speech was so messy. I thought maybe I could talk more normally if I touched my tongue to the roof of my mouth. "My boyfriend," I said again, then, "treated me pretty bad."

"Poor thing, poor thing," she whispered, then turned back to the car and rummaged in a back seat, coming up with a short-waisted Levi's jacket and holding it out to me.

I ducked my head and took the jacket. She gasped when I dropped my arms from my chest. I wrapped up in the jacket, which was roomy, but not long enough to cover my crotch. Then again, from the outside, my crotch didn't look so bad. I turned the collar up to cover my neck and the lower part of my face. "Thank you," I said.

Her eyes were wide, her broad face pale under her tan. "You need help," she said. "Hospital? Police?"

"Seattle," I said.

"Medical attention!"

"Won't help me now." I shrugged.

"You could get infections, die from septicemia or something. I have a first aid kit in the car. At least let me—"

"What would help me," I said, "a mirror."

She sighed, her shoulders lowering. She walked around the car and opened the passenger side door, and I followed her. I looked at the seat. It was so clean, and I was still goofer dusted. "Gonna get it dirty," I said.

"Lord, that's the last thing on my mind right now," she said. "Get in. Mirror's on the back of the visor."

I slid in and folded down the visor, sighed with relief when I saw my face. Nothing really wrong with it, except my chin was nearer to my nose than it should be, and my lips looked too dark and puffy. My eyes weren't blackened and my nose wasn't broken. I could pass. I gapped the collar just a little and winced at the angry dark rope marks around my neck, then clutched the collar closed.

The woman climbed into the driver's seat. "My name's Marti," she said, holding out a hand. Still keeping the coat closed with my left hand, I extended my right, and she shook it.

"Sheila," I said. It was the first time I'd ever said it out loud. She. La. Two words for woman put together. I smiled, then glanced quickly at the mirror, and saw that a smile was as bad as I'd thought. My mouth was a graveyard of broken teeth, brown with old blood. I hid my mouth with my hand again.

"Christ!" said Marti. "What's your boyfriend's name?"

"Don't worry about it," I said.

"If he did that to you, he could do it to others. My daughter lives in Renton. This has to be reported to the police. Who is he? Where does he live?"

"Near Sea-Tac. The airport."

She took a deep breath, let it out. "You understand, don't you, this is a matter for the authorities?"

I shook my head. The heat in my chest was scorching, urging me on. "I have to go to town now," I said, gripping the door handle.

"Put your seat belt on," she said, slammed her door, and started the car.

Once she got started, she was some ball-of-fire driver. Scared me—even though there wasn't anything I could think of that could hurt me.

"Where were we, anyway?" I asked after I got used to her tire-squealing cornering on curves.

"Well, I was coming down from Kanaskat. I'm on my way in to Renton to see my daughter. She's got a belly-dance recital tonight, and—" She stared at me, then shook her head and focused on the road.

The land was leveling a little. We hit a main road, Highway 169, and she turned north on it.

The burning in my chest raged up into my throat. "No," I said, reaching for her hand on the steering wheel.

"What?"

"No. That way." I pointed back to the other road we had been on. Actually the urge inside me was pulling from some direction between the two roads, but the smaller road aimed closer to where I had to go.

"Maple Valley's this way," she said, not turning, "and we can talk to the police there, and a doctor."

"No," I said.

She looked at me. "You're in no state to make rational decisions," she said.

I closed my hand around her wrist and squeezed. She cried out. She let go of the steering wheel and tried to shake off my grip. I stared at her and held on, remembering my grand-mère's tales of the strength of the dead.

"Stop," I said. I felt strange, totally strange, ordering a woman around the way a pimp would. I knew I was hurting her, too. I knew I could squeeze harder, break the bones in her arm, and I was ready to, but she pulled the car over to the shoulder and stamped on the brake.

"I got to go to Sea-Tac," I said. I released her arm and climbed out of the car. "Thanks for ride. You want the jacket back?" I fingered the denim.

"My Lord," she said, "you keep it, child." She was rubbing her hand over the wrist I had gripped. She heaved a huge sigh. "Get in. I'll take you where you want to go. I can't just leave you here."

"Your daughter's show?" I said.

"I'll phone. We're going someplace with phones, aren't we?"

I wasn't sure exactly where we would end up. I would know when we arrived. . . . I remembered the inside of Richie's apartment. But that was later. First he had pulled up next to where I was standing by the highway, rolled down the passenger window of his big gold four-door Buick, said he'd like to party and that he knew a good place. Standard lines, except I usually told johns the place, down one of the side streets and in the driveway behind an abandoned house. I had asked him how high he was willing to go. My pimp had been offering me coke off and on but I'd managed not to get hooked, so I was still a little picky about who I went with; but Richie looked clean-cut and just plain clean, and his car was a couple years old but expensive; I thought he might have money.

"I want it all," Richie had said. "I'll give you a hundred bucks."

I climbed into his car.

He took me down off the ridge where the Sea-Tac Strip is to a place like the one where I usually took my tricks, behind one of the abandoned houses near the airport that are due to be razed someday. There's two or three neighborhoods of them handy. I asked him for money and he handed me a hundred, so I got in back with him, but then things went seriously wrong. That was the first time I saw and felt his rope, the first time I heard his voice cursing me, the first time I tasted one of his sweaty socks, not the worst thing I'd ever tasted, but close.

When he had me gagged and tied up and shoved down on the back seat floor, he drove somewhere else. I couldn't tell how long the drive was; it felt like two hours but was probably only fifteen or twenty minutes. I could tell when the car drove into a parking garage because the sounds changed. He put a shopping bag over my head and carried me into an elevator, again something I could tell by feel, and then along a hall to his apartment. That was where I learned more about him than I had ever wanted to know about anybody.

I didn't know his apartment's address, but I knew where Richie was. If he was at the apartment, I would direct Marti there even without a map. The fire inside me reached for Richie like a magnet lusting for a hammer.

Shaping words carefully, I told Marti, "Going to the Strip. Plenty of phones."

"Right," she said.

"On the other road." I pointed behind us.

She sighed. "Get in."

I climbed into the car, and she waited for an RV to pass, then pulled out and turned around.

As soon as we were heading the way I wanted to go, the fire inside me cooled a little. I sat back and relaxed.

"Why are we going to the—to the Strip?" she asked. "What are you going to do when we get there?"

"Don't know," I said. We were driving toward the sun, which was going down. Glare had bothered me before my death, but now it was like dirt in my eyes, a minor annoyance. I blinked and considered this, then shrugged it off.

"Can't you even tell me your boyfriend's name?" she asked.

"Richie."

"Richie what?"

"Don't know."

"Are you going back to him?"

Fire rose in my throat like vomit. I felt like I could breathe it out and it would feel good. It felt good inside my belly already. I was drunk with it. "Oh, yes," I said.

"How can you?" she cried. She shook her head. "I can't take you back to someone who hurt you so much." But she didn't stop driving.

"I have to go back," I said.

"You don't. You can choose something else. There are shelters for battered women. The government should offer you some protection. The police. . . ."

"You don't understand," I said.

"I do," she said. Her voice got quieter. "I know what it's like to live with someone who doesn't respect you. I know how hard it is to get away. But you *are* away, Sheila. You can start over."

"No," I said, "I can't."

"You can. I'll help you. You can live in Kanaskat with me and he'll never find you. Or if you just want a bus ticket someplace—back home, wherever that is—I can do that for you, too."

"You don't understand," I said.

She was quiet for a long stretch of road. Then she said, "Help me understand."

I shook my braids back and opened the collar of the jacket, pulled down the lapels to bare my neck. I stared at her until she looked back.

She screamed and drove across the center lane. Fortunately there was no other traffic. Still screaming, she fought with the steering wheel until she straightened out the car. Then she pulled over to the shoulder and jumped out of the car, running away.

I shut off the car's engine, then climbed out. "Marti," I yelled. "Okay, I'm walking away now. The car's all yours. I'm leaving. It's safe. Thanks for the jacket. Bye." I buttoned up the jacket, put the collar up, buried my hands in the pockets, and started walking along the road toward Richie.

I had gone about about a quarter mile when she caught up with me again. The sun had set and twilight was deepening into night. Six cars had passed going my way, but I didn't hold out my thumb, and though some kid had yelled out a window at me, and somebody else had honked and swerved, nobody stopped.

It had been so easy to hitch before I met Richie. Somehow now I just couldn't do it.

I heard the Rabbit's sputter behind me and kept walking, not turning to look at her. But she slowed and kept pace with me. "Sheila?" she said in a hoarse voice. "Sheila?"

I stopped and looked toward her. I knew she was scared of me. I felt strong and strange, hearing her call me by a name I had given myself, as if I might once have had a chance to make up who I was instead of being shaped by what had happened to me. I couldn't see it being possible now, though, when I was only alive to do what the fire in me wanted.

Marti blinked, turned away, then turned back and faced me. "Get in," she said.

"You don't have to take me," I said. "I'll get there sooner or later. Doesn't matter when."

"Get in."

I got back into her car.

For half an hour we drove in silence. She crossed Interstate 5, paused when we hit 99, the Strip. "Which way?"

I pointed right. The fire was so hot in me now I felt like my fingertips might start smoking any second.

She turned the car and we cruised north toward the Sea-Tac Airport, my old stomping grounds. We passed expensive hotels and cheap motels, convenience stores and fancy restaurants. Lighted buildings alternated with dark gaps. The roar of planes taking off and landing, lights rising and descending in the sky ahead of us, turned rapidly into background. We drove past the Goldilocks Motel, where Blake and I had a room we rented by the week, and I didn't feel anything. But as we passed the intersection where the Red Lion sprawls on the corner of 188th Street and the Pacific Highway, fire flared under my skin. "Slowly," I said to Marti. She stared at me and slowed the car. A mile further, past the airport, one of the little roads led down off the ridge to the left. I pointed.

Marti got in the left-turn lane and made the turn, then pulled into a gas station on the corner and parked by the rest rooms. "Now, wait," she said. "What are we doing, here?"

"Richie," I whispered. I could feel his presence in the near distance; all my wounds were resonating with his nearness now, all the places he had pressed himself into me with his rope and his cigarette and his sock and his flaked stone knife and his penis, imprinting me as his possession. Surely as a knife slicing into a tree's bark, he had branded me with his heart.

"Yes," said Marti. "Richie. You have any plans for what you're going to do once you find him?"

I held my hands out, open, palms up. The heat was so strong I felt like anything I touched would burst into flame.

"What are you going to do, strangle him? Have you got something to do it with?" She sounded sarcastic.

I was having a hard time listening to her. All my attention was focused down the road. I knew Richie's car was there, and Richie in it. It was the place he had taken me to tie me up. He might be driving this way any second, and I didn't want to wait any longer for our reunion, though I knew there was no place he could hide where I couldn't find him. My love for him was what animated me now.

"Strangle," I said, and shook my head. I climbed out of the car.

"Sheila!" said Marti.

I let the sound of my self-given name fill me with what power it could, and stood still for a moment, fighting the fire inside. Then I walked into the street, stood in the center so a car coming up out of the dark would have to stop. I strode down into darkness, away from the lights and noise of the Strip. My feet felt like match-heads, as if a scrape could strike fire from them.

Presently the asphalt gave way to potholes and gravel; I could tell by the sound of pebbles sliding under my feet. I walked past the first three dark houses to the right and left, looming shapes in a darkness pierced by the flight lights of airplanes, but without stars. I turned left at the fourth house, dark like the others, but with a glow behind it I couldn't see with my eyes but could feel in my bones. Heat pulsed and danced inside me.

I pushed past an overgrown lilac bush at the side of the house and stepped into the broad drive in back. The car was there, as I had known it would be. Dark and quiet. Its doors were closed.

I heard a brief cry, and then the dome light went on in the car. Richie was sitting up in back, facing away from me.

Richie.

I walked across the crunching gravel, looking at his dark head. He wore a white shirt. He was staring down, focused, his arms moving. As I neared the car, I could see he was sitting on a woman. She still had her clothes on. (Richie hadn't taken my clothes off until he got me in his apartment.) Tape was across her mouth, and her head thrashed from side to side, her upper arms jerking as Richie bound his thin nylon rope around her wrists, her legs kicking. I stood a moment looking in the window. She saw me and her eyes widened. She made a gurgling swallowed sound behind the sock, the tape.

I thought: he doesn't need her. He has me.

I remembered the way my mind had struggled while my body struggled, screaming silently: no, oh no, Blake, where are you? No one will help me, the way no one has ever helped me, and I can't help myself. That hurts, that hurts. Maybe he'll play with me and let me go if I'm very, very good. Oh, God! What do you want? Just tell me, I can do it. You don't have to hurt me! Okay, rip me off, it's not like you're the first, but you don't have to hurt me!

Hurt me.

I love you. I love you so much.

I stared at him through the glass. The woman beneath him had stilled, and she was staring at me. Richie finally noticed, and whirled.

For a moment we stared at each other. Then I smiled, showing him the stumps of my teeth, and his blue eyes widened.

I reached for the door handle, opened it before he could lock it.

"Richie," I said.

"Don't!" he said. He shook his head, hard, as though he were a dog with wet fur. Slowly, he lifted one hand and rubbed his eye. He had a big bread knife in the other hand, had used it to cut the rope, then flicked it across the woman's cheek, leaving a streak of darkness. He looked at me again. His jaw worked.

"Richie."

"Don't! Don't . . . interrupt."

I held out my arms, my fingertips scorched black as if dyed or tattooed, made special, the wrists dark beyond the ends of my sleeves. "Richie," I said tenderly, the fire in me rising up like a firework, a burst of stars. "I'm yours."

"No," he said.

"You made me yours." I looked at him. He had made Tawanda his, and then he had erased her. He had made Mary his, and then erased her. Even though he had erased Tawanda and Mary, these feelings inside me were Tawanda's: *whoever hurts me controls me;* and Mary's: *I spoke up once and I got a curse on me I can't get rid of. If I'm quiet maybe I'll be okay.*

But Sheila? Richie hadn't erased Sheila; he had never even met her.

It was Tawanda who was talking. "You killed me and you made me yours," she said. My fingers went to the jacket, unbuttoned it, dropped it behind me. "What I am I owe to you."

"I—" he said, and coughed. "No," he said.

I heard the purr of car engines in the near distance, not the constant traffic of the Strip, but something closer.

I reached into the car and gripped Richie's arm. I pulled him out, even though he grabbed at the door handle with his free hand. I could feel the bone in his upper arm as my fingers pressed his muscles. "Richie," I whispered, and put my arms around him and laid my head on his shoulder.

For a while he was stiff, tense in my embrace. Then a shudder went through him and he loosened up. His arms came around me. "You're mine?" he said.

"Yours," said Tawanda.

"Does that mean you'll do what I say?" His voice sounded like a little boy's.

"Whatever you say," she said.

"Put your arms down," he said.

I lowered my arms.

"Stand real still." He backed away from me, then stood and studied me. He walked around, looking at me from all sides. "Wait a sec, I gotta get my flashlight." He went around to the trunk and opened it, pulled out a flashlight as long as his forearm, turned it on. He trained the beam on my breasts, my neck. "I did you," he said, nodding. "I did you. You were good. Almost as good as the first one. Show me your hands again."

I held them out and he stared at my blackened fingers. Slowly he smiled, then looked up and met my eyes.

"I was going to visit you," he said. "When I finished with this one. I was coming back to see you."

"I couldn't wait," said Tawanda.

"Don't talk," Richie said gently.

Don't talk! Tawanda and Mary accepted that without a problem, but I, Sheila, was tired of people telling me not to talk. What did I have to lose?

On the other hand, what did I have to say? I didn't even know what I wanted. Tawanda's love for Richie was hard to fight. It was the burning inside me, the sizzling under my skin, all I had left of life.

"Will you scream if I say so?" said Richie in his little boy's voice.

"Yes," said Tawanda; but suddenly lights went on around us, and bullhorn voices came out of the dark.

"Hold it right there, buddy! Put your hands up!"

Blinking in the sudden flood of light, Richie slowly lifted his hand, the knife glinting in the left one, the flashlight in the other.

"Step away from him, miss," said someone else. I looked around too, not blinking; glare didn't bother me. I couldn't see through it, though. I didn't know who was talking. "Miss, move away from him," said another voice from outside the light.

"Come here," Richie whispered, and I went to him. Releasing the flashlight, he dropped his arms around me, holding the knife to my neck, and yelled, "Stay back!"

"Sheila!" It was Marti's voice this time, not amplified.

I looked toward her.

"Sheila, get away from him!" Marti yelled. "Do you want him to escape?"

Tawanda did. Mary did. They, after all, had found the place where they belonged. In the circle of his arms, my body glowed, the fire banked but burning steady.

He put the blade closer to my twisted throat. I could almost feel it. I laid my head back on his shoulder, looking at his profile out of the corner of my eye. The light glare brought out the blue in his eye. His mouth was slightly open, the inside of his lower lip glistening. He turned to look down into my face, and a slight smile curved the corner of his mouth. "Okay," he whispered, "we're going to get into the car now." He raised his voice. "Do what I say and don't struggle." Keeping me between him and the lights, he kicked the back door closed and edged us around the car to the driver's side. Moving in tandem, with his arm still around my neck, we slid in behind the wheel, me going first. "Keep close," he said to me. "Slide down a little so I can use my arm to shift with, but keep close."

"Sheila!" screamed Marti. The driver's side window was open.

Richie started the car.

"Sheila! There's a live woman in the back of that car!"

Tawanda didn't care, and Mary didn't care, and I wasn't even sure *I* cared. Richie shifted from park into first and eased his foot off the brake and onto the gas pedal; I could feel his legs moving against my left shoulder. From the back seat I heard a muffled groan. I looked up at Richie's face. He was smiling.

Just as he gunned the engine, I reached up and grappled the steering-wheel-mounted gear shift into park. Then I broke the shift handle off.

"You said you'd obey me," he said, staring down into my face. He looked betrayed, his eyes wide, his brow furrowed, his mouth soft. The car's engine continued to snarl without effect.

Fire blossomed inside me, hurting me this time because I'd hurt him. Pain came alive. I coughed, choking on my own tongue, my throat swollen and burning, my wrists and ankles burning, my breasts burning, between my legs a column of flame raging up inside me. I tried to apologize, but I no longer had a voice.

"You promised," said Richie in his little boy's voice, looking down at me.

I coughed. I could feel the power leaving me; my arms and legs were stiffening the way a body is supposed to do after death. I lifted my crippling hands as high as I could, palms up, pleading, but by that point only my elbows could bend. It was Tawanda's last gesture.

"Don't make a move," said a voice. "Keep your hands on the wheel."

We looked. A man stood just outside the car, aiming a gun at Richie through the open window.

Richie edged a hand down the wheel toward me.

"Make a move for her and I'll shoot," said the man. Someone

else came up beside him, and he moved back, keeping his gun aimed at Richie's head, while the other man leaned in and put handcuffs on Richie.

"That's it," said the first man, and he and the second man heaved huge sighs.

▼▼▼

I lay curled on the seat, my arms bent at the elbows, my legs bent at the knees. When they pulled Richie out of the car I slipped off his lap and lay stiff, my neck bent at an angle so my head stuck up sideways. "This woman needs medical attention," someone yelled. I listened to them freeing the woman in the back seat, and thought about the death of Tawanda and Mary.

Tawanda had lifted me out of my grave and carried me for miles. Mary had probably mostly died when Grannie cursed me and drove me out of the house. But Sheila? In a way, I had been pregnant with Sheila for years, and she was born in the grave. She was still looking out of my eyes and listening with my ears even though the rest of me was dead. Even as the pain of death faded, leaving me with clear memories of how Richie had treated me before he took that final twist around my neck, the Sheila in me was awake and feeling things.

"She's in an advanced state of rigor," someone said. I felt a dim pressure around one of my arms. My body slid along the seat toward the door.

"Wait," said someone else. "I got to take pictures."

"What are you talking about?" said another. "Ten minutes ago she was walking and talking."

Lights flashed, but I didn't blink.

"Are you crazy?" said the first person. "Even rapid-onset rigor doesn't come on this fast."

"Ask anybody, Tony. We all saw her."

"You try feeling for a pulse. Are you sure he wasn't just propping her up and moving her around like a puppet? But that wouldn't explain. . . ."

"You done with the pictures yet, Crane?" said one of the cops.

Then, to me, in a light voice, "Honey, come on out of there. Don't just lie there and let him photograph you like a corpse. You don't know what he does with the pictures."

"Wait till the civilians are out of here before you start making jokes," said someone else. "Maybe she's just in shock."

"Sheila?" said Marti from the passenger side.

"Marti," I whispered.

Gasps.

"Sheila, you did it. You did it."

Did what? Let him kill me, then kill me again? Suddenly I was so angry I couldn't rest. Anger was like the fire that had filled me before, only a lower, slower heat. I shuddered and sat up.

Another gasp from one of the men at the driver's side door. "See?" said the one with the shock theory. One of them had a flashlight and shone it on me. I lifted my chin and stared at him, my microbraids brushing my shoulders.

"Kee-rist!"

"Oh, God!"

They fell back a step.

I sucked breath in past the swelling in my throat and said, "I need a ride. And feeling for a pulse? I think you'll be happier if you don't."

▼▼▼

Marti gave me back her jacket. I rode in her Rabbit; the cop cars and the van from the medical examiner's office tailed us. Marti had a better idea of where she had found me than I did.

"What's your full name?" she said when we were driving. "Is there anybody I can get in touch with for you?"

"No. I've been dead to them for a couple years already."

"Are you sure? Did you ever call to check with them?"

I waited for a while, then said, "If your daughter was a hooker and dead, would you want to know?"

"Yes," she said immediately. "Real information is much better than not knowing."

I kept silent for another while, then told her my parents' names and phone number. Ultimately, I didn't care if the information upset them or not.

She handed me a little notebook and asked me to write it down, turning on the dome light so I could see what I was doing. The pain of scorching had left my fingers again. Holding the pen was awkward, but I managed to write out what Marti wanted. When I finished, I slipped the notebook back into her purse and turned off the light.

"It was somewhere along here," she said half an hour later. "You have any feeling for it?"

"No." I didn't have a sense of my grave the way I had had a feeling for Richie. Marti's headlights flashed on three Coke cans lying together by the road, though, and I remembered seeing a cluster like that soon after I had climbed up the slope. "Here," I said.

She pulled over, and so did the three cars following us. Someone gave me a flashlight and I went to the edge of the slope and walked along, looking for my own footprints or anything else familiar. A broken bramble, a crushed fern, a tree with a hooked branch—I remembered them all from the afternoon. "Here," I said, pointing down the mountainside.

"Okay. Don't disturb anything," said the cop named Joe. One of the others started stringing up yellow tape along the road in both directions.

"But—" I was having a feeling now, a feeling that Sheila had lived as long as she wanted to. All I needed was my blanket of goofer dust, and I could go back to sleep. When Joe went back to his car to get something, I slipped over the edge and headed home.

I pushed the branches off the other two women and lay down beside their bodies, thinking about my brief life. I had helped somebody and I had hurt somebody, which I figured was as much as I'd done in my first two lives.

I pulled dirt up over me, even over my face, not blinking when it fell into my eyes; but then I thought, Marti's going to see me sooner or later, and she'd probably like it better if my eyes were closed. So I closed my eyes.

BIOGRAPHIES

Kevin J. Anderson's short horror fiction has appeared in *The Ultimate Dracula, The Ultimate Werewolf, Year's Best Fantasy Stories: 13, Fantasy & Science Fiction*, and others. His first novel. *Resurrection Inc.* was nominated for the Bram Stoker Award given by the Horror Writers of America. He has since published many other novels, including a serial killer thriller with Kristine Kathryn Rusch, *Afterimage*, as well as science fiction novels *Assemblers of Infinity, The Trinity Paradox*, and *Lifeline*, all written with physicist Doug Beason. He is also at work on a young adult fantasy coauthored with John Betancourt. Kevin's next solo novels will be three sequels to the *Star Wars* movies for Bantam Books. He is a part-time technical writer for the Lawrence Livermore National Laboratory.

John Betancourt began his editing career at the age of 19, working as an assistant on *Amazing Stories* magazine. He left five years later to start his own horror magazine, *Weird Tales*, with George Scithers and Darrell Schweitzer. Since then he has moved on to book editing for Byron Preiss Visual Publications, Inc. He is also a popular short story writer and novelist whose books include *Rememory, Johnny Zed*, and *The Blind Archer*. His next novel is a children's fantasy scheduled to appear from Atheneum in 1994, written in collaboration with Kevin J. Anderson.

Michael David Biegel was born in Detroit and raised in Northern New Jersey. He attended Syracuse University and spent one year after college working for a South Florida ad agency. Since 1985 he's been working as a freelance illustrator. His client list includes The Metropolitan Opera Guild, Avon Books, Scholastic Magazine, World Hunger Year, Milton Bradley Co. and more. He is currently President of the Self-employed Writer's and Artist's Network (SWAN) based in New Jersey.

Aside from illustration, music is integral in Biegel's life, as is his commitment to family and friendships. He cannot forget the Maine coast and its calling. It is the same sound he hears in the snow covered mountains of Vermont. In one of these two places he would like to bring his crow-quill pen to settle down with and ultimately call home.

JOHN BRUNNER was born in Oxfordshire, England, and attended Cheltenham College. As you might expect he is mainly self educated. Although he has written almost everything one can write and expect to get paid for, he is best known for his science fiction. Among other distinctions he has won the Hugo Award for best science fiction novel of the year, the British Fantasy Award, the British Science Fiction Award (twice), the French *Prix Apollo*, the Italian *Cometa d'Argento* (twice), the *Premio Italia*, the Spanish *Gigamesh*, the European SF Convention Special Award as best western European SF writer, and the Clark Ashton Smith award for fantasy poetry. He lives in what in olden days was called The Summer Country, to the south of the Vale of Avalon, and expects to die there—preferably not too soon because he is married to a beautiful Chinese artist called LiYi, and he likes it.

MATTHEW J. COSTELLO is a contributing editor at *Games* Magazine and a columnist for *Mystery Scene*. He has written for *Sports Illustrated, Writer's Digest*, and *Tower Video*. His interviews with Joan Rivers, Larry Hagman, Joel Silver, and others have appeared in *The Los Angeles Times* and *Amazing Stories*.

Costello's novel, *Midsummer*, was named one of the "Best Novels of 1990" by the *Science Fiction Chronicle*, as was *Beneath Still Waters* for the year 1989. Costello's recent novel, *Wurm*, was a best-seller on the Mystery Scene list. *Homecoming* was Berkley/Putnam's lead title for November 1992.

Costello lives in Ossining, New York, with his wife and three children.

DON D'AMMASSA has been reading and reviewing horror and SF for over 30 years. His first novel, *Blood Beast*, was published in 1988, and his short stories have appeared in *Hotter Blood, Chilled to the Bone, Analog, Pulphouse, Shock Rock*, and elsewhere. He is currently attempting to make the transition to full-time writing.

HARLAN ELLISON is the author of 58 books, more than 1,200 stories, essays, reviews, articles, motion picture scripts, and teleplays. He has won the Hugo Award 8½ times, the Nebula 3 times, the Edgar Allan Poe award of Mystery Writers of America twice, the Bram Stoker award of Horror writers of America twice, the World Fantasy Award, the British Fantasy Award, the Silver Pen award for journalism from P.E.N., and is the only scenarist in Hollywood ever to have won the Writers Guild of America award for Most Outstanding Teleplay 4 times for solo work. His latest books are *The Harlan Ellison Hornbook*, a 35-year retrospective of his work, *The Essential Ellison*, and forthcoming this year are *The City on the Edge of Forever*, the first book publication of his famous *Star Trek* script in its original (not the aired) version . . . and a new collection of stories, *Slippage*. He lives with his wife Susan in the Lost Aztec Temple of Mars somewhere in the Los Angeles area.

LIONEL FENN has had nine novels published to date (five of which are B-Movie adventures starring Kent Montana). His tenth (not a Kent Montana book) is *Once Upon a Time in the East*, the first book in a time-travel series called *Voyage of the Time Thing;* he's also had a number of short stories and novelettes published, all featuring Kent Montana. He lives in northern New Jersey in a luxurious basement apartment, has three published writer brothers (Geoffrey Marsh, Simon Lake, and Timothy Boggs), and is currently editing a bi-monthly newsletter called *Haggis*.

KAREN HABER'S short fiction has appeared in *The Magazine of Fantasy and Science Fiction, Isaac Asimov's Science Fiction Magazine, Full Spectrum 2, Women of Darkness*, and *Final Shadows*. Her books include *The Mutant Season* (co-written with her husband, Robert Silverberg), *The Mutant Prime, Mutant Star.* and *Mutant Legacy*. She is also co-editor of the *Universe* anthologies. She lives in the San Francisco Bay Area.

RICK HAUTALA is the author of nine novels, including *Dark Silence, Little Brothers, Cold Whisper,* and *Nightstone.* He has had nearly 30 short stories published in anthologies such as *Night Visions* 9, *Cold Blood,* and *Stalkers,* and magazines such as *Cemetery Dance* and *Horror Show.* He served one term as vice president of Horror Writers of America, and lives in southern Maine with his wife and three children.

BRIAN HODGE is the author of five novels, including *Nightlife, Deathgrip,* and *The Darker Saints,* all from Dell/Abyss. He is currently at work on his next, *Prototype,* a grimly existential look at psychosociochromosomal mutation. His short fiction has appeared in numerous unsavory magazines and anthologies, including *Book of the Dead, Final Shadows, Under the Fang, Solved,* and *Borderlands* 2. An avowed gothic/industrial music enthusiast, he has yet to beat an addiction to Ben & Jerry's Chocolate Fudge Brownie ice cream. Donations are appreciated.

NINA KIRIKI HOFFMAN has been pursuing a writing career for ten years and has sold more than 80 short stories, three short story collections, a novel (*The Thread that Binds the Bones*), one novella (*Unmasking*), and one collaborative young adult novel (*Child of an Ancient City* with Tad Williams). So far.

GEOFFREY A. LANDIS is a Hugo and Nebula award winning writer, and also a research physicist. His first short story collection, *Myths, Legends, and True History,* appeared in 1991 as volume 26 of the Pulphouse Publishing *Author's Choice* series. He is a scientist at the NASA Lewis Research Center, currently working on developing scientific instruments to be flown on a future probe to Mars. He is the author of over a hundred scientific papers in the fields of solar energy, semiconductor physics, and space flight, and holds a handful of patents on advanced solar cell designs.

Landis's science fiction and poetry have appeared in most of the SF magazines and several anthologies, including the *Year's Best Science*

Fiction. In 1990 he was awarded the Nebula Award for his short story "Ripples in the Dirac Sea," and in 1992 he won the Hugo Award for the short story "A Walk in the Sun."

Landis started writing in 1984, while he was working on his Ph.D. in physics at Brown University. His short stories have appeared in German, Dutch, Portugese, French, Japanese, Russian, Lithuanian, Finnish, and Czech.

Since 1987, **D. F. LEWIS** has had over 400 stories published in the United Kingdom and the United States, including British literary organs *Stand* and *Iron*.

Among the recent publications his stories have appeared in are *Signals, Best New Horror 1 & 2, The Year's Best Horror Stories XVIII, XIX & XX, Red Stains*, and *Darklands 2*.

F. A. MCMAHAN has written five novels (two horror, two fantasy, and one science fiction) that are under review at leading publishing houses. Her short fiction appears in several publications, including *Computer Edge, Strange Days, Prisoners of the Night*, and the horror anthology *Chilled to the Bone*.

While many successful authors claim they've "always" planned to be writers, **A.R. MORLAN** didn't come to that decision until, as an undergraduate, she found her fellow students offering to pay her to write papers for them. A professor got wind of the situation, and told Ms. Morlan, "No matter who turned in one of your papers, I'd know it was your work because your voice is so personal, so you."

"Nothing any teacher has said to me before or since," she says, "has ever pleased me so much." However, when the young writer decided to give freelancing a try, she soon learned she'd have to make that unique voice more flexible, to tune it, much as, she explains, "a singer learns to expand his or her range through constant practice and experimentation with new forms of expression."

And A.R. Morlan continues to practice, with more than 100 short stories, poems, novellas, and articles to her credit, along with two novels published (*The Amulet*, and *Dark Journey*) both of which will be published in Germany.

BYRON PREISS is the editor of the books *The Planets*, *The Universe*, *The Microverse*, and *The Dinosaurs: A New Look at a Lost Era*, which was featured in *Life* magazine. He has collaborated with Arthur C. Clarke, Isaac Asimov, and Ray Bradbury, and edited the Grammy Award winning *The Words of Gandhi*. His monograph on *The Art of Leo & Diane Dillon* was a Hugo Award nominee. He holds a B.A. from the University of Pennsylvania and an M.A. from Stanford University. He currently resides in New York City.

WILLIAM RELLING JR. was born in St. Louis, Missouri, in 1954. Over the years, he has worked as a carnival ride operator, supermarket clerk, produce truck driver, summer camp counselor, street crew worker, busboy, janitor, purveyor of fine wines and spirits, musician, hospital orderly, patio furniture salesman, magazine editor, high school teacher, and college instructor. In 1976-77 he lived on the Pine Ridge Indian Reservation in western South Dakota.

Relling moved to the Los Angeles area in 1978 (with the Colin Sphinctor Band) and has been there ever since. He has published more than a score of short stories in everything from *Omni* to *Cavalier*, as well as three novels: *Brujo* in 1986, *New Moon* in 1987, *Silent Moon* in 1990. In addition to working on two new novels and a short story collection, Relling recently broke into movie writing with a screenplay adaptation of Frank Lauria's novel *Blue Limbo*. He is collaborating on an original stage musical for children titled *Rainbow Pie* (in partnership with composer Timothy Bruneau) and a full-length play titled *A Saloon at the Edge of the World* (in partnership with poet Joseph Coulson). Married since 1978, he lives with his wife and son in a part of L.A. known as Silver Lake (see Jackson Browne's first album). His heroes include Groucho Marx, Albert Schweitzer, Albert Brooks, E.B. White, Ozzie Smith, Pete Townshend, and the Lone Ranger.

ANNE RICE is best known for her series of novels featuring the vampire L'Estat: *Interview With the Vampire*, *The Vampire Lestat*, *Queen* *of the Damned*, and *The Tale of the Body Thief*. She was born in New Orleans, where she still lives with her husband, the poet Stan Rice, and their son, Christopher.

ALAN RODGERS is the author of *Fire*, *Night*, *Blood of the Children*, and *New Life for the Dead*. *Blood of the Children* was a nominee for the Horror Writers of America Bram Stoker Award; his first story (actually a novelette), "The Boy Who Came Back from the Dead," won a Stoker and lost a World Fantasy Award. During the mid-eighties he edited the fondly-remembered horror digest, *Night Cry*. He lives in Manhattan with his wife, Amy Stout, and his two daughters, Alexandra and Andrea Rodgers.

ROBERT SILVERBERG was born in New York City, and educated at Columbia (Class of 1956). He has been a resident of the San Francisco Bay Area for many years. His first book, *Revolt on Alpha C*, was published in 1955.

He is the winner of four Hugo awards (1956, 1969, 1987, 1990) and five Nebulas (1970, 1972, 1972 again, 1975, 1986), as well as most of the other significant science fiction honors. He was president of the Science Fiction Writers of America in 1967-68.

Silverberg is the author of more than a hundred books and an uncounted number of short stories, which have appeared in such magazines as *Omni*, *Playboy*, and *Penthouse* and have been widely anthologized and chosen for best-of-the-year honors. Among the best-known book titles are: *Up the Line*, *Lord Valentine's Castle*, *The World Inside*, and *The Stochastic Man*.

He edited the *New Dimensions* series of anthologies from 1971 to 1980, the first volume of *The Science Fiction Hall of Fame* series, and *Robert Silverberg's World's of Wonder*, an anthology of great science fiction that is also a collection of his essays on the art of writing science fiction. With his wife Karen Haber he currently edits *Universe*, an anthology of original science fiction.

S. P. SOMTOW was born in Bangkok, Thailand, and grew up in Europe. He was educated at Eton College and at Cambridge, where he obtained his B.A. and M.A., receiving honors in English and music. Although he has received international acclaim as an avant-garde composer, he is most known for his best-selling horror novels, including *Valentine, Moon Dance,* and *Vampire Junction.* His work has been nominated for numerous awards and been translated into many languages. In 1981, he won the John W. Campbell Award for Best New Writer. His young adult novel *Forgetting Places* was honored by the "Books for Young Adults" program as an Outstanding Book of the Year. Currently he alternates between working on books and motion pictures; his films include *The Laughing Dead* and *Burial of the Rats,* which he scripted for Roger Corman.

LARRY TRITTEN is a veteran free-lance writer (Scriptor horribilis). His science fiction and horror have appeared in *The Magazine of Fantasy and Science Fiction, Asimov's Science Fiction Magazine, Amazing Stories,* the *Universe* anthology, *Rod Serling's The Twilight Zone Magazine, Pulphouse* and other genre sources. Some of his other publishing credits include *The New Yorker, Vanity Fair, Playboy, Harper's, Travel & Leisure, Penthouse, Spy,* and *Redbook.*

LAWRENCE WATT-EVANS was born and raised in Massachusetts, fourth of six children, in a house full of books. He taught himself to read at age five in order to read a comic book story called "Last of the Tree People," and began writing his own stories a couple of years later.

Upon reaching adulthood, he began trying to sell his writing, as well as trying a few other jobs—as a locksmith, bottle-washer, ladder assembler, cattle farmer, cook, bagboy, comic book dealer, and other things.

Eventually a fantasy novel, *The Lure of the Basilisk,* actually sold. Several more novels and dozens of stories have now made it into print, covering a wide range of fantasy, science fiction, and horror. He's also sold articles, poems, comic book scripts, and more, and is recognized as an expert on horror comics of the 1950s. His short story, "Why I Left Harry's All-Night Hamburgers," won the Hugo in 1988. "The Name of Fear," a fictional explanation of just what the connection is between the historical Dracula and vampires, appeared in *The Ultimate Dracula.*

He's married, has two children, and after living in New Jersey, Pennsylvania, and Kentucky, he's settled in the Maryland suburbs of Washington, D.C.

ROBERT WEINBERG is the only World Fantasy Award winning author to also serve as grand marshall of a rodeo parade. He is the author of four nonfiction books, four horror novels, and numerous horror and dark fantasy short stories. A noted collector of horror and supernatural fiction, he has edited nearly a hundred anthologies in this field. At present, he is working on the first two novels of a humorous fantasy series and putting the finishing touches on a contemporary horror novel about television.

GENE WOLFE'S father was from Ohio, his mother from North Carolina; he was born in New York while they were living in New Jersey. He grew up in Houston, where he attended Edgar Allan Poe Elementary School, an accident that seems to have shaped much of his life. Later he went to Texas A&M, dropped out, was drafted, and got the Combat Infantry Badge in the Korean War. He attended the University of Houston on the GI Bill and graduated as a BSME.

In the year that Wolfe graduated, he married Rosemary Frances Dietsch. They have four children: Roy, Maddie, Teri, and Matt. He moved to the Chicago area in 1972, when he became a senior editor on *Plant Engineering Magazine*; in 1984, he resigned that position to write full time.

Besides the four volumes that make up The Book of the New Sun (*The Shadow of the Torturer*, *The Claw of the Conciliator*, *The Sword of the Lictor*, and *The Citadel of the Autarch*), Wolfe is the author of *The Fifth Head of Cerberus*, *Peace*, *The Devil in a Forest*, *Free Live Free*, *Soldier of the Mist*, *The Urth of the New Sun*, *There are Doors*, *Soldier of Arete*, *Castleview*, and other books. Some of his short stories have been collected in *The Island of Doctor Death and Other Stories and Other Stories* (that's the title, not a typo), *Storeys* (ditto) *From the Old Hotel*, and *Endangered Species*.

Wolfe's work has won the John W. Campbell Memorial Award, the Prix Apollo, the British Fantasy Award, the British Science Fiction